LOST MISSION

Athol Dickson

LOST MISSION

HOWARD
Fiction
A DIVISION OF SIMON & SCHUSTER

NEW YORK LONDON
TORONTO SYDNEY

a Novel

Our purpose at Howard Books is to:
- *Increase faith* in the hearts of growing Christians
- *Inspire holiness* in the lives of believers
- *Instill hope* in the hearts of struggling people everywhere

Because He's coming again!

Published by Howard Books,
a division of Simon & Schuster, Inc.
1230 Avenue of the Americas, New York, NY 10020
www.howardpublishing.com

Lost Mission © 2009 Athol Dickson

In association with WordServe Literary Agency

Library of Congress Cataloging-in-Publication Data is available.

ISBN 978-1-4165-8347-9
ISBN 978-1-4391-6839-4 (ebook)

10 9 8 7 6 5 4 3 2 1

HOWARD and colophon are registered trademarks of Simon & Schuster, Inc.

Manufactured in the United States

For information regarding special discounts for bulk purchases,
please contact: Simon & Schuster Special Sales at 1-866-506-1949
or business@simonandschuster.com.

The Simon & Schuster Speakers Bureau can bring authors to your live event.
For more information or to book an event contact the Simon & Schuster
Speakers Bureau at 866-248-3049 or visit our website at www.simonspeakers.com.

Edited by Nicci Jordan Hubert
Cover design by Design Works
Interior design by Jaime Putorti

With thanks to Greg Johnson and Rachelle Gardner for slogging through an ugly early draft, and with deep appreciation to Nicci Jordan Hubert, editor extraordinaire, for her excellent work on this novel.

The two angels arrived
*   at Sodom in the evening,*
and Lot was sitting
*   in the gateway of the city.*
When he saw them,
*   he got up to meet them*
and bowed down
*   with his face*
*   to the ground.*

—THE BOOK OF GENESIS

*In the event of a suspicious find
those exposed should be re-vaccinated
and placed under medical supervision for 21 days . . .
The potential risk to public health is so great
that a contingency plan must be in place.*

—MARGARET COX,
"CRYPT ARCHAEOLOGY: AN APPROACH,"
INSTITUTE OF FIELD ARCHAEOLOGISTS,
PAPER NUMBER 3

LOST MISSION

CAPÍTULO 1

LET US BEGIN THE STORY of La Misión de Santa Dolores on the holy day of the three kings, in Italy, in Assisi. To commemorate his twentieth year among the Franciscan brothers, Fray Alejandro Tapia Valdez made a pilgrimage to his beloved San Francisco's humble chapel, the Porziuncola. For more than a week the friar prayed before the chapel's frescoes, rarely ceasing for food or sleep. But despite his lengthy praises and petitions, despite his passionate devotion to Almighty God, Fray Alejandro was a pragmatic man. He did not believe the rumor, common in his day, that the frescoes' perfection was beyond the ability of human hands. As we shall see, in time the friar would reconsider.

The Franciscan stood five feet four inches tall, an average Spaniard's height in the eighteenth century. He was broad and unattractive. Heavy whiskers lurked beneath the surface of his jaw, darkly threatening to burst forth. Fray Alejandro's brow was large and loomed above the recess of his eyes as if it were a cliff eroded by the pounding of the sea, ready to crash down at any moment. The black fullness of his hair had been shaved at the crown, leaving only a circular fringe around the edges of his head. His nose, once aquiline and proud, had become a perpetual reminder of the violence that had flattened it at some time in the past.

For all its ugliness, Fray Alejandro's visage could not mask the gentleness within. His crooked smile shed warmth upon his fellow man. His hands were ever ready with a touch to reassure or steady, or to simply grant the gift of human presence. When someone spoke, be that person wise or not, he inclined his head and listened with his entire being, as if the speaker's words had all the weight of holy writ. In his eyes was love.

Love does not defend against the sorrows of this world, of course. On the contrary, each day as Fray Alejandro knelt in prayer at the Porziuncola he became more deeply troubled. His imagination had recently been captured by strange stories of the heathen natives of the New World, isolated wretches with no knowledge of their Savior. This tragedy grew in Alejandro's mind until he groaned aloud in sympathy for their unhappy souls. Other brothers kneeling on his left and right cast covert glances at him. Many thought his noisy prayers an uncouth intrusion, but caught up as he was in sacred agony, Alejandro did not notice.

Then came that holy day of the three kings, when in the midst of his entreaties for the pagans of New Spain, Fray Alejandro suddenly felt a painful heat as if his body were ablaze. In this, the first of his three burnings, Alejandro became faint. He heard a whisper saying, "Go and save my children." The bells began to peal, although it was later said the ropes had not been touched. As startled pigeons burst forth from the bell tower, Alejandro rose.

How like the Holy Father to command such a journey on that day of days! Without a backward glance Fray Alejandro strode away from San Francisco's little chapel as if following a star, determined to return at once to Hornachuelos, in Córdoba, there to seek permission from the abbot of the monastery of Santa María de los Ángeles for a voyage to New Spain.

The abbot's assent was quickly given, but Fray Alejandro spent many months waiting on the vast bureaucracy of King Carlos III to approve his passage. Still, while the wheels of government turn slowly, slowly they do turn.

Finally, in late May of the year 1767, the good friar stood at the bulwarks of a galleon in the West Indian Fleet, tossed by the Atlantic, quite ill, and protected from the frigid spray by nothing but his robe of coarse handmade cloth. In spite of the pitching deck, always Alejandro faced New Spain, far beyond the horizon. His short, broad body seemed to strain against the wind and ocean waves with eagerness to be about his Father's business.

But let us be more patient than the friar, for this is just the first of many journeys we shall follow as our story leads us back and forth through space and time. Indeed, the events Fray Alejandro has set in motion have their culmination far into the future. Therefore, leaving the Franciscan and his solitary ship, we cross many miles to reach a village known as Rincón de Dolores, high among the Sierra Madre mountains of Jalisco, Mexico. And we fly further still, centuries ahead of Alejandro, to find ourselves in these, our modern times.

Accompanied by *norteño* music blaring from loudspeakers and by much celebratory honking of automobile horns, we observe the burning of a makeshift structure of twigs and sticks and painted cardboard, which seemed a more substantial thing once it was engulfed, as if the busy flames were masons hard at work with red adobe. The people of the village of Rincón de Dolores were encouraged by the firmness of the fire. All the village cheered as the imitation barracks burned before them. They cheered, and with their jolly voices dared a pair of boys to stay in the inferno just a little longer.

There was much to enjoy on that Feast Day of Fray Alejandro—the floral garlands, the children in their antique costumes, the pinwheels spun by crackling fireworks, the somber procession of the saints along the *avenida*—but one citizen did not join the festivities.

Guadalupe Soledad Consuelo de la Garza trembled as she watched the flaming reenactment of the tragedy of La Misión de Santa Dolores. Who knew, but possibly this year the boys would stay too long within the flames? Who knew, but possibly this time the sticks would burn, the cardboard become ash and rise into the sky, and "Alejandro" and "the Indian" would not emerge? Spurred to foolishness by those who called for courage, might this be the year when merrymaking turned to mourning? The young woman with the long name—let us call her merely Lupe—feared it might be so, while the imitation barracks burned and the boys remained inside.

As was their ancient custom, after the fire was set by eager boys in Indian costumes, the village people chanted, "*Muerte! Muerte! Muerte!* Death to Spaniards! Death to traitors!" Their refrain arose in tandem with the flames. Only when the fire ascended to the middle of the mock barracks' spindly walls did some within the crowd begin to yell, "*Salid! Salid! Salid!*" Come out! they called, a few of them at first, mostly girls

and women, then as the minutes slowly passed this call became predominant, until the entire village shouted it as one, Come out! and the
boys inside could flee the fire with honor.

Yet they did not come.

"*Agua!*" someone shouted, probably the boys' parents, and nearby
men with buckets hurried toward the crackling barracks walls. "*Agua,
rápido!*" they shouted, and the first man swung his bucket back, prepared to douse a small part of the flames.

Such wild and forceful flames, and so little water, thought young
Lupe. Holy Father, please protect them.

Even as she prayed, the first man thrust his bucket forward. Water
sizzled in the burning sticks and rose as steam, and from the conflagration burst two little figures. One boy came out robed from head to foot
in gray cloth, the cincture at his waist knotted in three places to bring
poverty, obedience, and chastity to mind. He carried a bundle, the
sacred *retablo* of Fray Alejandro concealed in crimson velvet, a small altarpiece which no one but Padre Hinojosa, the village priest, would
ever see. The other boy came nearly naked with only a covering of sackcloth, his bare arms and legs agleam with aloe sap as protection from
the heat. The fire around them roared.

Chased by swirling coals and sparks, the two brave boys went
charging through the crowd, yet no one turned to watch. It was as if
young Alejandro and the Indian were unseen, as if they were already
spirits on their way to heaven. All the village chanted, "*Muerte! Muerte!
Muerte!*" again. All the village faced the burning barracks. All of Rincón
de Dolores called for death to Spaniards, death to traitors, as the two
small figures fled invisibly across the plaza to the chapel, where they
entered and returned the treasure, the *retablo* handed down through
centuries.

Alone among the village people, only Lupe seemed to see the boys
escape. Watching from the shop door, she alone thanked God for yet
another year without a tragedy; she alone refused to play the game, the
foolish reenactment they all loved so well, pretending blindness as two
boys cheated death. Lupe's imagination would not let her join the celebration of their unofficial saint's escape from murderous pagans. She
had never felt the kiss of flames upon her flesh, but she had suffered
from flames nonetheless.

Often Lupe recalled the winter's night when her father had laid a bed of sticks within the corner fireplace. The flames took hold and a younger Lupe drew her blanket up above her head as other children did when told of ghosts. Even now the memory of resin snapping in the burning wood intruded on her dreams, conjuring a thousand nightmares drawn from Padre Hinojosa's homilies about Spanish saints who perished in the flames, Agathoclia and Eulalia of Mérida, and the *auto de fe,* that fearsome ritual of early Mexico, the stake, and acts of faith imposing pain on saint and heretic alike. Her most grievous loss and many sermons, dreams, and sacrifices of the flesh had left her terrified of fire.

Watching from the doorway, Lupe heard a voice. "Do you think this is how it was?"

Although she had not heard him come, a stranger stood beside her, a man in fine dark clothing with full black hair that shimmered slightly in the midday light like the feathers of a crow. From his appearance this man might have been her brother. Like Lupe, he was not tall. Like Lupe, his features called to mind stone carvings of the ancient Mayans. Like Lupe, he had a smooth sloped forehead, pendulous earlobes, and cheekbones high and proud. His golden skin was flawless, as was hers. Like hers, his lips were thick and sensuous, his teeth the flashing white of lightning, his eyes a pair of black pools without bottoms.

"Pardon me, señor?" said Lupe, unaware she might be looking at her twin.

"Do you think this is how it was?" asked the stranger once again. "With Fray Alejandro and the Indian?"

Lupe only shrugged. "Who knows, señor? It is a very old story."

The stranger nodded, his unfathomable eyes focused on the plaza.

Perhaps, being a stranger, he did not know the story of Fray Alejandro, how the Franciscan had walked two thousand four hundred kilometers to Alta California with two other Fernandino brothers. Because he was a stranger it was possible the man knew nothing of the apostate priests who corrupted Alejandro's efforts to advance the gospel, how his hope to be the hands and feet of Christ to pagan peoples in the north was undone by Spanish cruelty and indulgence, how Alejandro, forced to flee his beloved mission in the north, had escaped the burning buildings with the Indian, his trusted neophyte companion, the two of them miraculously unseen even as they passed among bloodthirsty savages, much as Saint Peter once had passed his guards in Herod's prison.

If the man knew nothing of this history he would surely learn that day, for every year at Alejandro's feast all was reenacted by the village children to commemorate the holy man's exploits. Rome had thus far not enshrined Fray Alejandro among the saints, but Rincón de Dolores had nonetheless adopted him as their patron, for the man of miracles had settled in their little mountain village when the pagans in the north rejected him, and through many acts of kindness he had become their eternally beloved padre, entrusting them with memories of the mission he had lost up north, somewhere in the hills of Alta California.

Lupe considered speaking to the stranger of these things, but he had departed unobserved. She searched the crowd beyond her door to find him. With the Burning of the Barracks finished now, people strolled throughout the village, passing in the shade of well-trimmed ficus trees around the plaza or along the tiles beneath arched porticos where they haggled with the vendors who had traveled from afar to set up booths for the fiesta. Some of the vendors offered plastic toys for children: balloons, whistles, and balls in a hundred riotous colors. Others hawked recordings of mariachi and *norteño* music. Sweets, hand tools, shawls, and pottery . . . everything was there. Near the chapel on the far side of the plaza one could purchase votive candles and *milagros,* those tiny metal charms that symbolized the miracles requested of the saints. In spite of so much competition, a few still patronized Lupe's *tiendita,* her little shop where soda pop and newspapers and other such necessities were offered to the good people of Rincón de Dolores, Jalisco, high in the Sierra Madre mountains.

Forgetting about the stranger, Lupe left her place in the doorway and tended to the customers who visited her shop all afternoon, both villagers and strangers. She took their pesos as the sun outside moved closer to the western mountains and the shadows lengthened. Finally it was almost time for the best part of Fray Alejandro's fiesta: the gathering at the plaza. The young woman stepped across the stone threshold of her little shop, where the sandals of a dozen generations had shaped a smooth depression. She closed the wooden door. She felt no need for locks. Dressed in a blue cotton skirt and white blouse with a traditional apron, wearing no jewelry and no makeup, with her pure black hair restrained only by a plastic clip, Lupe approached the plaza.

She followed the *familia* Delgado along the *avenida,* Rosa and Carlos in their finest clothing normally reserved for Sunday Mass. Rosa's blouse was perhaps a bit too tight and too low-cut in Lupe's opinion. Carlos was very handsome with silver tips and silver heel guards on his pointed boots. The three Delgado boys were likewise attired in formal fashion, and the youngest child, darling Linda, toddled on the cobblestones in patent-leather shoes, with petticoats and a pretty pink dress trimmed with sky blue ribbons.

Lupe sometimes wished for children. The thought arose in moments such as this, but it was always fleeting. At other times she praised the Holy Father for her call to chastity. It was good to be unmarried unless one burned with passion, as San Pablo said, and her passion was for Christ.

When Lupe reach the plaza, oh, such a festivity! She saw men at their carts selling little whimsies—empanadas and tamales and nopales from the prickly pear—and strolling toy vendors with helium balloons and plastic snakes on sticks, and groups of girls approaching marriage age who moved about the plaza casting covert glances at the boys whom they pretended to ignore. Soon everyone would laugh as mariachis in the central gazebo serenaded blushing grandmothers, then the people would ignore the mayor as he promised vast improvements through a needless megaphone, and they would admire Rincón de Dolores's own *ballet folklórico,* the handsome boys in black *charro* suits with felt sombreros and shoulders proudly squared, and the beautiful girls in swirling multicolored skirts like rose bouquets.

Lupe traversed the plaza, greeting all as friends, for she was a friend to everyone. Like Fray Alejandro, she longed to be the hands and feet of Christ to them. She went slowly, smiling on her way, touching this one, kissing that one, freely offering her kindness. Normally this bonhomie was as natural as breath to her, but that day it was a kind of sacrifice she offered. It came from force of will. She did not feel it in her heart, and she was uncertain why. Perhaps her dread had lingered since the moment when the barracks flames had nearly claimed two boys. Yes, probably it was only that. Yet she sensed something else at work within her heart, a conviction, and a fear.

On the far side of the plaza Lupe approached the embers of the imitation barracks, a mound of charcoal now, a black mark on the beauty of the day. It frightened her, yet drew her closer. Remarkably, it still emitted smoke. Only Lupe gave attention to that fact. All the others laughed and strolled and savored conversations unawares, but Lupe there beside the blackened ruins felt her pulse increase and heard the beating of her heart within her inner ear. She found it necessary to remind herself to breathe. She saw the smoke still rising like a slender column standing far above the village, straight and true, until it met the burning fringes of the sunset. She turned her face up to the sky and saw the strangest thing among the orange and purple clouds. She saw it, yet it could not be.

"Concha," called Lupe to a passing friend. "That smoke. Would you look at it?"

The woman, whose seven children swirled around her knees, replied, "I told those foolish men to pour more water on those ashes."

"But the wind . . ."

Concha and her perpetually squirming offspring had already passed into the crowd.

Lupe wiped sweating palms upon her apron and tried again to find someone to observe this thing and tell her it was real, but the mariachis had begun their brassy serenades and the people moved away from her, toward the gazebo in the center of the plaza. She stared up at the sky again and asked, "How can that be?"

Someone behind her said, "Perhaps it is a sign."

Guadalupe Soledad Consuelo de la Garza looked around and saw the stranger with dark hair that shimmered slightly like the feathers of a crow. She felt comforted immediately, for he too had seen the cause of her confusion; he too stood with face turned toward the sky, toward the smoke arising from Fray Alejandro's ruined mission, the smoke which drifted north against a wind that traveled south.

CAPÍTULO 2

MORE THAN TWO CENTURIES AGO, in a time when Mexico and the state of California were still part of the viceroyalty known as New Spain, Fray Alejandro Tapia Valdez endured the first of two assaults by Indians that he would suffer in his lifetime. It was just after vespers. The sky was alive with stars but the moon had not yet risen as Fray Alejandro searched for a place of privacy, his evening meal having been poorly received within his bowels.

While his discomfort was unwelcome, Alejandro was quite accustomed to the harsh realities of life beyond the reach of civilization. It had been many months since he left Mexico City, where he had been intensively schooled at La Universidad de San Fernando in the culture and the languages of California Indians, the better to teach them both the love of Christ and the skills of weaving and tanning by which they could support the missions, enrich mother Spain, and glorify the Lord. After completing his training at the university, Fray Alejandro had set out in the company of two other Franciscan brothers. One, Fray Benicio Eduardo de la Paz, had only recently made his solemn profession and commitment to the Order. The other, Fray Guillermo Manuel Espinosa, was to be the superior of the mission. On their long walk across the occidental range of the Sierra Madre mountains, together these men endured many trials and difficulties.

The three friars arrived at the port town of Guaymas, where they were joined by some fifty Spanish soldiers. A brigantine carried the

Franciscans along with the soldiers and their retinue of horses, mules, and cattle across the Sea of Cortez to the shores of Baja California. They disembarked near the Misión Nuestra Señora de Loreto Conchó. From there they made good progress northward on a well-traveled path, following the backbone of the parched and rocky Baja California peninsula from mission to mission. During this time they were never more than a three-day walk from a primitive Spanish outpost.

Finally they reached the Misión San Fernando Rey de España de Velicatá, the northernmost of all the missions then extant, and the one most recently established. There they rested while many neophytes (as converted Indians were then called) replenished their provisions with the salted meat of deerlike creatures called *berrendos,* and of desert hares and squirrels, along with many bags of maize. Then the expedition continued northward, led by a pair of Cochimí Indians who had been pressed into their service as trail guides.

Fray Alejandro objected to the Indians' forced servitude, but his superior, Fray Guillermo, deemed it necessary because above the Misión San Fernando lay a land without marked trails, or missions, or any other form of Spanish settlement. Although the famous explorers Cabrillo and de Fuca had observed the coastline from their ships and made landfall in a few places to claim the countryside for the Spanish crown, that had been more than two centuries before Fray Alejandro's journey. Few if any Europeans had entered the inland territory since then, so the land above Baja California remained almost entirely unexplored from Misión San Fernando all the way north to the arctic regions.

Thus it was that the gentle Fray Alejandro, whom we first met in the eminently civilized Italian city of Assisi, had crossed oceans, seas, and continents to arrive at the southern edge of a vast uncivilized expanse, where he was attacked quite by accident as he sought relief from the intestinal suffering so well known to travelers.

On the night in question he moved through the darkness quickly, for such matters will not wait. At a suitable location between two boulders, he gathered up his robe and assumed the usual position upon his haunches. Motionless and silent, he was unseen and unheard by the two frightened Cochimí Indians as they crept out from the camp, intent upon escape. Nor did Alejandro see or hear the approaching Indians until he arose from his place between the boulders. His sudden appearance in the blackness of the night horrified the Cochimís, who instantly assumed he was an evil spirit called up from the center of the earth through the magic of their Spanish captors. One of the Indians collapsed in terror, but the other lashed out with a stone, which struck Fray Alejandro on the temple.

Long after the fleeing Cochimís had vanished into the hills, Alejandro regained consciousness. Memory eluded him at first. Rolling onto his back, he stared up into the infinite cosmos, searching the star-dappled canopy for a clue to explain how he came to be lying on the ground in such a place. In his disorientation, he felt he had somehow slipped into another time. He heard the soft voices of the soldiers at their nearby campfires. A warm breeze trailed unseen fingers across his face. Eventually a memory returned of something in the darkness, a sudden movement, a flash of pain. He did not completely understand what had happened, but for the moment that was unimportant. Something else concerned Fray Alejandro as he lay staring at the sky, something quite impossible, for he saw smoke drift slowly past the powdered panorama of the Milky Way above, and although he felt the desert breeze upon his right cheek, the smoke came from the campfires on his left.

Along with Alejandro, let us pause now to consider smoke that flows into the wind. If it thusly moved against the physical laws of space, might it also transcend time? Might it cross from night to day? Might it drift three hundred miles north to find Fray Alejandro's destination, to find the very place where his mission would be built, and where more than two centuries later a wealthy man named Delano Wright stood at an open window looking at the modern world? In our own time, in the state of California, in the clutches of the canyon ridges on the left and right of this man Delano, might the palms like hazy silhouetted feather dusters brush away such wondrous smoke, just as they so often brushed the passing clouds? From the commanding position of his hilltop estate, might Delano Wright notice a sky so strange and glorious it overwhelmed the laws of nature? Or might this man so blessed with earthly fortune fail to see the marvels there before him? Might he fail to see the bountiful Pacific rolling toward him from the gently curved horizon, or the pelicans patrolling the foamy coast in

effortless formations, or the dappled swimsuit colors of sun worshippers along the beach below, or the pointillistic crimsons, corals, and
magentas streaming down the hill on cascades of bougainvillea? Might
he see no Eden there beyond his open window? In spite of all his wealth
and privilege, might he blindly look at such a world, while seeing only
ruin?

Behind him, Ana was speaking. "I didn't want you to find out on
your own. I wanted to tell you myself. I hate it that you heard like this."

Staring blindly through the window, Delano Wright noticed how
she seemed to start so many sentences with "I." After all their years together, the realization startled him. But he supposed it was good to still
be learning new things about her, even in this conversation.

"I'm sorry, Del." Beautiful, blond, and Spanish, she spoke with a
telltale hint of accent flirting at the edges of her English, the slight lisp
of a native-born Castilian. "I really am sorry. I know you won't believe
it, but I didn't have a choice."

"No?" he asked. "No other choice at all?"

"Please don't be sarcastic. I only meant you drove me to it."

"Did I?"

"I'm serious, Del. I don't think sarcasm is appropriate."

"I don't mean to be sarcastic. Sorry."

"Harry says—"

Delano interrupted. Turning away from the window, facing her, he
said. "Do we have to talk about Harry?"

"I don't see why we shouldn't. There's no need to pretend anymore."

"All right, then."

"Harry says we're different people now. Different from who we
were when we got married. I think he's right. I feel like a different
woman, and he says you're not the same."

"I'm the same, Ana. You're the one who changed."

"I *know*. Harry's wrong about you, but he's right about me. I've
changed, and you haven't. I'm more interested in life now. I need to try
new things. I have this . . . this new kind of energy I can't hold in, but
you're just the same old Del. I mean, you *can* see that, can't you? I'm
not the person you married anymore. I'm a new me, so how can we be
married? You can see that, right?"

"Oh, I can see you're not the same."

"Do you? I think that's great. We don't have to be ugly about this. I mean, we can still be friendly. I want to be, for Harmony's sake."

Delano tried to smile. "You want harmony for Harmony?"

Ana laughed a little and switched to Spanish, a sign she wanted to keep things light and easy. "I'm glad you still have a sense of humor."

Delano refused to speak her language, although he knew it well. He replied in his native English, on his terms. "What if I changed too?"

"I don't think—"

"You said you changed but I didn't. So what if I changed too? Would Harry still be in the picture?"

"I just don't think—"

"It's a fair question. You said you have energy. You're more interested. You try new things. What if I was that way too? Would it make a difference?"

"I need more."

"All right. What else?"

"You know this isn't working. We haven't been together, really together, in years. You can't even really say I was the first to . . . to leave."

"Leave? Is that what you want to call it?"

"Don't be ugly."

"I've never been unfaithful to you."

"You have! You left me for your work and for the church a long time ago."

"It's not the same."

"Maybe it's worse. How am I supposed to compete with a family legacy? How am I supposed to compete with God?"

"I could change, Ana. I could."

"Come on, Del. I mean, I don't want to hurt your feelings, but think about the sex. Could you change the way you are in bed? After all this time?"

"So Harry's good in bed?"

She faced him squarely. "As a matter of fact, he is. But even if he wasn't, at least he's *interested*."

He felt as if she had given him a kick between the legs, but he had to keep on trying. He had to do it for their daughter. "Why are you so angry with me, Ana? Just tell me and I'll make it right."

"Oh, Del." She sighed dramatically and left the living room, heading for the kitchen.

Delano followed. "What are you going to do?"

She held her purse in one hand. She dug through it with her other hand. She removed her keys.

"You're leaving? Now?"

"Absolutely. Let's not draw this out."

"But . . . but what about Harmony?"

"Don't worry, Del. I wouldn't leave you here alone."

"So you're leaving her too?"

"I'm not *leaving* her. I just . . . you need her more than I do." Ana would not meet his eyes. "I'll have Harry. It will be more fair this way."

"This is fair?"

"Don't be ugly. Just . . . just tell her I'll be back to see her soon."

"When?"

"Soon. A week or two, maybe. Harry wants to take a little trip to celebrate."

"Celebrate." He said the word flatly, because he knew he would have broken if he spoke it any other way.

He followed her to the back hall and down the steps to the door that opened on the garage. He watched as she bypassed the Bentley and the Range Rover to fold her long legs into the Porsche. Of course she would take the Porsche.

The overhead door rose. She started the engine and gunned it twice, as he had so often warned her not to do. One should wait a minute for the oil to rise. He tried to focus on the car, to distance his mind from what was happening in order to avoid saying something he would regret later. He knew he had to keep this civilized for Harmony's sake, but the thought of Harmony did not calm him. On the contrary, what Ana was doing to their daughter made him think of ruining his wife. There were so many ways it could be done. He let his imagination play with it a little, fantasizing. He could get her fired. Destroy her career. He could get her blacklisted at every club and charity that mattered. He was a friend of governors and senators, a confidant of CEOs and bankers. She must be insane to tempt him in this way.

Ana lowered the car top and then reversed out of the garage onto the granite driveway. He thought she looked very chic behind the wheel, with her round sunglasses and the Southern California sunshine on her short blond hair. Somehow the way she looked made him long to let it out this once, to do what he never did. He was tired of being afraid to show his feelings, tired of being afraid of himself. Maybe if I just don't raise my voice, he thought. Maybe that would be okay.

He walked out into the sunshine to stand beside the car. In the same flat tone that he had used before, he spoke the name, "Jezebel."

She stared up at him, her eyes obscured by sunglasses. "What?"

It was essential to be calm, so he said it again, exactly as before. "Jezebel."

"Is that supposed to make me feel bad? You calling me some Old Testament thing?"

"Fornicator," he said in a conversational tone. "Adulteress."

Ana said, "See? This is why, exactly. Talking to me like you're Moses or something . . . *this* is why I did it, Del!"

"I'm just saying what you are."

"I'm not perfect, but this is not my fault. You—"

"'Such is the way of an adulterous woman; she eateth, and wipeth her mouth, and saith, I have done no wickedness.'"

"What is that? A Bible verse? You're going to quote the Bible to me now?"

"Better than listening to your excuses."

"Excuses? Why would I need excuses when I have you? You're *boring,* Del. You don't know how to have fun. You tip fifteen percent, to the penny. You go to bed too early. You work too much. You're never late or early. You look down your nose at a person just because she likes to have a little wine with dinner. You won't do anything about that belly of yours, and you haven't changed your haircut in twenty years. I mean, look at where we live, and you don't even have a *tan!*"

He smiled. "So you're leaving me because I'm white?" He said it knowing how much pride she took in her pure Spanish blood, how it offended her when ignorant Americans expressed surprise at her pale hair and complexion. He said it knowing she would be reminded of his parents' objections to their marriage on that very basis, their concern that he had married below his station. He said it knowing it might never be forgiven.

He listened as she cursed him in her native language. He listened quietly to every word, understanding perfectly, knowing that he should have held his tongue, knowing he had failed his daughter for the sake of foolish pride.

When Delano did not reply in kind, Ana seemed to run out of expletives. She gunned the Porsche's engine again and popped the clutch. The tires smoked as she shot down the hill toward the front gate. Watching her go, he felt a momentary fear for her safety, driving crazy like she was. Then he realized he had lost the right to worry about Ana, and for some reason that thought hurt him more than any other.

When she was through the gate and gone, he turned and went back into the house. In the kitchen he suddenly thought of a dinner just the week before when he had tipped twenty percent. He wished he had remembered it in time to refute her accusation in a reasonable way. He was ashamed of all his name-calling. He sighed. He picked up the phone and dialed Jim Silverman's number from memory.

"Jim?" he said. "I know it's a little late in the day for this, but I need a favor."

"Sure, Del," came the man's perpetually bright voice. "What's up?"

"That new brokerage account I asked for last week . . ."

"Oh, no."

"Yeah. It's time."

After a pause, Jim Silverman said, "I'm as sorry as I can be."

"Thank you."

"I never thought she'd really do it, Del. I never did."

"Me either."

"If there's anything I can do . . . anything at all. Just ask."

"I appreciate that. Just make the transfers for now."

"Everything we talked about?"

"Everything except for her deferred accounts, of course."

"Of course. Consider it done."

"When will that take effect?"

"Well, the markets are all closed at the moment, you know, but I had a talk with Bill Chung in Singapore and Nick Halden in London, so they're kind of, uh, kind of prepared, I guess you'd say. And of course New York answers to me, so you know that's handled. We should have everything moved over within the hour. Two at most. And remember, she can't touch your land. Only direct descendants can participate. The trust is very clear about that."

"Good man," said Delano Wright, staring out the kitchen window. He hung up the telephone, his eyes directed toward the lush tropical landscaping around the swimming pool. A hummingbird, fast as a bullet, shot from one purple flower to another. His eyes followed the movement, but his mind did not register the meaning of it, what it was, the exquisite beauty of the flashing ruby at its tiny throat. He was blind again, as he had been before when Ana began to leave him. This explained how Harmony could be suddenly beside him at the kitchen counter when he had not even realized she was in the room.

"Are you all right?" she asked.

Startled, he turned toward her. He forced himself to smile. "Sure I am, Button."

She was so beautiful, his Harmony, the image of her mother at fifteen years of age, a surfer's tan and sun-bleached hair long and straight and parted down the middle, and those adorable freckles on her cheeks. She said, "I heard Momma," putting the accent on the final syllable like a European, a pretentious affectation Ana had imposed upon the girl.

Delano's smile disappeared. "What did you hear?"

"Everything."

He sighed. He opened his arms. She stepped into them. He said, "I'm so sorry, Button."

With her cheek against his chest, she said, "Momma kept talking about 'Harry.' Who is that?"

"Harry Martin, from church."

"But . . . Mr. Martin? He's my Sunday school teacher."

"I know, honey."

"We were supposed to go to his house for a weekend retreat in two weeks."

"Well, that's off, Button. Mr. Martin won't be involved with the youth group anymore."

"But I don't want the kids to think I ruined the retreat."

"You didn't do anything wrong."

"They'll still think it's my fault."

He sighed. "Maybe you guys could camp out on the forty-twelve." The forty-twelve was one of his closest parcels of open land, Harmony's favorite out of all his holdings, four thousand and twelve acres of un-touched hill country alongside the canyon road to Wilson City. "I could have some of the hands put up safari tents around a big fire pit. They could come by with a string of horses. Maybe set up an archery range? Volleyball? Whatever you guys like."

Harmony said nothing. The shampoo scent in her hair reminded him of something. The connection seemed so strong . . . yes, he had it now. The spice markets in Thailand. He tried to remember if Harmony had been with them on that trip. No, come to think of it, they had left her at home with a nanny. She must have been only one or two; far too young to travel. He and Ana had enjoyed Thailand. But of course Harmony was plenty old enough to travel with him now. Maybe they should do that. Ana was going on a trip. To celebrate. Maybe he and Harmony should do the same.

Absentmindedly Delano said, "We're going to be all right."

Harmony pushed away a little and looked up at him, doubt inside her liquid eyes. He knew he had to be more honest. With his thumb he wiped away the moisture on her cheek. He said, "It's going to be hard for a while, but we'll be okay. I promise." He kissed her forehead and let her go and crossed to one of the refrigerators. Opening it, he searched the brightly lit interior. "Doesn't Flora keep the tomato juice in here?"

"Flora quit last week."

"Last week? How come nobody told me?"

"I think Momma did."

"No. I'd remember that." He found a small bottle of apple juice. He removed the cap and drank. Looking at the shelves in the refrigerator, he said, "Your mother could have hired someone, at least. Someone has to buy some groceries."

Behind him Harmony said, "Will we really be okay, Daddy?"

At the plaintive sound of her voice he felt the flood of anger rise again. He did his best to swallow it along with the juice. He turned to face his daughter. "Don't you worry, Button. God will not be mocked."

CAPÍTULO 3

AT FRAY GUILLERMO'S INSISTENCE, TEN soldiers pursued the escaped Cochimís. The Indians were perfectly at home in that country, while the Spaniards were strangers. The soldiers' quarry easily eluded them. They abandoned the search and returned, only to find an Indian standing in the camp. How the savage got there, no one knew. Although the camp was guarded by three men and many others loitered all around, no one saw him enter. The returning soldiers, embarrassed perhaps by their failure to apprehend the fugitives, or perhaps by the Indian's ability to penetrate their camp unnoticed, formed a circle around him and began to shove him back and forth with many slaps and curses.

Observing this, Fray Alejandro pushed two of the bullies aside without a word. Striding to the center of their circle, he helped the Indian rise to his feet. When he was certain the man had not been seriously harmed, he stood glaring at the soldiers silently, his ugly face made much more awful by his anger. One by one the men dispersed until only Alejandro and the Cochimí and a sergeant remained. With many apologies, the sergeant began to bind the Indian's hands with a rope. Alejandro objected, but the sergeant had his orders.

"We cannot let him run away again," called Fray Guillermo, who had observed everything from a distance.

"Again?" Alejandro frowned. "But this man is not one of the fugitives."

"How can you be sure?" asked the redheaded Fray Guillermo, his tonsured scalp peeling in the sun. "One of them is very like another. What is more, it does not matter. A guide is needed."

Pulling gently on the rope, the sergeant led the Cochimí away.

After a brief pause on that barren plain to celebrate the Annunciation of the Blessed Virgin, they resumed their northward journey through the desert hills of Baja California, following the captive Indian. Alejandro's sandals were meager protection from the baking rocks, his thick robes unsuited to the temperature, yet his perspiration was not altogether from the heat. It was also a form of sympathy, for Fray Guillermo had ordered the "renegade" Cochimí to carry a heavy stone in penance for deserting them. The stone was bound with stout rope, one end of which was tied around the Indian's neck. Just ahead of the Spanish column, the nearly naked man staggered with his grievous burden through low-lying brush and cactus. Sometimes he would drop the stone and fall. Then, prodded by a silent soldier's lance, he would lift it and trudge on.

His guard and tormentor was one of New Spain's famous leather-jacket soldiers, so called because of the stiff deer-hide vests they wore as proof against the stone-tipped weaponry of native peoples. The balance of their uniform consisted of flat-brimmed black sombreros and pantaloons and blouses of raw cotton. Some were armed with lances and a small leather shield. Some bore muskets. Either way, the soldiers' skill at fighting from a horse's back was legendary.

Many of the soldiers were short and wide, with dark black hair and faces innocent of whiskers. They were *mestizos,* of mixed Spanish and native blood. A few of higher rank wore long sideburns and flowing mustaches in the fashion of the day. These few were *criollos,* like young Fray Benicio, born to parents of pure Spanish blood but not actually born on the peninsula of Spain, and therefore socially inferior to Fray Alejandro and Fray Guillermo. The older friars were pure-blooded *peninsulares,* born in Spain itself, as was Don Filipe Joachim Ortiz, the captain of the expedition.

A weathered fellow of thirty-nine and a master horseman, Don Felipe displayed perfectly erect posture, meticulous grooming, and impeccable manners. He had assumed command of the expedition in order to escape from creditors who demanded payment of certain debts incurred in the gaming houses of Guadalajara. For their part, some of Don Felipe's men were petty criminals who had been sentenced to the expedition as a punishment, but most had volunteered, lured by the promise of a fresh start in the north with the possibility of land and a little hacienda as a reward for their service, and perhaps a native girl to ease their loneliness. Each was one part soldier, one part colonist, and one part evangelist, for in a time when the dreaded Inquisition still afflicted New Spain, all the soldiers were devoutly Catholic. It was quite dangerous to be otherwise.

Perhaps that danger explained why no soldier questioned Fray Guillermo's order as the Cochimí staggered northward with the heavy burden in his hands, but it did not explain Alejandro's silence. Although the injustice weighed upon his heart as surely as the stone weighed down the Indian, obedience was valued only slightly less than poverty within the Franciscan Order, and after half a lifetime guided by such wisdom Alejandro could not bring himself to question his superior's command.

On the other hand, young Benicio, only recently a friar, felt no such compunction. Trudging beside Fray Guillermo, he said, "Surely this is not the way to lead these men to Christ."

"I know of no better way," replied Guillermo.

"But it is barbaric!"

"Barbaric? Come now my young friend. Recall your training at La Universidad de San Fernando and carefully consider what you say. Do you not remember how these pagans live? Do you not recall their so-called second harvest, in which they pluck pitahaya cactus seeds from their own dried excrement in order to consume them? Do you not recall the barbaric practice of *maroma,* in which they tie a string around a piece of meat and swallow, only to pull it up again and share it with their friends, who then go on to do likewise?"

"Such things are disturbing, but to make him bear that stone this way . . ."

"You have a soft heart, Benicio. In some ways, that is admirable. But you must not let it interfere with our Lord's work. Look for yourself." The bowlegged Guillermo gestured toward the unfortunate pagan before them. "You see how meek he has become. To sanctify these heathens one must first pacify them, and to pacify them one must put their hands to labor, even if by force."

"Surely not, brother! Surely Christ never made a slave of anyone."

"Well now, Benicio, am I not a slave of Christ?" Guillermo's sunburned face became a mask of mock severity. "Besides, this is not slavery for its own sake. 'Work is prayer,' as San Benedicto often said. Never forget that, my young friend."

Always the theologian, Fray Alejandro paused to lean upon his staff and shake his dripping head. He had read the Benedictine Rule and it said no such thing. Their own beloved San Francisco never gave them that command, nor did the contemplative Alejandro think Guillermo's motto wise, for seldom were such broad pronouncements accurate in every case. Surely one could work without engaging the divine.

In this last point perhaps we can agree. Consider, for example, Guadalupe Soledad Consuelo de la Garza, tossing bucketfuls of steaming water onto the cobblestones before her little shop. As electric lights gave way to the first glow of morning, Lupe swept the liquid briskly to and fro, scratching with her broom at confetti in the cracks, the multicolored remnants the Feast Day of Fray Alejandro. This labor kept dust to a minimum, reduced the stench of dog droppings and rotten fruit, and made possible an exchange of pleasantries with neighbor women doing likewise. It was certainly work. It was almost liturgical in its regularity—Lupe did it every morning—but she would not have called it prayer, for although she was preoccupied with thoughts of higher things, on that particular morning she did not think of God. Instead she worked and thought of little else but smoke that traveled north against the wind. She worked and wondered if it might truly be a sign.

When her task was complete, Lupe entered her little shop, passed through a curtain at the rear, and on into her small apartment. She crossed the salon into the kitchen, where she put the broom and bucket in their place. She then returned from her apartment through the curtain to her shop out front. She carried a wire display rack onto the sidewalk beside the open door and stocked it with the latest glossy magazines and yesterday's newspapers. Today's newspapers would not arrive until tomorrow. She hung a chalkboard from a small hook on the wall. Pausing just a moment to consider her inventory, she began to write a list of offerings: *tortas, cocktel de frutas, gorditas, snow cones, Chiclets*. Satisfied, she reentered the shop and set about her daily straightening of the items on her shelves.

Soon her regular customers would stop by on their walk to work, making their usual purchases, mostly snacks for those whose wives or mothers had not fed them well at home. Then would come a lull, followed by the children on their way to school, all of whom knew they could count upon a free piece of candy from Señorita Lupe. After that she might receive a visit from a neighbor or two, in search perhaps of soap or bleach or maybe just a little conversation. At lunchtime she would be her busiest, serving *tortas* and *gorditas* and cans of Coca-Cola and orange soda. Then she would close the door and indulge in a light meal herself, followed by the day's siesta, until Padre Hinojosa rang the chapel bell for the afternoon rosary, and she reopened the shop. For the rest of the day Lupe would sit upon her stool behind the short counter at the door, or else stand on the stone threshold watching friends and neighbors pass along the *avenida*. Possibly she would sell a few pesos' worth of something now and then. Long after the sun went down, at last she would close her shop.

Such was the course of a normal day. But this day, after Lupe had finished straightening the items on her shelves, she could not bear to merely sit and wait for customers to come. Restlessly she moved around the shop, making small adjustments to the way her products were arranged, all the changes pointless. An aimless need to act had almost overwhelmed her. It was not boredom. She had a great capacity for stillness, both of mind and body. It was not apprehension. Except for fire, she obeyed her Savior's command not to worry. It was instead a sense she should be doing something, yet she did not know what to do.

Lupe tried to remember when her normal calm had first been disturbed. Long before the strange events of yesterday, something had begun to agitate her mind. Not suddenly, not powerfully, but gently and gradually over many weeks, she had become aware of this impatience to act. Several times she had entreated God for understanding. In her small apartment Lupe had prayed before her little statue of the Virgen de Guadalupe, her namesake, who gazed down stoically as tongues of golden flames (or was it light?) burst out all around her pale blue robes. More than once at holy Mass, Lupe had prayed for discernment. Now, on the first morning after the Feast Day of Fray Alejandro, Lupe believed perhaps her prayers were being answered. She had seen what she had seen: smoke from the mock barracks strangely flowing north against a southerly wind. It had been a miracle undoubtedly, yet she did not know its meaning.

Lupe paused in the middle of her work and prayed, "Holy Father, please reveal your perfect will."

Just then Don Pedro, an aged cobbler who lived next door, turned on his radio. Because of his affliction, he always played it very loud. Lupe disliked the noise but Don Pedro was nearly deaf, therefore she had long ago decided to ignore it. The music was not bad, but the commercials and the news were like a barking dog at midnight. *Saturday! Saturday! Saturday! At Cantina Julia, it's Los Hermanos Gutierrez and Mario Caldon performing their Super! Super! Super! hit song "I'm Going Now!" Doors open at Nine! Nine! Nine! Ladies enter Free! Free! Free!* On and on like that, every day Don Pedro's radio shouted at the world, hawking bullfights, football games, and concerts in distant cities Lupe would never visit, and selling things that she would never buy.

But it wasn't all so bad. Sometimes the radio produced hymns and Protestant sermons, which Lupe secretly enjoyed. Besides, the radio seemed to make Don Pedro happy, so Lupe endured it for his sake. As the Savior said, one must love one's neighbor as oneself, and as Padre Hinojosa had so often taught, love is what you do, not how you feel.

The sages tell us sacrifice is sometimes rendered moot by habit. Lupe had made this sacrifice many times. It no longer cost her much. Sometimes whole days passed without a single thought for the noisy radio. But that morning, as Lupe moved through her little shop needlessly changing this and that and asking the Holy Father to explain her agitation, her mind, normally so calm, was captured by the frantic shouts that blasted through the wall and filled her ears and would not give her peace. With a sigh, Lupe abandoned work and prayer to listen.

What she heard was heartbreaking. Between commercials every minute the radio broadcasted international news, mostly from north of the border. The news announcer spoke of foolish famous ones in the United States, rich in money, poor in every other way, living public lives of debauchery. He spoke of drug overdoses, unmarried pregnancies, public nudity, scandalous divorce. He spoke of other people in that wealthy northern country, previously unknown, now also famous for their sins.

Finally the news gave way to music. Lupe stepped outside onto the sidewalk. Standing by the display rack, she read the headlines on the Spanish-language versions of American magazines. HEIRESS'S BODY FOUND AT GARBAGE DUMP. SWASTIKAS DEFACE SYNAGOGUE. TEACHER SENTENCED IN SEX CASE. She sold many of those magazines. People loved to read about the crazy gringos, even in the quiet mountain town of Rincón de Dolores.

How often had she seen such words without responding? How many days had she ignored the announcer on the far side of her wall? And why could she not ignore the words on this day, this first morning after the Feast Day of Fray Alejandro? Lupe raised her face up toward the sky and watched the clouds, still streaming south. She implored the Holy Father. Could this be the answer? She watched the clouds for several minutes, and then, "But who am I?" she asked aloud. She cocked her head. One might easily have thought she listened to the music on the radio, the braying of a donkey, or Señora Ibarro in the distance, calling to her sister. "But I do not have the words," she said. And finally, after a longer pause in which she seemed to listen still more closely to the sounds of Rincón de Dolores, she said, "Yes, Señor, of course I will."

Although the men had not yet come for their early morning snacks, although she had given not one free Chiclet to a child, Guadalupe Soledad Consuelo de la Garza closed the doorway to her little shop and set out walking down the *avenida*. She paused at the corner to drop a few centavos into the plastic cup beside poor old Señora Torres, who sat in her usual place upon the sidewalk, dressed against the morning chill in gray woolen stockings and an apron. Warmed by the señora's mumbled blessings, Lupe reached the plaza and continued underneath the ficus trees beside the fine gazebo. She altered her direction slightly to pass as far as possible from the smokeless ashes of the imitation barracks, which she sincerely hoped the men would quickly clear away, for one could not be too careful where fire was concerned.

Scattering a flock of pigeons, Lupe ascended the chapel steps and passed through the open doors. She turned right at the tall wooden screen beyond and paused at the stone font. Touching the holy water, she made the sign of the cross as she faced the little wooden crucifix. Then she walked along the central aisle between the pews, the tapping of her heels against the tiles repeated in an echo from the vaulted stucco ceiling.

The *capilla*, or chapel, of Santa Dolores was small, but many thought it very beautiful. The length and height and width of it were pleasing in proportion; the antique statues of the saints in niches on the walls were nicely carved; the altar, before which Lupe now briefly knelt to cross herself again, was gilded in the center section, where the Christ stood in his place of honor, one hand lifted in a blessing, the other pulling back his robes to reveal his sacred heart.

Rising from before the altar, Lupe turned left into the shallow transept, where she entered a low doorway. On the far side was the room where Padre Hinojosa conducted parish business, a room first occupied by Fray Alejandro, where that saintly man had spent the last years of his life. Indeed, it was the very room where Alejandro had nodded off to sleep and never woke again.

From his seat behind a mountainous collection of papers on a wooden table, the priest looked up. "Ah, Lupe. What a pleasure. May I have a little moment, please?"

"Of course, Padre."

Lupe stood patiently as the old man wrote upon a piece of paper. Above her, a single lightbulb hung from a long cord. It cast a stark glow on the little room. She felt no need to sit, which was just as well, since the only other chair besides the one where Padre Hinojosa reposed was occupied by a tall stack of books. On the floor along the walls were many other books in random piles, and the single set of shelves behind the priest had been packed with other books to overflowing. So many words, thought Lupe. So much wisdom.

The old man laid his pen aside. "Thank you for waiting, daughter. How may I serve you?"

She hardly knew where to begin. "I . . . I believe the Holy Father has given me a sign."

"Indeed? Please tell me more."

Lupe explained about the smoke.

The priest said, "And this sign, what does it mean?"

This question took her by surprise. Did he not know the meaning? It occurred to Lupe that she might be mistaken. What if all of this was only her imagination? It was not good to interrupt the padre with superstitious nonsense. Filled with new misgiving, Lupe said, "I . . . I do not know."

"Are you sure?"

The old man smiled. Her confidence returned. The words came rushing out. "I think maybe the Holy Father has given me a quest. Maybe he wishes me to tell the Americanos about our Savior."

His eyes went wide. "You think they do not know about the Christ?"

"Did our Lord not tell us we would know believers by their fruit?"

Padre Hinojosa frowned. She felt her prior misgivings return, but then he nodded. "That is so."

"Yes, Padre. And consider their fruit. Everything with them is always sex or money or violence. They persecute each other in their courts over matters we would resolve with a simple conversation. They divorce as often as they marry. Even the pastors of our separated brethren have no respect for marriage. The men prey upon the women. The priests—forgive me, Padre—but the priests prey upon the children. And the parents, they let their daughters dress as harlots, and the mothers kill their babies in their wombs, and their sons carry weapons into schools, and they—"

"Stop," the old man interrupted. "Please say no more, daughter."

"It is horrible, I know. My heart should ache for them. I should long to tell them of our Savior. They are lost. I hear it on the radio each day, Padre, and I see it in the magazines, but may the Holy Father forgive me, I have not suffered for them until now. I was shown my sin this morning, Padre, and I think that I must go to them as a penance for my apathy."

"Yes, I see your point, daughter. A moment, please."

The old man pressed the back of his bald head against the topmost slat on his straight wooden chair, his face turned toward the ceiling. He laced his crooked fingers together and rested them upon his ample belly. He closed his eyes, and did not move. Lupe waited patiently again. She considered all the wisdom in his mind. So many books. So many years. She stood silently, awaiting his reply, prepared to do exactly as he said. With her great capacity for stillness, she did not move a muscle for many minutes, but as the priest's breathing seemed so regular, eventually she wondered if he might be asleep. He was an old man, after all.

"Padre?" she asked very softly, unwilling to awaken him.

He replied immediately, without opening his eyes. "Yes, daughter?"

"Oh. Are you praying?"

"Of course."

"May I pray with you?"

"Of course."

So she closed her eyes as well, and she laced her fingers together and raised her clasped hands to her chin, but unlike Padre Hinojosa she bowed her head down toward the floor. Within her mind she prayed, Dear Holy Father, please reveal your will to Padre Hinojosa. Please confirm this feeling that I have, or please do not confirm it if I am mistaken. Should I go to tell the gringos about Jesus? I thought I heard you say it just this morning. You remember, Holy Father: it was when I stood on the sidewalk looking at the sky. I suppose I could have been mistaken. Sometimes I do misunderstand you. Or it might have been Don Pedro's radio making me a little crazy. I am not complaining about Don Pedro, or his radio. Don Pedro is a good man, and he makes good shoes. I am sure it is my ears that are too sensitive. But if they are too sensitive, how is it that I do not always understand you when you speak? It is a mystery, perhaps, and certainly confusing. So you see why I desire some kind of confirmation, Holy Father, just a word from you to this wise man. If only you will—

"It blew against the wind, you say? Toward the north?"

Lupe opened her eyes to find the padre as he was before: his eyes closed, face up, hands upon his belly. "Yes, Padre."

His eyes snapped open. "In that case, come with me."

The old man put his hands upon the table and he rose. He turned and removed a small metal box from the shelf behind his desk. From the box, he took a large iron key which, unknown to Lupe, had been handed through the generations, brother to brother, priest to priest, from Fray Alejandro for this very moment. Moving carefully, Padre Hinojosa walked among the piles of books and papers on the floor, and led Lupe back out through the narrow doorway to the chapel.

Upon reaching the transept he turned right, toward the nearest side aisle. Obviously he intended to take her confession. Perhaps she had been wrong to suggest the Lord had spoken to her of a quest, perhaps headstrong, or prideful. She would confess it freely, for she knew she was quite capable of pride.

Lupe followed the priest toward the single confessional where the Sacrament of Penance had so often relieved her of her burdens, but to her surprise Padre Hinojosa did not pause to enter the small booth. Of course, the padre was before her, so there was no one offering a confession, but Lupe still covered her right ear as she passed by, a habitual gesture of respect lest she overhear the whispers of a penitent.

On the far side of the confessional, the priest stopped to insert the large key into a lock on an iron gate. Lupe maintained a respectful distance. This gate sealed the niche of the *retablo* where Fray Alejandro's altarpiece was kept, except for once each year when it was wrapped in crimson velvet and put into the care of whatever privileged son of Rincón de Dolores would play the role of Alejandro in the Feast Day reenactment. After the last of many vignettes, after his escape from the burning barracks, the chosen boy would then return the altarpiece to Padre Hinojosa to be restored to its place within the deep shadows of the niche for yet another year. It had been this way for more than two centuries, and in that time only Padre Hinojosa had ever seen the altarpiece itself—the Padre and, of course, the eleven predeceasing chapel priests of Rincón de Dolores who had gone before him.

The old man turned the key and pulled. The ancient gate swung outward. The priest stepped into the niche and beckoned her to follow. Lupe was speechless. In more than two hundred years, no layperson had set foot beyond that gate. Who was she to violate such an ancient tradition?

But a stronger reason for her hesitation was less easily explained. She sensed a presence just beyond the gate, something waiting there to seize her will and mold it to an unpredictable design. Lupe wavered on the edge of a deep and dangerous decision, for she somehow knew to follow Padre Hinojosa was to leave herself behind.

Lupe made no move.

The priest's voice came from the shadows. "Come with me, daughter. Have no fear."

"But Padre—"

"Lupe, do you have faith in our Lord?"

"Yes, Padre. I do."

"Then come."

And thus commanded, Lupe bowed her head and entered.

CAPÍTULO 4

THE HAPLESS COCHIMÍ LED THEM on, ever northward, even as he staggered from the weight of Fray Guillermo's punishment. His sweat soaked into the tan stone that he carried, rendering it dark brown. In spite of heavy calluses, his hands began to bleed.

When a sergeant mentioned this to Don Filipe, the captain waved the soldier away with an airy motion. Young Fray Benicio, tall and awkward underneath his coarse gray robe, received much the same reaction when he tried again to sway Guillermo. "His punishment is just," replied the older friar. "Did he not forsake us? Did he not assault our brother Alejandro in the night?"

"He did not," spoke Fray Alejandro. "This is not that man. Look closely at his features. You will see he is a different person altogether."

"My brother," said Guillermo. "Kindly do not speak with certainty of what you cannot know."

"Yes, brother," replied Alejandro, for San Francisco's Rule strictly bound him to obey.

Fray Benicio, bound by this same Rule, nonetheless found many ways to display his disgust with the injustice. He pretended deafness, forcing Fray Guillermo to repeat himself in conversation. He ceased to use Guillermo's Christian name and would not call him "brother," addressing the man only formally as "abbot." He moved with exquisite slowness in obedience to Guillermo's commands.

Fearing young Benicio would go too far, Alejandro again privately entreated their superior to show mercy, but if anything it seemed Benicio's campaign of passive protest had hardened Fray Guillermo's will.

Between their prayers at sext and none that afternoon, Benicio fell in beside Alejandro. "Something must be done," he said.

"Pray," replied Fray Alejandro.

"Surely more than that."

"No act of man is more than that."

"Of course, brother. But what does the scripture say? 'If a brother or sister be naked, and destitute of daily food, and one of you say unto them, Depart in peace, be ye warmed and filled; notwithstanding ye give them not those things which are needful to the body; what doth it profit?'"

Trudging on behind the Indian, Alejandro simply nodded.

A few minutes later, Fray Benicio interrupted Alejandro's thoughts. "I will toss that stone aside myself."

"Do not," replied Alejandro. "The soldiers have their orders. We must not force them into a crisis of conscience."

"I had not thought of that. But surely we must do something."

"Let me think," said the good friar, and Fray Benicio was silent. Then, after a few minutes, Alejandro said, "Yes, the time has come."

Fray Alejandro quickened his pace. With Benicio behind, soon the two friars passed the Indian and took the lead. On Alejandro walked, outdistancing the rest of the expedition, searching the ground ahead.

"What are we doing, brother?" asked the younger friar.

Alejandro strode on in silence until at last he found the object of his search. Laying his staff upon the ground, he stooped and lifted up a large stone, easily a match for the one the Cochimí bore. Thusly burdened, the sturdy Alejandro waited for the Indian to reach their position, then he set out walking at the tormented man's side.

"Brilliant!" said young Benicio. "Absolutely brilliant! This will show the fool."

"Do not call him such a thing, Benicio. He is your superior, appointed by the Lord. More than that, he is your brother."

Saying nothing, Benicio went ahead in search of a large stone to bear, even as Fray Guillermo hurried to the front, red in the face from sun and haste. "Alejandro," said the abbot. "Drop that rock immediately."

"Alas, I cannot."

"Cannot? What do you mean, cannot?"

"I am the cause of this man's punishment, for I allowed the others to escape. In the name of justice, how can I allow him to continue suffering alone, when I am the guilty one and he is innocent?"

"Innocent or not, I command you to put down that rock!"

"Please believe that I am grieved to say it is not possible."

"Not possible! Not possible, you say?"

"Sadly, no, brother. I am compelled by conscience."

"I have ordered this heathen to do penance all the way to Alta California. Are you prepared to go so far?"

"If he must, I must."

"Very well, then. Let it be as you wish."

Unwilling to command a brother in a matter of his conscience, Fray Guillermo fell back among the soldiers, while Benicio, having found an even larger stone, joined Alejandro and the Indian.

Thus day after day the two friars and the Cochimí suffered together, the brothers speaking to the silent Indian of Christ, their muscles aching as they stumbled forward until vespers on the third evening, when Don Felipe announced that they had entered Alta California. The Indian, of no further use as a guide outside his territory, was allowed to lay his burden down and depart.

Fray Alejandro watched the Cochimí scramble up a hillside between the rocks until he paused upon a ridge and turned to look down on the friar. Silhouetted against the setting sun's last glow, the Indian's long hair reflected oranges and reds as if it were alight. He raised his palm toward the friar. Something in the gesture seemed to go beyond a mere acknowledgment of parting. Could it be a blessing? A benediction? Alejandro smiled his ugly, crooked smile and raised his hand as well. In an instant, the Indian was gone.

The following morning at lauds Fray Alejandro knelt beside Benicio and Guillermo to recite the five required Our Fathers. He could not focus on his prayers. He pondered Fray Guillermo's unjust discipline. He hoped the Cochimí might believe what he had learned of Christ. His thoughts flew about at random until they landed on an intriguing question. How could the captain be so certain they had passed from one land to another?

The friar knew nothing of geography, but he had seen no line upon the ground, no barricade along the border. To him the animals and plants and soil had all seemed the same when Don Felipe pronounced the land "Alta California" and the Indian went free.

Pondering the power of such an invisible difference, Alejandro wondered what drove men to call one land different from another. Even if there had been some kind of marker at the border, what did it truly signify? A bird upon the wind would pass from here to there unchanged, and whether the wind blew from the south or north it did not pause at walls or fences, yet a man born on one side of a line upon a map might be forced to carry heavy burdens like an animal, while with a different accident of birth the same man might be blessed to ride a horse. Ideas, it seemed, were the most substantial thing in the universe.

Since ideas could modify the very earth beneath one's feet, could determine wealth or poverty, slavery or freedom, might they linger in the very atmosphere? From fires in Rincón de Dolores and encampments in the wilderness we have seen the proof that smoke can travel across time and space. Perhaps we should expect the same of our ideas. Perhaps we should not be surprised if Alejandro's musings drifted east across the Sonoran Desert to hang within the ether for eleven generations, until a moment not so very long ago when they passed into the mind of a young man named Ramón Rodríguez.

A citizen of Mexico, Ramón Rodríguez sat with his back against a mesquite tree, contemplating the rusting barricade of steel which divided the small town of Naco, Sonora, in Mexico, from Naco, Arizona, in the United States of America. The wall extended two kilometers into the empty desert to the east and west of the small town, where it was abruptly replaced by a barbed-wire fence. With typical Mexican ingenuity, the south side of the unwelcome border wall had been covered by spray paint and vinyl signs advertising everything from dentistry to rebuilt transmissions. In full view of these signs Ramón moved his legs, pulling his dusty boots into the shade. The hotel room he shared with three strangers was unbearable in the desert heat, so he had spent most of the day in the dry and dusty park named for Benito Juárez. In this spot beneath the mesquite tree, he stared at the forbidding corrugated wall that kept him from the dream which had already failed him twice.

On his first attempt to traverse the arbitrary line across the land, Ramón had agreed to pay twenty thousand pesos to a "coyote," or guide. Ramón had then walked into the night, circumventing the corrugated wall with about a dozen others, only to be caught within one hour of his crossing. La Migra, the U.S. Border Patrol, had carried them in vans to a cool concrete building. There the Americanos fed them, took their names, fingerprinted them, and allowed them to rest. As the night progressed, the building slowly filled with more and more unfortunates captured on the north side of the border.

About noon the next day Ramón and almost two hundred others were returned to Mexico on buses, which discharged them at the crossing between Douglas, Arizona, and Agua Prieta. On the south side of the crossing, a sweating Mexican beside a van offered Ramón a ride back west to Naco for one hundred pesos. During the drive Ramón and the other passengers learned this was the man's business, transporting *"pollos,"* or chickens—those who hoped to travel north without the proper papers—back to Naco, where they could wait to try again.

Ramón had been discouraged by the fact that such a business could exist, for it meant his capture was predictable.

On the second attempt, which cost another twenty thousand pesos, La Migra caught them even sooner, and a few hours later he was returned to Mexico, and the same sweaty man drove him back to Naco, where Ramón now sat beneath the mesquite tree watching a hot wind stir the dust and wondering if he should try a third time.

He had only fifteen thousand pesos left, the last of his life's savings. The minute he set foot on U.S. soil, he would have to pay it to the coyote. Then if he was caught again, he would be forced to return to his village somehow, much worse off than when he left. On the other hand, if he gave up now and went back home, at least he would have a little money, enough perhaps to support Raquel and the boys for a year. Yes, if he added the pesos to be earned in Señor Diego's clay pits, and if his dear Raquel and the boys stayed healthy enough to gather sticks for sale as firewood, they could last nearly a year. Afterward he did not know how they would live.

Since the closing of the copper mine, there had not been enough work in Ramón's hometown to support a family. Señor Diego employed a few men to dig clay for pottery, but ten hard hours in the pit yielded just two hundred pesos—about twenty U.S. dollars—which would feed him and Raquel and their three boys well enough, but left little for clothes or rent.

When Raquel's father died she had inherited twenty-four hectares of land outside of town, a parcel scorched and overgrown with cactus. Working alone and without mechanical equipment it would have taken many years for Ramón and Raquel to convert it into farmland, so they had sold it with the hope that the sixty-thousand-peso price would fund his journey to the northern land of plenty. There he would get a job and send as much money as possible back home to Raquel and the boys. They would save enough to buy a place in town and start a little restaurant. Then he could go home again.

Ramón had left five thousand pesos with Raquel and taken the rest, knowing it was necessary to pay guides a great deal of money to get across the border.

He and Raquel had not kissed in their final moments together, for they were standing in the street and a kiss in public would be scandalous. But he had knelt to kiss each of the boys, and he had hugged them, and kissed them again, and then he rose to look into Raquel's welling eyes a final time before he turned and carried off the memory of tears. How strange that turning was. He had been in the presence of his family, and he had started walking, and then quite soon he looked back to find them gone already, gone beyond a bend in the road. He had not known they could be so easily separated, but he had only walked a little while, and truly, they were gone.

The thought of it still frightened him.

Having lost his heart so easily, Ramón felt himself becoming lost in every other way. It had only been five days, but already he had moments when he could not quite remember his boys' faces. He had no photographs, of course. Such an extravagance was not to be considered. It terrified him that the day might come when he would try and fail to bring Raquel's face to mind. On that day, he would be alone completely. He remembered something he had heard a priest say one time. To save one's life, one must lose it. But he had lost his life already, and forty thousand pesos besides, and so far his life—his Raquel and his boys—had not been saved.

So the hard question remained beneath the mesquite tree. Should he try again, or should he return home? Everything within him longed to see his wife and boys. But he was fortunate the coyote had agreed to take him for so little this time. One more try for his last fifteen thousand pesos. It would leave Raquel and him with nearly nothing, but it was a bargain price. Besides, was it not the reason he had come, to reach the so-called Land of Opportunity?

He had been told the gringos called it that among themselves, but sitting underneath the mesquite tree, staring at the ugly wall, he thought it was a strange name for a land so inhospitable to those in greatest need of opportunity.

A black beetle approached Ramón's legs, which were stretched out in the dirt before him. He watched as the insect's antenna tapped the fabric of his trousers. It turned toward his knee and walked a few centimeters. It paused to investigate his leg again. It reversed direction and tried again to find a way around. Back and forth like this it went until finally it began to climb. The beetle reached the top of his thigh. He allowed it to crawl onto his hand. Gently, he returned the insect to the ground on the far side of his legs. It continued on its way.

In the Sonoran Desert heat, Ramón closed his eyes. It was important to get all the rest he could, for the beetle's perseverance had inspired him. He had decided to make a final try that night.

With his eyes closed, Ramón heard an iron bar beaten with a hammer, a little boy at work, calling people to bring refuse outside for a garbage truck. He heard barking dogs, of course, and the roar of cars and trucks with antiquated mufflers, and the chirp of traffic police whistles, and whining power saws and tolling church bells . . . so many noises that reminded him of home. Sleep was impossible. He opened his eyes and saw a woman on the sidewalk opposite the park. Instantly he stood.

Raquel! She had followed him somehow!

The joy that brought Ramón Rodríguez to his feet was quickly overshadowed by a sense of dread. The boys were not there with her. As he rushed across Benito Juárez Park, he realized only bad news could have brought Raquel to Naco. Dear God, he thought, don't let it be the boys.

He reached the sidewalk on the far side of the street from her. She stood with her back to him, dressed in a man's white cotton shirt and a pair of denim trousers. It was strange to see her wearing trousers. Usually she wore a skirt and blouse and apron. Over one of her shoulders was a loop of plain hemp rope tied to a burlap bag. Over the other shoulder was a backpack. She must have purchased the backpack and the clothes with some of the pesos he had left for her.

Fully focused on his wife, Ramón stepped into the street. A horn blared. He barely managed to leap back in time before the truck sped by. A self-important policeman blew a whistle at him. Frowning, the man gestured with white gloves that Ramón must remain on the sidewalk. The policeman waved more trucks and autos through the intersection. As Ramón waited for a chance to cross, his wife walked toward a distant street corner. "Raquel!" he called. "Wait for me!" But a bus accelerated with a mighty roar at just that moment and she did not hear.

When the policeman finally allowed him to cross, she was gone.

Ramón ran to the corner and looked up the street. There she was, half a block away. He tried to tell himself the news might not be so bad after all. Maybe she had brought the boys and left them someplace in the town to wait while she went looking for him. Yes, probably that was it. Ramón imagined seeing the boys again, buying each of them some *pan dulce,* or pastries, with the money in his wallet, and all five of them returning home together. Oh, how could he have ever thought of going north without them? They would find a way to live somehow, all of them together as it should be.

He was nearly with her, just a few meters to go. He decided to surprise her. He approached her, very close, and he grabbed her from behind in a great bear hug, lifting her into the air.

"My heart!" He laughed into her ear. "I am here!"

She screamed, and it was not her voice.

Startled, Ramón set her down and said, "Raquel?" But it was only a woman who looked like Raquel from the back: the same perfectly clear skin, the same raven-colored hair shining like a liquid, the same regal Mayan profile. "I am sorry, señorita," said Ramón. "I thought you were my wife."

The woman stared at him warily. "You do not know your own wife, señor?"

"You look like her a little, and I have not seen her for so long, and I was excited, so I . . . I am very sorry."

The woman's wariness receded. "You saw whom you wished to see."

"Yes, señorita. I suppose that is true."

A softness entered in her eyes. "How long since you were with her?"

"Five days, señorita."

"Only *five*?"

"It is a lifetime!"

She laughed. He thought it was a pretty laugh. He thought she was a pretty girl, but not as pretty as Raquel. She said, "I am Guadalupe Soledad Consuelo de la Garza, a shopkeeper."

He shook her hand. "Much pleasure, señorita. I am Ramón Ernesto Rodríguez Obregón, a traveler."

"Are you traveling to the United States?"

"I hope so. To Wilson City, in California. I have a friend there."

"You are not from Naco?"

"No. I live in Hércules, in Coahuila."

"I have never heard of it."

"It is a small town."

"I too am from a small town. Rincón de Dolores, in Jalisco."

"Jalisco? You have come far."

A shadow crossed her face. "For no reason, apparently."

"But why, señorita?"

"I did not know it cost so much to hire a guide."

"You do not have enough?"

"No."

She put so much sorrow in that single word, Ramón felt the weight of it. "You have a family in Rincón de Dolores, loved ones who depend on you to cross?"

She shook her head. "I have no family."

He thought to ask her to explain her sorrow at not crossing, but his questions had already gone beyond civility. Besides, he had sadness enough of his own. "Then," he said, "good luck."

As he turned to go, she said, "Do you know how to get around that wall?"

"It goes out into the desert on each side of the town. Only walk beside it to the end."

"And then you cross?"

"Not at the end of the wall, señorita. They watch that area most carefully."

"So I must walk farther? How far, do you think?"

"Señorita, do you plan to go alone?"

"I have no choice."

"It is a big desert, with little water. To get lost is to die."

"I know."

"La Migra has night-vision binoculars to keep watch from moving platforms high up in the air—'cherry pickers,' the Americanos call them—and when your footsteps shake the ground they have machines that speak of your position to men in buildings many miles away. Just beyond the border other men in white trucks with green stripes listen to their radios for reports from those machines. They are very fine hunters, señorita. Like the cougar, which also prowls the desert, they can fall on you without a sound."

She nodded. "I have heard all of this before."

"When you get to the other side, how will you reach a town?"

"I will walk."

Ramón shook his head. "It is too far. You must get a ride."

"Do you have a ride?"

"It is part of the guide service. They have someone on the other side to pick us up when we reach the road."

"I understand."

"But still you plan to cross alone? Without a ride arranged?"

"I must."

"But why?"

She stared into the distance. "I have seen something . . . a miracle. It compels me to go. I must save the Americanos."

He stared at her a moment, trying to decide if she was crazy. But she truly did remind him of Raquel, who also believed in miracles. What if Raquel were in the desert, alone and lost? He said, "I will cross tonight with many others. The coyote, he comes for us at seven o'clock. We meet in the park across the street back there. If you follow at a distance, I do not think he can stop you. Then perhaps you can sneak onto his truck on the other side of the border."

"Yes?" She brightened. "I can do this?"

"You must be very careful. If you follow us too closely, he will probably force you away. Some of these fellows are not good men, you know. Many of them smuggle drugs as well as people. But if you fall too far back behind, you will lose us. The trails are not well marked. You must not become lost in the desert, señorita. Upon your life, you must not."

"I understand."

"If you do not get lost and die of thirst or get a bite from a rattlesnake before you find the road, the most likely one to pick you up will be La Migra. They will then return you back to Mexico and it will be for nothing. I myself have tried and failed two times, and that was with a coyote to guide me."

"I do understand, señor. Truly I do. But I must go."

He thought for a moment. "Listen. I will walk behind the others, as far back as I can without losing them myself. That way you need only to follow me, and if the coyote stays with the rest, as he surely will, he will have less chance of noticing you."

"God bless you, señor."

"Forgive me, but I must be satisfied in my own mind that you understand the risks. If you cannot sneak onto the coyote's truck with us you will be stranded many days' walk away from water. You will certainly die. Are you absolutely sure you wish to cross?"

"I must."

"Very well, Señorita de la Garza. Until tonight in the park, at seven."

They shook hands and the woman who was not Raquel said, "Until then, Señor Rodríguez."

CAPÍTULO 5

ALTA CALIFORNIA WAS A HARD country. Sun, dust, thorns, and serpents pressed them on all sides, yet Fray Benicio seemed undaunted. The tall young man spoke earnestly of God's purity and glory as revealed by the land's austerity and rustic beauty. His ceaseless enthusiasm did not win him friends among his miserable companions. Most of the soldiers preferred complaints; indeed, even Fray Alejandro was tempted to resent the brother's naïve enthusiasm. Caught up in his struggle with the land, the good friar sometimes forgot why he was there. Then, remembering his calling at the Porziuncola and ashamed of this failing in himself, Alejandro prayed for such a faith as Fray Benicio's, and for the clarity of mind to see that land as a pristine, shining thing even as he suffered from the broiling air and omnipresent dust.

The leather-jacket soldiers shed their jerkins, shunning protection from arrows in the hope of some slight relief from the awful heat. Don Felipe, normally reserved and urbane, laced his orders with obscenities. Fray Guillermo, red and fair, suffered greatly. His pale skin blistered and peeled where it emerged from his robes. To protect his tonsured scalp he often raised his hood, but then the heat tormented him beneath the heavy cloth so he put it down again. His only solace from this devil's alternative seemed to come from taking daily stock of their provisions.

Although Fray Alejandro did not doubt the abbot's vow of poverty, to him it sometimes seemed Guillermo reviewed their possessions as if the inventory were a kind of creed: so many reams of paper, so many blankets, so many yards of sackcloth and green baize, and maguey cloth, and red pepper bales, and dried beef, cotton seed, vine cuttings, wine, lentils, flour, rice, lard, and of course there was the herd of cattle to be counted twice each day. Alejandro thought this preoccupation with quantities and numbers a strange form of comfort for a Franciscan. They were taught to place their trust in God alone, who never changes. Guillermo's weights and measures, on the other hand, could not even be relied upon from one place to the next. For example, Alejandro had heard it said air weighs very little on a mountaintop, but by the sea that same air weighs much more. Crisp and delightful at the higher elevations, taxing and oppressive in that harsh and bitter land . . . of what use were Guillermo's lists and inventories when the very ether of existence was so fickle?

Many years away into the future and far to the east of Alejandro's position, in the Sonoran Desert a little south of the state of Arizona, Guadalupe Soledad Consuelo de la Garza, having only recently descended from the light air of the Sierra Madre, also suffered from the brooding weight of lower altitudes. Nevertheless, she pursued Ramón Rodríguez's distant silhouette through the arid landscape. Panting in the leaden atmosphere, burdened by a burlap bag hung from a rope over one shoulder and by plastic water bottles in a backpack over the other, she blessed that good man when he fell behind the little group of travelers at the ragged edge of town, exactly as he had promised.

It was night, and the moon, a mere sliver, gave little guiding light. Lupe followed from as far behind Señor Rodríguez as she dared. In the desert beyond town she looked down to check her footing, only to look up again and find him nowhere to be seen. She continued walking— what else could she do?—and he appeared ahead again. The following was easy at first, the trail wide and well cleared, but that changed little by little until eventually she realized there was no proper trail at all. The low desert plants drew close to prick her trousers. Unseen creatures scurried off at her approach. She tried not to think of rattlesnakes.

She reached a barbed-wire fence almost as high as her shoulders. The man's black form was on the other side, disappearing over a low rise. She dropped her backpack and her burlap burden to the dirt beside the wire. She stepped onto the lowest strand and climbed. Barbs sank into her palms. She continued climbing. She swung one leg over the top and another barb bit her inner thigh. Crying out, she fell and landed on her back with the fabric of one trouser leg caught up in the wire. She ripped herself free. She reached through the fence and dragged her backpack and the other burden underneath the lower strand. She stood, and searched the desert for Ramón Rodríguez.

Vague in the gray moonlight were the towering forms of saguaro cacti. Beneath these she saw other, less impressive plants. She did not see the man. Strapping the water-laden pack upon her back and carrying the contents of the burlap bag as if it were a precious infant, Guadalupe Soledad Consuelo de la Garza walked into America.

She remembered what Señor Rodríguez had said: with so many men and machines arrayed against them, most travelers were caught. It was usually by trying many times that one finally entered and remained. This did not concern her. If she was successful, she would begin her work in a few days in some town or village. On the other hand, if she was caught it would be a chance to tell an Americano of the cross and empty tomb that very night, to pray for them, these poor lost people she had come to save. How she yearned to pray for them in person, to lay her hands on them, to show the love of Christ to them! One way or the other, in a few days or tonight, she would have a chance. This thought made her burden light.

Ignoring her bleeding palms, Lupe reached the edge of an arroyo, a dry streambed about five feet deep. She scrambled down the side until she stood on the level bottom, where the sand was very fine. In the dim moonlight she saw many footprints in the sand, hundreds of them headed in the same direction. Surely Señor Rodríguez and the others must have passed this way, as had many more before them. Surely La Migra knew of such a well-used path. Surely they would watch it. She listened, hoping to hear the others, and, listening, she heard many desert sounds—barks and calls and clicks—but nothing human. She decided not to walk in the arroyo. She climbed the far embankment, where, keeping the dry streambed to her left, she continued north.

Her one concern was for the miracle she carried. If she was caught, and the Americanos did not let her keep it, how would she face Padre Hinojosa? Thinking of this, she did not notice a large stone in her path. She tripped and stumbled to her knees.

It was a posture she adopted often. It reminded her of the morning, many days before, when she had gone to see the padre and told him of the feeling, the voice, which had called her to this quest, when Padre Hinojosa had opened the iron gate and entered the deep niche that sheltered Fray Alejandro's *retablo* and beckoned her to follow. She had remained as motionless as any of the chapel's wooden saints, thinking surely this was wrong, but the padre had insisted. "Come with me, daughter. Have no fear."

"But Padre—"

"Lupe, do you have faith in our Lord?"

"Yes, Padre. I do."

"Then come."

Thus commanded, Lupe entered, but filled with fear and veneration she had not moved very far. Great was the inertia of sacred tradition.

From deeper in the shadows the old priest returned to clasp her two hands in his. "Lupe, if you will only trust me you will see there is good reason. I have waited most of my life for this moment. I have watched you carefully. As you grew from child to woman I became more certain. But it was not for me to tell you what to do. The calling has been yours alone to answer. Now you say our Lord has spoken, so come with me, gentle daughter. Come and see the miracle awaiting you."

He pulled upon her hands, and she followed him into the darkness of the niche.

On her knees in the Sonoran Desert, Lupe remembered another moment many years before, when she, a wayward child, had entered the chapel of Santa Dolores alone. In that lofty space the echoes of her footsteps had threatened to betray her, but she crossed the central nave quite boldly, determined to kneel at the iron gate guarding the niche, to peer between the bars and see for herself the pictures on Fray Alejandro's mysterious *retablo*. At that much younger age Lupe somehow felt she had a right to see the pictures. In the chapel where she knew she should not go alone, the child she used to be had knelt and stared into the darkness. She had pressed her small forehead against the iron to move as close as possible. She had opened her eyelids wide, the better to admit what little light there was. Deep inside the niche she had seen three small panels standing upright on a crudely carved wood table, a twin of the credence table on which the bread and wine of the Eucharist were kept. The little altarpiece was not covered or hidden in any way, yet eternal shadows in the niche concealed the image on the *retablo*'s surface. In frustration, little Lupe had tried to open the gate. Iron had rattled loudly against iron, the sound greatly amplified by the hard stucco walls and vaulted ceiling. Lupe fled.

Later, she had been ashamed of her behavior. She had resolved never to look between the bars into the niche again, and she had kept her resolution perfectly until the day when Padre Hinojosa beckoned and she had followed him to stand before the table in the shadows.

The old man whispered, "Prepare yourself." Then the wooden match had flared, and Lupe flinched and backed away. The padre, who understood the reason for her fear, spoke soothingly. "It is only a little match, and a single candle. Do not be afraid. Come close now and see." The candle was ignited. Fray Alejandro's *retablo* was illuminated. Despite her trepidation, Lupe approached.

She saw nothing miraculous about the altarpiece. She saw only three small panels hinged together like a folding screen, the two outer panels swinging open from the middle one, allowing the *retablo* to stand upright on its own. Strangely, the central panel bore no image. It was only a simple piece of wood, unfinished and unadorned, about half a meter tall and a quarter meter wide. In contrast, the two outer panels were trimmed with gilded frames which sparkled in the candlelight, their surfaces covered with colorful and intricate paintings. On each side panel she saw a man upon a cross. Obviously these were the two thieves who were crucified with her Savior. Beneath one thief she saw a crowd of people, ugly people, frozen by a master artist's hand in postures of derision and mockery, shouting and shaking their fists toward the empty central panel. Beneath the other thief she saw a few mourners around a woman who could only be the Virgen de Guadalupe, surrounded as she was by golden flames. Behind and above the crosses

Lupe saw a hillside in profile, apparently Golgotha. Arrayed upon the hillside she saw many angels looking toward the unpainted wooden panel in the center.

In spite of such an ugly scene, the blood, the tortured men, Lupe thought the two side panels were quite lovely, alive with light and color. Yet lovely though they were, still she saw no miracle. Lupe said, "I don't understand, Padre. Why was it necessary to conceal this from the people?"

"You must look more carefully. Draw closer, daughter."

She tried, but the flicker of the candle's flame filled her with foreboding. Seeing the reason for her hesitation, Padre Hinojosa lifted the candle with one hand and held it near the painted panel on the right. He placed his other hand upon her arm. "See?" he said. "I will hold the candle for you. It is perfectly safe. Have courage, Lupe, and behold."

Ashamed of her cowardice before the flame, Lupe inched a little closer. In the flickering candlelight the images upon the small altarpiece seemed to move with life. On the left, the mocking crowd shook fists toward the empty central panel. On the right, the mourners gazed up toward it sorrowfully. Then Lupe saw the mourners and the Virgin . . . and she thought it could not be, and yet . . .

Lupe collapsed.

Much as she would later trip over a stone and fall to her knees beside a nameless arroyo in the Sonoran Desert, Lupe fell before Fray Alejandro's *retablo*. Only Padre Hinojosa's hand around her arm rescued her from injury upon the hard tile floor. Kneeling, she stared at the altarpiece and trembled.

"Do not fear it, Lupe," said Padre Hinojosa, bending down beside her with a grunt, for he was not young. "It was ordained in love more than two centuries ago."

"But it is blasphemy!"

"Blasphemy? No, daughter. Not that."

"It *must* be blasphemy! I am only an unworthy sinner."

"As were Peter, Paul, and the apostles, and every other saint who ever lived."

"Saint? I am not a saint!"

"Ah. The protest of them all."

She shook her head. "No, Padre. This cannot be."

"Yet look, and see it is."

Lupe would not look. What she had seen within the painting must have been wrong. Lifting clasped hands to her chin, she bowed her head to pray. Padre Hinojosa did the same. In the dim light of a single candle, the two of them knelt side by side before the miracle. In time, still in her prayerful posture, the woman asked, "What must I do?"

"Earlier you said you had received a quest."

"I might have been mistaken."

"Mistaken? Look at the *retablo*, Lupe."

Still she would not look. Gazing at the floor in supplication, she said, "I am just a simple woman, Padre. I have no fine words."

"What were the words of Moses when our Lord commanded him to lead Israel out of bondage?"

Lupe remembered. "'Who am I, of uncircumcised lips?'"

"Yes, daughter. You have been an excellent pupil. And now perhaps you understand why I asked you alone, out of all the people in this village, to study with me privately. Gripping the table edge for support, the old priest rose. On his feet above her he said, "Tell me this as well: Jonah, who tried to escape the calling of our Lord, what was the result?"

"He . . . he was pursued. And chastised."

"Do not make the same mistake, my daughter."

"But—"

"Do not make the same mistake!"

Carefully, the old man folded the *retablo*. From a drawer in the center of the table he withdrew a crimson velvet sack, the one Lupe had seen many times in the hands of an honored village boy on the Feast Day of Fray Alejandro. The priest slipped the *retablo* into the velvet sack and said, "Rise, daughter."

Lupe did as he commanded, and the padre placed the burden of the sack into her hands, saying, "It will be your guide."

Kneeling alone beside the arroyo in the desert of Sonora, in the state of Arizona, in the United States of America, the woman prayed for courage. Strangely, she could sense no answer. She rose to her feet. She dusted off her knees and adjusted the straps of her backpack and peered into the darkness, hoping for a glimpse of Ramón Rodríguez.

Seeing nothing but the moonlit sand and cacti, she bent to lift her burden, a velvet bundle in a burlap sack. The sun had been down for some time, and it was getting cold. She had not expected that. Shivering, she set out again beside the arroyo, hoping she was heading north. She had no compass. She knew not how to read the stars. She had no watch to track the time. Hours passed without a glimpse of Señor Rodríguez, and when at last the pitiless sun arose again to burn the earth, she was surely lost.

CAPÍTULO 6

ARRIVING AT A SHALLOW CANYON near the coast, the Spanish expedition found a small creek in which the slightest trickle remained. They decided to make camp. It was the first sign of fresh water in six days and along the canyon floor were many sycamores, which blessed the earth with shade. Water and shade—how priceless were such luxuries. Guillermo and Don Felipe decided to remain an extra day to rest the men and horses and to celebrate the Feast of our Savior's Ascension.

Among the deep shadows of the canyon, a Mass was held at terce the next morning. Fray Guillermo officiated, with Benicio attending. Wary of the savages in that region who were rumored to dine on human flesh, Don Felipe insisted on a guard. He stationed six men around the camp, one upstream, one downstream and two on each side, up along the canyon ridges. He also insisted that the remaining men attend the Mass in battle dress, with their hardened leather jerkins, shields, and pikes. Thus it was that a young *mestizo* soldier named Modesto became the means through which the mission site was chosen. Just as the sun appeared above the canyon ridge a pure white dove alighted on the soldier's pike. Then the sunshine racing down along the canyon wall rested on the dove, which became blinding in its brilliance.

All agreed it was a holy sign, and after much prayer Fray Guillermo chose that place for the Misión de Santa Dolores. At his direction, the soldiers built a cross of sycamore. It was raised and blessed to the great joy of all, except perhaps for Guillermo himself. Even as the enthusiastic Benicio led everyone in hymns, Alejandro saw the abbot, very stern of visage, taking stock of their provisions yet again.

That night as he lay down to sleep Fray Alejandro pondered the abbot's actions. It seemed to him earthly wealth offered nothing to those who were determined to be miserable. Power, safety, and liberty were commodities for those who could afford the price; even justice could be purchased, yet none of these most precious acquisitions could lift a soul from sadness.

If this was true in Alejandro's time, it was all the more so true in the complicated modern times of Delano Wright, who remained helpless before heartbreak in spite of his considerable fortune. Sitting in a high school counselor's office, he tried to defend himself against yet another wave of misery by giving it a name. "You think she's clinically depressed?" he said. "Is that what you're saying?"

Dr. Simmons seemed to force his personality across the room at Delano, leaning forward with an innocent, searching expression. "'Clinically depressed' has a specific meaning, Mr. Wright. Before we can answer your question we need more information about Harmony."

The doctor was one of those tanned, hard-bodied men, a lifelong surfer, probably. He made Delano feel pale and naked, as if it were obvious how out of shape he was in spite of his loose clothes. Delano said, "What kind of information?"

The school counselor lifted a piece of paper from his desk and handed it to Delano. "We should begin with this."

Taking the paper, Delano read the heading. "Beck Depression Inventory?"

"It's a list of questions we use to determine the presence of unipolar depression, or clinical depression, as you called it."

"So give it to her."

"I tried. She wouldn't answer it."

"Why not?"

"She wouldn't say, exactly. She just said she'd rather not."

Delano scanned the questionnaire. "It asks about sex. If she's interested in sex."

"A decline in libido is one sign of severe depression."

"She's only fifteen."

The man smiled, his naïve eyes belied by what he said. "Surely you're aware that fifteen-year-old girls are interested in sex, Mr. Wright."

"Not Harmony."

"I'm not saying she's sexually active. I'm only saying—"

"Not Harmony. She knows better than that."

Delano remembered Ana's parting accusation, the way she had compared him to Harry. At least he's *interested.* Delano extended the paper toward the man. "Let's move on."

Dr. Simmons leaned forward to receive the questionnaire. "All right. But without this kind of input, I really don't see how I can help."

"Help with what, exactly? That's the question."

"As I've tried to explain, several people here have noticed Harmony doesn't seem herself. From what I've seen I have to agree with them."

"But what is the *problem,* exactly? Not being herself tells me nothing."

"Haven't you noticed a change in Harmony at home, Mr. Wright? Listlessness? Lack of interest? Inability to socialize?"

Delano thought of their awful evening meals together, him trying desperately to make small talk, Harmony's monosyllabic replies, the dreadful strain of being cheerful even with disaster happening before his eyes, an acid undercurrent which he must try to ignore because acknowledgment would only hasten the collapse. He sighed. "She has good reasons for all that. Sometimes depression is normal, right?"

"Certainly. It depends on the reasons."

"You do know her mother left us?"

"Yes, of course she told me. I'm very sorry."

"Thanks. But don't you think that explains it? I mean, her mother didn't just leave me. She left Harmony too."

"It's a difficult thing for a child to accept."

"Accept? Her mother *left* her, Doctor. Her mother said she'd drop by in a few weeks and then she drove off in the Porsche and that was that. So of course Harmony's depressed. Any kid would be depressed. *I'm* depressed. It's only natural."

"When you say you're depressed, what do you mean, exactly?"

Delano crossed one leg over the other and gripped his ankle with both hands, a defensive move, a way to regain some of the distance he had lost with his unwise admission. This doctor had somehow managed to get him to admit his feelings. Certainly he was depressed, but that was no one's business but his own. He stared directly at the man, willing his eyes to become hard, his face a perfect mask, revealing no emotion whatsoever. He spoke blithely, as if discussing some minor piece of business. "We're not here to talk about me."

The man flashed his sycophantic smile. "Just trying to be helpful."

"I'm fine."

"That's what Harmony said."

"Maybe she meant it."

"Mr. Wright, I'm sorry. We're not making any progress. This might have been a mistake."

Delano uncrossed his legs and leaned forward, earnest now, pressing his advantage. "Listen. I appreciate what you're trying to do. It's just, I think Harmony needs to work through this in her own way, you know?"

"That's very possible. But if she could be properly diagnosed, we have medications that can help."

So that was it. Forget discipline. Forget the possibility that growth might come through suffering. Fill in all the valleys even if it means lopping off the peaks. Avoid all pain at all costs. "You have medications that can help?" he said. "Really? Something to help bring her mother to her senses? Help her to come home?"

"Now, Mr. Wright, I don't—"

"I'm serious. If anybody's crazy here it's my wife, not Harmony."

"I'm not saying Harmony is crazy."

"Ill, then. Mentally ill. You're obviously saying she's mentally ill, or you wouldn't want to give her drugs."

"I'm only saying psychotropic medications offer some patients time to get their thoughts in order. To adjust to circumstances, if you will."

"Circumstances?" Delano Wright stood up. "I thought this was a Christian school."

"Of course."

"We're not dealing with circumstances. This is a trial we're in. A trial to build our faith, to make us stronger."

"I understand, but—"

"Then why are you so quick to offer drugs? Harmony doesn't need them. She has her faith. She has God, and me."

Delano left the office of that ignorant man, who had no idea what an awful price one paid for standing fearfully at a distance from the wild and rushing river of sentiment, no concept of the jealousy one suffered watching others dive in freely, the bitterness of being branded as unfeeling by the very ones you hoped to spare from an embarrassment of emotions if ever once the dam you built were breached. Their conversation had disinterred a memory as if raising up the dead, an image of a frightened boy of six or maybe seven, at any rate too young for his feet to touch the ground as he waited on a wooden bench outside the headmaster's office at a prestigious West Coast preparatory school.

His father would have much preferred to keep his son at home, but Delano's mother, a Driscol of the Philadelphia Driscols, had strong ideas about the way a child of privilege should be raised. "Boys must not be coddled," was her frequent admonition. Years went by before Delano realized the word 'coddled' was as antiquated as his mother's ideas on the subject.

When the headmaster's door had opened and his mother had emerged, young Delano had leapt up from the wooden bench to stand in eager expectation. June was upon them, and a break from school for two whole months. Never was a boy more ready to go home. But it was not to be.

She stood high above him, looking down. "Delano," she said. (She never called him "Del," as his father did.) "I know this will be a disappointment, but your father and I have agreed it's best for you to stay at school this summer."

"But—"

"Don't interrupt. Your grades are not what they should be. Your French and Spanish are atrocious. So we have to do something about that, don't we? Dr. Headley has agreed to see that you are tutored properly."

"But—"

"Don't snivel. Stand up straight. This is what happens when you don't work on your lessons hard enough, you see?"

"But don't you want me to come home?"

"Of course we do. Your father and I will return for you one week before the end of summer break, unless you fail to satisfy your tutors. All you have to do . . . What is that? Tears? Oh come *on*, Delano. It's only seven weeks for goodness' sake. Try not to be so childish."

Delano Wright had not relived that memory in years, but once it came it would not quickly go. It lingered still at five thirty in the afternoon as he sat waiting for Harmony at the Wilson City Stables. She rode her palomino, Rowdy, after school on Mondays, Wednesdays, and most Fridays. From inside the Range Rover he saw her come across the lawn in heather green jodhpurs and knee-high riding boots with a white helmet carried under her arm. Her beautiful blond hair was pulled back in a ponytail. She stared at the dead grass at her feet as she came. A pair of girls intercepted her, laughing. She paused to speak with them. The girls were clearly in a playful mood, giggling and jostling each other. Watching Harmony, he had the feeling nothing she saw made it to her brain. It was as if she had glass eyes.

When she sat beside him in the Range Rover, Delano said, "Are those girls friends of yours?"

Staring ahead through the windshield, she said, "Sort of."

"They really seem to like you."

"I guess."

He drove silently along the canyon road, the bluffs beside them shades of amber and sienna, the view composed of dried grass, stone, and naked soil. Passing the forty-twelve, one of many large parcels of untouched property he owned along the road, Delano remembered making a casual remark about the money they could get for the land, and Harmony, too young to realize he was only thinking out loud, begging her mother not to let him sell. Then it was Ana on the attack as usual: Why couldn't he be more sensitive? Did he not care how much his daughter loved to ride Rowdy on the forty-twelve? Did he not remember it was where they'd buried Pepper? Taking Harmony's side against him, as usual, bringing up her horse and her dead dog, accusing him of greed, accusing him of caring more for money than for family.

He drove beside his property for another ten minutes. He owned almost everything from Wilson City to Blanco Beach. Finally he steered around a gentle bend and the deep turquoise Pacific appeared in the distance, the welcome coolness of it framed by steep slopes on the left and right. At the edge of Blanco Beach he turned into a side canyon, following the steep road up toward his estate. Except for the slight hiss of bone-dry air slipping past the windows, the interior of the British vehicle was nearly silent, even as the engine labored up the hill. Glancing at Harmony's profile, he asked, "Want to turn on the radio?"

"No, thanks."

"I don't mind."

"That's okay. We're almost there."

He stopped at the gate, pressing the remote control above his sun visor and waiting until the steel barricade slid out of the way. Driving on, he soon reached the granite pavement outside the garage. As Harmony opened her door, he said, "You know I love you, right?"

She looked at him. "Sure, Daddy."

"Okay. Just so you know."

She said, "Sure," again, and stepped out and closed the door, leaving him alone in the Range Rover.

He sat there, watching her walk away. He thought of Christian men who seduced other men's wives. He thought of Christian women who allowed themselves to be seduced. He thought of all his friends at church who had been divorced, and all the ones who drank too much, who told ribald jokes on the golf course and spent their tithes on luxuries. He thought of doctors peddling medication instead of letting people feel the things that ought to hurt. He thought of that some more. Suddenly he gave his head a little shake, and he got out and went inside the house.

Harmony was nowhere to be seen. It was possible for two people to spend all day in his huge house without seeing or hearing each other, but he had decided not to downsize after Ana left. Given what had happened, he believed it would be best for Harmony if he kept everything as normal as possible. So he and Harmony would continue living in what some might call a mansion, at least for the time being.

He passed through the entry gallery and down a long corridor, turning right into his study. Closing the door, he felt himself relax. This was his favorite place. Surrounded by his books in shelves from floor to ceiling, whether sitting at the eighteenth century American walnut desk or in one of the leather wingback chairs beside the fireplace, he could indulge himself in his love affair with the written word.

He selected one of many Bibles on a shelf and sat down to read. Turning to a page marked by a ribbon, he found himself in Proverbs:

> *Wisdom will save you from the ways of wicked men,*
> *from men whose words are perverse,*
> *who leave the straight paths*
> *to walk in dark ways,*
> *who delight in doing wrong*
> *and rejoice in the perverseness of evil,*
> *whose paths are crooked*
> *and who are devious in their ways.*
> *It will save you also from the adulteress,*
> *from the wayward wife with her seductive words,*
> *who has left the partner of her youth*
> *and ignored the covenant she made before God.*

He read the passage once again, convinced it had been written just for him. He continued reading, and lost himself within the words. Across the library were two pairs of tall French doors flanked by silken curtains. Through the doors the angle of daylight slowly shifted, until the beam struck him in the moments just before the sun slipped below the surface of the sea. Annoyed by the glare, he shifted his position and continued reading. Soon the sun was gone. In the afterglow he switched on the reading lamp beside his chair. He had found another reference to adulterous women, and another . . . seven at least in the book of Proverbs alone.

"Daddy?"

It was Harmony's voice on the intercom.

Looking up, he spoke as if she were with him in the room. "Yes?"

"Dinner's ready."

"All right, Button. I'm coming."

Before he rose, he pulled a fountain pen from his shirt pocket. Carefully, he underlined a section of the page he had been reading. The pressure of the lines drove deep into the sheets of tissue-thin paper underneath. The thickness of the ink almost made the words themselves illegible.

Upon entering the morning room beside the kitchen he found Harmony already at the table. He sat across from his daughter. Dinner had been nicely arranged, complete with place mats and matching linen napkins, bright blue and yellow fabric, which Ana had purchased at a shop in Cabo San Lucas, if he remembered correctly.

He breathed deeply through his nose. "This smells great. Hey, peanuts! Must be Thai."

Harmony nodded. "Uh-huh. Massaman curry."

"Great. You want to say the blessing?"

Harmony bowed her head and said, "Thank you for this food. Amen." He watched her as they started eating. She kept her eyes down on her plate. She ate only a little, and then mostly stirred her food around, slowly cutting it into smaller and smaller portions, seldom lifting her fork to her mouth.

"That Rosa, she's a real find," he said.

"I guess."

"Well, she's a better cook than Flora ever was, that's for sure."

Harmony looked up at him. "You think so?"

"Sure. Don't you? This is a wonderful dinner."

"I cooked it."

"No."

"Uh-huh."

"Well, Button, I'm impressed. This is just a wonderful dinner. Really."

"Thanks." She dropped her eyes again.

They ate silently for a while; then Delano asked, "So, what made you decide to cook the dinner?"

"Someone had to do it."

"What about Rosa?"

"She left early."

"How come?"

"I don't know."

"She just left without explaining?"

"She said her boyfriend was down at the gate and she had to go, is all."

Delano took another bite, and chewed it slowly. He swallowed and said, "She talked about a boyfriend? Are you sure?"

"Yes."

After dinner, he helped Harmony with the dishes. His daughter went upstairs to finish her homework. He returned to the study. Walking behind his antique desk, he opened a drawer and selected a manila file folder. From it, he removed a piece of paper. He examined it to verify his recollection that Rosa Gomez had told him she was married. Yes, there it was in black and white: husband, Mario, and a cellular telephone number for the man in case of emergencies. Yet a boyfriend picked her up at work.

Delano put the folder back in the desk drawer and crossed to the wingback reading chair. On the table by the chair lay the open Bible. The text he had underlined before dinner was clearly visible in the light of the reading lamp:

If a man commits adultery with another man's wife—with the wife of his neighbor—both the adulterer and the adulteress must be put to death.

He sat down and considered what to do about these women and their boyfriends.

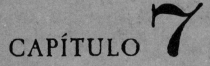

CAPÍTULO 7

WORK BEGAN IMMEDIATELY UPON THE chapel. Hastened by the ceaseless lashing of Fray Guillermo's tongue, the leatherjacket soldiers erected thick walls of tan adobe bricks to a height of seven *varas* in a few short weeks. Then the roof became a problem. Most of the surrounding sycamores had been contorted into crooked shapes by constant ocean breezes. It was impossible to find straight trees tall enough to bridge the span from one side of the chapel to the other. Fortunately, one of the soldiers devised a cunning way to splice short lengths together. While a team of men logged the best trees in the grove, Alejandro and Benicio followed the creek bed inland, harvesting short saplings to be used as *latillas,* or lathing, for the chapel ceiling between the beams. Thus the friars came to stand among a cluster of low bushes when three heathens appeared in the arroyo just below.

Their forms did not support the myths so often told of them. Cannibals should be large and frightening—so thought Alejandro—yet these men were small in stature, broad and bowlegged as if victimized by rickets. With their wide noses and black eyes they were perhaps as ugly as Fray Alejandro himself, but certainly not terrible or fearsome. Rather than a sense of dread as he looked down on them, Alejandro felt only amazement at their shamelessness, for they did not seem to notice their own nudity. The ever-zealous Fray Benicio did not seem to notice either. Smiling broadly, he did his best to speak with them while Alejandro stood by, silenced with astonishment.

Unlike the Cochimí farther south, these Indians wore nothing but small leather pouches. They carried only throwing sticks. Alejandro marveled that they could live in such a hostile place with so little. It reminded him of what he had been taught at La Universidad de San Fernando in Mexico City while preparing for his work. Survival in the elements is a matter of the rule of three. One perishes in three minutes without air, three hours in cold weather without proper clothing, and three days without water.

Today we know these rules should not be taken literally. Many people have survived much longer. Many perish sooner. The record is ten minutes seventeen seconds without air. In the desert of Sonora, in an Arizona summer, without water, Guadalupe Soledad Consuelo de la Garza might well die in fewer days than three.

It had been thirty hours since she emptied the last plastic bottle and dropped her backpack to the ground. Sitting in the shade of a rock overhang, she prayed while waiting for the sunset. Only in the dark did Lupe dare to move. She knew nothing of the rule of three, but unless she was rescued sometime in the night she did believe the next day would be her last.

Nevertheless, the young woman prayed with confidence. She had asked for rescue long ago, and did not bother her Creator with additional requests. Her prayers now were mostly words of praise. She praised the Holy Father for her health, which had allowed her to survive up to that moment. She praised Him for her old friends in Rincón de Dolores, and for Padre Hinojosa, who had led her in the Way. She praised God for her Savior, who had rescued her from a fate much worse than this. She praised God for the beauty of the desert, which was a reflection of his majesty, and for this chance to witness a new aspect of him after all her years in cool and verdant mountains.

Padre Hinojosa had taught her the Holy Father could be beautifully fearsome. She remembered Aaron's sons, Moses' nephews, who approached too close to the Most Holy Place without the proper preparation and were consumed by flames which flashed out from the Presence of the Lord. She shivered in the heat to think of such a fire. High in the cool mountains of Rincón de Dolores she could never have imagined such a fearsome God, but now she knew what Aaron's sons had seen in their last moment: a splendid furnace like the gloriously shimmering desert, a beauty worth the horror of the flames.

In spite of her parched mouth and throat, when she was not praying Lupe tried to sing. She remembered melodies from Don Pedro's radio, from the Protestant station the deaf cobbler had tried to listen to sometimes. One song in particular she liked very much. Amazing grace, how sweet the sound that saved a wretch like me. She understood it was a very famous hymn among the Americanos.

She did not think the Holy Father minded that she listened to such words. The preachers and the singers on the Protestant radio station seemed to love the Savior as she did, even if they were perhaps mistaken on some details. But she would never mention the radio station to Padre Hinojosa.

Lupe sang softly, I once was lost, but now am found, and before her eyes a serpent crawled across the soil. She fell silent, watching from the shadow of the rock as it traveled in an S-shaped fashion. It passed out of sight beneath a low-lying bush without leaves. It was of course a rattlesnake.

She thought of the serpent that deceived the first man and woman. She did not think the Evil One had been a serpent in the same way as this little thing which crawled before her humbly on its belly, seeking shade as she herself had done. She felt pity for the snake beneath the bush. She believed it knew only the horror of the heat, and nothing of the desert's beauty.

She had no fear of death. The Holy Father's ways were not her ways, of course, yet it would be very strange if he had sent her on a quest, only to let her perish in the desert before she had a chance to speak to one single person of the Savior. She remembered what the priest of Rincón de Dolores had taught her of the prophet Moses, who remained upon the mountain forty days and nights, and the Savior himself, who suffered forty days of temptation in a wilderness. Israel was very dry and very hot, or so the padre said. If the Savior and the prophet Moses had been tested in a place like this, a place where one might learn to see the Holy Father's fearsome beauty, perhaps this desert was her place of testing too.

Holy Father, if that is so, give me strength, for I am weak.

When I am weak, then I am strong. The words came to mind as if San Pablo himself had whispered in her ear. Lupe knew it was important to conserve her strength, but joy rose in her irresistibly. She began to sing again. In the lonely shade below the rock she longed to teach the song to the Americanos if in fact they did not know it. I once was lost but now am found. Perhaps it was a prophecy.

When evening came at last, she arose with Alejandro's burden in her arms and walked into the gloaming. It was her last chance. "Señor serpent," she said beside the leafless bush, "please allow me passage through your land."

With the glow of sunset fading on her left, she walked. One by one the stars awoke. Below the darkening sky she tried to find the proper star to follow. She had done the same the night before, but the stars she picked had slowly fallen to the earth and disappeared. She had heard of a star in the north that did not move, but did not know which one it was, so she selected a light at random and tried to judge its movement, making small adjustments in her own direction as she went. When at last the final remnant of the sunset had departed, the sparkles in the heavens became countless. Some were densely packed together and reminded Lupe of powdered sugar, others stood out bright and clear.

Lupe paused to stare up in wonder. She was such a tiny creature. Above her was a bowl of glittering ebony that stretched into forever. She thought, I once was lost but now am found, was blind, but now I see. She thanked her Holy Father for his vastness, praying with her eyes wide open and turned upward, toward the Mighty One she served. Spinning slowly around in wonder—seeing—she clutched Fray Alejandro's burden closely to her breast.

The desert in the night grew quickly cold. How this could be after such a fierce heat in the day she did not know. She only knew she had to walk to remain warm. Beneath her shoes the earth crackled and crunched with every step, shifting sometimes on the slopes, causing her to stumble. Rarely did she fall, but when she did she tried to fall beneath her burden, and not on top of it. Several times she brushed against the thorns of a cactus. Her trousers and her lower legs had been slashed in many places. Sometimes she encountered barbed-wire fences. These were not as tall or well made as the one she had climbed at the border, but they were still a challenge. Her palms stung in all the places where the wires had pierced them.

Late in the night it became impossible to sing. Her mouth was dry as ashes. Still, she prayed within her mind.

Later still, even prayer became too difficult. Impossible ideas began to fill her thoughts. Memories of the dead wandered in and out among the living, and she could not tell the difference. Padre Hinojosa walked beside her for a while, and her mother on the other side, and her younger sisters and her father before her and behind. They all had a little talk, although she herself said nothing. The air became insufferably cold. She shivered without ceasing. Her heart began to beat too quickly. In a rare moment of sanity Lupe realized she was dying.

The night passed and it was morning. Long after the sun arose, the muscles in her legs began to cramp. Lupe fell to her knees. Smelling wood smoke, she knew she was on fire. This was to be her *auto de fe*, her burning in the barracks. She thought of martyred Spanish saints and remembered the golden flames around the Virgen de Guadalupe and knew she was not worthy of this death. She rolled onto her back and closed her eyes against the pitiless sun. Her head hurt very much, as if the hottest portion of the flames consumed her mind. Clutching Fray Alejandro's burden to her chest, she thought it would be good to sleep awhile before she burned. She would rest; then she would burn. The sun glowed through her eyelids. The wood smoke filled her nostrils. She was burning, and must sleep.

Suddenly a cooling darkness came.

Opening her eyes, she saw a man above her silhouetted by the sun, his figure framed by solar flares which shot out all around like fire erupting from the Presence of the Lord. With his back to the sun, she could not see the man's face as he bent near. Perhaps it was Ramón Rodríguez from Hércules, Coahuila, that good man who had tried to help.

The black figure spoke, saying, "Arise, and walk."

"Upon my word, señor, I fear I cannot."

"Fear not," he said. "You can."

Then he shifted his position and the sun came from behind and blinded her. She closed her eyes and turned her head away. She thought about his words, and hers in reply. Had she really spoken? If she could speak in spite of all these ashes in her mouth, perhaps she truly could arise and walk. She resolved to try, and trying, found herself successful. On her feet somehow, clutching Fray Alejandro's burden to her breast, she squinted toward the west. There he was, standing far away. He lifted up a hand. A blessing? A benediction? A beckoning?

Silently, she followed.

On the constant verge of falling, she moved among the thorny cacti. Sometimes when she looked the man was nowhere to be seen, as it had been two days earlier with Señor Rodríguez. Other times she looked and he was there, always in the distance with his upraised hand. Once she saw him clearly—so she thought—a Latino gentleman with handsome features, full black hair combed straight back from a smooth forehead, hair shimmering in the sunlight, and widely spaced dark eyes, high cheekbones, and a strong square chin, nothing marring his perfection. She did not realize how like her he looked. She did not know if he was truly there, or if his face was just a memory. She could only follow.

The smell of burning wood grew stronger. She thought of timber stacked beneath a martyr's stake. She thought of sticks within her father's fireplace. Ahead she saw a thin plume of smoke. She remembered Moses in the wilderness, a man of uncircumcised lips following a column of fire. Holy Father preserve me from all fire! Yet let it be with me exactly as you wish. She feared to approach, but the man had said, "Fear not," and was this not great wisdom? So on she stumbled toward her fiery death, and drawing very close she raised her eyes to see the thin plume of smoke trail west, against the wind.

CAPÍTULO 8

FRAY BENICIO DREW MANY PAGANS to the fledgling mission. The enthusiastic friar sought to learn their ways, practicing poorly with a throwing stick to the great amusement of the men, wading through the lagoon with a long line of women to drive boiling schools of fish into cunning traps, and harvesting the acorns that constituted a large part of the pagans' diet. In these ways he helped to feed them, gained their trust, and led them by the dozens to become neophytes who confessed faith in the Holy Cross.

One day after prayers at sext, Abbot Guillermo stood with Fray Alejandro in the coolness of the chapel's shadows. The pale man said, "You see how eagerly he leaves, Alejandro?"

"Yes," said the friar, turning his unfortunate features toward the door as Benicio hurried away, all rushing legs and gangling elbows.

"That young man would rather be out there with the pagans than here at prayer with us."

"Indeed, he is a natural evangelist."

"Certainly he has some success in terms of numbers, but are the heathens truly penitent before the cross, or is it merely that a god who bleeds and hangs upon a tree appeals to their cannibalistic instincts?"

"Benicio believes the rumors of their love for human flesh are false."

"Yes, yes. I have heard him say it, but one wonders. . . ."

In the days and weeks that followed, if Guillermo was uncomfortable with Fray Benicio's methods, Alejandro could not fail to also notice the abbot's eagerness to take full advantage of their young companion's results. With so many neophytes added to their resources, it was possible to make quick progress on the mission. The chapel was complete, as was their second building, a strong storehouse with just one door and no windows, where Fray Guillermo's precious inventory of grain and cloth and other riches could be safely kept.

Next the abbot put the converted Indians to work upon a tannery, a series of round holes in the ground lined with fire-baked bricks. When the tannery was complete, the abbot set many of the neophytes to building barracks for the friars and soldiers, and the rest he charged with hunting deer, skinning them, soaking the hides in brine vats, and staking them to dry. The deer were very small and their hides offered a poor reward for so much labor, but Guillermo called it worthy practice for the real work which would start the following year, once their cattle herd began to calve.

The neophytes involved in tanning obeyed sullenly. It was filthy labor and the odor was most difficult. As usual, Fray Benicio joined cheerfully in their work. Fray Alejandro also gathered up his robe about his loins to engage in the distasteful business. Thus it was that the gentle, ugly man stood knee-deep in a stinking vat when he glimpsed the Indian.

Always a few idlers stood about the camp and mission grounds. Some hoped for a meal but did not wish to work to get it. Some were simply curious. The Indian stood among them, staring at Alejandro. He was short and broad, with flawless skin the color of the golden soil of California. His long hair was as black as night and glittered as if sprinkled by the stars. Their eyes met. A thrill of recognition shot through the friar. He felt he might have known those eyes before the birth of memory.

Alejandro longed to linger in the pleasure of his gaze, but with slow deliberation, the Indian shifted his attention to a neophyte nearby, a woman who stood with covered head and a child in her arms, much like the blessed Virgin Mother. The man's motion had the strength of a command, so Alejandro also turned his kindly eyes toward the woman and her baby.

The sight of the child filled Fray Alejandro with unholy envy. Immediately ashamed, he looked down at the filthy brine about his legs. Then, remembering the Indian, he looked up again, but in that impossibly brief moment the man had somehow slipped away.

This simple incident, unknown and unobserved by all but Alejandro, haunted him unmercifully. Had he been shown the woman's child to raise a jealous specter? Was this envy in him drawn up to the surface so he might recall the weakness of his flesh?

He confessed his sin to Guillermo after lauds. Of course he did not regret the vows San Francisco required—poverty, obedience, and chastity are great blessings—but chastity means childlessness, and Fray Alejandro did sometimes covet other people's children. He longed to be a father, to live in a newborn's presence every moment, for they filled him with an urgent fascination. It seemed great wisdom haunted babies' eyes, yet what truth could newborns know? Did they come to earth with memories of angels? "I thirst!" they cried, and mother's milk was given, but still they cried. Did they lament the ebb of heaven from their minds as the corrupted world slipped in? Did it pain them as perfection fell away? He saw them grow. He mourned their passing innocence. He watched their pristine trustfulness erode and knew it was a lifetime's quest to gain it back. He watched and felt great loss; for he was once a newborn too, and surely then remembered paradise.

With such thoughts Alejandro proved himself enlightened, yet there is a kind of wisdom that transcends learning, a kind of knowing that was always known. There are a precious few who never quite forget the time—if time existed then—before the womb, when they were known by God and they knew him. In their eyes we find a trace of infant wisdom still. Consider for example Tucker Rue, a recent seminary graduate, who was such a blessed one as that.

On the day after Tucker's commencement ceremony in Pasadena, California, when his proud parents and grandparents had returned to their homes, he bought two tarps, a sleeping bag, some cord, a Swiss Army knife, and a flashlight. He also purchased many cans of food, many batteries for the flashlight, and fifty plastic jugs of water. Then, with a full tank of gas in his ancient Toyota pickup truck and a map of the state of Arizona, he set out.

He drove without a definite objective. Having only just completed studies at Fuller Seminary, being unordained and unemployed and eager to embark upon the service of the Lord, Tucker Rue had decided to begin his years of ministry in the wilderness, much as Jesus did. He drove into Arizona, searching for a place where he could be alone for forty days with God. He drove from the interstate highway onto an Arizona state highway, to a Cochise County road, to a gravel road, and finally he stopped at the end of a faint dirt track in the Sonoran Desert, one mile south of Gleeson, which was nothing but a ghost town.

There he arranged the tarps: one stretched between the top of his car and a creosote bush, the other underneath it on the ground. He collected many stones and arranged them in a circle. He gathered wood and lit a fire within the circle, and resolved to keep it burning. Using the screwdriver on his Swiss Army knife, he removed the truck's passenger seat and placed it on the ground below the tarp next to his car. He sat on the seat. He opened his Bible.

So it was, thirty-eight days later, that Tucker Rue sat in the middle of a desert beneath a tarp beside his old Toyota and looked up from the scriptures when the woman stumbled in.

The young man laid her on his sleeping bag and pried her fingers from the burlap bag she carried. He laid the bag aside and brought her water. Lifting her head, he tipped a cupful to her mouth. When first the water touched her lips, she did not respond.

"Drink," he begged her. "Drink." Still, she did not swallow. He realized he was speaking English. He tried his rusty Spanish, speaking formally, too out of practice for contractions, urging her, cajoling her, and finally her lips parted.

Once she had taken that first sip, she tried to drink it greedily. His instincts warned him to restrain her. "Only a little now," he said. "You are going to have more in a little moment."

He removed her filthy shirt and shoes and socks and bloody tattered trousers and laid her down upon the sleeping bag again, dressed only in her underwear. He poured a little water on her shirt and slowly wiped her body, watching as the moisture quickly vanished into the atmosphere. He lifted her head again and gave her more to drink. Slowly, slowly, he saw the blotches on her skin begin to fade.

Hours passed. He wiped her with the wet shirt. He fanned her with it. He gave her water, ounce by ounce. At sunset her eyes opened. She did not look at him. She stared up at the plastic tarp above. Her eyes fluttered, then they shut again.

At the usual time, the disciples started howling. Peter, Paul, and James, as he had named them, the coyotes who had called out every evening for thirty-eight nights straight, preaching in the wilderness. Usually Tucker amused himself by preaching back to them. At first he had been unable to delude them for more than a few minutes before they fell silent, but over time his coyote had become quite good, and now they were convinced his doctrine was authentic. Their theological debates sometimes lasted hours. He had the gift of languages. With practice, he could preach to anyone.

He rose to tend the fire. It had nearly been extinguished while he cared for the woman, but underneath the ashes he discovered glowing coals. Soon he had it roaring. Shadows leapt about the camp, a ghost dance driven by convulsive flames. Wood crackled. Sparks arose like fairies. Below the tarp the woman moaned. He hurried back to her.

Her eyes were open, staring at the fire. She seemed to shrink away from it, although she barely moved. "Have no fear," he said in stilted Spanish. "All is well."

He sat between her and the fire, blocking her view of it. This seemed to grant her peace. He raised her head again and gave her more to drink. This time he let her drink all that she wished. When she had finished and reclined upon his sleeping bag again, she whispered something much too quietly.

"What?" he said. "I do not understand."

She tried again, and he leaned very close. Her cracked lips brushed his ear. He thought she said, "What will happen when you die?"

Delirious, he thought. She is delirious.

She slept.

Tucker settled down onto the seat from his old Toyota truck, which was beside the sleeping woman underneath the tarp. He switched on his flashlight and began to read the Bible. After a while he looked at her. She had drunk nearly a gallon in the last six or seven hours. He believed she would be fine. Perhaps something to eat next time, along with the water. Saltine crackers, maybe. Something bland. He continued reading. He was in the book of Job.

It started to get cold, as it always did that time of night. He set aside his Bible and moved to kneel beside the woman. He laid his palm upon her forehead, her stomach, her thigh. Satisfied with her temperature, the young man walked around to the other side of the truck, opened the door, and leaned inside to search through his belongings. He found what he was seeking. He walked back and stooped beneath the tarp and spread the blanket over her. He did not think she needed to remain uncovered anymore, not in the cool desert night air, and when she finally awoke in her right mind he did not wish her to be frightened, lying only in her underwear with a strange man at her side. He laid more wood upon the fire and slipped into his jacket. He returned to Job.

For nearly forty days he had pursued the Lord out in the wilderness. He had prayed and read the Word without ceasing. He had entered the Sonoran Desert with no idea what his purpose was. He knew he lived to serve the Lord, but how, exactly? He had gone to seminary in part to get the answer to that question, but the question had remained when his schooling was complete. It was still the question when he had parked his truck there in the middle of the desert, and it remained the question now. What should he do? He was desperate for an answer, but he could only pray and seek an answer in the Bible. As he tried to follow the words his eyes lost their focus. His vision faded.

When Tucker Rue awoke, the eastern sky glowed lavender and the fire was almost out again. He roused himself and went to lay more wood upon the coals. Leaning down, he felt the heat of smoldering embers embrace his cheeks. He blew, and the finer tinder caught. He blew some more, and flames began to crawl up through the sticks. Satisfied, the young man rocked back on his haunches to watch the resurrected fire, now thirty-nine days old. It hypnotized him.

Why was fire so fascinating? He sensed a lesson there, something of importance, but he could not think what it might be. Was something of the Lord in it? Those who had drawn closest to their Maker often spoke of the experience in terms of light. Yet the prophets also spoke of hell in terms of heat, of eternal burning. Might fire be a marker at a crossroads? Heat and light together, a place where hell and heaven met upon the earth? The flames called out to him; that was certain. They seemed to call to everyone.

The woman moaned.

He went to her.

Underneath the tarp, underneath the blanket, with open eyes she shivered.

"Hello," he said, remembering to speak Spanish. "My name is Tucker. Do you have cold? You could go into the . . ." He paused. He did not know the word for "sleeping bag." He said, "There are bedclothes below you. You could go below them if you have cold."

Wide with fright, her eyes shifted from the fire to him. Somehow, he knew it was not him she feared. He smiled. He poured some water into the cup and offered it. This time she tried to grasp the cup herself. It was a good sign.

When she had finished half the water he said, "One moment, please. I go for food." He rose and went around the truck and came back with a box of saltine crackers. He offered one. She took it and ate slowly. She took another, and another. She took another drink. She tried to speak. Again, her voice was a mere whisper. Again, he placed his ear close to her mouth. Again, he thought he heard her say, "What will happen when you die?"

A crazy question under the circumstances. He began to worry. It was one thing to care for someone who was dehydrated. It was quite another thing to deal with insanity. He thought of the long trip back to civilization. While driving, could he trust her? What if she erupted into madness on the highway at seventy miles per hour?

"What will happen when you die, señor?"

This time her voice was stronger. There was no mistaking her meaning. In the formal Spanish of the classroom, he said, "Why do you ask me this? I will not die. Neither will you. We will both be fine."

"All people die, señor, even you. Then what will happen?"

He decided to treat her question seriously. "I will be with God."

"Why? Do you think you are a good man because you saved me? 'No one is good, except God alone.'"

Even in Spanish, he recognized the quote. He stared at her, amazed, and continued it. "'You know the commandments: . . .'"

She finished it with cracked and bleeding lips. "'. . . Do not commit adultery, do not murder, do not steal, do not give false testimony, honor your father and mother.'"

Tucker Rue laughed. "Do you wish to save my soul, señorita?"

"I do, if you need saving."

"No, thank you. I am a Christian."

She smiled, although it must have pained her. "That is good." Her eyes seemed to lose their focus as they strayed toward the fire. Her blistered face expressed a hint of fear again, or maybe sorrow. She said, "Can you help me find the others?"

"Who? What others?"

"The ones who do not know our Savior."

"Ah. Sadly, they are everywhere."

She nodded. "That is what I thought."

Tucker watched as she stared silently into the fire. Several minutes passed. With the blanket pulled around her shoulders like a poncho, she endeavored to sit up. He helped her, and she put her back against his truck. Side by side they sat. He watched her profile closely. Underneath the dirt and damage from the sun, he saw a steady dignity. It made her beautiful. She seemed to sense his eyes on her and turned to look him squarely in the face. She gasped.

"What is it?" he asked.

She stared as if shocked by the sight of him. Finally, she looked away. "My bag. Did I come here with a bag?"

"It is here." He pulled it from beneath the truck between them.

She took it from him eagerly. "Señor, would you please turn away?"

"Certainly." He shifted his position and stared into the desert. "You are going to dress?"

"Of course."

He waited, hearing the rustle of fabric and her groans as she moved. After a little while, he said, "Ready?"

"Not yet, please."

"Okay." He kept his eyes averted, thinking this was taking a long time, but of course she was very weak. Then it crossed his mind again she might be crazy, maybe doing damage to his truck or crawling toward him with a knife. He turned to look.

The woman had something in her hands, three wooden boards of some kind. From the way she held them he could see the upper surface of only one board. It was covered with a painted image, like an icon. The three panels were held together with little leather straps. Beneath them on her lap he saw a piece of bright red fabric, and the burlap bag.

She stared at him intently over the boards in her hands, as if spying on him while pretending to read a newspaper. Seeing his eyes on the panels, she quickly shifted them so he could no longer see the painted surface. "Señor!" she said. "You promised!"

"Sorry." He looked away again.

Another long minute passed with the rustling of fabric, and then she said, "Very well."

He looked again and found her fully clothed, albeit in filthy rags, with the burlap sack upon the sleeping bag beside her, and no sign of the painting or the red cloth. He said, "I do not wish to . . . violate? Yes, to violate your privacy, but please to tell me what is in that bag?"

"I cannot, señor."

"Call me Tucker. And you? I am sorry, I do not know your name."

"Lupe."

"Good. So, Lupe, why can you not tell me what it is?"

She shifted her position, as if placing herself between him and the bag. She said nothing.

Tucker said, "It is only a painting, is it not?"

She said nothing.

He said, "Is it stolen?"

"No!"

"Then there is some other reason you hide what is in the bag? Do you have drugs?"

"Drugs? No! Of course not drugs!"

"Many people come from Mexico with drugs. They are called mules."

"I am *not* a mule."

"You are here illegally, yes?"

She said nothing.

"All right," said Tucker after a moment. "But I am in much trouble if you carry stolen things or drugs. Do you understand?"

"Yes. . . ." She lowered her eyes to the ground a moment, obviously thinking. "I can tell you this: It is a guide for me. To help me find my way."

"Like a map?"

"Like a map, yes."

"I saw wood. The map is on wood?"

"Yes. May we talk of this no more?"

"You promise there is no illegal thing in the bag?"

"I do."

"You swear it?"

She looked at him sternly. "Tucker, you should never ask a person to swear. It is a sin."

"Thank you. I will try to do better."

"It is greatly to be hoped."

He laughed. "Would you like some more water? A thing to eat?"

"Yes, please."

He rose from the truck seat on the ground and went to get his last plastic gallon jug of water. He returned with it, more saltine crackers, and a jar of peanut butter. "Here," he said, putting the things on the ground beside her. "Please take the seat. It is more comfortable."

"I could not."

"Please. I wish it."

She scooted over to the seat. He dropped onto the sleeping bag beside her, poured some water in a cup, and offered it. As she drank, he used the Swiss Army knife to spread peanut butter on a cracker, which she also took, and ate. After he had sipped a little water from the jug and spread more peanut butter on more crackers, he said, "That is the final water. Tomorrow we must go."

"I am sorry. I used too much of your water."

"No, tomorrow is forty days since I came here. I go anyway."

"Forty days?" she asked. "Like our Savior?"

"It is the idea."

After a minute, she said, "Did you find what you came here for, Tucker?"

He looked at her thoughtfully. "Maybe."

They talked and napped. He read aloud from the Bible, translating from the English very poorly as he went. Sometimes she corrected him, but gently. The sun went down. The sun came up. That next day he allowed the fire to perish. He scattered the circle of stones and spread the ashes with a stick. With Lupe's help, he folded the two tarps and reattached the passenger seat. They gathered up the few remaining signs of their presence in that place and packed them in the old truck. Then they got inside.

"Cross your fingers," said the young man as he prepared to turn the key in the ignition.

"I do not understand 'cross your fingers,'" said the young woman. As with so many things, it did not translate well into Spanish.

The engine came to life on the first try. "It does not matter," said Tucker. He put the truck into gear and set out along the faint dirt track. "Where are we going?"

She looked at him. "It is your truck."

"But you are the one with the guide in a bag."

After a moment's silence, she said, "I met a very kind man, who led me into the desert. He said he was going to a place called Wilson City. In California. Do you know it?"

"No."

"We could find it on a map?"

"We could use your guide."

"Tucker," she said, admonishing him.

He laughed. "I am only playing. Look in there."

She opened the glove box and found the map of California. After much inspection she told him where they had to go.

They rode and talked for hours. She asked him many questions about his time at seminary. She seemed impressed to learn he was a doctor, until she realized he knew nothing about medicine. She did not seem impressed that he had received his doctorate at the age of twenty-two. He tried to explain. "I'm the youngest doctor of ministry ever to graduate from Fuller."

"It is important? This doctor of ministry?"

"I thought it was."

"You worked very hard for this doctor of ministry?"

"Yes. Very hard."

"Why?"

"I want to help people."

She nodded. "I want that also. It is why I came to your country. To tell the pagan people here about the Savior."

"So you are a missionary?" He laughed and said in English, "A wetback missionary."

"Tucker. I do not like this word, 'wetback.' I have heard it before and I do not think it is very nice."

Surprised she had understood his English, he stopped smiling. He felt like a schoolboy caught misbehaving by his teacher. "That is true. Sorry."

"Besides," she said, "what is funny? The people of this country are lost. They need missionaries."

Minutes passed as Tucker Rue thought about that. "Are other missionaries coming from the south?"

"I do not know."

"Who are you with?"

"With? I am with you."

"No, I mean, what group or church. Who sent you?"

"I was sent by the Holy Father."

"The Pope?"

She smiled. "No. His Holy Father."

"So, you just came on your own?"

"I am never on my own."

"Touché."

"I do not understand this 'touché.'"

Tucker explained, and then he asked, "Do you have friends in Wilson City? Someone who can take you into their home?"

"The only people I know in the United States are you and Señor Rodríguez. He is not a friend, although he is kind, like you. I hope he is not lost in the desert."

"How will you start your ministry?"

"I do not know."

"I have a Mexican friend from the seminary, a Mexican-American, I mean. I can introduce you. Maybe he can help you meet the Latinos in Wilson City."

"I did not come for them."

"Then who . . . ?"

"Americanos."

"Do you speak English?"

"No."

"How will you tell Americans about Jesus without English?"

She looked at him, her eyes very wide. "I did not think of that."

He laughed again, and immediately regretted it. She stared at him just as she had stared the day before over the top of the strange boards she carried in the bag. The intensity of her gaze embarrassed him. He said, "Do not worry."

"Thank you. I will not. Worry is a sin."

They covered a mile or two in silence, then Tucker said, "We have a long drive ahead. I can teach you a few words."

"Truly? You will teach me English?"

"Maybe a little between here and Wilson City. What is the first thing you want to learn to say?"

Looking through the windshield at the lethal desert of Sonora, Lupe said, "What will happen when you die?"

CAPÍTULO 9

FRAY GUILLERMO, PALLID AS A corpse within the shadow of his cowl, appeared one morning at the door of Alejandro's cell. "Come, brother," said the abbot. "We go to the village." Twenty minutes later the two Franciscans trudged along a dry arroyo down into the plain below the mission grounds. Their errand was not unexpected. Fray Benicio had been three days and nights among the Indians without the abbot's leave.

In the heat along the trail the abbot said, "His mind has been poisoned by the savages, brother. It is the only explanation."

Remembering Benicio's reaction when the abbot forced the Cochimí to bear the stone, Fray Alejandro believed there might be other reasons, but he had no desire to contradict the superior. He said nothing.

Guillermo did not notice Alejandro's silence, but continued, "I only hope we do not find him piece by piece in cooking pots."

Following the abbot down the arroyo, Alejandro tried to remain silent. To their left and right rose rugged hills, covered sparsely by dried grass, cacti, and low shrubs. From a cloudless sky the sun shone sickly yellow on Guillermo's naked hands and feet. Alejandro feared for the abbot's health, sallow and unsuited as he was for such a climate. And although he did not wish to rouse the abbot's passions more than Benicio had already done, Guillermo's words disturbed him. How were they to lead these people to the Church and Mother Spain if the abbot saw

them in that way? He sighed. He spoke. "I am not certain they are cannibals, Abbot."

"So you often say," replied the superior.

The two Franciscans reached a bend in the dry streambed not far
from the mission. Within the elbow of this gentle curve was a small
plateau, protected on three sides by the steep walls of the arroyo, which
had been eroded by countless flash floods through the centuries.

The plateau supported perhaps two hundred *kis,* the Indian word
for their low-domed houses made of tule rushes and willow saplings.
At the center stood a storehouse and a sweat lodge used for certain reli-
gious ceremonies. These too were built of saplings and rushes. From
dozens of campfires scattered about, slender tendrils of smoke arose
straight and true through the perfectly still air, like enchanted columns
holding up the sky. Everywhere were naked men, women, and children.
The women did not pause in their activities to watch the two friars
come. The men, most of whom were idle, did not rise to greet them.
Fray Alejandro felt their stares upon his back after they passed, and
worried at the hardness of their eyes.

"Do not look at them," cautioned Fray Guillermo. "Look only
ahead."

Beside the sweat lodge they found Fray Benicio sitting cross-legged
on the ground among about a dozen men. In the center of the little
group a wizened patriarch spoke softly. Paying close attention, the
young friar did not notice Alejandro or the abbot until they were
almost standing over him.

The pale Guillermo said, "Arise, brother. You neglect your duties."

Startled, Fray Benicio scrambled to his feet. Without another glance
at him, Guillermo walked away.

Alejandro whispered, "Come, Benicio. You have been here far too
long."

"How long?" asked the friar.

Alejandro creased his brow. "Do you not know?"

"I . . . I seem to have lost track of time."

"Have you partaken of their herbs?"

"Just a little. The smallest portion possible. It was necessary to
build a bond of friendship."

"Oh, Benicio." Alejandro pinched the bridge of his broad nose between two fingers, as if warding off a headache. "Your heart is kind, but sometimes I fear you are a fool."

"I do not understand the problem. It was only just a little. The effects were very mild."

"You have been here for three days, brother. Three days and three nights."

"*Three?*"

"Indeed. That is why the abbot was so curt."

"But how is this possible?"

"*Now,* brothers!" shouted Guillermo from a distance, and Alejandro quickly followed, with Benicio behind.

Outside of the village, ascending toward the mission, the two friars caught up with their abbot. Without looking back at them, the pale, redheaded man said, "Alejandro, I have been thinking. I want you to fashion a small altarpiece, a triptych, which can be folded in upon itself and easily carried. Perhaps with such a reminder to aid his work in the villages, Fray Benicio will not again forget his purpose there."

Young Benicio said, "Abbot, I assure you—"

The superior cut him off. "I have seven gold coins which can be beaten into leaf for gilding. In Córdoba you worked in a scriptorium, I believe. You have the skills to produce a serviceable altarpiece as I have described?"

"Yes, Abbot," replied Alejandro. "I do."

"Very good. I wish you to begin work on it immediately."

Minutes later, close beside him Benicio whispered. "Coins? Where did he get coins?" It was an excellent question, for Franciscans were forbidden to hold money, but Fray Alejandro did not reply. Behind the question was an accusation, the thin edge of another wedge between his brothers. Alejandro raised his cowl, bowed his head, and crossed his arms at his chest, tucking his hands into his sleeves. In that posture of contemplation, he walked between Guillermo and Benicio all the way back to the mission, saying nothing.

During the days following, Fray Alejandro was loath to start the altarpiece. He did not wish to sit and paint alone while Benicio and Guillermo labored at cross-purposes, yet they themselves admonished him to do it. In this one thing they were unified, and he had to admit they were correct. The new chapel did need an altarpiece, and Benicio required it to be portable so he might carry it to outlying villages from time to time. Alejandro should have begun work on the altarpiece immediately, as Fray Guillermo ordered, but he longed for the fellowship of others in that lonely place. He therefore lingered overlong on other chores among the neophytes and soldiers, and did not take up brush or paint.

Whether packing mud into the brick molds, scraping hides, or tilling soil for cultivation in the newly cleared maize field, Alejandro knew he was in sin. His was a transgression of omission, most insidious. It is the besetting sin of many holy people, the devil's favorite tool in such a case, for it requires no shameful passion, no overt rebellion, nothing but inaction. And as it thus afflicted Alejandro in the eighteenth century, so it was with Lupe in these modern times. That good woman told herself she only lingered there with Tucker because she lacked the English. Better to wait until she had learned the necessary words. But when two weeks had passed and she had mastered all the sounds required, if not the exact meanings, still she lingered.

With her first excuse removed, she told herself it was an obligation. Had not the handsome young Americano saved her life? Had he not sheltered her, and given her water and food? (She must not think about him passing cooling cloths across her flesh.) Did she not owe him something in return?

Soon after their arrival from Arizona, Tucker Rue had announced his plan to start a storefront mission for the Latinos of Wilson City. He said God had sent him to the wilderness to find his calling, and met him there through Lupe. Because of Lupe, he had seen a world he did not know, a world of decent people risking life itself for their families, people suffering from want of everything in a land of plenty. Her quest to save the pagan people of America, and the desperate journeys others risked to provide for loved ones back home . . . this had been his inspiration. As she had come to serve the Anglos, so he hoped to serve Latinos, and in this worthy enterprise he had asked for her assistance.

She told herself she had no choice. Honor made demands. She was a debtor, and must repay the man as best she could. She told herself she lingered just to teach him of her culture: the traditions, the unwritten rules. Although his Spanish was improving, she would help him learn the things one could not find in any textbook. She would go with him into the barrio that Wilson City had become. She would help him meet the people there, and by her presence at his side become the bridge he needed to traverse the cultural divide. She told herself she lingered for these reasons.

But it must be said she also saw the raffish way his hair fell into those strangely naïve eyes which somehow combined youth with age-less wisdom. She observed his ready smile, his direct manner of speaking, and the way her people warmed to him in minutes, accepting him like family. Even the *cholos*, the brash young men with low-slung trousers, slicked-back hair, menacing tattoos and strange mannerisms, even they seemed quick to call him "*vato*" and "*ese*," as if he were an honorary Chicano, somehow one of them. And it must be noticed as she lingered, that Lupe sometimes appraised Tucker's wide shoulders, and slender hips, and the graceful way he moved as if always on the verge of breaking into dance. It seemed to her no man in Rincon de Dolores had ever moved that way, charmed so quickly, or looked into a person's eyes so frankly. Indeed, there were no men at all like Tucker Rue in Lupe's village, and so she found him . . . interesting.

Tucker somehow raised the money to rent a small warehouse at the western edge of Wilson City, one of a row of hard concrete buildings dividing a sunburned neighborhood of chapped and peeling apartments from the irrigated farmland outside the town. Beyond the row of warehouses was a vista to the hills, the air laden with pale blue haze, the ground—which had once been desert—level and plowed and planted for many kilometers in all directions. These fields, and Blanco Beach on the far side of the hills, explained why twelve thousand Latinos lived in Wilson City.

Each day they fanned out from the town in battered vans and trucks. Some parked along the edges of the fields where they picked in broad-brimmed straw hats with bandannas draped behind to guard their necks from the brutal sun. Other pickers climbed ladders among orange and almond trees, or repaired irrigation pipes, or mowed endless fields of sod advertised on billboards as "stadium quality," or adjusted turnstiles to send water through the rows from irrigation canals where snowy egrets lurked among the dangling tendrils of solitary willows. Still other Wilson City residents left the flatlands every day to cross the hills, the men in trucks bearing leaf blowers and lawn mowers, the women in tiny neon-colored cars from Japan and Korea with "European Maid Service" written inexplicably upon the doors. They sped along the canyon road to Blanco Beach to serve rich Anglos there in hillside bungalows with multimillion-dollar views of the Pacific. Six days a week the people of Wilson City picked and plowed and cleaned and mowed and washed until the sun went down, when they drove back from the fields, or east along the canyon road, exhausted.

At the western fringes of their neighborhood, Tucker named the little warehouse "Sanctuario." On the wall of concrete blocks beside the door, with Lupe's help, he painted that word large in blood-red letters. Then he moved into the building, to live among the people. Although conscious of the impropriety, Lupe moved in too. They strung ropes from the rafters and draped blankets over them to serve as walls. She slept beside Fray Alejandro's *retablo* on a mattress on the floor at one end of the empty space. Tucker slept far away, at the other end. They shared the one bathroom and cooked together on the same butane camp stove. They cleaned the building together—the interior littered with broken beer bottles and fast-food wrappers—and together they painted over the graffiti on the walls. Working together, they often sang—he in English, she in Spanish—the same Protestant hymns she had learned from Don Pedro's radio. To her surprise, Tucker seemed to know them all.

One day they sat side by side at a folding table, working. To save money they made fliers by hand, announcements of Tucker's plan to begin preaching in the warehouse every Sunday. On each blank piece of paper Tucker drew a border and wrote the main words in red across the top: "*Sanctuario: Dios y Desayuno.*" He then passed the paper to Lupe, who added details below in her cursive hand: the time, the place, the explanation that there would be a sermon followed by a free breakfast and a time of fellowship. Lupe believed Tucker's handwriting was very beautiful. His words flowed gracefully across the top of every page, like calligraphy. She felt her own clumsy writing, poorly learned from Padre Hinojosa, ruined the fliers. She begged Tucker to let her help in a different way, but he insisted that she sit beside him so they could work together.

The table was very small. Often Tucker's arm or leg brushed against Lupe as they worked. Each time this happened, he apologized. Finally she said, "Tucker, you do not have to say you're sorry when you touch me. I do not mind."

He looked at her. "No?"

Lupe lowered her eyes.

They worked on in silence, Lupe doing her best to keep up with him. They hoped to finish two hundred of their handmade fliers in time to distribute them around the town before sunset.

"I couldn't do this without you," said Tucker, using the contraction, speaking Spanish much more fluidly each day.

"Oh, our Holy Father would send someone else," she replied. "I am not special."

"You *are* special! The Lord sent you to help me. Nobody but you."

Lupe felt a strange exhilaration, and immediately asked her Maker for forgiveness. Pride was such a fickle path to tread.

After a few minutes Tucker filled the silence. "I am glad."

"You are? Glad for what?"

On the table between them, he covered her hand with his. "I am glad you do not mind if I touch you." He lifted her palm to his lips, closed his eyes, and kissed the place where barbed wire had scarred her.

Lupe felt as if her heart would rise into the sky. Yet she had no experience in such feelings. Because she knew not what to say or do, she said nothing and did nothing. She longed for the wisdom to respond as he expected, but what did he expect? The moment became awkward. The fine young man released her hand, and she could think of nothing else but to withdraw it.

"I am sorry," he said. He would not look at her.

That night a dream awoke Lupe. She lay in darkness, listening to Tucker Rue's snores. It had just occurred to her—she must have realized this in her dream—that Tucker made her sad. In her sleep the emotion had nearly overwhelmed her. Now, as the handsome young man snored on the far side of the warehouse, separated from her only by a hanging blanket, Lupe wondered why she felt such sorrow. She did not grieve for his immortal soul. She was aware some Catholics believed all Protestants were bound for hell, even Padre Hinojosa might possibly believe it, but many hours of listening to their sermons and hymns on Don Pedro's radio had convinced Lupe that Protestants were merely Catholics who did not understand some details of the faith. No man who loved the Savior as Tucker Rue did could be at risk of condemnation . . . so if she was not sad for Tucker's soul, why did she dream of him and grieve?

Lying in the dark beside Fray Alejandro's burden, breathing in the scent of fresh paint and a musky mattress, Lupe faced the question squarely. She remembered Tucker's praise of her that day. God had chosen her to help him. She remembered her pride at that thought, and her immediate shame at feeling pride. She remembered the lightness of her spirit followed by the horrible awkwardness when he kissed her hand. Alone in the darkness, Lupe thought of many ways to respond to his kiss. If only she had leaned toward him a little, closed the space between them. . . .

Lupe was a simple person, neither foolish nor naïve, but simple. She believed everything which tempts us must be evil. It is not true, of course. Although beauty can evoke illicit desire, beauty is not wicked. Nor is safety wrongful in itself, yet who has not abandoned duty for security at times? Friendship, patriotism, honor, religion . . . all these things are good, but sometimes they inspire horrific sins. And the one that causes greater misery than all others is intemperate love. Guadalupe Soledad Consuelo de la Garza, a simple woman, did not understand this. For her, love had always been attired in virtue. Love for her had led to misery, but never to temptation until now.

Lying in the dark, she did not fully understand why she had felt pride, or why her pride had shamed her, or why she had dreamed grief. She did not know the true reason why she had not encouraged Tucker Rue's advances when everything within her longed for what he offered. She only knew she had lingered overlong with him, pretending a concern for learning and for teaching, for obligation, when those were mere excuses. She knew her duty languished in another place, abandoned, although it grieved her to admit it.

"Please forgive me," whispered Lupe to her Maker.

To her very great surprise, the answer she received was silence.

Later, after breakfast, Lupe sat upon the mattress with Fray Alejandro's burden in her hands. She stared at it intently. There could be no doubt that it had led her to that place, and to that man, but who was the man, really? Gazing at two figures in the paintings, she tried to decide, would Tucker be with her in paradise, or was he unrepentant? And what of her own burden? What of the millions she had come to save? If she did not know which man Tucker was, at least she could be certain of her calling. She returned the *retablo* to its crimson covering. She stood and crossed the warehouse. She said to Tucker, "I must go."

At the bathroom sink, washing their breakfast dishes, Tucker said, "Where?"

"To the Anglos," she replied.

He came toward her, drying his hands on his shirt. On his face was sadness. Lupe forced herself to look away. How she longed to give herself to him! She wondered if her love for God could stand this sacrifice.

He said, "What I did yesterday . . . I am sorry."

"There is no need to apologize."

"Then don't leave."

"I must."

"What about Sanctuario?"

"You do not need me anymore," she said. "The people have accepted you."

"You can still stay here. I'll drive you back and forth and help you with the people over there the way you have helped me here."

Lupe shook her head, stubborn in the face of grave desire. "That would take too much of your time. I do not wish to interfere with your work."

"It would not interfere. It—"

"Please, Tucker. Please. Do not tempt me."

He saw the welling in her eyes. He seemed confused. And again he said, "I am sorry."

CAPÍTULO 10

EL DÍA DE LOS MUERTOS, LUNES,
2 DE NOVIEMBRE DE 1772

BECAUSE OF BENICIO'S THREE DAYS of willful disobedience at the Indian village, the abbot ordered Fray Alejandro to assist him at the All Souls' Day requiem Mass in rebuke of the younger friar, who had always served in that capacity before. So it was that Fray Benicio knelt among the neophytes and soldiers in the newly completed chapel while Alejandro stood within a shaft of sunlight from a window high above the transept, holding the abbot's missal and turning the heavy leaves as the Latin Mass was chanted. While Fray Guillermo made entreaties for the dead, Alejandro solemnly resolved to devote himself at last to the altarpiece. The painting was a lonely form of service, but necessary, and he had been too long in accepting it.

That evening after lauds Alejandro confessed his willfulness to Fray Guillermo. He could not completely explain his hesitance to paint. It was no longer just desire for companionship, a wish to avoid long hours alone within his cell. He had begun to feel he ought to wait for some extraordinary occurrence. What such an event might be he did not know, but the friar believed it would be glorious. He tried to describe this strange sense of impending destiny to Fray Guillermo, but in the midst of his confession the superior interrupted.

"All this talk of destiny and miracles is meaningless, brother. Your hesitation merely comes from selfishness. Say twenty-four Our Fathers with the laymen at matins for one week, and begin the altarpiece immediately."

In the darkness of his cell that night, Alejandro pondered Fray Guillermo's words. Did his resistance to the altarpiece truly spring from selfishness? The Franciscan knew self-absorption is a blackened room, and only those who look into the light beyond their lives can hope to recognize the forces that persuade them. It was strange therefore that the good friar did not understand the reason for his actions. Yet just as Alejandro failed to recognize the voice that whispered he should wait, so Lupe did not understand her overwhelming sense that she must go.

Although she had seen only goodness and mercy in Tucker Rue, and although a deep longing of her heart railed against leaving, her quest drove her out of Sanctuario. With Fray Alejandro's altarpiece suspended from her shoulder, without a doubt that she must go, she went, for she had not been called to work among her own people. Although she did not understand how it would come to be, she had traveled far to save the native people of that land, the Americanos.

In tears she wandered Wilson City's streets, where dried weeds lined each crack and trash lined every gutter. Aimlessly she wandered, until she found the canyon road and a sign that said it led to Blanco Beach. She stared at the sign. She had heard about this town. It lay across the hills, and was a place where many souls were desperately in need of God.

Lupe set out alongside the road. In less than fifteen minutes a pickup truck pulled to a stop beside her, and a man with a gray mustache and kind eyes offered her a ride. She climbed into the back to join the two young men who sat among the gardening tools. They greeted her politely and allowed her to listen to their conversation, which was about the wealth of gringos. Shouting into the wind as the rocks and brush and dusty slopes sped by, they spoke of homes and cars costing vast amounts of money. Lupe believed they were mistaken. No house or car could cost so much. Silly exaggerations did not interest her. She turned her attention to the passing scenery.

The mountains of her Jalisco home wore verdant robes of evergreens and ferns and lichens, but the hills in California were not as well attired. With only a tattered fabric of sun-baked grass and dormant brush to clothe them, massive sandy boulders emerged from the steep slopes above the road like the naked breasts and pregnant bellies of dormant giants. Lupe half expected one of them to shift position in its slumber, disturbed by the truck's noisy passage, sending down an avalanche of stones and sand in sleepy protest. She watched the hillsides carefully. Here and there she witnessed prickly pears and twisted oak trees in gullies carved by long-forgotten rains. She saw one hawk circling high above the canyon, and then a second hawk, a little farther up. She was glad there were two birds of prey, for it meant they were not lonely.

Her eyes filled with tears again. She told herself it was the passing wind.

Half an hour later Lupe stood upon a sidewalk, watching as her brothers traveled on. She felt a little better now. Finally it was time to tell America about the Savior. But as she turned and walked into the town, Blanco Beach surprised her. It was clean and orderly and pleasant. All the streets were paved, unlike Rincón de Dolores or Wilson City. And unlike those towns where poverty imposed a kind of uniformity to the construction, in Blanco Beach she saw many different styles of buildings. Some made her think of Mexico, with stucco walls and clay tile roofs and colorful mosaics around the entrances. One shop looked like something from a picture book she had once seen, a book of fairy tales. It had intricately cut boards along the eaves, and crisscrossed timbers set at angles, and straw upon the roof. Farther down along the street Lupe saw trees growing up from holes in metal grates, and wooden benches here and there for sitting, and a delightful fountain at one corner of an intersection, and dozens of different kinds of flowers, red, yellow, pink, and white. She smelled the flowers in the air, inhaling their perfume deeply. Just standing there, it was as if her nose were buried in a rich bouquet. A pair of hummingbirds buzzed past her, shooting like fiesta fireworks toward a cascade of bougainvillea near a sidewalk café where people dined at round tables, each of which was sheltered from the sun by a green-fabric umbrella.

Among the Anglos at the café and along the sidewalk Lupe saw no obvious drunks or drug addicts. The girls and women did not seem to fear the men, nor did the men seem eager to indulge in violence. A little boy ran laughing through a flock of pigeons, setting off mass panic and a minor hurricane of beating wings. Watching the birds rise into the blue, Lupe heard a church bell ring. It was not like the simple bell above the Chapel of Santa Dolores. This one played a complicated melody. Listening, she recognized a hymn that she had learned from Don Pedro's radio, a lovely hymn that praised the Creator, a hymn she had sung with Tucker. How great thou art. How great thou art.

Had she come so far in vain? It seemed these people already knew the Savior.

A woman came her way along the sidewalk, tall and fair. Assuming she was a native of the region, Lupe said, "Hello." She was embarrassed to attempt the English word. The woman turned away and passed in silence, and Lupe looked after her, astonished. Such a thing had never happened, not once, in all her life. Another native woman came, and again Lupe said, "Hello." This woman returned the greeting, but only in a cursory way, without a smile or a meeting of the eyes.

Uncertain of the meaning of such ill-bred behavior, Lupe went along the sidewalk, passing many small shops with strange and beautiful things for sale in their windows: shiny surfboards, shockingly small swimsuits, crystals dangling from strings, paintings of seascapes in golden frames. Ahead on the sidewalk she saw a man kneel down to pet a dog. She saw him smile. "Hello," she said as she passed by. The dog regarded her with kindness, but the man's face changed to stone.

Suddenly, in spite of clean sidewalks and church bell melodies, Lupe knew her quest had not been futile. Here was work to do, a fertile field to plant and harvest, just as she was told. To stroll the streets of Rincón de Dolores was to greet and to be greeted, to reinforce old friendships, to enjoy the company of neighbors. It had been that way in Naco, too, and in Wilson City, but in Blanco Beach dogs were greeted with compassion and affection while human beings were greeted as if they were only dogs. These poor people did not know the Savior. How could they? No Christian ever acted thusly.

Lupe walked on. A sound like rushing wind in distant trees came to her ear, a sound that seemed to rise and fall. She wished to ask a passerby to explain it, but did not have the English. As she walked, the sound increased until she turned a corner at a clothing store and saw a vast magnificence.

She had reached a busy thoroughfare. Many people filled the sidewalks; many autos filled the road. On the far side of it lay an impossibly enormous thing, a thing so grand it filled the world to the horizon. Amazed by the endless panorama, Lupe felt as if her mind and heart and time itself had stopped. She could only stare and marvel, although all around her no one else took notice. She gestured toward the thing and spoke aloud to those who hurried by, saying, "But . . . but . . . but look!"

It was the sea, of course, the *Océano Pacífico*, and the rushing sound that she had heard was the eternal sigh of breakers. She had seen the ocean on a neighbor's television set and many times in photographs, but nothing could prepare a person for the majesty of the real thing, for the grandness of it, the splendor of it.

"Holy Father," cried Lupe. "Your works are glorious, and you are beautiful beyond description!"

She said it very loudly, with her face and palms raised up toward heaven. Arm in arm, a passing man and woman looked away.

Lupe ran along the sidewalk, casting sideways glances toward the vision that amazed her. At a traffic light she joined a crowd of Americanos waiting to cross the busy road. She looked around at them and said, "Hello," but nobody responded. On the other side she dashed across the beach until she reached the ocean's edge, where she stooped to remove her shoes. Rolling up her trousers, she waded into the salt water, a thing she had never dreamed of doing, a marvelous thing no one in her mountain village had ever done except perhaps for Fray Alejandro, hundreds of years ago. She laughed and skipped along the waterline, sometimes only in it to her ankles, sometimes to her knees. Silly little birds with sticks for legs went running on before her, while other, larger birds soared and shrieked above her head. Many people sat upon the beach and swam within the water, some with children, some with friends, some alone. Like the people on the sidewalks up in town, no one seemed to see her, even when they looked directly at her.

Lupe tired of running. She sat upon the sand to watch the waves. Above the roar of breakers she heard laughter. Looking over her shoulder, she saw about forty people standing in a large circle around a brown and skinny man. All of them wore shorts or swimming suits. All of them were barefoot. All of them laughed loudly, as if the man was very funny. Lupe watched, trying to understand the reason for their hilarity. The skinny man said something in English and instantly their laughter stopped. He paced within the circle speaking to the people. Then everyone began to laugh again, all at once.

Lupe smiled. At last, here were people who took pleasure in that glorious place. Caught up in hilarity, some of them flung hands into the air, much as she herself had done to praise the Holy Father for the ocean. Others bent forward at the waist and slapped their knees, laughing and laughing, on and on, delighted for some reason.

Laughing like the others, the weathered man placed his palms together underneath his chin and bowed to one of those around him in the circle. Immediately all the others did the same, turning toward each other, breaking ranks to mill about like ants after the nest is stirred, dividing into pairs, bowing with their hands in the attitude of prayer, and then walking to the next person to bow and laugh some more. One of the laughing men noticed Lupe staring. Their eyes met across a distance of five meters. In spite of his hilarity, his eyes were hard and distant.

A woman left the circle and began to move along the beach, passing out small yellow fliers. She gave one to Lupe. It had a headline: "Laughing Yoga." Lupe did not understand the first word, but she had seen the second in her magazines in Mexico. She believed it had something to do with Eastern religions, pagan gods with many breasts and many arms and yellow eyes and fierce blue faces. Watching the unnatural laughter of the beachfront native ritual, Lupe no longer felt a bold desire to preach. Instead, she shivered in the heat.

What evil place was this, where people languished deaf to greetings, blind to neighbors, isolated in the middle of a crowd? What wicked mesmerism numbed them to the undulating glory of the sparkling sea? What devil drove them to attempt this imitation happiness, this counterfeit laughter, when the true delight of God's creation lay in all directions?

"Holy Father," she whispered, "please protect me."

She felt no answer to her prayer. It was as if the people of that place had somehow blocked the voice of God.

Awash in dread, Lupe thought of Tucker Rue, of how the man had rescued her from death, and how safe she felt when he was near. She longed to flee these joyless laughing pagans. She longed to fly back to Sanctuario, to return to Tucker, to be helpful to him, and with him to serve her own people, whom she understood. She longed to gaze at Tucker when he did not realize she was looking, perhaps to touch his arm, his face, to lift his palm up to her lips as he had done to hers. And if that handsome man refused her, she longed for Rincón de Dolores, her shop, her street, the plaza and the chapel, the simple pleasures of a bucketful of steaming water and a brisk broom on the sidewalk in the morning in the company of neighbors, and the joy of giving candy to the children, the peace of a siesta until dear old Padre Hinojosa rang the simple chapel bell.

None of that was possible. She had come upon a holy quest, driven north against her wishes like a plume of smoke against the wind. Compared to such an ordination, these longings of her heart were unimportant. They only meant the devil in that place desired to take her.

"Lead me not into temptation," Lupe whispered. "And deliver me from evil."

She rose, dusted the sand from her trousers, and passed the rope strap over her shoulder, once again accepting Alejandro's burden. With a boldness that she did not feel, Lupe approached the laughing pagans. The sounds she had so carefully memorized at Sanctuario seemed disordered in her head. She had no idea how to say, "Excuse me," or "May I speak?" Instead she said, *"Oiga, por favor,"* and when that failed, *"Señoras y caballeros, perdonenme!"*

On they went with their senseless laughing, milling about, ignoring her. She took a deep breath and started with the first sounds she had learned from Tucker Rue. She shouted to be heard above their grotesque hilarity.

"Wat weel ap-een ween jew die?"

On she went, shouting to be heard above their laughter, shouting sounds she did not understand, trusting what she had been taught, trying to speak the truth in a tongue she did not know. By the time she reached the end of her speech, the part where she hoped they would pray a prayer of faith, the laughing pagans had all turned to face her. They watched with barren eyes, even as their mouths gaped wide with counterfeit hilarity, teeth and tonsils open to her, faces red, hands flying up into the air and then down onto their knees.

Finally, their surrealistic mirth had found a focus.

Lupe shouted out the question Tucker Rue had taught her, the sounds, "Do jew troost Hey-soos Christos as jer Lord an save-or?"

They laughed all the louder.

Beginning over again, she repeated all the sounds that she had memorized. Apparently they did not understand that they were bound for hell, or if they understood they did not care. Lupe felt the sadness of that and her helplessness before it. Devastated for them, she could only turn away. She walked to the edge of the ocean, to the place where God's waves reached farthest up into that pagan land. She stared at the horizon. Again, she thought of home. The joyless laughter carried on behind her, different somehow, now that she knew they were laughing at her Savior.

Someone spoke nearby and touched her shoulder. Wiping her eyes, Lupe turned to find a young girl standing close, a beautiful child of perhaps fifteen, with perfectly clear skin, freckles, and long straight hair the color of corn. The girl spoke again.

Lupe replied, "English, no."

The girl switched to bad Spanish, which to Lupe sounded like, "No speak English?"

"No," said Lupe.

"I am thinking you speak English because of words you speak to people."

"That was just some things I memorized."

"Memorized? What is?"

"Memorized," repeated Lupe in Spanish. "To learn a thing. To remember it."

The girl shook her head. Clearly, she did not understand. She said, "My Spanish no good, but want to say you very good for talking to the people there."

Lupe tried to smile. "Did you understand what I said?"

"Understand?" The girl frowned, as if search her memory. "Oh, *understand*. Yes. I think so."

"What will happen when you die?"

"I go to God."

"How do you know that?"

"I am . . . belief? Yes, belief in Jesus."

The girl looked solemn as she said it, almost mournful. To hear the Savior's name upon this native's lips was a soothing balm to Lupe, who felt a strong desire to hug her. "That is good," she said. "You should be happy."

The girl turned her head down and frowned. "I am happy."

Lupe's laughter joined that of the maniacs. "Happy? You call this happy?"

The girl looked up. A deep sadness in her eyes silenced Lupe. "It is my mother. She is . . . she is . . . not with me."

"Missing? She is missing?"

"Yes. I think that is the word."

"Did you call the police?"

"No. Not that. She is not knowing Jesus. No God. Missing."

"Oh, you mean she is *lost*," said Lupe, using the Spanish word. "I'm very sorry."

"I wish you talk to her."

"Does your mother speak my language?"

"Yes. My mother is from Spain. My father lives there for a time. Before me."

"Is your father Spanish too?"

"No. Is American."

"Where is your mother?" Lupe looked around the beach. "I will tell her about the Savior."

The girl shook her head. "Not with us."

"Can you take me to her?"

"She not with us, my father and me. Gone. Long time past."

"Your parents are divorced?"

"Divorced. Yes."

Again, Lupe longed to put an arm around this girl. "Would you like to sit and talk?"

"Okay," said the child.

They settled down upon the beach beside each other. Facing the incoming waves, Lupe did her best to offer comfort. She distracted the girl with many questions. What is your name? How old are you? Do you go to school? What do you study? Do you have a boyfriend? Gradually, the girl's solemnity lifted. She spoke of a horse, her horse, which she loved. She kept the horse in a stable in a place called Wilson City, which was not far away, inland.

"Yes," said Lupe, trying not to think about the handsome man who lived there. "I know Wilson City."

The girl spoke of her home, and pointed to a hill above the town. She and her father lived up there, in that house there, just the two of them. Squinting up at the mansion, Lupe said, "Only two of you?"

"A woman lives there for a time, after my mother go. Now she goes too."

"Ah," said Lupe, nodding. "Your father lived with a woman." It explained the divorce.

"Oh, no! No woman for my father. A woman for to help with the house. She clean and cook and to be with me."

"Yes," said Lupe. "I understand."

A wave, bigger than the rest, crashed against the beach and rushed up almost to their bare toes. Lupe wondered why that one wave was much larger than the others. All around her were so many things she did not understand.

The lovely blond girl said, "You wish to come to our house?"

"Me? Why?"

"To clean and cook and to . . . to be with me." As the child spoke, her lips turned down, the mournfulness returning.

Lupe wished she could agree, could go with the sad girl and somehow help her through the agony of loss. But this too was temptation. The purpose of Lupe's quest lay among the suffering pagans in the town, not with a believer high upon a hill. She said, "I am sorry. I cannot."

"You are sure? My father pay you very much."

The girl mentioned a figure and Lupe stared at her, amazed. It was ten times the amount Lupe could earn at her store in Rincón de Dolores. But money was the least of her temptations. "No," she said. "I have other work to do."

"Okay." The girl began to rise.

Lupe said, "Don't go. Stay and keep me company."

"What is 'company'?"

"To not be alone," said Lupe.

"Oh," replied the girl. "Okay."

They sat beside each other, burdened in their different ways as waves approached and fled and the fools behind them laughed without a reason. A shadow fell across the sand.

"Hi, Daddy," said the girl in English. Then, in grade-school Spanish she said, "Allow me present my father, Delano Wright. Father, is Lupe."

Lupe looked up, shielding her eyes with one hand. The man stood over her with the sun at his back, framed by solar flares which shot out all around like fire erupting from the presence of the Lord. Lupe felt she had been in that very moment somewhere else before. Was this memory? Was it fantasy? In her mind she heard the words, *Fear not.* She lifted her hand toward the man above her, his features lost within the blackness of his silhouette. "Much pleasure," she said in Spanish.

He shook her hand and replied with a fine Castilian accent, "The pleasure is mine." Then he shifted his position and the sun came blinding from behind him and she had to look away.

"Father," said the girl, still struggling in Spanish, "I ask Lupe to work for us."

"Indeed?" said the man in the same language. "And what did Señorita Lupe reply?"

"Reply? What is 'reply'?"

"Her answer. What did she say?"

"Oh. She say no."

At the sadness in the child's voice Lupe said, "I am honored by the offer, señor, and truly wish it could be possible. Unfortunately, I have other work to do."

"Yes? What is your work, if I may ask?"

"I have come to America to save the lost people here. To tell them about the Savior." Again she shielded her eyes from the sun, looking toward his black silhouette. "Señor, what will happen when you die?"

In his cultured Spanish he said, "I will surely go to my eternal reward, by the grace of God in Christ."

"Well said, señor! I am delighted to hear it."

"You say you came to our country to tell us about Jesus?"

"I did."

"What makes you think we need a missionary?"

Lupe pointed toward the laughing fools. "Is it not obvious?"

The man turned to follow her gesture, and for the first time she saw something of his features, a fleeting glimpse of them in profile. She sensed familiarity in them, which reinforced the strangeness of the moment, the overwhelming feeling she had lived through this before. Then he turned back toward her, and against the sun his face was lost in silhouette again. "It is good work," he said. "May God richly bless you."

"And you, señor."

The man said, "Señorita Lupe, may I ask a question which is somewhat indiscreet? And will you trust that it is not as it may sound?"

"Yes, señor."

"Do you have a husband, or a boyfriend?"

Lupe frowned. "No, señor. I do not, and I do not desire one."

"You do not desire one? Why is that?"

"My work, señor. It is better to be . . . celibate."

"Yes. Yes, certainly." The man allowed a moment to pass by before he said, "You are sure you do not wish to work for us?"

"I must do the work our Father has commanded."

"Of course. I understand completely. This has been a pleasure." With that he switched to English. "Come on, Button. Time to go."

The girl touched Lupe's arm lightly, then she rose to stand beside her father. Feeling awkward at their feet, Lupe rose as well. Only then, with the sun no longer at his back, did she see the man's face clearly, and when she saw him as he was, Alejandro's burden pressed down on her shoulder; it moved as if alive, and she knew she must be careful.

She had come to America believing the Holy Father would prepare the pagan people of that land. She never dreamed they would refuse the gospel, yet the foolish ones upon the beach had met the good news with mockery and laughter. Then the daughter of this man appeared, this particular man out of all men, at that particular moment. Now that she had seen him fully as he was, could she really let them walk away? Had not Fray Alejandro's precious burden led her to that very place, these very people?

Even with Fray Alejandro's burden as a guide, she did not see the path ahead with clarity. She could only choose the right thing in the moment. So if this portion of her duty was not as she had imagined it would be, what of that? Heaven forbid her to deny the miracle before her eyes.

"Señor," said Lupe. "May we speak a little more about that job?"

FRAY ALEJANDRO SAT UPON A three-legged stool, surrounded by the raw adobe walls of his little cell. Before him on a rough-hewn table was the first wing of the altarpiece. His horsehair brushes inched across the wooden panel, adding to the image bit by tiny bit. He worked in a shifting square of sunlight cast through a single window high on the southern wall. Following the light across his cell, he rose to move his stool and table. He did this every hour or so as time crawled like a tortoise.

Often Alejandro paused to stare out through the narrow doorway. In truth, he spent as much time staring as he spent at his work. Outside, soldiers and neophytes toiled together, erecting a palisade of sharpened sycamore logs to complete the plaza rectangle. On the other three sides of the rectangle were the chapel, the barracks for the friars and leather-jacket soldiers, the kitchen, refactory, and storerooms. The plaza was quite large, about eleven thousand square *varas,* or almost two of our modern acres. Near the center stood a well. In the northwest corner was a corral, and beside the corral a garden, very fertile because of the proximity of manure. The tannery lay beyond the walls. Also outside the plaza were crude lean-to shelters made of limbs and rushes. These shelters backed against the blank adobe exterior walls of the mission's primary structures. In them lived the neophytes.

Such details may interest us today, but Alejandro paid them no attention whatsoever. Staring through the doorway of his little cell, the friar's thoughts had been captured by a sullen sense of doom which had descended on the mission. Alejandro did not understand it. All seemed well, yet his brothers were aloof and disobliging. Furthermore, the altarpiece progressed more slowly than it should. Although he had worked for many days, barely one-quarter of the first wing had been painted. Fray Alejandro did not understand how this was possible. He painted, did he not? All day long he painted. While he was about his work it seemed to progress normally, yet each time he stopped for meals or prayers or sleep, upon his return the panel seemed no closer to completion. He sensed another's hand in this, but did not know if it was God's.

Although it is a sin to worry, that is what he did. Every day the abbot warned Benicio against the liberties he took with the Indians, and at every warning young Benicio's disdain for Fray Guillermo came a little closer to the surface. So Alejandro worried. He sensed calamity approaching, as it comes to every life, cloaked in secrecy or brazen as a lion. The wise accept it on its terms. The unwise dread its coming in the future or torture themselves with regrets about the past. Looking back, they search for a moment of decision, a turning point when they might have said "This," instead of "That," and thus postponed the inevitable.

Such regrets are futile, for our most crucial choices often come like all the rest, importance unannounced, and therefore cannot be more carefully considered. Yet Delano Wright would long regret a crucial choice he made one day, more than two centuries after Alejandro's time. To Delano it seemed a normal day, a day that followed many other normal days. Indeed, five years of normal days had passed since last we saw Delano upon a beach with Harmony and Lupe. For five years the three of them had lived together in his mansion on the hill, and in five years' time a man may forget certain things. He may let his guard grow lax. He may become dangerously complacent.

The crucial choice drew close when Lupe entered the morning room. Delano Wright glanced up from the wingback chair where he sat reading a newspaper. Speaking English to Harmony, who was cooking in the kitchen, the Mexican woman said, "Do you want some help?"

Harmony shook her head. "Not on your day off."

"I don't mind," said Lupe, approaching.

Harmony brandished a paring knife in a mock warning. "I'm serious. You stay out of here."

"Let me baste the roast."

"Dad, will you please talk to her?"

Delano smiled. "There's no way I'm getting in the middle of this."

"But she never lets me do anything. Tell her it's okay to take a break."

Lupe said, "I let you help me with the groceries, yes?"

"Only because you don't drive."

"You are splitting hairs."

Noticing her correct use of the idiom, Delano admired Lupe's command of English. Although she still put the accent on the wrong syllable sometimes, seldom used contractions, and had a problem with *Y* sounds (which came out more like *J*), for the most part Lupe had trained herself to speak the language fluently. And thanks to Lupe, Harmony now spoke Spanish almost like a native, which was more than Delano had been able to accomplish with his daughter during her formative years.

The two young women often chatted in a mix of English and Spanish, slipping from one language to the other and back again as if there were no difference. It reminded Delano of how things once had been with Ana and him, freely choosing words to suit the moment, English for precision, Spanish for emotion and romance. Theirs had been a world too large for just one language. They had fallen in love in Spanish and broken up in English. Even with over five years to think it through since the divorce, Delano still had not identified the moment when the Spanish started fading.

It had been more than two years since Ana had been in touch. On Harmony's eighteenth birthday she had called from somewhere in Florida. Harmony would not speak with her, and of course Ana had blamed Delano for that, accusing him of poisoning their daughter's mind. There had been anger, there had been insults, then the sound of sobs, embarrassing tears, and he had realized she was drinking. Then, with schizophrenic abruptness Ana went from accusations to entreaties, speaking in that full-throated Barcelona accent of hers. Three years had gone by and suddenly there she was again, using all the old amorous endearments. She had spoken words that only sounded right in Spanish—my love, my heart, my affection, my wish—pleading to come home, but all he heard were words from the King James: Jezebel, fornicator, adulteress.

"Forgive me, love," she had begged in Spanish.

"Of course," he had replied in English, before hanging up the phone. Later, in the shower, he had wept.

Now, as the two stood side by side, Lupe's diminutive stature made Harmony look even taller than she was. Delano's daughter had reached five feet ten inches, exactly the same height as Ana, and like Ana, she was spectacularly beautiful. Sometimes Delano wished she had a blemish, a crooked nose, eyes too close together, a jaw a bit too large, some small flaw inherited from him to remedy her beauty. In Ana he had witnessed the cruel temptation that was physical perfection.

Harmony playfully bumped Lupe with her hip, nudging the smaller woman away from the kitchen counter.

"All right, all right," said Lupe. "Have it your way, you large bully."

Harmony laughed. "'Big bully' would be better."

"Big and large are the same thing."

"Trust me. It's just better."

"*Gracias, profesora grande,*" replied Lupe, crossing back into the morning room.

Delano chuckled as she took part of the newspaper from the pile on the table and settled into a wingback chair opposite him. "Mister," she said. It was her usual form of address to Delano, a direct translation of "señor." Even after five years of living together—or almost together, with him and Harmony in the house and Lupe in the apartment out back above the pool house—she still refused to adopt the familiarity of his given name. "Mister, may I borrow a pen?"

Delano removed a Montblanc from his shirt pocket and passed it to her. "Harmony," he said. "You'd better apologize. She's over here circling ads in the help wanted section."

Harmony chuckled. "Good luck with that. I don't think they have a lot of openings for obsessive-compulsives."

Lupe looked at Delano. "Obsessive-compulsive?"

Smiling, he explained.

"Oh," she said, feigning indignation. "Harmony, you be nice!" Then she leaned closer to Delano. "Do not worry, mister. I am only going to play with the crossword puzzle."

"That's a relief," said Delano, smiling to let her know he wasn't really worried. One benefit to employing people of her status was the fact that they rarely left a job once they had found it, regardless of the pay or working conditions. Not that he relied on that, of course. He treated Lupe much like family, and thought her compensation very fair.

A bell rang. Someone had pressed the call button at the gate down the hill.

"Who's that?" asked Delano.

"I asked a friend over for dinner," said Harmony.

"I will go," said Lupe, heading for the intercom and the switch to open the gate, but Harmony dashed around the kitchen counter, beating Lupe to the gallery. When she had left them, Lupe spoke to Delano. "I think she wants me to be fat and lazy."

Delano turned another page in his newspaper. "She just wants to take care of you."

"It is supposed to be another way around."

"She doesn't need us to take care of her anymore."

Lupe sighed and focused on the puzzle. Delano glanced at her profile. Her sigh intrigued him. He sometimes saw a subtle undercurrent within Lupe, a hint of melancholy in unguarded moments, something so slight it would not concern him except for its contrast with the rest of her character. On the whole, this wandering Mexicana they had found like flotsam on a beach was most amazing. When Delano had first begun to realize she was different from the others, from Flora and Rosa and that other one who only lasted for one week, he worried Harmony might invest too much hope in her, might create an unhealthy surrogate to fill the maternal gap. Fortunately, Harmony and Lupe had never formed that kind of bond. It was more like they were sisters.

Almost from the moment Lupe had come to live with them, Harmony had begun to recover from her mother's betrayal. The gloom that had settled on their house simply could not stand against Lupe's relentless optimism. Where she went, the sun shone, birds sang, the bitter past retreated and a hopeful future beckoned. Life with Lupe overflowed with reminders to slow down, pay attention, and appreciate the moment. She took great delight in hummingbirds, for instance. She applauded sunsets. She interrupted conversations to demand that everybody listen to the roar of crashing waves. Yet sometimes there were sighs.

He suspected a deep sorrow in her past, but she spoke little of her history. He had learned she came from a small mountain village in Jalisco, where she once owned a shop of some kind. She never mentioned parents or siblings, so he assumed she had been raised an orphan. Civility restrained him from asking for more details. As for men, he had been gratified to find her behavior above reproach. Indeed, Lupe had to some extent restored his confidence in women.

Although she was a Catholic, he believed her devotion to the Lord rivaled his own. He knew she kept a Bible open on her bedstand, and twice each week she walked to the little Catholic church down in the village, where she attended Mass. But more important were two incidents when he had observed the power of her faith.

The first occurred down in the village near the spot where he first met her. Delano had been driving along the Pacific Coast Highway on a Sunday after church when he happened to glance over and see Lupe standing on a low concrete wall along the boardwalk, wildly waving one hand while she held what seemed to be an open book in the other. Intrigued, he parked a block away and walked back toward the spot. Soon he heard Lupe's voice, even above the traffic noise and waves. For some reason he did not want Lupe to know he was there. He stood behind a palm tree. Peering around the trunk, he realized she was preaching from an open Bible. A hundred people passed along the beach before her while he watched, and not one paused to listen. She did not seem to care. Delano listened for a long time. He thought her sermon was quite good.

The second incident had occurred one afternoon about a year later. He arrived home before the normal time. Entering from the garage he heard someone shouting, and realized it was Lupe. At first he thought she might be practicing for her usual Sunday sermon on the beach. Then he heard the anger in her voice. Clearly she was arguing with someone, but who could it be? She should have been alone at that time of day.

She screamed.

Suddenly afraid, Delano thought of burglars. He paused in the kitchen to withdraw a long knife from a drawer. He slipped off his shoes, the better to approach the confrontation silently. Creeping along the gallery, he heard Lupe more clearly with each step. "Is this all you want?" she shouted, speaking Spanish. "I don't see why! It's not worth anything!"

He heard the vacuum cleaner whining and her continued shouts. "Why won't you let me leave? Just let me leave! No one will believe me! Not one single person! There's no reason for me to stay! Please, just let me go!" She was begging for her life, begging the criminals to let her leave them to their evil work.

Very close now, just outside the bedroom where she was, Delano gripped the knife more firmly. With his other hand upon the doorknob, he prayed, Lord help me. Turning the handle, he opened the door just an inch. Through the crack he saw Lupe with her back to him. He saw nobody else. She pushed and pulled the vacuum cleaner viciously as if wrestling with an enemy, arms and elbows flying, shouting all the while.

"I came a long way, you know! I almost died that time! It wasn't so easy, following you here! Why did you make me do this? I want an explanation!"

With a flash of understanding he realized she was shouting prayers over the vacuum cleaner's roar, as if the Maker of the universe could not understand her otherwise. Delano gently closed the door, but he remained outside and listened.

"Have I done something to offend you? Tell me what it is! I gave him up for you! I gave him up! Shouldn't I be doing something more than this, if I had to give him up? Why do you make me wait? Let me serve you! All I want is something that's worth doing!"

Never in his life had Delano Wright heard such a prayer. He knew some people shouted *to* the Lord, but this woman shouted *at* him. He heard such suffering, such frustration, and such passion in her words. To pray as she did would have terrified him. Yet it also made him jealous. The woman's faith was very strong, possibly even stronger than his own. These were the words of someone who was absolutely certain she was being heard.

Awed by his housekeeper's faith, Delano then realized something else. Clearly, Lupe was not as happy in his home as she appeared. He would be forever grateful for her influence on Harmony when his daughter had teetered on the brink of clinical depression. He had long ago begun to think of Lupe as more than just a servant or employee and he had assumed she felt the same about Harmony and him, that she felt lucky to be with them, glad for the work, for the money, for the shelter, for their friendship. He had always assumed he was doing her a favor, as she had done for him. But all this time, apparently, she had longed to be elsewhere.

Delano had walked away that afternoon deep in thought, and many times since then he had wondered what it was that made her want to leave, and why she stayed.

Now Harmony returned to the morning room, drawing him back into the present. Rather than passing on into the kitchen, his daughter paused before the table. "Daddy? My friend's in the front living room, but before we go in there I have something to tell you about him."

"Him?" Delano folded his newspaper. "Your friend is a man?"

Lupe looked up from her crossword puzzle.

"Yes, and he's kind of special."

"What do you mean, special?"

"It means this man is not just a friend, I think," said Lupe.

"I know that, thank you," said Delano. "Harmony, who is this guy?"

"He really means a lot to me, Daddy. That's the thing. And I just know you're going to love him."

"*Love* him? Wait a minute—"

Lupe interrupted. "Go in there, you both. I will finish the cooking."

Harmony said, "But—"

"Go, okay? Is not a problem, really. You know I love to cook."

Frowning, Delano rose and crossed the morning room. "Come on, Button. I want to meet this friend of yours."

Delano and Harmony walked along the gallery and joined their guest in the living room, a lofty space with dark wood paneling, an antique wooden floor, and a set of ten-point elk antlers above an imposing limestone hearth and mantel. The young man sat on the edge of one of the brown leather sofas, his rigid back several inches away from the cushions. He rose quickly to his feet and extended his hand. Delano was surprised to recognize him, a minister of some kind who had recently made an excellent presentation at church.

They sat down and began to speak about the chairman of the church's benevolence committee, a mutual acquaintance, and then unfortunately the fellow mentioned football, which had never been Delano's game. Delano was a hunter and a golfer, and except for supporting Harmony's love of riding, he did not care one bit about other sports. He wished they could bypass all the small talk and get right to the reason for his visit. He saw that look in the man's eyes, the look all men got around his daughter. Young or old, married or single, she brought it out in them. How he feared for her sometimes.

"What's your favorite team?" asked Harmony. The fellow answered, and Harmony asked another question. Although Delano knew she cared no more for football than he did, he watched her keep the conversation going, faking fascination, and as he watched he saw something else, something startling. She had the same hungry look he had seen in the young man.

Delano resolved to stop this foolishness before it started. His plans for Harmony did not include a love affair with some poor minister. He would not idly watch while she repeated the mistake he had made with Ana, marrying someone from another world. How he wished he had listened to his parents' objections all those years ago. How wise they had been. Marriage was difficult enough without that kind of added pressure. No, Harmony would not repeat his mistakes. She would complete her bachelor's degree in management at Biola and then go on to get her MBA at Stanford. She would return to Blanco Beach and work at his side, managing the family holdings, which he had inherited from his father, and which had been passed down before him through three generations.

Harmony would inherit everything one day. So much land and money was a great responsibility. The time would come for her to choose a partner for her life, but that time was in the future, after she had laid the necessary foundation. And when she chose a man he would not be a man like this. He would be someone who had been raised as she had been, someone with the same heritage and background, someone who could stand beside her as an equal.

"Button," he said. "Why don't you offer our guest a drink?"

"Sure," said Harmony. "What would you like?"

He asked only for a glass of water. Delano asked for juice—any kind would do—and watched his daughter leave the room.

"What do you think of Harmony?" he said.

"Excuse me?"

"My daughter. What do you think of her?"

The young man adjusted his position on the sofa. "She's a wonderful person, Mr. Wright."

"Oh, she is. She's very nice. But she's only twenty. Did you know that?"

"Yes, but I don't—"

"I know she seems older, but she was just a teenager a few months ago."

"Mr. Wright, I—"

"Call me Del."

"Okay, uh, Del, I don't know wh—"

"How old are you, by the way?"

"Uh, I'm twenty-seven."

"Married, are you?"

"No, sir."

"Want to get married?"

"Well, one of these days, I guess."

"Good. A man of God ought to be married. 'Husband of one wife' and all that, right?"

"I guess so."

"How did you two meet?"

"At your church, actually. I have a booth there every year at the 'Local Missions Sunday.' You know, when you guys invite people to come ask for donations for their ministries? She was very interested in my work."

"Do you believe opposites attract?"

"I'm not sure."

"They do. But let me tell you, it never works out."

"Mr. Wright, really, I don't think we need to have this conversation."

"Well, just humor me a second, okay? You know, I'm a very wealthy man. I give a lot to charities. Millions every year."

The young man's face turned red.

"Now, don't be embarrassed. Let me offer some advice." Delano leaned closer. "There's nothing wrong with asking rich Christians for money. 'The worker is worthy of his meat.' Don't you ever forget that."

The young man looked Del in the eye, and Del admired him for it. "I won't."

"Good. Good." Del leaned even closer. "Just make sure that's all you ever ask me for, okay? My daughter's not available."

Harmony came in. "What are you guys talking about?"

"Money," replied Delano, smiling.

"Oh, brother," said his daughter. "That again."

"Where are our drinks?" asked Delano.

"She wouldn't let me in the kitchen. Said she'll bring them right out."

Delano sat back and let the young people carry most of the conversation. He could see his point had been well taken by the fellow, whose eyes had definitely lost that hungry look. Maybe he and Harmony would keep things on the proper level, and Delano would be able to help with his ministry.

Watching the young people did make Delano feel old . . . old, and tired, and very lonely. Loneliness brought Ana back to mind. How amazing, after so much time, that he could still ache for his beautiful mistake. Ana had her talents. She would have found a more tactful way to warn this young man off, some approach less mercenary than the one he had just used. How he hated speaking to the fellow as he had, but he knew no other options. Delano was not one for subtlety or small talk. He had never mastered those arts. He had—

A crash of breaking glass behind him.

Delano twisted on the sofa to look back. He saw Lupe standing in the gallery, standing with both hands covering her mouth, her wide eyes locked upon their guest, the drinking glasses shattered at her feet.

"What's wrong?" asked Harmony, rising. "Lupe, what's wrong?"

"Lupe?" said the young man, also coming to his feet.

As the visitor spoke her name Lupe backed away. She turned. She ran, and Harmony set out after her.

The young women's fleeing footsteps echoed through his massive home. Delano looked back from the empty gallery to find upon the man's face a mirror of the Mexicana's anguish, and in that moment Delano—a wiser man for having learned from Ana's betrayal—had a sudden revelation. He remembered Lupe's strange prayer, and he supposed he understood why she so often sighed.

Thus arrived the hidden moment of decision, the deceptive turning point when Delano Wright might have said "This," instead of "That," and postponed the inevitable. In the years to come he would yearn to travel back through time to live that instant just once more, to tell the man to leave, leave immediately, before it was too late. But curiosity is a seductive temptress, and like most crucial choices, the decision came upon him with no fanfare, importance unannounced. So Delano Wright did not tell the man to go. Instead he spoke the words that sealed his fate, and that of many others.

He said, "Tell me, Tucker, how do you know our Lupe?"

CAPÍTULO 12

DURING THE ADVENT OF THEIR Lord's birth, the friars of the Misión de Santa Dolores went looking for lost livestock, walking through the wilderness like the fabled three kings of the Orient following a star. Fray Alejandro did not understand this task, for the neophytes were much more capable of finding missing cattle, and the abbot seldom did a thing himself that could be delegated. But as the men of God strolled along a ridge peering down into the canyons on each side, Fray Guillermo spoke of vast, eternal things and Alejandro came to understand the enterprise was just a ploy. The abbot hoped to lure Benicio away from the cares and distractions of the mission and remind him of their higher calling, thus awakening the young friar to his errors. Benicio was hesitant to respond at first, but Fray Guillermo drew him out most masterfully. Soon the friars were deep in a discussion of the Gnostic error, and Benicio began to sound like a Franciscan again.

Fray Alejandro approved of Guillermo's plan wholeheartedly, although it must be said the good friar owed much of his enthusiasm to the delightful prospect of escaping from his cell and from the tedium of work upon the altarpiece, if only for a little while. He walked ahead, his attention on the bushes about them and the sun-baked soil below, alert for stray cattle and malicious serpents. The trail they followed curved around a boulder shaped like a massive skull, which stuck up from the shoulder of the hill.

Fray Alejandro picked his way around the looming obstruction, only to confront a most bizarre sight: a pile of flat stones stacked one upon the other, higher than his head and thickly covered by beads, carved bits of wood, feathers, and seashells.

"Those are offerings," said Fray Benicio, reaching Alejandro's side. "The people call them *pooish*."

"Offerings?" Fray Guillermo was the last to round the boulder. He squinted at the strange apparition suspiciously. "What offerings?"

"You see the structure yonder, Abbot? It is an altar to their god. Cooksuy, I believe they call him. I learned of this while sitting in the elders' circle at the village. They throw those trinkets on the altar every time they pass, as a sort of homage to the spirit of this holy place."

"Holy place?" exclaimed Fray Guillermo. "It is no such thing! It is an abomination!" Casting his staff aside, the abbot charged down to the altar and began to tear the offerings from the stones, hurling them as far into the surrounding bushes as he could. He shouted, "Cunning serpent be gone from this place! Most infernal demons be dispersed! The power of Christ commands you! The power of our most Holy Virgin commands you!"

Fray Benicio called, "Stop, Abbot! You must stop!" He ran forward to restrain Guillermo, but the older friar moaned with rage and twisted from Benicio's grasp, and fell upon the pagan altar with renewed vigor, scooping up the offerings and throwing them in all directions like a dog who furiously desired to dig a rodent from its hole. "Get thee behind me, Satan!" screamed the abbot. "By the might of God the Father I command you to be gone, Prince of Lies! By the power of the Holy Ghost I order you away, Author of Destruction!"

In the end Benicio and Alejandro could only watch until at last their superior, spent with holy zeal, fell onto the soil beside the pagan altar. Then together they assisted the pale man back down along the ridge and through the canyon to the mission.

With his arm around the trembling Fray Guillermo, Alejandro marveled that a pile of stones could wield such power over men of faith. Indians adored it. Catholics abhorred it. If stones could summon up such opposites as love and hate, did the altar truly have inherent power, or were such sentiments the spawn of human minds alone? He thought of his own work, the altarpiece that had been ordered by

Guillermo. Surely it was merely paint upon a piece of wood, yet the thing did seem to resist him as if it had an independent will. He thought of miracles allegedly received on pious knees before carved saints in chapels all around the world, of hard hearts softened by the majesty of Saint Peter's Basilica or the fabled Sistine Chapel ceiling. He thought of the frescoes at San Francisco's Porziuncola, of those who said such absolute perfection could not have come from human hands. He recalled the power in that place, the way that power seemed to fill him as he knelt in prayer.

Alejandro knew it was not faith to bow before created things; it was magic and not miracles, tricks instead of truth. Yet he also knew the story written in the primal symbols of the Christian faith—the cross and empty tomb—had saved countless lives. By them some men were transformed into saints. Others (he thought of the Inquisition) became monsters.

Certainly we know a symbol can bring change to lesser things than souls. Consider a town like Wilson City, assailed by heat and dust, abraded by a scorching wind, refuse in the gutters. Amid such devastation let us marvel at the transformation wrought by lily garlands tracing a converted warehouse doorframe, by colorful balloons bobbing on the cords that bound them to the roof, by virginal white ribbons tied to the burglar bars over the windows.

The merrymakers who had converted such somber poverty into a gay oasis came and went with happy burdens: flowers, food, and drink, and gifts in silver paper. Asked by a passing stranger to explain these glad preparations, one of them paused and smiled—for who could do such work without a smile?—and said, A wedding! A wedding here tomorrow!

From the lily-covered door emerged a man not thirty years of age, wide of shoulder, slim of waist, with very much to do. He pointed far, and people went; he pointed near, and people came. Everyone consulted him. All the people wished to please. He might have been a wealthy man, an employer, or a government official wielding the great power of his office. But this was only Tucker Rue, poor and simple Tucker Rue, who had arrived there as a stranger not so very long ago, a man who possessed nothing, yet who now encountered love and admiration everywhere.

Would the peoples' admiration fade if the details of his courtship became known? Tucker watched them make arrangements for his wedding and recalled the bargain he had struck in Delano Wright's living room, the condition placed by that rich man upon his tithes. Tucker had agreed to take only the man's money, and since that night he had surely taken much of that for the sake of Sanctuario and the poor. But in spite of his agreement to the contrary, Tucker had also taken something for himself.

A Chevrolet approached. Tucker Rue watched it come and told himself to think only of love. Some might call his actions shameful, but if he had acted for love of the people and the love of the woman, how could that be true? Could love ever be shameful? Tucker watched her come and thought of what it meant for her to drive such a modest car. He lived in poverty among the people, but it is easy to abandon what you never had. This woman, on the other hand, had decided to abandon riches he could not imagine. She could be at a Bentley's wheel, yet she came in a Chevrolet Impala, which was not even new. She could be shopping in Beverly Hills or lying in the sun at Saint-Tropez, but she was in Wilson City; she was with him, Harmony, his bride-to-be.

Her Impala stopped in front of Sanctuario. Before she could emerge, Tucker was in front of it, waving one arm toward the garlands at the doorway and the ribbons at the windows. "What do you think?"

"It's perfect, honey," said Harmony, emerging from the car. "It's just perfect."

When she stood beside him, he glanced around to see if anyone was watching. It would not do to kiss her on the street, not in that conservative community, even with their marriage just a day away. But what man could resist a woman such as this, knowing he was free to draw her near? Tucker pulled Harmony's lithe body to himself and pressed his lips to hers. She yielded instantly, molding herself to him. He felt heat rise in his belly. Breaking the kiss, but only for a moment, he whispered, "I can't wait for tomorrow."

"Me, either," replied Harmony. Her voice was husky as he kissed her ear and neck. "But right now we're not alone."

"Mmm?" he mumbled, nuzzling her hair.

"Seriously, honey. Lupe's in the car."

"What?" He looked toward the windshield. The sun's reflection on it dazzled his eyes. He could not see inside. "She's sitting in there?" he asked.

"Uh-huh."

Pushing away from Harmony he said, "You should have told me."

He turned and entered Sanctuario, passing underneath the lush white lilies.

Harmony was at his heels. "Honey? What's the matter?"

Tucker walked on through the lobby and turned to stride along a corridor. On his right was a row of small rooms and on the other side a large meeting hall. He thought of the last time Lupe had been there. He thought of carpet now where once bare concrete had been, and walls where once he had been separated from her by mere ropes and hanging blankets.

A lady on a stepladder teased him in her native Spanish as he passed. "Don't walk so fast," she said. "You'll need your strength tomorrow night." This was followed by much giggling as she and another woman strung crepe paper, helping with the preparation, proud to be a part of this great moment in his life.

At a pair of doors outside the meeting hall Tucker paused to let his fiancée catch up. "Whose idea was it to bring her here?"

"Why? What's the matter?"

"I'll bet it wasn't her idea. Did your father order her to come?"

Harmony stared at him. "*Order* her? Lupe's our friend, honey. We don't order her to do anything. She's here because she wants to help us get ready for the wedding."

"You told her about the wedding? Why would you do that?"

Harmony reached for his hand, but it remained a fist. "What's going on, honey?"

"It's just . . . why is she here? She doesn't like me very much. You saw how she was that time at your house."

"She was surprised. She told me it was like seeing a ghost, you showing up after five years."

Tucker moved closer. He touched Harmony's arm. "Listen. Your father doesn't want us to be together, so he—"

"Oh, come on, honey. Let's not go over that again.

"You're supposed to marry a Rockefeller or something, not someone like me."

"He'll learn to love you."

"I don't think so. Not after he finds out we got married. I think he sent Lupe here to keep an eye on you. What if she tells him about the wedding?"

Harmony laughed. "That's ridiculous. She would never— Oh, hello, Lupe."

From behind him came, "Hello," and Tucker turned to get his first long look at her in years. She had run away too quickly that time at Delano Wright's house; he had barely caught a glimpse of her. In the months since then he had often wished they could have spoken, maybe cleared the air a little, but of course another visit to Harmony's house had been out of the question. Her father would have guessed the truth about Tucker and his daughter immediately. Now that Lupe stood before him calmly, face to face, he saw she was much as he had so often remembered: cheekbones high and proud, bronzed skin flawless, pure black hair alive with dancing sparkles in the incandescent light. She stared at him, and her eyes, so darkly incomprehensible, seemed to drill into his mind as if his every thought were naked for her scrutiny. Something writhed within him, pinned in place by the needles in those eyes, a formless, irrational emotion, based only on . . . what?

He had nothing to feel guilty for, standing there at the heart of a growing ministry to worthy people, with the woman he would marry at his side, a good woman who would help him serve the poor, Lupe's own people. If his bride was tall but Lupe was short, if Harmony was pale and blond while Lupe's skin was the rich brown of café con leche and her hair as black as night, if he was marrying the richest woman in southern California while Lupe owned nothing, what did it matter? The contrasts were coincidence. None of it meant anything.

"Hello, Lupe," he said. "It's been a long time."

"You have changed many things here."

"Yes," he said, wrapping his arm around Harmony's shoulders. "There have been a lot of changes."

Harmony said, "Don't you think it's neat that you two knew each other before Tucker and I met?"

Lupe shrugged. "It was only for a little while, a long time in the past."

"Don't let her kid you," said Tucker. "She was a huge help back then. We were sorry to see her go."

Lupe smiled at that, a flash of teeth, and it was gone. He had forgotten how white and pure her smile could look against the golden color of her skin. The fleeting beauty of it distracted him a moment, then he realized why she had smiled. He tried to laugh at his pomposity. "I mean, *I* was sorry. There was no 'we' back then, of course. Just me."

"Just you and Lupe, you mean?" asked Harmony.

He did not answer, for he did not trust his tongue. Lupe continued to stare at him with eyes unwavering, as if she were a charmer and he a snake. He longed to know her thoughts, why she was there on that day of all days, but the question would not do. He said, "Would you like to see the place? See what's changed?"

"Yes," she said. "That would be nice."

With Harmony beside him he led her through the building, pausing at each room he had built within the old warehouse, beginning with the food pantry, its shelves stocked to the ceiling with canned meats and vegetables, and then the learning center, where children studied on computers after school and adults learned English as a second language. In the corner of a storeroom Tucker showed them about a hundred plastic milk jugs filled with water. "The people bring them in from home and fill them here with boiling tap water, so we know they're clean," he said. "Then we take them out into the desert for the *pollos*." They reached the little library, stocked with several hundred books in Spanish and in English, and then the secondhand clothing closet, where the homeless and the desperately poor could dress themselves and their children.

"You have done much," said Lupe.

"I couldn't even have started without your help," he said.

Lupe paused at another door. "What is here?"

"Nothing. Just my room."

"You've got to see this, Lupe," said Harmony. She opened the door and Lupe peered in. It was a very small room, about the size of the kitchen pantry at the Wright mansion. On the left was a bed, neatly made and barely large enough for one. Beside it was a nightstand with a lamp and Bible. There was a single wooden chair and space enough for nothing else. The walls were bare. The floor was bare. "Tucker lives here like a monk," said Harmony.

"I don't need much," he said.

His fiancée looked at Lupe. "Is this how Tucker lived when you knew him before?"

"We were not so comfortable," said Lupe.

"We?"

"Hey," said Tucker. "We got those covers for the folding chairs this morning. You want to see?"

"Okay . . ." said Harmony, her eyes still locked on Lupe.

He led them into the meeting hall, where all was almost ready for the wedding. Crisp white fabric covered several dozen folding chairs arranged in rows to face a lily-adorned arbor. White and silver crepe paper streamed along the ceiling. Bouquets of white roses stood in pairs of tall stands at the ends of every second row down the central aisle, and brass candlesticks with dozens of white tapers flanked the arbor, ready to be lit.

"Oh, Tucker," said Harmony.

"I know it's not very fancy, but the ladies did their best. . . ."

"It's lovely! It's absolutely perfect! Oh, honey, I love you!"

She pulled him close and clung to him.

With slack arms Tucker stood in Harmony's embrace. He stared over her shoulder at Lupe, who watched impassively. Slowly he wrapped his arms around his fiancée. He closed his eyes and said, "I love you too." When he opened his eyes again, Lupe had walked away.

Harmony and Lupe remained about an hour. Slight changes were made to the decorations at Harmony's request. She greeted many of the ladies there, speaking Spanish with them, praising all the work they had done, thanking them, charming everyone. She would be an asset to his ministry; of that, Tucker Rue had no doubt.

Meanwhile, he watched Lupe bringing things inside from Harmony's Impala: glass bowls, ceramic platters, steel serving spoons, and paper cups and plates. All of this she carried into Sanctuario's new kitchen, which had just been constructed with Delano Wright's donations.

When Harmony went into the restroom, Tucker entered the

kitchen to find Lupe laying out the serving bowls, preparing them for tomorrow's reception.

"This is very kind of you," he said.

"It is nothing."

"No, to come here like this, to help out with our wedding when you feel the way you do . . . it's a fine gesture."

Lupe fixed her obscure stare upon him. "When I feel the way I do?"

"You know . . . about me."

"I am happy for you, Tucker."

"Really?"

"Of course. I wish you and Harmony great happiness."

"Are you sure? Because, you know, after the way you left that time . . . I thought . . ."

Lupe did not fill the silence. She did not look at him. Her hands were very busy.

"You left so suddenly and never came back. I thought you were angry at me, or you didn't like me, or maybe I offended you when I . . . when I kissed your hand."

"I was not offended."

"I looked for you."

"Yes?"

"For months."

"I am sorry."

"You remember that I kissed your hand?"

"Of course."

"Were you angry then? I made you angry?"

"No. Not angry."

Watching her work, he drew a shuddering breath, and realized he was terrified. "All this time I've wondered what I did that was so wrong. Why you didn't like me."

"I never said you did anything wrong. I never said I do not like you."

He thought he saw her eyes go a little wider. He thought he saw emotion there.

She turned away from him to do something with a platter. "We should not speak of this."

"If I thought you cared about me . . ."

"Please."

"Are you saying 'please' because you do care, or because you don't?"

"I am saying tomorrow is your wedding, and I have work to do."

"Lupe, I just want to—"

"Tucker," she interrupted, still showing him her back, still busy with her hands. "You are marrying my friend tomorrow."

He watched her for a moment. Then he said, "Of course you're right." He left her in the kitchen and went to look for his bride-to-be.

Ten minutes later, Harmony backed out of her parking spot in the yellow Impala, with Lupe beside her in the passenger seat. Through the windshield Lupe stared at Tucker where he stood before the letters that spelled "Sanctuario," the letters she had helped him paint in blood red on the concrete wall. He waved as they departed. Harmony returned his wave. Lupe did not.

CAPÍTULO 13

IN THE THIRD WEEK OF Advent the altarpiece remained unfinished. Indeed, Fray Alejandro had not yet completed even the first wing of the triptych. This failure must not be held against him, for every morning except on the Sabbath the friar had attacked the project with great vigor, determined to produce results, but as he worked an atmospheric thickness descended on his little cell. It enslaved his movements. His hand upon the brush seemed impossibly distant. His thoughts were shattered into disconnected pieces as if a malevolent presence had dashed them wickedly against the inside of his skull. Each day dragged on as if for months, yet in the evenings it seemed they had passed in an instant, and when at last the setting sun made further work impossible, he escaped exhausted from his cell like a ghost ship emerging from a fog.

In the night this obscurity lifted just as strangely as it came. Even the memory of his struggle faded. At vespers he still felt certain of the fact of it; at compline he was not so certain what was true and what might be a construct of imagination, and by lauds each morning he could not recall the miasma which had so bedeviled him. Thus the Franciscan put his brush to work again each day in a state of renewed ignorance, and thusly unprepared, the lowering veil again enshrouded him, rendering his efforts fruitless.

While supping in the refectory, Fray Guillermo often asked about the altarpiece. "It must be finished," said the abbot one evening, "before Christmas."

"I will do my best," replied the exhausted Alejandro.

"You perspire overmuch, brother. You are pale and shaking. Are you ill?"

"I do not think so."

"Yet your progress on the altarpiece is sluggish. What excuse can you offer?"

"None, Abbot, except that I am slow."

"You apply yourself with diligence?"

"Yes, Abbot."

At this the spectral abbot frowned. "One often wonders, brother. One truly does."

Fray Benicio witnessed this exchange and others like it often, but he offered Alejandro little sympathy, for the young friar's concerns lay elsewhere.

To attempt amends for Fray Guillermo's desecration of their altar, Benicio had asked for one small basket of grain, to be taken to the closest village for the Indians' use in some sort of sacred ritual. Fray Benicio would have done better to omit the grain's intended use from his request, for Fray Guillermo swore to grant them nothing, not even such a pittance, so revolted was he by the Indians' false religion and so great was his offense that some from their village had not yet converted to the one true faith.

In spite of his disinterest in Alejandro's troubles, Benicio appealed to him for support. The abbot in his turn assumed Fray Alejandro was an ally in such matters. The good friar, finding much to praise and fault in both positions, endeavored for neutrality. Yet rather than appeasing Guillermo or Benicio, it seemed Alejandro's position in the middle displeased both. Each withdrew in his own way, until the three friars became as separate islands. Benicio quite literally avoided contact with Alejandro and Guillermo except at meals and daily prayers. The abbot was not so obvious, but he did limit dialogue with the other friars to that required by his office. At table Alejandro's brothers remained silent, save for the barest of civilities. Elsewhere no greeting was returned when Alejandro offered one, not even nods while passing in the plaza.

The leather-jacket soldiers held Fray Alejandro in high regard, as did many of the neophytes, for the friar's kindness to them was unceasing. But the scriptures tell us it is not good for man to be alone, and this was written even as the first man walked the garden with his Maker. We must infer therefore that a longing for the company of one's own kind is possible even in the company of God, and if such a thing is true, a Franciscan might find fraternity unsatisfactory among those outside his Order. As was the case with God and Adam, the gulf of education and of interests was too vast between the homely friar and the Indians and soldiers. Only a brother Franciscan could have assuaged the loneliness he felt in that remote and forbidding place.

If such a thing was true more than two centuries ago, it remains true in our time, for we have touched on changeless human nature. Thus Ramón Ernesto Rodríguez Obregón, late of Hércules, Mexico, but now living in the town of Wilson City, California, USA, also longed for the companionship of the one most like himself: his woman, whom he had not seen in more than five long years.

In the years since Ramón Rodríguez had risked a crossing of the southern Arizona desert to save his wife and sons from direst poverty he had been richly blessed. He had sent more than thirty thousand dollars home to his Raquel. In the United States, money was not so very hard to find. All one had to do was stand outside the lumberyard and wait for rich gringos to come and offer work. He had earned as much as eighty dollars in one day. Usually the pay was less than that, but he still made more in one hour than he could make all day in Mexico.

He had also made many friends, five of whom now sat beside him drinking beer and watching as the sun sank toward the western hills. Because of the five brothers who lived with him and shared the rent, he could afford a fine place to live, a two-bedroom duplex with a soft mattress on the floor. One could drink the water from the faucet. The electricity was on at all times. There was a refrigerator. It was rarely empty, and when it was empty the place across town—Sanctuario, they called it—was always willing to provide a meal. One of his roommates even had a vehicle, a truck with fringe above the windows and his name across the rear window. A fine white truck only slightly older than Ramón himself that was reliable and could be used to travel anywhere, so long as there was money for the gasoline.

Truly, Ramón Rodríguez was richly blessed. He possessed more than he had ever dreamed was possible, yet even at the risk of ingratitude he thought only of Raquel and his sons, the absent blessings who made all other blessings meaningless, and whom he had not seen in far too many years.

Fernando Amador emerged from the back door. "My friends," he said, "I have bad news. Some son of a mangy dog has taken all our beer."

Paco Medina, the man sitting to Ramón's left, crushed the empty beer can in his hand and tossed it to the ground. "Who would do such a thing?" he asked innocently.

"It is a great mystery," said Fernando. "But do not fear. I know a way to solve it."

"Tell us how," said Paco. "And it shall be done."

"We must set a trap for this criminal. We must purchase more beer and place it in the refrigerator, then watch it very carefully. He will return for it, and we will have him."

"What if the beer we purchase is not good enough to tempt him?" said Paco. "Perhaps we should test it, just in case."

"A fine point, my friend. Let us add it to the plan."

"How much money do you have?"

"For beer? My entire fortune!"

"Very good, but how big is your fortune?"

Fernando frowned. "Perhaps three dollars."

"We will not capture this shameless cur with three dollars' worth of beer. Who else can contribute?"

"I can spare five dollars," said Trini Gallego, the youngest of them all.

"I have four," said Felix Diaz, who wore his hair in a ponytail like a woman.

"I too have four dollars," said the one they called Lobo, who would not give his true name, for some reason.

This left only Ramón, who did not wish to spend his money on beer. But what could he do? His compatriots had spoken. "I have six dollars," he said. "And I am sober. I will drive."

"No! It is my truck; I will drive," said Lobo. He added a few curses, for he was a quarrelsome drinker. Then he said again, "I will drive!" But when Lobo tried to stand, he fell back to the ground.

"Lobo, my friend," said Fernando. "Thank you for your brave offer, but I believe we need you here to help prepare the trap."

"Trap?" said Lobo from the ground, where he propped his head up with his hand. "What trap?"

"I will explain everything, but we must hurry. Please give our bald friend Ramón your keys, and your money."

Ramón was not bald, at least not yet, although he had perhaps begun to lose some hair. One morning Trini claimed he had discovered a small bare patch at the back of Ramón's head. Ramón had denied it. The more he refused to believe, the larger the bald patch had grown in Trini's telling, until now his friends sometimes insisted he had merely a small fringe of hair remaining, which grew only in the places he could see in a mirror. Oh, they had great fun with him, these, his drunken friends, but Ramón did not mind. He took Lobo's keys, accepted money from them all, and set out toward the truck.

"I will come along," said Trini.

"And I," said Lobo, rising to his feet unsteadily. "It is my truck! Mine!"

With much patience, the men again persuaded Lobo to allow Ramón to drive. Trini sat next to the door, with Lobo in the middle beside Ramón. The engine started, which was always a relief, and Ramón backed out of the dirt driveway. At the last moment, when they were already rolling, Felix climbed into the open truck bed behind them.

In future days he never ceased to blame himself for what would happen next. If only he had not allowed the quarrelsome Lobo to sit beside him. He should have known the drunken man might rise up from his stupor to cause mayhem, but as Ramón Rodríguez drove away he did not think about such dangers. How could he, when his soul was starving for Raquel?

CAPÍTULO 14

ON A MISTY MORNING SHORTLY before Christmas, Fray Alejandro raised his paintbrush from the altarpiece and gazed out through the narrow door. The slender strip of plaza he could see beyond his cell lay wrapped in feathery whiteness, as if the veil which shrouded Alejandro's mind had spread throughout the mission. The thick fog muffled sound and created the illusion of great stillness, although the mission's work progressed as always.

Alejandro was just about to return his attention to his work when he thought he saw a shadow in the shifting haze, a hint of something more substantial. Suddenly Fray Benicio appeared as if arriving from an imaginary place, a fact from an illusion. Mist and gray robes merging interchangeably, Benicio strode across the plaza with a bundle in his arms. His manner warned of an emergency. Alejandro fought the miasma in his mind and forced himself to concentrate. As Benicio came closer, Alejandro clearly saw the bundle carried by the young friar was a child.

With a mighty effort of his will, Alejandro rose up from his stool to follow.

Fray Benicio entered the refectory and with great tenderness laid the child upon the table there. When he stepped back, the ugly Alejandro peered at the little one and drew in a startled breath. The child, an Indian of course, lay drenched in perspiration.

"Can you help this boy?" asked young Fray Benicio, his first words to Alejandro in three days.

"I will try," replied the good friar. He had been well trained in the healing arts. It was the principal reason he had been chosen for the mission.

Stepping forward, he laid a meaty palm upon the boy's forehead. As suspected, the skin was very hot. When the boy opened his eyes, they remained unfocused. Speaking the child's language, Alejandro asked, "Can you hear me, my son?"

The boy slowly nodded.

"Do you have pain in your head?"

Again, the hint of a nod.

"Where else do you have a pain?"

"My back," mumbled the boy. He closed his eyes. He moaned.

Alejandro placed a hand beneath the child and lifted him into a seated position. "Help me," he said to Benicio. "Hold him just like this." Then, with the young friar steadying the boy, Alejandro laid an ear against his back. He listened for a moment, then stood back and tapped the boy in many places with a finger, asking, "Does this hurt? Does this?" At first the boy tried to reply, but soon his mumbling trailed off into silence. "Try to stay awake," said Alejandro. "Son? My son? Can you hear me?"

The boy gave no response.

"Lay him down again," said Alejandro. When this was done he said, "Bring cool water and some cloths."

"Yes, brother," replied Benicio, all hint of former rancor gone. But in leaving the refectory he passed the abbot coming in. Neither man acknowledged the other. Alejandro merely frowned while peering into the child's mouth.

With Benicio no longer in the room, Fray Guillermo spoke. "What have we here?"

"A sick child, Abbot."

"What is the poor boy's malady?"

"I am not yet certain."

"Measles, perhaps? You see the lesions on his face."

"Yes, but I do not think so."

"Why not?"

"He does not cough, you see? And his nose and eyes are normal."

"What then, brother? You must have some idea."

Alejandro felt the sides of the boy's neck, and pressed his fingers into the child's armpits. He tapped his chest, listening closely. Then he examined the boy's palms and drew in a sharp breath.

"What, brother?" asked the abbot.

Shaking his head, Alejandro moved to the bottom of the table. There he bent to peer at the soles of the boy's feet.

"What?" demanded Fray Guillermo. "Give your diagnosis!"

"On his palms and soles and face are tiny blisters. He complains of pain in his head and back. I have seen these signs before, when I myself was still a child in Ibiza."

"But what does it mean?"

When Alejandro answered Fray Guillermo's question, the pale monk crossed himself and backed away, saying, "It is God's judgment on them." Then, using the loose sleeve of his robe to cover nose and mouth, he turned and fled from the refectory.

Alone there with the child, Alejandro prayed for his recovery. He prayed the mission might be spared the horror that had emptied many houses on his childhood island home. Even in his prayers it must be admitted Fray Alejandro feared for the boy, and for the mission. Thinking of his hands touching the boy, he also feared for himself, but he did not let dread drive him into panic. He believed surrender in such battles between faith and fear was sinful.

Still today the Christian faith would have us understand that we are judged on what we think as well as what we do. To curse a person in one's heart is to commit murder. To lust for someone other than one's spouse is to commit adultery. But are we judged on how we feel as well as what we think? And if we are, who can stand before such judgment? Who can choose to feel or not to feel a certain way when life's outrageous circumstances intervene?

Just as Alejandro fought against grave fears, so Guadalupe Soledad Consuelo de la Garza suffered grave misgivings. Riding in the Chevrolet Impala, she turned away from her friend Harmony to watch the graffiti-blemished walls of Wilson City passing by her window. She watched, but did not truly see. Instead she pondered what she felt for Tucker Rue.

If Harmony and Tucker were to be married, could she bear it? It was the question she had hoped to answer on this, her first return to Sanctuario since she had left it more than half a decade before.

Often in her years among the Anglos she had removed Fray Alejandro's sacred altarpiece from its velvet sanctuary and placed it on the little table in her apartment above the pool house. Often she had stared into its images to confirm what she already knew: the Holy Father's quest had led her to this exact place and no farther, to these exact people and no others. Although she did not understand the reason, although she sometimes railed against the inertia of her situation, the apparent uselessness of it, although she yearned to travel out among the people of that pagan land to talk about their Savior, Lupe had received no hint that God desired her to move on. The *retablo* of Fray Alejandro revealed just what it always had, therefore she must stay.

But could she bear it?

It had not been long since Harmony had come to her, filled to bursting with a secret. She had sworn Lupe to secrecy, or not sworn, exactly, for that would have been sinful, but Lupe had been asked to promise never to reveal the knowledge of their coming wedding. For some reason, Harmony believed the Mister would oppose them.

As Harmony began to share her plans to marry Tucker, Lupe fought a bitter battle in her heart. Oh, what it had cost Lupe to receive her friend's confidences! How often she had longed to tell her friend to send the man away! But what could she say? Tucker Rue was a scoundrel? A cheat? A weak man, or a coward? No, it was not possible because of course the man was no such thing. And Lupe could hardly tell her friend to send the man away because he was humble, or fair, or strong and brave, the very qualities that had caused her own temptation.

So Lupe had decided to conduct a test, to go with Harmony to Sanctuario, to witness her dear friend with the man whom she would marry on the morrow, to see the two of them together in the setting of her fondest memories, to learn if she could bear it, and hopefully to cauterize her broken heart forever.

How could she have known it was a trap? Throughout her troubles never had she thought there might be another aspect to the matter, a circumstance as painful as her own. Never had she dreamed that Tucker Rue might still feel as he had on that day almost six years ago, when he had kissed her hand.

She did not judge him for it. She of all people knew how strong the heart's desire could be, and she knew the awful weight of loneliness. She had given him no hope in her case, so he had quite reasonably looked elsewhere. For this, she only blamed herself.

With all of this in mind as she rode away from Tucker in his fiancée's car, Lupe turned to face the side window. She closed her eyes against the poverty outside. She pressed her forehead to the glass. She did not fear the future for herself. She hoped she would be strong if Tucker Rue again showed weakness, and she hoped if she were ever weak, the Holy Ghost would give him moral strength. But what of Harmony? What woman could be happily married in these circumstances? Surely she would sense a shortfall in her husband, a holding back where everything should be surrendered. She might never understand it, but—

"Tell me about him, Lupe."

Lupe opened her eyes. Beyond the glass was an apartment building, all the windows open in the heat, laundry drying on the balconies. Two small girls sat in a patch of dirt beside the stoop, watching as the car went past.

"It's obvious something happened between you," continued Harmony. "Don't you think I have a right to know about that?"

"Yes," said Lupe. As the tenement disappeared behind them, she asked her Holy Father for the words. At her next confession she would beg forgiveness for this foolish test of hers, this choice to go to Sanctuario on that day of days. She should have stayed away.

They stopped at a red light, the only vehicle at the intersection.

Harmony said, "It was a long time ago, right? That part is true? You haven't seen him for a long time?"

"Yes, a very long time."

"Except for when he came to our house once, of course. When you broke those glasses."

Remembering her joy and terror, Lupe replied, "Yes."

"I was just thinking about that day. The way you acted at first. I guess I understand it now."

Lupe said nothing.

"I'm not angry or anything," said her friend.

"Thank you."

The light changed to green and Harmony drove into the intersection, saying, "I just wish you would have told me."

Ready to confess her weakness, Lupe turned toward Harmony, and beyond her dear friend's lovely profile she saw the front grille of a speeding truck in that final instant before the crash. Then came the buckling metal and the flying glass, and the whole world changing.

Children longing for the liberation of adulthood believe time passes slowly. Old men longing for their vanished youth believe it moves too fast. Science has no measurement for time except for time itself, so who can say if it is regular, or random? Guadalupe Soledad Consuelo de la Garza only knew each second was an hour as the yellow Chevrolet Impala gracefully ascended to the sky, then rolled, then came to earth again to glide along the pavement on its roof. She had time enough to see a crow against a cloud, a man flying arms and legs akimbo through the atmosphere, an oil patch on the asphalt, each scene revolving on to be replaced by others: a pedestrian's engrossed expression, a purse—Harmony's—defying gravity before her in midair. Although there was time enough to think of taking action, little could be done. Lupe only watched, noting details at her leisure as the tragedy revealed its full dimensions.

When the warping metal ceased its screaming, time completely stopped. Lupe hung upside down, suspended in an eerie silence by the safety strap across her lap and shoulder. She saw the road above as if it were a sky, and the earthen sky below. All was perfectly inert in that arrested universe: no sound, no motion, no thought except unthinking wonder, and in this place of timelessness was peace.

Then the wave of life crashed down again, and with it came raw chaos: a ceaseless blaring horn, a barking dog, the brimstone scents of metal sparks and melting rubber. She saw her arms at rest against the ceiling of the car. She moved, and woke a monster. Ferociously it sank its fangs into her flesh, ripping at the tissue, gnawing on her bones. She moaned and fell into a welcome blackness.

Flames lit up the darkness, chasing shadows on adobe walls. She was a child again, engaged in her own *auto de fe*. She lay in bed and listened to her mother's cries. She dreamed of Spanish saints alight, the act of faith demanded by inquisitors. She lay motionless as her childhood home burned all around her, motionless and trusting that her father would appear to save her from the pungency of burning pine and the silent smoke that fanned across the ceiling. The heat caressed her skin, the cost of faith approaching. Still she lay unmoving, for to rise would mean she did not trust, she had no faith, she was not worthy of this test. Her father would come, and if he did not, she would die for God.

Lupe lay unmoving, though her blanket smoldered, though the air no longer satisfied her lungs. She heard the crackling of the fire and through the fading darkness saw a pair of boots traverse the asphalt overhead, sparkling shards of windshield crackling underneath those boots as if they trod on crystal flames. Suspended from the seat belt, she felt pounding blood engorge her temples. She knew she was alive. She did not dare attract the beast again by moving.

Through the twisted opening where the windshield used to be she watched the boots approach, seeing only the man's legs from his knees down, noting the worn spots on the toes and the frayed cuffs of his trousers. She saw the way the boots moved without rhythm, stepping and then pausing strangely before moving on. Was this her father coming? Was her faith to be rewarded?

He knelt before the vanished windshield, or rose, as it appeared from where she hung. He bent to peer into the car. Even with his head awash with blood, she knew the man was not her father, for she had just remembered she was not a little girl, and her father was long dead. Crouching on the road, clinging to it upside down, the man stared in and spoke to her in Spanish. From his head blood dripped onto the ground.

"I am very sorry. Lobo was asleep beside me, but he awoke and tried to take the wheel. He was a crazy man. Lobo is very drunk, you see, and drinking makes him crazy. He thought I was a thief, I think. But I am not a thief, and I am not drunk, señorita. I have had no beer, I swear."

She wished to tell him not to swear, but he continued talking.

"It is why I was the one to drive, you understand. I was the sober one. Now look what I have done. Felix is over there on the street. He is dead, I think. I think . . . It is only that my head, you see, it hurts a little bit. I think maybe I am having some kind of a problem, because everything is moving. Are you moving? How are you, señorita? I myself am just a little . . ."

The man seemed to forget her. He lay upon the asphalt, which was above her. He closed his eyes and went to sleep.

"Help me," whispered Lupe.

His eyes remained closed.

Lupe remembered something. She risked awakening the beast to turn her head. It bit her flesh again with the movement, but not as deeply as before. What she saw confirmed her memory: Harmony there beside her, also hanging from a strap, long hair drifting in a growing pool of red that spread along the ceiling of the car and spilled onto the asphalt.

Just beyond her on the road a dog stood licking up the blood, and beyond the dog a spirit passed, a shadow, or perhaps a little smoke. Smoke. Yes, it must be smoke. But what was burning? Was that flame from the car?

"Señor," she whispered. "You must help us now, or we will die."

Opening his eyes, he placed a palm upon the road and pressed, rising up a little. "Yes," he said. "Yes." But as he rose another man appeared. Of this one, she saw only boots. Then a pair of hands came into view to help the man. Unsteadily the first one reached his feet.

"Come, Ramón. We have to go."

"But the señoritas . . ."

"The police will tend to them. Listen, you can hear them coming."

A siren in the distance.

"We must help. . . ."

"They will arrest us. They will put us in a jail."

"It was not our fault. Lobo did this. Lobo is the one to punish."

"They will put us in their jail, I tell you."

"But we must still help. . . ."

The man collapsed upon the pavement again. This time Lupe saw his features fringed with blood and in her growing consciousness she knew him, saw him walking far behind the others in the desert, risking death to help her find her way. More than anyone alive she knew the cost the man had paid to be there in that place. She heard the sirens nearing. She remembered what the man had told her of a wife and sons in Mexico, selling sticks of firewood to survive.

"Go with God, señor," she whispered, and then she saw the pair of hands come down again to lift Ramón Rodríguez, and she saw a pair of boots shuffle away, struggling beneath the burden of a friend.

Across the space between them flowed the roiling spirits cloaked in black and gray, many more than just a while ago, attracted to the misery and thick enough to hide the fleeing men.

A bitter scent of rubber smoke and burning plastic insulted her nostrils. She thought of barracks burning, of martyred saints and flaming pyres. She thought of Padre Hinojosa's stories, of the *auto de fe,* and she thought about the gasoline and shook with fear and would have withheld this, her final sacrifice, if she only could. She remembered fleeing from her bed, unwilling in the end to wait beneath the smoldering blankets when her father did not come, breaking faith. Having escaped wrongfully before, all her life she had feared another testing of her faith. Smoke like demons danced around the pyre, mocking all her childhood dreams of Alejandro's brave escape. What mattered was not death, but failure. She had received a quest, a sacred task, yet what had she accomplished?

Very soon now—surely in a few minutes only—she would stand before the Holy Father. How it grieved her to have done so little! She had left her home and traveled to that foreign place. She had preached the gospel every Sunday on the beach. But she knew of course her offerings were rubbish. Her hope lay in the Savior's sacrifice alone, yet how she wished she could have thanked Him with a crowd of converts! So many lost souls in that pagan land, the damned were all around her, yet for all her boardwalk preaching she had led not one of them to God. How could she ascend to heaven so ungratefully?

"Lupe," came a strange man's voice. Peering through the wreckage and the mocking smoke, she saw him watching at a distance: a handsome man with black hair combed back from a smooth bronze forehead, hair that shimmered as if he himself were burning.

"Here I am," she said.

"Rise up!"

"Señor, I cannot."

"You can," he said. "You must."

She could only whisper. "Were you also in the accident?"

"You believe this is an accident?"

"Surely Señor Rodríguez did not crash into our car on purpose."

"Nonetheless, rise up."

"Very well, señor," said Lupe. She moved her hand toward the clasp on the seat belt, and a furious agony attacked, wrapping her in blackness. She knew nothing from that moment until the next, when she somehow lay upon the road beyond the burning wreckage as a pair of Anglo men in uniforms ran toward her with a stretcher. Remembering, she asked them about Harmony. She received no answer.

CAPÍTULO 15

THAT FIRST SUNDAY AFTER CHRISTMAS, the good Fray Alejandro walked outside the mission walls in deep contemplation of the Nativity. His tonsured scalp exposed to the sun, his hands tucked into the folds of his sleeves, he measured every step. Passing by a lean-to shelter, one of many where the neophytes resided, he heard a feeble moan. He paused, unwilling to take liberties with the Indians' privacy. He heard another moan. Concern overcame propriety. He called, "Hello? Are you in need of help?" Receiving no answer, he bent at the waist and entered the small structure.

Sitting on the soil before him were three people in the shadows. He recognized the Madonna-like young woman and her baby. They were the neophytes to whom the Indian with shining hair had once called his attention. With them also was a man. The father held the mother, and she in turn sat cradling the child as if in imitation of a Christmas crèche. Their postures startled Alejandro, who only moments earlier had been deep in meditation on the solemnity of the Holy Family.

He greeted them in their own language, but neither the father nor the mother bothered to look up. Like an adoring shepherd, the Franciscan knelt beside them. He realized all three were unconscious—the parents' bodies propping up each other, the baby senseless in its mother's arms—and all three neophytes were drenched with sweat. Filled with dread, Fray Alejandro looked much closer. On their faces, palms, and soles the friar found many lesions.

"Holy Son of God, protect us," said Alejandro. His hand trembled as he crossed himself before rising. "Holy Mother of God, pray for us now and in the hour of our death."

The abbot chose the refectory to be used as a sickroom, for it had already been contaminated when Benicio unwisely laid the boy upon the dining table there. Don Felipe, the captain, posted a guard at the door. Only the three friars were allowed to enter.

On the following Monday, a group of tribal elders from the village beside the arroyo came demanding grain. They blamed the sickness on the Spaniards, for desecrating holy places, destroying the altar to their god Cooksuy, and building the Misión de Santa Dolores in a sacred grove of sycamores. Fray Guillermo mocked their superstition.

On Tuesday morning the abbot emerged from the storehouse in a rage. It seemed a bag of grain was missing, the very thing the pagans had demanded. Guillermo sent the leather-jackets for the elders, who were dragged back to the mission at the ends of ropes, restrained beside the water well in the center of the plaza, and whipped. When Benicio tried to intervene, the abbot also had the younger friar restrained.

How the ugly features of Fray Alejandro writhed to watch this punishment! Conscious of the malady at work in the refectory, he wept that Guillermo might add more suffering to the awful trials imposed by nature. Unlike the abbot, he knew the face of death too well, having seen it leer across the hills and planes of Ibiza, his childhood island home.

Many times since then had Alejandro contemplated the frailty of life. In the end he knew we do not fade away as some believe. There is no gradation, no spectrum or scale between this life and the next. Our spirits vanish in one final breath and at one final time and place. We are here, then we are not, and the brute fact of the difference, the stark unthinking apathy of it, sometimes leads the unprepared to madness.

At funerals and wakes the first hints of this madness often rise within the eyes of the bereaved. So it was with Delano Wright, who had survived the funeral only to find his majestic home inexplicably overrun by people from his church, employees, partners, neighbors—strangers, really—arriving unexpectedly with flowers, food, and words.

Someone had organized a reception afterward. He did not know who. He did not remember giving his assent. He only knew he wandered through a field of platitudes. So sorry for your loss. Such a fine young woman. Shocking. A terrible thing. So sorry. Is there anything that we can do? All you have to do is ask. Anything at all.

Delano stood outside himself, watching as he met them graciously, listening as he said the proper things. So grateful for your concern. Such a comfort at this time. Having learned of Harmony's wedding plan, the real Delano, the one observing people from a distance, thought it interesting that none of them was Tucker Rue.

He looked around the room for Lupe, wondering why she wasn't taking care of the guests. Then he remembered she was in the hospital. He had gone to see her just the day before. How could he forget that? It was a good thing someone, probably one of the funeral home people, had arranged for temporary servants to cater to these unexpected guests. He would not have thought of it. He couldn't even remember who most of these people were, although many of them seemed to know each other. They enjoyed each other's company. The food and drink were good. They lingered overlong. They talked and talked and talked.

During a rare uninterrupted moment, Delano had an idea, something that might make some sense of the situation. Returning back into himself, he made a telephone call, and then he slipped away.

In the perfect silence of the Range Rover he crossed the village of Blanco Beach, rolling slowly past happy strangers bearing beach chairs, ice chests, bags, and towels in primary colors. The sun was bright, but out over the ocean he saw cumulus clouds building. It would rain, and then the hopes of all those happy strangers would be dashed.

Palm trees, perfectly straight and regular, like columns in a temple, marked the edges of the road. Orange bougainvillea flowed across a stucco wall of pristine white. At the eastern edge of town, he accelerated onto the canyon road for Wilson City.

Arriving there, he found the block where it had happened: four well-traveled lanes of bubbling blacktop stretched between two rows of weary clapboard bungalows, which had been thrown up in a hurry for GIs returning from the Second World War. Behind low wire fences children born in troubled southern countries played on hard-packed dirt and withered straw that passed for lawns.

A black-and-white police cruiser and a plain white sedan waited for him in the glaring sunshine at the curb. Delano left the stream of rushing traffic to park behind them. From the sedan emerged Warren Roderson, the Wilson City chief of police, whom Delano had met once at a fundraiser. Two patrolmen in blue uniforms got out of the cruiser. Delano stepped from his vehicle to meet them on a concrete sidewalk buckled by the roots of a large tree. The tree had been chopped down long ago.

"Mr. Wright," said Chief Roderson, extending his hand. "It's good to see you again."

"I appreciate your time."

"Oh, don't mention it. Least we could do for you, under the circumstances."

"Thank you."

"Ah, let me introduce Officers Harris and Valle."

Delano shook hands with them both. The taller one, the blond, said he was sorry for Delano's loss. "Thank you," replied Delano. "You were here at the accident?"

"Yes sir. We arrived just afterwards."

Delano turned to look at the street. "Would you tell me how it happened?"

"Well, as best we were able to reconstruct it, your daughter, she came from that direction." He pointed to the west. "And the truck ran the light, coming from that direction." He pointed south. "The guy was going about fifty. He made no attempt to stop until about two seconds before the impact. Your daughter must have seen him coming, because she tried to swerve away. The force of the collision shoved her vehicle toward that little berm over there, where it flipped and slid back down onto the street."

Delano said, "Were there any witnesses?"

"Some, yes sir. But their stories weren't consistent."

Chief Roderson said, "That's typical in these kinds of situations, Mr. Wright."

"The driver of the truck left a passenger behind, I understand."

"That's right. Apparently he was riding in the truck bed. Went flying and broke his neck."

"A Mexican, right? Here illegally?"

The chief nodded. "There's a lot of that in Wilson City."

"And drunk?"

"A lot of that too, yes sir."

"How was it possible for the truck to drive away from something like this? Shouldn't it have been badly wrecked?"

"Presumably they didn't make it very far. Hid the truck in a garage somewhere, probably."

"You have a description?"

"Yes sir. It's a white, early-model Ford or Chevrolet with fringe around the headliner and a word across the rear window. Probably the owner's name. Mexicans like to put their names in the rear window of vehicles."

"And you're looking for it, right?"

"Of course we are, Mr. Wright. I promise you that. We'll find the truck eventually, and then we'll find the driver. But we don't get a lot of cooperation from the Latino community. When undocumented immigrants are involved in a crime, it takes a little longer."

"I understand there was a man who helped Lupe, uh, the passenger, to get out of the car. Did anyone describe him?"

Chief Roderson looked at the taller patrolman. "Bill?"

The patrolman removed a notepad from his shirt pocket, flipped through it, stopped at a page, and read for a moment. Then he said, "We had two descriptions of him, actually. Both said he was a short Latino. Only one of the witnesses saw his face. Dark, she said, with shiny black hair combed straight back from his forehead. Pretty average description for most men around here, except for the hair. Both witnesses said his hair sparkled in the sunshine like he had glitter in it or something."

"Was he in the truck?" asked Delano.

"She didn't think so. The driver of the truck and one of his passengers went over to look at your daughter's car, then they drove away when they heard our siren. This other guy, he showed up after that."

"Then what? He just left?"

"Yes sir. He must have slipped away after we got here."

"Could you show me where the car was? The exact spot?"

The patrolman pointed across the road. "See that telephone pole over there? And the bus stop sign across the street? If you draw a straight line between them, the car was pretty close to the middle."

"Thank you."

Delano stepped into the street.

"Uh, Mr. Wright?" called the police chief. "You need to be careful of the traffic here."

Ignoring him, Delano continued walking across the road. A car changed lanes to avoid him, honking as it passed. He did not notice. In the center of the street he followed a pair of yellow lines until he reached a place where the paint vanished below a ragged patch of black, darker than the asphalt.

In the sooty middle of that blackness, Delano stopped. Standing there, he closed his eyes and tried to see her. As cars and trucks and vans roared past on his left and right, he stood very still. If there was something left of her, this would be the place to find it. He inhaled deeply. Opening his eyes, he knelt upon the asphalt. On his knees, he bent to place both palms against the black stain that encircled him. He lowered his face until it was an inch above the pavement. He inhaled again. Gasoline and rubber came to him, and behind them an aroma, very slight, that he recognized. He had first smelled it many years before, when they brought her to him wrapped in a pink blanket, yawning wide and toothless. He had held her to himself that morning; pressed his nose into her tiny cheek. He had smelled it many times since then, Harmony's particular scent, in her clothes and on her pillow. It had come to him with every hug. Some might say he was imagining things, but he could smell it, on his hands and knees, in the middle of the street. Some might call him crazy, but it was there. She was there.

"Mr. Wright? This is dangerous, sir. Please."

He looked up. The police chief stood above him while the two patrolmen stood on either side, waving traffic off. "She died right here," said Delano.

"Yes sir. I'm very sorry."

"Right in this very spot," he said, brushing the pavement with his hand, sweeping little bits of debris aside. Somehow it seemed too simple. Out of all the places in the world, all the places she had been, how could there be a single spot where she had ceased to be? If it had to be that way, then that place should be a country, or a continent. It should be the entire planet.

"Please, Mr. Wright," said the police chief again.

This time Delano arose. "I'm sorry."

"No need to be sorry, sir. Let's just get back on the sidewalk."

Later, as he drove home again along the canyon road, Harmony's scent remained with him. He left the windows up and the air conditioner off, lest she fade away. He took her in with every breath, his nostrils flaring widely, the aroma causing free associations in his memory. He thought of her in knee boots and jodhpurs after riding at the stables. So many times he had driven her between those very hills with the smell of horseflesh strong upon her, but even that had never masked her sweetness. He inhaled deeply and she was there again. She was there.

His land appeared along the left, the forty-twelve. Out of all the family's old ranch holdings across that part of California, this land had been Harmony's favorite. Thus reminded, he spoke aloud to her. He told her how he felt, the things that he would never say to anyone alive, the things that were too personal. He felt her there beside him, listening. He said he knew she had never meant to leave him, to marry behind his back, to deceive him. She herself had been deceived by that young minister. The man had broken his promise to Delano. That seemed very clear.

Still ten miles from the coast, he slowed and turned through a construction gate. Following a short gravel road, he reached a compound of cream-colored metal trailers, the project offices, where the contractor's supervisors oversaw his new development. Harmony had been angry when she learned about the project, but it would mean at least a hundred million dollars in tithes over the next decade. He believed she would have come to understand that proper stewardship of God's gifts demanded sacrifices. He could not bear to believe otherwise, could not bear the remorseful thought that he had made his Harmony unhappy, even for an instant.

He parked between a pair of pickup trucks and stepped onto the temporary lot. He stared up the hill, watching as a bulldozer rumbled

slowly along a newly graded road. It had been almost seven months
since they broke ground, and still the earthmovers worked the land,
carving level places in the hillsides where concrete pads would bear the
multimillion-dollar homes that soon would rise.

The bulldozer above him faded for a moment, replaced by a vision
of his daughter on her palomino, riding English style, her long hair
gilded by the California sunshine. He blinked, and the yellow machine
reappeared.

"Mr. Wright? Can I help you, sir?"

He turned. A lanky man with a deep tan and a white hard hat approached from one of the job trailers. Delano did his best to smile. "No,
thank you, Jimmy. Just dropped by to watch."

The man walked closer, then stopped a few feet away. "I heard
about your daughter. I'm . . . me and all the guys, we're just as sorry as
we can be."

"Thank you."

"If there's anything we can do . . ."

"Thank you, Jimmy. I appreciate it."

The man kicked at the gravel gently. "Would you like a tour? We
made real good progress over on Tract A this week."

"I think I'll just walk a little, Jimmy. If that's all right."

"Of course, Mr. Wright. You take care, okay?"

"Will do."

An old cow trail angled up the hillside. Delano Wright set out
slowly, with no destination in mind. Above and to his left, the bulldozer's diesel engine idled, then went silent. Delano checked his wristwatch. Lunchtime. He heard other equipment shutting down in the
distance. Soon the little canyon where he walked was quiet, not sound-
less, but free from the construction noise. He heard mockingbirds and
crows, and the faint hum of the interstate highway, about two miles
away beyond the hills. From that distance the speeding traffic whispered like wind in trees, or far-off rushing surf. He remembered Harmony griping once about the highway noise.

It's annoying, she had said. It's unnatural.

He had been ready with an answer. Nobody complains when
seagulls make a racket or foul the rocks with guano, or when a beaver
builds a dam or an eagle builds a nest. Why should we complain when

people make noises and messes and build buildings? It's not unnatural. We're just God's creatures, doing what God created us to do, like all the other creatures.

Thinking back, it sounded more like a sermon than an answer. He wished he had said a little less and listened more.

Strange, the guilt he felt.

Thirty minutes later Delano reached the hilltop, his shirt soaked at the underarms and between his shoulder blades, his Italian loafers covered with dust. Breathing heavily, he sat on a low rock jutting from the ground. He wiped sweat from his eyes.

In all directions was a commanding view. Far to the west gray clouds sailed above the ocean. It had not rained for many months, but it was coming. To the east the Santa Ana Mountains were just visible, far beyond the hills. The slope between his position and the canyon road had been sculpted into many level terraces, like a giant's stair steps, regular and clean. In the other direction, rugged hills rolled away from the road, covered by the random browns and olive greens of manzanita and deer brush and sage. Somewhere out there ghostly coyotes ranged across their ancient territory, and mountain lions slept in shady places deep among the giant sandstone outcroppings.

No human being could survive for long among the hostile brush and boulders of those untamed hills. The possibility of a safe life lay only in the level places where his equipment had arranged the earth more suitably. Security came with strong foundations, walls of stone and stucco and solid roofs above. Delano remembered Harmony's resistance to the roads and building sites he had carved into that land. She had never understood the planning it took, the order and the rules, to provide a place where decent people could live in peace. It took deed restrictions. Homeowner's association covenants. Architectural guidelines. Building codes. It took laws. The Word of God. The Ten Commandments.

All you got when people tried to live among the untamed scrub and boulders of this life was a drunkard at the wheel, an illegal alien who had no business living in that country in the first place, no driver's license, no insurance, no shame, and no morality. And you got people like that Tucker Rue, giving sanctuary to criminals.

Sanctuario.

The man had not even come to her wake.

Delano ground an Italian heel into the earth.

How could he have ever given money to a man like that? Taken part in feeding criminals, clothing them? Made it easier for them to come into his country without permission, helped them live outside the law? He had been a fool. He saw that now. You couldn't coddle people that way, or you got gangs and criminals and drunks, and life not making any kind of sense anymore, brush and boulders where there ought to be clean terraces, predators awakened in the shade and prowling, hunting for your little girl.

Since the day Ana left him, he had felt he ought to do something about that kind of rampant immorality, but he had let six years go by without acting. Was that why Harmony was taken? Was he being punished?

No, of course not. This was not his fault. He must control that kind of thinking. Still, if he had acted earlier, things might have been different, and even now if he failed to act, things might still get worse.

What could he do? He felt the answer was quite near, something elegant, a single solution to it all, if only he could open up his heart to inspiration.

He considered the grave evils of this fallen world: the pagan culture that rejected truth in favor of its hedonistic lies, the attacks from every quarter on God's people. How he longed for safety! But not for himself. Oh, no. He could bear this trial. He could. He only wished to spare other Christian families from it. There must be a way to protect God's people from the scum outside the church. To act, to stand against this emptiness and do *something*, to honor Harmony, to give meaning to her life and death, and to . . . to impose some kind of justice for that young man's betrayal.

Was that not a worthy purpose?

Suddenly, as if ambushed by emotions without warning, Delano Wright groaned aloud. It was the bursting of a dam. He clasped his hands together, fingers interlaced, clenched and white like bloodless fists at war. He heaved raw prayers up from his belly like a retching dog. High above the wilderness, alone with God, he beat his forehead with his praying fists and shook them clasped and trembling up at heaven.

He fell from rock to knee before the Lord. In agony he fell still farther to his face. He lay that way for hours, high upon the hill, on his miserable belly, pressed low into the dirt, arms cast out like Jesus on the cross.

He screamed, "Show me what you want!" and sobbed and beat the ground.

The impact of his fists went rippling out into the earth. The planet shook, sifting sand from stone, rock from boulder. The hillside shivered as if sympathizing, sending loose soil streaming downward along crevices on both sides of the hill, through the clean and level preparations to the north, and out into the southern wilderness. Delano Wright knew his prayer was answered. He had received a revelation.

He rose to his feet. Standing on the land that once had been his father's father's father's, he looked across the hills and saw the future. He had gone into the wilderness, up to the mountaintop, and there the Lord had met him with a vision of a place where evil could not enter, where innocence and righteousness would rule. He would build a place where believers could be safe, a shining city on a hill constructed with the tithes of half a million Christians. He would dedicate it to his daughter, build it for his neighbors, and see to it that no one had a penny left for Tucker Rue and his so-called sanctuary.

Far below, the bulldozer pushed stones and brush along before it, carving out another level building pad near a stand of eucalyptus trees. It was wrong, all wrong, a waste of time and effort.

He hurried down the hillside, his face and clothing coated in tan dust. About halfway to the bulldozer he slipped and rolled a dozen feet and came to rest against a rock the size of a casket. He rose, his shoulder aching from the impact. He continued down along the old cow path. Wild and filthy like the Baptist in the desert, he emerged onto the level place where men were working. He saw a white man on the bulldozer and two Latinos in hard hats and bright yellow safety vests standing by with shovels. He called to them.

"Stop! Stop what you're doing there! This is the wrong place!"

They stared as he approached, and in their eyes he saw they thought him mad.

"You okay, mister?" asked the man on the bulldozer.

"I'm fine. I just fell down and got a little dirty."

His clothes were torn, his entire body caked with dust. A twig clung to his hair. "You need to move up there." He pointed toward another hill, the tallest of them all, the one called Camel Mountain. "We're going to focus everything on the top of that hill."

"Look, buddy, I don't know who you are or what—"

"This is my land!" Delano shouted, moving closer. "You work for me!"

The man called to the others in Spanish. "Be careful, boys."

"Why should they be careful? Are these men illegals? I don't want illegals on my land!"

The man began to climb down from the bulldozer. "Stand back a little, buddy, till we get this figured out."

"There's nothing to figure out. Just head up to the top of that hill. I want the top of it leveled."

The man came walking toward him. "We can't do that, buddy."

"Then I'll do it!"

Delano ran around the man and grabbed a handhold on the bulldozer. The earth beneath him shook before he got his foot onto the lower step.

Someone shouted, "Another one!" in Spanish.

Delano fell to the ground and lay there while the eucalyptus swayed above him and the soil below him danced. When all was still again he felt a strong hand grip his arm.

"You need to get out of here, mister," said the Anglo, helping Delano to his feet.

Delano shook a finger in the man's face. "You're making a mistake. Call Jimmy Shields. He'll tell you who I am."

"You know Jimmy?"

"Of course! You have a radio, don't you? Call him. Tell him Delano Wright wants everything focused on that hill."

Five minutes later Delano stood alone on the terraced ground, watching the bulldozer rumble toward the taller hill with the two laborers walking behind. His revelation under way, Delano descended along a winding trail toward the job trailers below. Beneath his feet the angry earth now slept again, but soil would trickle down the hill for hours to come, burying some things, exposing others. He gave no thought to this. His mind was on the revelation, the sweet distraction from his grief. He had no time for other mysteries, summoned to the surface by the tremors. Thus he passed unknowingly beside a newly liberated secret hidden by a stand of bitterbrush, a human skull which gazed upon a sky it had not seen for centuries.

CAPÍTULO 16

ALEJANDRO MET EACH MORNING WITH a heart weighed down by sorrow for the infirm in the rectory and the elders from the village who had been so sorely used by Fray Guillermo. Yet the instant he sat down to work before the altarpiece these benevolent concerns began to perish in an eerie haze which choked his thoughts. The good Franciscan dipped a brush in handmade pigment. Moments later the paint was somehow hard among the bristles. He frowned in confusion. Surely no paint ever dried so quickly.

Could he but rise outside himself, Alejandro would have seen the hours pass while he sat motionless before the altarpiece. He would have known the minutes between dipping brush in paint and finding it had hardened were not really minutes after all, but entire mornings, afternoons, and days. He would have seen his unfortunate features hanging slackly as if in death. He would have felt his eyes grow dry from want of blinking. But the ether which descended on him never lifted in the light of day, so he never knew what happened to his mind, what stole his thoughts and robbed him of himself.

It was not until the sun set outside Alejandro's cell that the awful power gripping him arose, and he was left alone before the unchanged altarpiece. Then, stuporous and befuddled, he stumbled out to relieve Fray Benicio, who remained with the sick neophytes each day while Alejandro struggled in his cell. The homely friar labored in the refectory until dawn, cooling the poor souls as best he could with washcloths soaked in water, and whispering continuous prayers for their survival. Rarely did he sleep.

One night after compline, Alejandro approached the refectory with a water bucket. Along the way he passed Fray Guillermo's cell. In the flicker of a single torch he saw the abbot on his knees before a crucifix, facing away from the cell door. The superior's robe lay gathered down around his waist. His pale back flamed with bloody welts. At first glance Alejandro feared Guillermo had contracted the disease, but then he saw the wounds were continuous and long, not small pustules as with the neophytes. Still, such wounds required attention.

Alejandro turned to enter, but before his sandals crossed the threshold of the abbot's cell, Guillermo slapped a leather strap across his back. As Alejandro watched, the thin man rhythmically attacked himself with the same whip he had caused a leather-jacket soldier to use on the tribal elders. Again and again the whip came whistling over Fray Guillermo's shoulders, curling around to bite into his exposed flesh. In conformance to the rhythm of the blows the abbot prayed, "O my God. . . ." He struck himself. "I am heartily sorry for having offended you. . . ." Again he struck. "And I detest all my sins. . . ." Another blow. "Because of your just punishments. . . ." And another. "But most of all because they offend you. . . ." And so it went, that revolting act of contrition, until Fray Alejandro could no more bear it witness.

Careful to keep silence and deep in thought, the ugly brother walked away. He wondered what tormented his poor abbot so, and how a man consumed with such intense self-loathing could achieve so much. Pausing in the moonlight, Alejandro gazed around at the chapel, barracks, palisade, and storehouse, built in just eight months because of Guillermo's strong will. It had seemed a glorious accomplishment, equal in its way to great monuments to faith in Spain such as the sacred Catedral de Santiago de Compostela, which contained the venerable bones of Saint James, or the ancient Catedral de Valencia, where the Holy Grail resided. Fortunes had been spent to raise such grandiose expressions of man's piety, but compared to the humble Misión de Santa Dolores, they were mere Towers of Babel, monuments to the misuse of man's blessings, piles of stone where loaves of bread would better have been offered. At least that had been Fray Alejandro's opinion and his hope. Then he witnessed Fray

Guillermo's terrible self-flagellation and began to wonder what it really was that they had built in Alta California.

Not far from the site of the mission but many lifetimes later, Tucker Rue considered much the same question from the comfort of a padded chair within the vast expanse of Grace Tabernacle. Somewhere he had read about the stained-glass panels towering behind the stage, which were reported to exceed the size of those at Chartres and Notre Dame. The electrical system included enough wire to span the state of California from top to bottom and back again. The air-conditioning fans, if combined, could blow enough wind to keep a commercial airliner aloft, and the baptistery (a swimming pool, really) could accommodate the simultaneous submergence of two dozen newly consecrated souls.

Fully one percent of Orange County's population worshipped in that space, nearly eighty thousand of them in three services, drawn by their communal love of God, or perhaps by their love of spectacle, for a worship service at Grace Tabernacle was indeed a spectacle. Each week brought the promise of a different star performer tempted there from Hollywood, or else the possibility of a stage production worthy of the Great White Way, such as full-sized crucifixion scenes complete with earthquake at Easter, or levitating angels over vast barnyard menageries at Christmastime.

Tucker Rue had come because of Local Missions Sunday at Grace Tabernacle, an annual opportunity to appeal directly for support from one of the world's largest Christian congregations. Each year many storefront missions, charities, and parachurches were invited to attend. A fortunate few were given three minutes to present their needs on-stage. All were given space for booths in the massive entry lobby, where Grace Tabernacle members milled around to discuss tithing opportunities before and after each of the Sunday services.

It resembled a sales convention floor, and many of the ministries in attendance treated it that way, with elaborate booths displaying video presentations and large glossy photographs and trinkets of all kinds to give away as small reminders. Unlike the more well-established ministries, Tucker Rue simply had a folding table, a handwritten sign on an easel, and a stack of photocopied mission statements about Sanctuario. The first two years he had come to the event with those meager tools it had been enough. In fact, he thought the more high-profile ministries did themselves a disservice, for surely people knew the money for those fancy displays came out of their tithes. But this year, when the first worship service was over and the doors were opened and the flood of Christians poured into the massive lobby, everyone had passed his booth—and most of the other booths besides—without stopping.

Tucker did not usually attend Grace Tabernacle worship services—the pomp and pageantry annoyed him, for he had more humble views on how to practice Christianity—but the dismal showing after the first service convinced him he had better sit in on the second, just to find out what was said.

It began with opening music, intricately orchestrated and carefully designed to please God while offending the fewest people possible: the words of ancient hymns set to new pop melodies. Then came church announcements with full video support on multiple big screens, including impressive animation and special effects, a cinematic presentation comparable to the finest Hollywood could offer. The lights went down. A deep voice boomed into the darkness and quotations from the Bible flowed through a hundred loudspeakers. Then the lights were up again and panning wildly over two rows of black-clad dancers, who exploded into motion on the stage while a pleasant-looking fellow with strangely spiked platinum hair sang into a microphone cantilevered from behind his ear. Tucker rolled his eyes and sank low in his seat.

After several highly choreographed musical numbers involving set changes, a small orchestra, and a large cast of dancers and choral singers, finally the senior pastor literally ran onto the stage. He was a fit man in his mid-fifties with a face well known by most Christians in America and by many unbelievers. Exuding the same laid-back California style so prominent in his congregation, the pastor wore blue jeans and a long-sleeved shirt with the shirttail out. He spoke about the privilege of giving. He quoted the Bible, of course, the Lord loves a cheerful giver, and then he said a few words about their special Local Missions Sunday.

Ordinarily, he said, they would allow several ministries to come onstage and speak directly to the congregation, and as everyone had seen on the way in, it was still possible to learn about those great organizations face to face out in the lobby, but this year they had such an amazing ministry to talk about, such an awesome gift from God, he felt compelled to give all the stage time to just one opportunity.

"Delano," said the pastor. "Would you come on up here?"

Tucker sat up straight.

Far below he saw a little figure walk across the stage. As one of the camera operators went in for a close-up, Delano Wright's face appeared on all the auditorium's large screens. He reached the pastor's side, smiled widely, and the men shook hands.

"Many of you know my dear friend Delano Wright," said the pastor. "He donated the land for this church. We'll always love him for that." The audience broke into polite applause and Delano looked down at his feet as the pastor continued. "How long have you been a member here, Del?"

"Almost thirty years," said the man.

"Has it really been that long? Man. You're making me feel old. But those were the days, weren't they?"

"Sure were," said Delano. "Back then it was just you and Penny and me and my wife and about ten other people in Jim and Marti's house."

The pastor looked straight at a camera, his smiling face huge upon the screens. "Most of you are still here after all this time."

"You won't let us leave," said Delano Wright.

The audience erupted into laughter.

"That's right," said the pastor, after joining in the laughter. "I need you guys around to keep me humble."

"You have a lot to be proud of," said Delano, and the crowd's laughter turned into applause.

The pastor held his palms up. "No, no. This is all God's thing. And believe me, he's just getting started. Del has come to us with a proposition so amazing, so huge, I'm still trying to take it all in. Why don't you explain it to us, Del?"

The camera focused tightly on Delano. "Well, I lost my daughter in a car wreck a little while ago. A drunk driver ran her off the road. When a thing like that happens, it makes you think about how short life is, and what you want to do with the time you have left." The pastor put his arm around Delano's shoulders as he continued. "So the other day I went to the top of a hill over on some property I'm developing, and I asked the Lord to help me make some sense of things.

When Harmony—that's my daughter, Harmony—when she, uh, when she died, it meant the end of our family. My wife is gone, and we didn't have any other kids, and I was an only child myself, so there aren't any brothers or sisters or nephews or nieces. I won't be having more children at my age, of course, so when Harmony died, she left me all alone."

The man's voice wavered on those last few words. The large woman seated beside Tucker, a stranger, sniffled. Tucker stared at Delano's image on the screen and wondered why he himself was sitting there dry-eyed. It bothered him that he had not yet cried for Harmony, but just as he had sometimes found it hard to sense the presence of the living God, so he could not seem to think of Harmony as a person who had truly lived. She had passed into a place where life's full dimensions became flat and abstract, just as Jesus sometimes seemed merely theoretical, may the Lord forgive him.

But did he need forgiveness, really? His intentions had been good. When Harmony stood before him in the flesh, beautiful in every way, he had been convinced—truly convinced—that he loved her. He would never have proposed marriage otherwise. Even after seeing Lupe that one time at Delano Wright's house, he had managed to convince himself she no longer had a place within his heart. Then had come that awful day before the wedding when Lupe had returned to make his mistake clear, and then the wreck, the panic, and the overwhelming fear—but not for Harmony—and in the weeks since the accident, he had spent most of his spare time at the hospital, watching over Lupe as she slept, praying during her several operations, cherishing the rare minutes when she was awake and lucid, joyous when it seemed she would survive and terrified that she might make him leave. In those weeks he had learned he did not need forgiveness so much as forgetfulness, for although he should be mourning his fiancée it seemed Harmony had already faded, while one unguarded thought could easily, instantly, summon Lupe up within him.

Down on the stage Delano cleared his throat. "Anyway, this land has been passed down through the generations from my great-great-grandfather, and now it's going to go to someone else, someone outside my family, and I was up there on the hill, pretty sad about all that, and I asked the Lord for wisdom, you know. Then suddenly I remembered I still have a family right here. All my brothers and sisters in this church."

The pastor pulled Delano a little closer and patted his shoulder. "That's right, Del. It's one of the wonderful things about being a Christian. We're all brothers and sisters, children of the Lord."

"That's what I remembered while I was praying on top of that hill, over where we're building a little residential development, you know, and all of a sudden I realized there was a way to honor Harmony and let the land be a blessing to my other family, a blessing to you all. I decided to give it to the church. The land, I mean."

The pastor said, "We're not talking about an acre or two for a new parking lot or something like that, are we, Del?"

"Oh, no. It's four thousand and twelve acres."

A murmur of astonishment swept across the audience.

"Four *thousand* acres!" said the pastor, turning toward the audience. "What do you think the Lord could do with *that*?"

Many people rose to their feet, waving hands and shouting, while all the audience broke into wild applause. The pastor removed his arm from Del's shoulder and held up his hands for quiet. "Wait a minute, folks. We're just getting started here. Believe it or not, this is gonna get a lot more interesting." When the clapping had died down, he said, "Okay Del, tell us the rest of your idea. The part that takes it from a gift into a ministry where we all play a role."

"Well, after I decided to do this, I kept thinking about what a shame it is that a good Christian woman like my Harmony can be driving down the road and get killed by a drunk. The man who killed her, he was an illegal alien, see. He wasn't even supposed to be here in our country. And that got me thinking about all the ways Americans are under attack, especially Christian Americans, in our schools and in the media, in the streets, our government, the movie people, and the television. I don't want to get political, but I'm sure everybody here knows what I mean."

Several people shouted out agreement.

"So like I said, I already have the ball rolling over there on a residential development, and I thought, wouldn't it be great if we didn't have to worry about these things, for ourselves or for our children?"

The pastor said, "That does sound great, Del. Where do I sign up?"

Del said, "Actually, I want everybody here to sign up. The idea is, I'm not only giving the land to the church, I'm looking for investment partners. You know the parable about the rich man who gave money to three servants and rewarded the ones who invested wisely? I want everybody here to invest wisely with me in the future of our church. As undeveloped land, this property is worth about a quarter million dollars per acre. That's about a billion dollars altogether. But if we develop this land instead of just selling it, we can increase that figure at least five times."

The pastor said, "Five times? You mean our church could turn this gift of yours into five *billion* dollars for the Lord?"

"That's right. But only if everybody here will tithe enough to develop the property. We'd have to raise about five hundred million dollars over the next few years for grading, roads, utilities, and so forth. But the return will be immense. Enough to fund our benevolence work for decades to come. So I'm here today to ask my brothers and sisters if they'll do that."

The pastor turned to look out at the audience. He stood completely still. The massive room was silent. Then, scattered here and there among the crowd, a few people began to clap. More people joined in, and then more and more, until nearly twenty thousand Christians stood up to shout and clap approval.

After the applause died down, Tucker listened for a few more minutes as Delano and the pastor spoke about the details. When Tucker began to realize what it meant for Sanctuario, he left his seat and walked out to the lobby. He went to his simple little booth and collected his materials. With the roar of the crowd full in his ears, he put the photocopied fliers in a box and turned the table on its side and folded it. He removed his handwritten sign and collapsed the easel, and by the time the auditorium doors swung open to release the ecstatic congregation, he had already gone.

Driving slowly lest his old Toyota pickup truck fail him, Tucker left the endless field of costly automobiles in the church parking lot and followed the narrow streets of Blanco Beach to the canyon road. Turning east, he drove for over half an hour. He reached Wilson City and the remodeled warehouse that was Sanctuario, where he unloaded the table, easel, and fliers. He went into his cell-like room and changed into old boots, blue jeans, and a white T-shirt. Then he and a teenage volunteer named Vincente set to work filling his small truck bed with plastic bottles, over two hundred gallons of tap water in many different-sized containers, all of them recycled by Sanctuario families and carefully washed, sterilized, and filled by volunteers working in the new kitchen. Finally, he and Vincente laid a wheelbarrow upside down on top of the water containers.

Vincente offered to ride with him, but Tucker knew the boy's illegal status and would not take the chance. Besides, he wished to be alone. He had to think.

Straining under the weight of so much water, the old truck creaked and groaned as he turned it toward the south. The sun was high, and through the open window the air blew hot and dry against his face as he rolled along the valley's perfectly straight roads, passing field after bountiful field of lettuce, cantaloupes, and onions. Pickers sprawled in the shade of orange trees, eating lunches they had packed in paper bags. Rainbows flashed scarlet, yellow, and indigo in the spray of irrigation sprinklers. Eventually the flat farmland began to rise. It became too dense with stones and boulders to be cultivated. Among the rugged hills, cactus replaced vegetables and sod. Spidery black mesquite branches replaced neatly trimmed rows of citrus and almond trees.

After an hour's drive Tucker was well into the eastern edge of San Diego County, or maybe western Imperial County; it was hard to tell for sure. He reached a crossroads where an old filling station stood, a relic of the 1940s. Parked in the shade of its overhang was a white SUV with a green stripe along the side, the Border Patrol. Tucker turned onto a small asphalt road, which led west between a pair of low, boulder-studded hills. He watched his rearview mirror carefully. The Border Patrol truck remained where it was until he lost sight of it around a bend.

About five miles farther on he turned south again onto a gravel road. There were no fences, power lines, or other human signs alongside the road. He drove slowly to save his aged truck and to avoid stirring up a cloud of dust which would give away his position should the Border Patrol be following. Every now and then he leaned forward to peer up through the windshield, searching the clear sky for helicopters. Ahead he saw a giant rock shaped like an upright pear. He followed the curve around this obstruction and turned sharply behind it, rolling with the truck's motion as it crossed a shallow ditch. He drove on about a hundred yards until he was sure he could not be seen from the road. He killed the engine and sat still, listening.

He heard no birds, no wind, no hum of distant traffic. He loved the silence of the desert, the sense of total isolation. It reminded him of those peaceful days out in the wilderness just after he had graduated from the seminary, reading his Bible and praying and searching for God's will.

Tucker stepped out of the truck and cocked his ear, listening hard for sounds of interlopers. It would not do to let the border guards discover him at work. After a few minutes, satisfied with his solitude, he removed the wheelbarrow from the truck bed and loaded it with plastic water bottles. Gripping the wooden handles, he set out into the desert.

He walked half a mile, following a subtle impression in the soil, a trail he himself had blazed on previous occasions. It was hot work, and sweat soon soaked the wheelbarrow handles, making them more difficult to grip. As he walked, he thought about Delano Wright's idea.

People often gave real estate to churches. It was usually sold to raise cash, but Delano's proposition was different. By putting in the roads and utilities themselves and then offering the individual lots for sale, the church could look forward to a perpetual source of funds. The only thing required from the people of Grace Tabernacle was a commitment to pay for the development costs, and four thousand acres of prime real estate was theirs. The profits from such a huge development could ensure that the poor and homeless of the county would never want for food or shelter or health care again, but such a major commitment of their tithes would mean cutting back on support of other ministries. Tucker knew that meant Sanctuario. So, just like that he was out, and Delano Wright's big idea was in.

At last Tucker reached his destination: a slight depression in the ground alongside a low sandstone escarpment. He rolled the wheelbarrow to the edge of a brown and gray camouflaged tarpaulin. Stooping, he removed several stones that weighed down the tarp, and then he pulled it back to reveal a pair of common wooden shipping pallets. On the pallets were about a dozen plastic bottles filled with water, and several dozen more, which were empty. Good, thought Tucker Rue. Good.

The last time he was there, he had left over one hundred such contain-ers. Most had been consumed, therefore many had been saved.

Beside the pallets lay a square of plywood painted with these words in Spanish:

Drink all you want. Take what you can carry.
Please hide empty bottles underneath the tarp
and cover your tracks when you leave.
Help us keep the secret of this place for future travelers.

Working quickly, Tucker transferred the water from the wheelbar-row to the pallets. When he was done, he covered them again and set out for the truck to get another load. His thoughts returned to Delano's big plan.

As the man had explained it, there had been mill towns, mining towns, and railroad towns before; Chicago had its Little Italy and so did New York City. San Francisco had its Chinatown, so why not build a Christian town? It would be a peaceful village focused on the Bible and the Lord, a safe haven where believers could walk the streets in safety, where the cable and the satellite TV companies would know better than to come around offering pornographic channels, where there would be no bars or nightclubs or liquor stores, where prayer in school would be encouraged, and Christian kids would be taught the truth about cre-ation. That was Delano's big vision, and the people of Grace Tabernacle had loved it.

The whole idea made Tucker Rue sick.

What kind of a Christian sent his kids to schools with other Chris-tian kids instead of out into the world where they could make a differ-ence? What kind of a Christian dreamed of life in neighborhoods of other Christians, instead of life surrounded by unbelievers who desper-ately need the gospel? What kind of Christian hid from those beyond the church, instead of going out among the sick and lame and poor and lost to spread the love of Jesus?

Hypocrites, of course. Hypocrites and Pharisees.

At the truck, Tucker paused to drink a little water, then filled the wheelbarrow again and turned it around and set out for the water cache. Trudging through the desert, he thought of the sea of expensive automobiles outside Grace Tabernacle, all that money sitting there while desperate people risked their lives just a few hours' drive away, humble people, good people, starving for the freedom so much wealth could bring, willing to risk the horror of a death from dehydration and exposure just to walk into the same America where those rich so-called Christians—who were themselves the descendants of immigrants—planned a billion-dollar town to hide behind.

Tucker fantasized about simply taking what was needed from those greedy hypocrites. If he took just ten thousand dollars from every member of Grace Tabernacle he could change the lives of all the poor in Wilson City. Ten thousand dollars was peanuts to those people. They would not even notice.

Later, with the wheelbarrow back in the truck and a hundred and fifty gallons still to go, Tucker drove onto the gravel road, heading for the next cache. He had three more to replenish that day. He had arranged them with several "coyotes" down along the border, in Tecate and Mexicali. Every six months or so he shifted the water cache locations and went down there to give maps to the smugglers so they could tell their *pollos*—the immigrants—where to go. He hid the water along the edges of arroyos or escarpments, natural features of the landscape that a person could spot easily in order to find the water. Still, people perished in the desert every week. Tucker could not spread the word to everyone, and when the border guards found the water, they removed it.

This was one part of his ministry that Tucker Rue never mentioned in his fundraising. Too many of the fine churchgoing hypocrites in Blanco Beach would view it as support for criminals. But what was he supposed to do? Let them perish for the sake of the law? Tucker would never forget the sight of Lupe on the verge of death. That memory tormented him, the thought of such a gentle soul cruelly suffering. Even if it was against the law, he would not remain idle while there was a way to save a few.

CAPÍTULO 17

ON THE MORNING OF THE day all Catholics around the world celebrated their Savior's baptism, the first of the stricken neophytes expired. The progress of the boy's decline had confirmed Fray Alejandro's fears. It was indeed the same disease that had so devastated the island of Ibiza in his youth, therefore the boy's death was only a beginning. The family who had reminded him of the Nativity would surely be the next to perish, and the Misión de Santa Dolores, already a somber place, would begin to reek of death. So disturbed was Alejandro's mind that he abandoned every pretense of working on the altarpiece. He sat alone before the unfinished painting in his cell, forsaking his duty to complete it. Exhausted from his ministrations to the ill and from his struggles with the strange oppressive force that had so often thwarted him, the good friar merely stared at the wooden panels and lost himself in somber thoughts.

Of all creatures on the earth, Alejandro believed man alone imagines death, and this foreknowledge very often leads us to despair. Some might live many years without once conceding the grim reaper's approach. Then a thing happens, a tragedy, and with a rush of vertigo a dread of death begins to haunt the love of present life. A great depression settles down. The mind, once capable of moving easily between so many sentiments, suddenly conceives of nothing but its suffering. Powers of imagination become extraordinary in their single focus, stronger even than the will. Morbidity gains force with every revolution in this downward spiral, until at last the very thing imagination dreads, imagination brings to pass.

Humanity has learned much since Alejandro's time, but all our knowledge is as nothing in the face of this malaise. Captured in that downward spiral, Delano Wright walked along a hospital corridor. He moved like a sleepwalker along the polished vinyl floor until he found Lupe's room.

Through a small square of glass he viewed Tucker Rue inside, sprawled on a reclining chair, apparently asleep.

Delano Wright drew a deep breath and sighed. Unshaved whiskers scratched his collar. His shirttail was out. He wore no socks. His hair had not been combed. He was not himself, and would never be again.

He pushed on the door and entered. He ignored the sleeping man. He moved to stand beside the bed. Lupe lay unconscious there, her left arm in a plaster cast to the shoulder, her neck and right cheek swathed in bandages. She had suffered many injuries. It had been several weeks, yet still they operated on her.

Delano drew his fingertips along the sleeping woman's hair, although in his imagination it was not the Mexicana's pure black hair he stroked, but that of another, which gleamed like golden sunshine. He gazed at Lupe and for the thousandth time he tried to understand his world as it now was.

"Don't touch her," came a soft voice behind him. "She'll wake up."

Ignoring this, he stroked the woman's hair again.

"Seriously," whispered Tucker Rue. "She's in a lot of pain. She needs to sleep."

Delano backed away and sat down heavily upon a brown steel chair beside her bed. He admired her Mayan profile. In spite of the cast and bandages, in spite of the tubes feeding oxygen into her nose and liquid into her veins, she was elegant in repose, stately, like a queen.

After each of Lupe's operations he had come to visit. Each time he had come in hopes of finding something that would tie him to the world again, some unbroken connection, but he barely recognized this person on the bed. Although she had been part of his household for six years, she was not a part of him. No one on the surface of the earth was a part of him. His wife was gone. His daughter, gone. His parents had been buried years ago. He was utterly alone in life, an orphan, a prisoner in solitary confinement, awaiting the fellowship of death.

"She woke up a little while ago," said the so-called minister from the comfort of the recliner at the foot of the bed. "She asked me to tell you something. She said Harmony was already unconscious before the fire got to her."

Delano refused to think about the meaning of those words. He merely sat and watched the pure white sheet over Lupe rise and fall, her breath, like his, continuing even with his daughter in the ground.

"She wanted you to know Harmony didn't suffer."

He roused himself and turned toward the young cleric. "How long have you been here?"

"Well, uh, since before they operated. Five this morning."

"Every time I've come to visit, you've been here. Why is that?"

The man looked away. "She . . . I thought Lupe might need me."

"I knew there was something wrong with you. I knew it from the look on her face that night when she screamed and dropped the tray." Delano turned away from the man. He preferred to watch the woman breathe, to try to understand how such a thing was possible. "I should have made you leave right then. Then Harmony would be alive."

"You can't really think this is my fault."

"You dragged her down into that world of yours. Gangs. Illegal aliens. Drunks."

"Harmony wanted to help with the ministry."

"You shouldn't have allowed it. You broke your promise."

"What promise?"

"You know exactly what I mean. You made a promise that night. We had an oral contract, and I paid you a lot of money based on it."

"You never paid me anything. That was tithe money."

Delano saw the man's awareness of his guilt within his eyes. He spoke with perfect calmness. "Don't tell me what it was. I know what it was, and I know what you are. You thought you could attach yourself to me, get more money, if you married my daughter. You never really cared about her."

"That's not true! I . . . I loved Harmony!"

"If you loved her, why didn't you go to her wake?"

"I thought you wouldn't want me there."

"Don't lie to me, young man. You're no good at it." He said it quietly, lest the woman be awakened. Inexplicably, the pure white sheet over her chest still rose and fell.

"I'm not lying," said the so-called minister.

"I know Lupe had some kind of procedure the day of the funeral. I know you were here for that when you should have been mourning your fiancée. You've been here for everything, ever since the accident. If you loved Harmony, why were you here? With her?" Delano gestured toward the woman on the bed. When Tucker did not answer, Delano looked at him again. The young man sat with his eyes focused down on the clasped hands in his lap.

Delano shifted in his seat. He spoke with no hint of emotion. "You want to know why I think Lupe screamed that time? I think she was scared of you."

"Scared of me? That's crazy."

"I think you should leave. I don't think Lupe would want you here. She knows what kind of man you are. You're a thief. You stole my daughter. You got her killed."

"It was an accident, Mr. Wright. It wasn't my fault. You need to calm down."

"I've never been more calm."

Delano rose. He touched the sleeping woman's hair a final time. He turned and walked away from her. Her breathing offered nothing.

At the door he paused. Inhaling deeply through his nose, he caught Harmony's scent again. It caused a momentary softening in him. Although he did not bother looking at the man, he thought about giving Tucker Rue fair warning. But he was greatly burdened by the heavy combination of a good imagination and an aching heart, hopelessly overmatched in his quest for cosmic mercy. Delano longed to see a certain kind of dreadful knowledge rise behind the eyes of that young man, the same kind of horror that afflicted Delano himself: a vision of the coming years without the future he had planned.

Delano felt no pity for the fellow. He had hired watchers. He knew about the aid the man had offered criminals who came north to steal jobs from Americans. He had proof of food and clothing given to illegal aliens who had no right to be here. He had paid for photographs of Tucker leaving water for those outlaws in the desert, no better than a smuggler. He knew the man had tempted Harmony to join the very lawlessness which had enticed her murderers across the desert.

Justice simply must be done.

Delano did not wish to disgrace a Christian minister in the public eye. He would pursue his justice in another way. An eye for an eye, a tooth for a tooth . . . a dream for a life. The death of Tucker's dream, his so-called Sanctuario, would not equal the death of Delano's daughter, nor would it fill the emptiness that spread around about him like a stagnant sea, but Delano was a civilized man, so it would have to do.

What little comfort he had found—and it was very slight—lay in the knowledge that his instrument of justice, the development, would serve many righteous purposes. He would convince every major Sanctuario donor in Southern California to support his plan. Not only would Tucker Rue's future be justly ruined for the life he had destroyed, but many other lives would be protected from the kinds of crimes that caused that loss of life. The profits would support future acts of charity. Also, the development would be a monument to Harmony. Delano would immortalize his daughter through the good thing that rose upon the hills she had once loved.

With so much good accomplished by one project, Delano Wright never doubted that his inspiration was divine. Was it not a hallmark of God's guiding hand to bring a multitude of benefits from a single act? Still, while he knew he should be pleased about the protection and the benefits to others that would come from the development, the act of justice it involved gave such slight consolation.

Standing by the hospital room door, he thought perhaps it might be more gratifying if he explained things to the man, told him just exactly how his life would soon be ruined. Delano turned back toward Tucker Rue. His mouth opened, but he could not bring himself to say the words. He felt them far too deeply. He left the room and walked outside.

In the parking lot, in the insulated silence of his Range Rover, Delano remained perfectly still for several minutes. Then he roused himself and turned the key and drove away, heading inland.

His family's land had been beside him for three miles when he saw a trespasser standing in plain sight a short distance from the road. Delano's head swiveled as he passed, staring at the man. He slowed, then stopped. He turned around, drove back, and parked off the pavement. The trespasser remained where he was, on a gentle slope at the bottom of a hill about one hundred yards beyond the fence, where "No Trespassing" signs were clearly posted. It was hard to tell for certain at that distance, but based on height, hair color, and complexion, Delano believed he was a Latino.

Delano stepped out of his Range Rover and called up to the man. "You're trespassing on my land."

Immediately the fellow started climbing up the hill. Standing beside the open door, Delano removed his cell phone from his pocket. He would call the sheriff and tell him to send deputies to come and get this . . . this wetback. But deep inside the canyon as he was, the phone received no signal. Delano walked around beside the road, holding the cell phone at different angles in hopes of a connection. He had no success. Looking up along the slope, he saw the trespasser still climbing. He returned to the Range Rover, to the passenger side this time, and removed his binoculars. Focusing on the trespasser, he shouted as loudly as he could, "You up on the hill! Get off of my land!"

The man paused and looked down. Through the binoculars Delano saw a short Latino with Mayan features and black hair combed straight back from a high, proud forehead.

Delano lowered the binoculars. He raised them and looked again, but the man had resumed his climb. His face was turned away. Just for a moment the man's hair shimmered brightly in the sun; suddenly it seemed to glow pure white, and then he moved and it was black again. Delano remembered the patrolman's words. *His hair sparkled in the sunshine. . . .*

A guttural, growling sound escaped from Delano's throat. With no thought for anything except pursuit, he dropped the binoculars to the ground and set out running. He reached the fence and began to climb. The barbed wire ripped his trousers, but then he was over and scrambling up the gentle slope. Soon the land inclined more steeply. Breathing became difficult. He slowed to a fast walk. Then he was climbing, gripping bushes, searching out small level places for his footing. He reached a kind of gully carved into the hillside by centuries of downward-rushing water. There the going was a little easier. He moved from rock to rock, glancing upward often. Sometimes he caught glimpses of the man above, still climbing. Usually, he did not.

Almost an hour later, atop the hill at last, Delano looked back. Far below he saw his Range Rover parked beside the road. The driver's-side door was open. The passenger-side door was open. He wished he had not been so hasty. What if the trespasser chose to turn around and confront him? If things got physical Delano did not believe he would fare well. He was not a young man. The wisest choice would be to call the sheriff. Now that he was high up on the hill he probably had a cell phone signal. He had no doubt the sheriff would send a helicopter. After all, he was Delano Wright, and at the very least this trespasser might be a witness to his daughter's murder.

Suddenly he saw the man again. In the narrow valley at the bottom of the other side of the hill, far below, the trespasser disappeared beneath the canopy of a sycamore grove. Although he had never been up this far, Delano knew the valley. It had been carved by a small creek that flowed part of the year. About two miles farther to the west the creek and its little valley turned to run behind Camel Mountain and the area where the development was being built.

Watching the sycamore grove carefully, Delano did not see the man emerge on the other side. Maybe he had a camp within the grove. There would be water and shade. But it was a long way up and over the hill to reach the canyon road. A lot of trouble. Wasn't the whole point of sneaking into America to get work, make money, and send it home? That would be impractical for anyone living so far from transportation. Why would this man travel all the way from Mexico, only to live down there like a hermit? It made no sense unless . . . he must be hiding. Because he was involved somehow in the hit-and-run, he was hiding.

Delano began to scramble down the hill. The going was a little faster than the climb had been, but it was also dangerous, because he could not pay attention to his footing. He had to watch the sycamores below, lest the trespasser move on and elude him.

Finally he reached the valley floor. Only then did he remember his plan to call the sheriff, but by then he had lost the cellular signal again, so it was too late. He would have to deal with this himself.

Running while bent over at the waist, pausing now and then to kneel behind a bush or boulder, Delano approached the sycamores. He drew close enough to hear their leaves rattling listlessly in the breeze. Beyond their peeling white and gray trunks he saw the sunlit side of the far hill, a pinkish line of stone and a heap of tan-colored gravel, a small landslide from higher up, probably disturbed by the recent tremors. A narrow trail of stones along the ground beside him, white and round like skulls, marked the course of the dry creek. In the shade of the grove where he had expected to find the trespasser's camp, Delano saw nothing. It seemed impossible. He had been so careful to keep watch on the grove during his descent. Where could the man be?

He advanced. It did not cross his mind that this might be a trap. He passed into the welcome shade but did not linger there. The man he sought had moved on, so out the other side went Delano, through the grove and on along the valley floor, beside the winding creek.

On his left and right the hills rose very steeply. He did not think the trespasser had climbed again. The man would have been too easily seen. But the way between the hills was serpentine, with one hill pressing forward to conceal the valley floor beyond, and then the opposite hill asserting itself back again the other way, the creek turning now left, now right, the view ahead never clear for more than a few hundred yards. The man was likely just beyond the next bend in the valley, moving as Delano moved, heading toward the main canyon and the road to the sea.

Brush huddled thickly up against the watercourse. All along the valley floor, on the hillsides and in places farthest from the creek, the plants stood dry and tan and gray, with a rare hint of weak olive green. Closer to the creek small red flowers balanced on delicate stems about hip-high, with petals like splatter patterns, as if heaven had rained down drops of scarlet paint. Another type of flower clung to long stalks, the coral-colored blossoms shaped like trumpets. All such blooms were unexpected in that arid place. They reminded Delano of his daughter's delight in secret desert flowers. Harmony would have picked a bouquet as she passed, or woven blossoms in her hair.

Suddenly Delano realized he could not sense her presence anymore. Her scent had left him somehow.

He came upon a boulder almost as tall as himself, out of place in the middle of the narrow valley floor, a rounded sandstone monster tinged with pink and clutching many smaller rocks within its marrow. Atop the boulder sprawled a lizard in the sun.

At Delano's approach the scaly creature bobbed quickly up and down on spindly front legs, as if doing push-ups. Between the boulder and the nearest hill he saw a trail of devastation: bushes flattened, soil upturned. Obviously, the great stone had recently crashed down from the hill above, wreaking havoc in its path. Like the little landslide he had seen beside the sycamore grove, Delano assumed this was the work of recent tremors. He remembered beating the earth in his grief and the way the shocks had rippled outward from his sorrow.

He looked back along the boulder's path and noticed a level place about twenty feet up along the hillside. The soil below it was a little darker then the rest, as if it had just lately tumbled down from farther up. He walked along the path cleared by the boulder through the brush. He climbed to the level place, hoping to see farther off between the hills from that vantage point, hoping to spot the trespasser.

He wiped sweat from his eyes. Looking down into the valley, he saw birds flitting here and there among the brush, and drifting clouds of gnats, gilded by the sun, and far beyond all that the bright yellow frame of an earthmover, tiny in the distance. Looking higher, he saw the distinctive profile of Camel Mountain. So he had walked all the way down to the development. Delano sighed. The witness to his daughter's murder had eluded him.

Sweat stung his right eye. Blinking, he ran a palm across his face again and turned to descend. Looking down to check his footing, he noticed sunlight shining into a newly opened crack in the ground. He paused. He stooped. He knelt and stared into the crack. About one foot below the surface he saw an exposed piece of stone, and carved into the stone he saw a word.

Delano scratched at the dry ground with his bare hands. Frustrated at his lack of progress, he rose and went in search of a tool. Returning with a short stick, he began to dig in earnest. Soon he had exposed a flat stone, about the size of a bed pillow but only two inches thick, like a small tombstone. The face of the stone was engraved in Latin: SI COM-PREHENDIS NON EST DEUS. Latin was not one of his languages, but this was close enough to Spanish to decipher.

If you understand, it is not God.

He gripped the stone and lifted it from the hole. It came easily. Setting it aside, Delano looked back down into the earth and saw he had exposed a rectangle made of four similar thin stones, except these were turned on end and inserted down into the ground to form the sides of a box, a recess in the soil, like a smaller version of the metal vault where they had lowered Harmony. Within the stones lay a wooden box about one-third the size of her casket. Had he uncovered a baby's grave?

Carefully, Delano reached down and lifted the wooden box.

The iron hinges were remarkably free of rust. He opened the lid to find the box contained a painting, a crucifixion scene in a compelling primitive style, rendered in rich colors on what appeared to be a wooden board. In the center hung the figure of Jesus, and on his left and right were two hands nailed to timbers. The rest of the two thieves and their crosses were not shown. The top and bottom were bound by a brightly gilded molding. Strangely, the molding did not extend along the left and right edges. He had the feeling this was just the center of a painting, as if parts of the board had been cut off on the sides.

In the foreground, just below the crosses, he saw a building that could only be a Christian chapel with a small cross mounted on a low bell tower. Strange, that the artist would show a church at the crucifixion, as if the effect had preceded the cause. Above that odd anachronism and the figure on the cross he saw the shape of Golgotha, the famous hill where Jesus died, and his curiosity deepened. Against a sky alive with angels, the top of Golgotha had a distinctive silhouette, the shape of a camel's back, the shape of the very hill above him at that moment.

Even stranger than all this, beneath the little chapel lay an image that could only be Christ's empty tomb, complete with a giant round stone rolled away. Yet this tomb was not empty. Within it, the artist had cunningly painted men and women in various stages of decomposition, yet the people somehow seemed to be alive, writhing in agony, their bodies overcome by bursting boils. It must have been an image of perdition, for below it Delano read these words in flowing gilded script: *El Cristo resucitado ha enterrado el infierno.*

This, in Spanish, he understood immediately. The risen Christ has buried hell.

Delano sat back upon his haunches. What could such a bizarre painting mean? Who would bury it in that remote location?

A sense of foreboding overtook him. The small stone vault must have been exposed when this section of the hillside slid away. Why would anyone bury it here? It made no sense. Unless . . . unless it had been hidden in the little vault a long time ago, long enough for a covering of topsoil to develop out of windblown dust and the composting of many generations of fallen leaves and twigs, not to mention all the other little landslides from earthquakes of prior generations.

It certainly looked old. Delano leaned forward to inspect the painting more closely. In the lower right corner he found more words. These had not been painted prominently, nor had the artist used expensive gilding. They were written in pure black, and at first he had not noticed them against the dark gray field that was the hillside near the painting's hellish tomb. It was more Latin: *Anno Domini 1773.*

Delano Wright felt a sudden sinking in his belly. He had been in this position once before, on a development near Newport Beach when a backhoe had uncovered an ancient Indian skeleton. Government bureaucrats had descended like a plague of locusts. The development was shut down pending an archaeological survey. For three years he had waited on an endless process of delicate excavation, the entire area uncovered inch by excruciating inch with hand trowels and little brushes, universities involved, archaeologists, historians, and scientists, every bit of it beyond his control. If they would do all that just because of an Indian grave, imagine what might happen if he let them know about the painting in his hands. Delano's new development might be delayed for years, perhaps even forever, his whole scheme drowning in a bureaucratic flood of paperwork and regulations.

He sat beside the open hole for a few more minutes, thinking. It did not occur to him to question how he came to find the painting. He only thought about the trouble it might cause. He stood. He stared toward the earthmoving equipment in the distance. Satisfied he had not been seen, Delano dropped the wooden box and the engraved capstone into the hole. He knelt and pushed soil in over them. When they were completely buried, Delano picked up the painting and set out up the valley, hurrying back the way he had come, away from the development, with his newfound secret in his arms.

CAPÍTULO 18

THE WOMAN AND HER BABY were dead. So too was the father. All three of the neophytes who had so reminded Alejandro of the Holy Family died at Candlemas, the day devoted to the memory of Joseph and Mary's redemption of the baby Jesus at the temple. The good friar spent little time in contemplation of this irony. He was far too busy tending to the nine newly afflicted neophytes.

Together with Fray Benicio, he bathed the feverish wretches with soft cloths soaked in cooling water. He had also found a kind of cactus similar to aloe, which yielded a clear sap. This he harvested from the surrounding countryside and applied to the victims' spreading boils in hopes of soothing them a little.

At Fray Guillermo's insistence, smoldering punks were carried through the refectory every hour. Although Alejandro did not believe the smoke gave any benefit, it seemed to cause no harm except for stinging eyes and a slight irritation of the nose and throat. Prayers for the sick were offered by the brothers when they gathered for the canonical offices, and Alejandro entreated God for mercy at many other times throughout the day and night. None of this availed. Fray Alejandro expected at least four more deaths within the week.

Several times while crossing the plaza from the well to the refectory, the Franciscan felt he was the object of someone's particular attention. He cast covert glances left and right, but it was impossible to identify the source of this sensation. In a plaza filled with dozens of neophytes and soldiers engaged in the constant work essential to the mission, anyone or everyone might watch him pass.

Then, late in the afternoon Alejandro saw the Indian again. Like any neophyte the man was short and broad, very dark, and dressed in simple sackcloth. There would have been no reason to notice him among the others, save for the curious shimmer in his hair. Rather than a mere reflection of the sun, it seemed as if a strong light glowed behind his head.

Their eyes met. The man lifted a hand as if offering a blessing or a benediction. In a sudden rush of memory Alejandro thought of the Cochimí who had paused upon a hilltop to turn and gesture in that same way after carrying Fray Guillermo's unjust burden. Fray Alejandro's common sense insisted this comparison was false. The Cochimís lived far to the south. The Indian before him was from a different tribe, and only one more neophyte among many.

Still, something stronger than mere curiosity made the friar forget his duty to the ill. He began to cross the plaza toward the man. Just then a pair of mounted leather-jacket soldiers rode between them. By the time his path was clear again the Indian had vanished.

During the following days the homely friar thought often of that man. The unfortunate Cochimí who was so poorly used by Fray Guillermo had remained in his mind, and inexplicably the Indian across the plaza merged with that memory. The man also became somehow connected in Alejandro's imagination with the unfinished altarpiece which lay neglected in his cell, and with the victims perishing in the refectory.

These odd associations found their nexus in a growing sense of guilt. Alejandro felt it every time his thoughts touched on the altarpiece, which should have been long completed. He had been called to mission service at San Francisco's Porziuncola in Assisi, called to travel across many years and miles to convey the love of Christ to the strange people of that unfamiliar land, yet while Fray Benicio had been wildly successful, Alejandro had not led one pagan to salvation. He had not even finished a simple altarpiece to assist his young brother's work. He could not forget his shame at the Cochimí's torture, his inability to stop it, his meager act of comfort which had been limited to joining in it. And each time Alejandro entered the refectory to tend the sick, he became more burdened by the fact that most of the stricken neophytes would die despite his efforts.

In all these things he believed himself a failure. Thus, although Fray Alejandro had begun his quest with hopes of converting others for the better, by the power of these morbid thoughts he himself became converted for the worse.

The good friar's transformation should cause us no surprise, for possibility is the offspring of ideas. Matter can be altered by a human thought. The heat of fire, the force of wind, the strength of mighty animals . . . all of this the human mind had harnessed to its will three thousand years before the good friar's time. Nothing in creation can surpass the power of our thoughts.

If this was true for Alejandro centuries ago, it was doubly true for Ramón Rodríguez, who lived in an age when human thought had lifted men and women from our planet's surface and sent them flying out among the stars.

Two long years had passed since the accident in Wilson City, two years since the death of Harmony Wright, and in every month of those two years, in every day and hour and minute, Ramón had waged a ceaseless struggle against a stricken conscience which threatened to corrupt him.

His battle had begun the morning after the wreck, when the enemy inside his head attacked him physically. On that morning he had remained upon his mattress on the floor with his palms pressed against his throbbing temples. Because there were no curtains, newspapers had been fastened over the bedroom window, but sunlight overwhelmed that poor attempt at privacy.

A wicked heat had attacked his eyelids. His brain burned. Every sound seemed amplified a thousand times. His only hope had been the sweet release of sleep. Fernando, Paco, Trini, and Lobo returned home that night to find him still upon the mattress with his palms against his head. Ramón claimed nausea when they offered food, and begged them to be silent.

It took three days, but at last the headache faded. During that time Ramón had sometimes seen the accident inside his mind. Passing in and out of consciousness, he was never certain what was true and what was a false nightmare. On the third morning he arose and shuffled out to the garage. He saw Lobo's truck squatting in the darkness, its grille and fender mangled. Although the pain inside his head had gone, another kind of torment took its place.

When Fernando and the others had returned home, Ramón asked for details. At the table in the front room, Trini showed him an English-language newspaper with the accident described on the front page. Two days earlier the men had pooled their limited understanding to decipher the words. It seemed the Mexicana had survived. Unfortunately, the driver, the blond girl, had not been so fortunate.

Moaning at this news, Ramón had covered his eyes as the others watched him silently. Finally, he said, "I must go to the police."

Fernando said, "My friend, that is impossible."

"It is not. It is only difficult."

Fernando shook his head. "Think. What will happen then to us?"

"Why should anything happen to you? I was the driver."

Trini, the youngest of them, said, "Lobo and I were with you. We would be arrested."

"And I would be deported," said Fernando.

"And I," agreed Paco.

"But . . . a woman was killed!" said Ramón. "Felix was killed!"

"It was not your fault," said Trini quietly.

"But I was the driver!"

"But it was not your fault," repeated the young man. "Do you not remember?"

At this, Lobo strode out of the house, slamming the door behind himself.

Puzzled, Ramón asked, "Why is he so angry?"

Fernando shrugged. "Why not? He is always angry."

"But—"

"Ramón," said Trini. "You truly do not remember what he did?"

Ramón rubbed his temples. "I remember. . . . We were at the store, then we were driving back to here. I remember that, and then I do not remember much except for a woman in a car, the wrong side of the car was up, and I knew her."

"You knew her?" asked Paco. "How?"

"I met her in Naco, on the day I came across the border. She is beautiful. She looks like my Raquel."

"Did she recognize you?" asked Fernando.

"I do not know."

"Think! It is important."

"She recognized him," said Trini. "They talked to each other."

"You saw her too?" asked Ramón.

"I carried you away."

"Away?" His fingers moved more rapidly against the power in his mind, pressing deep into the flesh at his temples. "I remember now. I left, and did not help her."

Trini smiled, but there was sadness in his eyes. "You could not help her."

Ramón stood up from the table. "I left her there? I left her?"

"You were hurt, my friend. And the police were coming. What else could we do?"

Ramón walked unsteadily to the back room where his mattress lay.

Down the hallway Trini called, "It was Lobo's fault. The drunken fool attacked you at the wheel."

Those words did not matter. The change within Rámon was complete.

The next morning he had arisen and dressed and made a sandwich from ham and a piece of cheese, and put the sandwich in a bag and walked out of the house with all the others. Fernando had found work for everyone at a large construction project on the canyon road. The bosses there had asked if Ramón was allowed to work in the United States, and he had said yes and signed a piece of paper. He had been uncomfortable with the lie, but what else could he do? Raquel and the boys depended on the money he sent home. What kind of father would he be, to tell the truth and let his family go hungry?

For two years after that, every morning when Ramón and his friends arrived at the work site they were given plastic hard hats and bright yellow safety vests, and then sent to different places in the hills. It was a very large project. Ramón believed the purpose was to make flat places in the land for future houses, although this had never been explained to him. Compared to digging in the clay pits outside his hometown of Hércules, the work was not so hard. Mostly Ramón walked behind bulldozers, using a shovel to move small piles of earth the machines had left behind. Often, he simply stood and waited for someone to tell him what to do. He worried when he had to stand and wait, and when given something to do he worked very hard, for he wished to keep his job.

Each evening, Ramón and his friends met at the same place beside the job trailers to begin their journey home. Ramón seldom spoke throughout those days as he and the others prepared sack lunches in the kitchen, as they rode along the canyon together on the bus, or at night when they were home. The accident had dampened everyone's good cheer at first, but as the months went by Trini, so young and full of life, could not contain his natural geniality. Neither could Fernando, the wise one, or Paco, who always had a friendly word. In time, it was as if the three of them had somehow managed to forget.

For Ramón those two years passed as if they were two decades. His thoughts were never far from painful places. Every evening he sat by himself in silence, haunted by the specter of their dead friend, Felix, while Lobo loitered at the edge of conversations, glowering.

Meanwhile, in the hills along the canyon between Blanco Beach and Wilson City, roads were paved, houses raised, and guards in uniforms were posted at the gates. Beside the gates large signs proclaimed this place was called "New Harmony."

"What does it mean?" asked young Trini on the day the first sign was erected.

"It has to do with music," replied the wise Fernando. "You would not understand."

Ramón Rodríguez and his friends continued working. They had never kept a job so long. One day when his work was done, Ramón approached the others by the office trailer. For the first time in many dusty and dry months, it began to rain. The rain was very soft, with tiny drops that seemed to settle down upon the earth instead of falling. Trini, Paco, and Fernando enjoyed the feeling of it on their faces. Joking with each other, they stood nearby while Ramón returned his hard hat and safety vest to the woman who collected them each night. Finally Lobo came down from the hills, and the five friends set out together.

As they walked, Trini said, "What is this stuff falling from the sky? It seems familiar, but I cannot remember."

"You are too young, my son," replied Fernando. "This is your first time."

"Yes," agreed Paco. "He has a lot to learn about the world. Probably he thinks it is tequila."

Trini stuck out his tongue to catch a few drops. "Is this the taste of tequila?"

"No," replied Fernando. "Tequila is less wet."

"You see?" said Paco. "The boy knows nothing."

"This," said Fernando, holding his palm out toward the sky, "Is something we call rain. It is composed of *poblano* tears."

"Why are the *poblanos* crying?" asked Trini, grinning as he glanced at Lobo. They all watched the sour man pretend to ignore them, knowing as a citizen of Puebla, Mexico—a *poblano*—Lobo certainly understood the reason for this jest. He had drunk eight beers the night before while listening to the radio as his football team, known simply as the Stripe, had suffered an ignoble defeat at the hands of Monterrey.

Fernando said, "They cry because the Stripe has been disgraced, dear boy."

"How disgraced?" ask the youngest.

"Four to zero," said Fernando. "If it can be believed."

"*Zero?*" asked Trini with mock incredulity.

"Zero!" replied Fernando and Paco together.

Cursing, Lobo stalked off ahead of the small group. Behind him, the three lighthearted ones laughed.

"You should not tease him so," said Ramón quietly.

Still laughing, Fernando said, "It is impossible to avoid. Last night he cried like a baby when his team lost."

"Are you sure?"

"Of course. We all saw it."

"But the reason why he cried," said Ramón. "Are you sure it was the game?"

Fernando and the other men fell silent.

On they walked. As the gentle rain descended, the ground beneath their boots began to turn to mud. Rivulets from higher up the hill now crossed the path, carving little valleys in the soil. Their clothing was soon soaked through to the skin, and although the air itself was warm, they sometimes shivered.

Silenced by the meaning of Ramón's question, the men followed a shortcut up a low hill toward the bus stop on the far side at the canyon road. Lobo, still muttering, remained far ahead, alone. Near the ridge of the hill they heard him give a little yelp, like the startled cry of his namesake, the wolf. Then he disappeared from view.

"What happened?" asked young Trini.

"I think he fell," said Paco.

Fernando and Ramón, saying nothing, broke into a run.

At the ridge, they found no sign of their friend among the bushes and the boulders. Because of the clouds it was already almost dark, and difficult to see.

"It is a trick," said Paco, joining them. "He wants vengeance for our insults."

"Lobo!" called Fernando loudly. "Come out!"

"We are sorry!" added Trini, arriving last. "Your team is very good, except when they are losing!"

Paco laughed.

"Shhh!" said Ramón. "Listen!"

The men stood still. Mixed with the sound of rain, they heard distant weeping.

"He's crying again," said Trini.

"Ramón was right," said Fernando. "We should not have teased him."

"Where is he?" asked Trini.

"Over here," called Paco.

Ramón, Trini, and Fernando moved to stand beside Paco, at the edge of a short but steep incline. Below, they saw a small level place where the bulldozers had left their mark. "We worked down there a long time ago," said Paco. "Remember?"

"Yes," said Fernando. "When the *patrón* came and told us we must move."

"I remember because he was very strange that day. He had torn and filthy clothing and eyes like a wild man."

"Like San Juan Bautista," agreed Fernando.

"Look. Here is where Lobo fell." Paco pointed to skid marks in the mud, which followed the slope down toward the little naked plain below. The marks were filled with rain, a pair of little waterfalls.

Ramón walked to the edge.

"It is too steep," said Paco.

"He might be hurt," said Ramón.

"Lobo! Are you hurt?" shouted Fernando.

Again the men stood quietly. Again they heard low weeping in the rain.

"He is surely hurt," said Paco.

"Do you see him?" asked Trini. "I cannot see him anywhere."

"It is too dark."

Ramón squatted down and backed over the edge, gripping a bitter-brush branch.

"Be careful," suggested Fernando.

A few feet down Ramón slipped in the mud. He slid upon his belly. His chin bounced on a stone. At the bottom of the slope he heard Fernando call, "Are you all right?"

"Yes," replied Ramón.

"I told you to be careful."

"Yes," replied Ramón again, rising to his feet.

"Can you see him?"

"No," said Ramón. "I need to listen for a moment. Please be silent."

The sound of weeping was much louder. In fact, it was so loud that Ramón felt he must be standing right on top of Lobo. But look as he might, he could not see the man.

"Lobo," he said. "Where are you?"

He heard nothing but a thousand little impacts of the rain on bush and stone and mud, and of course, the weeping.

"Perhaps the pain is too great," called Fernando. "Perhaps he cannot speak."

"Will you please be silent?" said Ramón. "So I can listen?"

"I only want to help."

"Yes," replied Ramón, covered as he was with mud. "Many thanks."

It was strange to hear Lobo's cries, obviously so close, and yet not see him. Had Lobo somehow become invisible? Ramón bent over at the waist and spread his eyelids wide, the better to see the ground in the dark.

He walked slowly out onto the level place, searching at his feet and saying, "Lobo? Lobo? Declare yourself. Where are you?" He followed the flow of water as it streamed across the nearly level ground to a place where it fell down the hill again on the far side of that flat scar in the earth. There, finally, Ramón found him.

Lobo lay in a shallow depression lately carved out by the rain. He was camouflaged by mud, which coated him completely. He seemed to disappear into the dark background of sticks and roots and smooth stones all around him, which had been exposed by the little waterfall. Ramón knelt and said, "Tell me where it hurts."

Lobo merely wept.

Ramón ran his hands along the fellow's legs, waiting for a reaction when he reached a broken bone. He did the same to Lobo's arms and ribs. The man trembled underneath his touch, as if he were very cold, or terrified. Finally, Ramón said, "Lobo, you must tell me what is wrong."

Still trembling, the weeping man whispered, "Do you not see them?"

"Who, my friend? We are all alone here."

Lobo merely wept.

Ramón did not know what to do. He sat back to watch Lobo. As he watched, a section of soil, eroded by the flowing water, slipped into the shallow pit where Lobo lay. Newly exposed by this fallen soil, another rounded stone appeared in the clutches of the earth. Except it was not a stone. It had two circular holes for eyes, and a ragged hole where the nose once was, and a few remaining teeth, and on the cheeks and forehead were fleshy remnants marred by ugly pocks. Suddenly Ramón saw everything around him as it really was and, seeing, understood Lobo's trembling and his tears, for these were not sticks and roots and stones at all, but were instead the arms and legs and ribs and heads of many bodies, once preserved by a deep covering of dry desert soil, now exposed and rotting in the rain.

CAPÍTULO 19

WHEN FIVE MORE DIED AT the Misión de Santa Dolores, Fray Alejandro began to think the mission's name prophetic, for *Dolores* is related to the Spanish word for "pain". Eight souls had fled the mortal flesh within the mission walls—two women, three men, two children, and a baby—their earthly remains the first to be interred in the sanctified ground beside the chapel. Seventeen more now languished in the refectory. Yet in truth the matter was much worse, for Benicio had heard of seven deaths among the unconverted at the nearest village, and many others lying ill within their willow huts.

The altarpiece, on which Fray Alejandro had labored long and accomplished little, had now been forgotten. He rarely ate or slept. He prayed almost constantly while moving among the suffering, dispensing little mercies. A moist cloth on a forehead here, a bit of cactus balm there, a gentle touch (Alejandro had ceased to worry about touching them), yet always he endured the bitter truth that he could not save their lives. Just two souls had survived the disease so far. Was this merely by chance or was it perhaps the grace of God? The homely friar wasted no time trying to discern the difference.

Amid the stench of sickness within the shadows of the refectory, Alejandro knelt beside a girl of eight or nine. From a wooden spoon he dispensed a few drops of water to moisten her disfigured lips. She could not see him, blinded as she was by the disease's blisters. Yet, stirred to sensibility by the touch of water, the girl whispered the word "Mother" in her language.

"Your mother is nearby," replied Alejandro, which was not strictly a falsehood, for the woman was indeed quite near, beneath the ground. "She desires you to drink this water."

The child allowed him to drip a little more between her lips and then she turned her swollen face toward the refectory's mud wall.

Alejandro rose. With the wooden water bucket in his hand, he moved to the next pallet, where an old man lay completely motionless, staring at the ceiling. The friar looked down upon him, watching for the rise and fall of his sunken chest. Seeing no movement whatsoever, Alejandro knelt, set the bucket on the dirt floor at his side, and made the sign of the cross above the body.

After reaching out to close the man's eyelids, he began to whisper, "I beseech you most Holy Father, forgive the soul of this your servant from all constraints of sin, that being raised in the glory of the resurrection, he may be reinvigorated among the Saints and Elect through the eternal grace and mercy of Jesus Christ our Lord." In this fashion the good friar continued praying, asking the Creator to have mercy on the man, to ensure that his suffering in purgatory might be brief so he might pass swiftly into the Holy Presence.

While he was on his knees, with his tonsured head bowed above the body and rosary beads clasped in his fingers, Alejandro's whisperings expanded in significance, spreading out beyond the dead man before him to include every soul within the mission, and then traveling still farther to encompass all the villages beyond.

Thusly lost in supplication, at first the good Franciscan did not hear the angry words which rose outside the refectory, but those distractions grew in volume until they could not be ignored. Alejandro's lips fell silent. He listened. Identifying the two shouting voices, he sighed. He arose and went outside.

Blinking in the dazzling sunlight after many hours in the refectory shadows, it took Fray Alejandro several seconds to recognize the abbot in the center of the plaza, with Don Felipe at his elbow. The abbot stood with cowl thrown back, his fair skin flaming with emotion. The captain stood with a hand upon the pommel of his sheathed sword. Behind them was a small group of leather-jacket soldiers bearing pikes.

Facing the armed Spaniards was a crowd of Indians. From their naked-ness Alejandro knew they were not neophytes. By the welts crisscross-ing their backs he recognized some of them as the same tribal elders Fray Guillermo had caused to be whipped beside the plaza well. In the space between these two groups of men stood young Fray Benicio, holding his arms extended in each direction as if to keep them back from one another.

"Abbot, I entreat you!" said Benicio. "They ask only for a few hand-fuls of grain. An insignificant amount. Why should we continue to deny them? It is for symbolic value only. It is a way of apologizing for our offense."

With a false tone of innocence, Guillermo asked, "And what is our offense, pray tell?"

"You know their complaints, brother. The altar, the sycamore grove. Now the sickness has attacked their villages. They believe it is because we desecrated their holy places."

Guillermo turned to Don Felipe, who observed the exchange with mocking smile. "A pile of stones, my dear captain. A few trees. A hand-ful of grain. That is where these godless heathens seek protection from disease."

Fray Benicio said, "They are dying and we cannot save them. Should we withhold a little solace? Are mere symbols so important?"

Spying Alejandro standing at a distance, Fray Guillermo raised his voice. "Brother, get you hither and give heed! Here is this friar speaking as if symbols do not matter!"

"Yes, Abbot," replied Alejandro, his unfortunate features betraying much concern as he approached.

"The cross! The sacred heart! The dove! Do these things mean nothing?"

"No, Abbot," replied Alejandro. "But perhaps if we considered Benicio's—"

"No indeed! These savages stole our grain before, and now they dare to come demanding more? No I say!" The abbot turned toward Fray Benicio again. "Tell these shameless dogs a thousand times no!"

The village Indians did not understand his words, but they under-stood his tone. With dark scowls and murmurs, they pressed forward. Speaking quickly in their language, Fray Benicio placed his palms against the naked chests of the two closest men. Then he said, "Abbot, I entreat you—"

"Enough! Captain, drive these creatures out!"

At a nod from Don Felipe, the leather-jacket soldiers lowered their pikes toward the bellies of the Indians. The Spanish men advanced. The Indians fell back, with Benicio among them. Fray Alejandro thought the expression on their faces terrible to behold. When they were beyond the mission walls the abbot called out through the open gate, "Heed me, Fray Benicio! I will not allow my authority and our religion to be insulted by a mob of heathens led by a *criollo!*"

Wincing at Guillermo's insult, Alejandro longed to comfort Fray Benicio, but the young friar did not pause to give him time. Instead he walked into the countryside at some distance from the Indians. Alejandro assumed he would brood alone before returning for their prayers at vespers.

Meanwhile, still red in the face, Fray Guillermo strode across the plaza to the garden, where he barked orders at the neophytes engaged in labor. Don Felipe and his leather-jacket soldiers dispersed throughout the mission. For his part, remembering the old man in the refectory, Alejandro walked to the chapel yard, where he took up a shovel and began to dig another grave.

The simple work allowed him time to think. Benicio was the son of Spanish parents, but unlike Fray Guillermo and Don Filipe and Alejandro himself, the young friar had not been born on the Spanish peninsula. He was a native of New Spain, thus his social status was inferior to that of a *peninsular,* a true Spaniard. He could never hold a high position in the Franciscan Order, nor in politics, nor the military. There would always be many who considered him less intelligent, less honorable, and less trustworthy than a man of authentic Spanish blood. In short, he was inferior by birth according to the mores of society, and as an inferior, men like Fray Guillermo might deride him as a mere *criollo.*

While scratching with his shovel at the parched soil of that new world, the ugly friar considered the grim meaning of his work. *Criollo* or king, it did not matter; all human life was a journey toward a hole in the ground. Since all men came to the same end, how unwise it was to define men by their beginnings. What lunacy to celebrate one kind of man as "better," or more "beautiful," while discounting others. It was a self-destructive impulse at its core, for Nature drew herself most beautifully in contrasts—day and night, land and sea, spring and autumn, birth and death—and without such counterpoints the world would be a dreary one indeed. What insanity to hold a single standard as the most desirable, when that very standard would be meaningless without alternatives.

This madness did not die with Alejandro's generation, of course. It remains with us today. It could be seen in the women of Blanco Beach, who were mostly tall and blond, because the wealthy men of that small town preferred them so.

In a place where beauty had thus been so narrowly defined, a dark woman of slight stature might be excused for deeming herself common, as did Guadalupe Soledad Consuelo de la Garza. In Rincón de Dolores she had believed she was only one among the many of her kind, an average sort of woman. She was all the more unable to believe herself attractive in a wealthy world preoccupied with her physical opposite.

Thus it was that Lupe could easily accept the pink scars on her shoulder, neck, and cheek. A woman who had never counted outer beauty as an asset, who had never used her comeliness to seek a man's affections, had less to fear than most from such disfiguration. How ironic that she did not recognize the effect of Nature's law of contrasts: the burn on one cheek only served to underscore the beauty of the other.

But the burns had left her scarred in other ways, less easily ignored. At night she often moaned upon her bed, her dreams a montage of horrific images: the wreck in Wilson City, her childhood family tragedy, a dreadful vision of two village boys in flames on the Feast Day of Fray Alejandro, the many nameless saints who had been bound to blazing stakes as inquisitors watched coldly, and a friar and Indian alight within a burning mission. Often Lupe cried out, and awoke, and found herself alone in her small apartment above the pool house, alone among a pagan people she had come to save. In those solitary sleepless hours she endured the condemnation of her conscience. She had saved not one soul in eight long years of preaching on the beach. On the contrary, she had lost her precious Harmony, and now Delano Wright seemed intent upon destruction.

Soon after the accident, her employer had begun to gather every book he could find on the subject of Spanish missions. At first his newfound interest had excited Lupe. She hoped there might be some connection to that sainted patron of her village, Fray Alejandro, to his miraculous legacy, the *retablo,* and her quest. She hoped at last to understand her calling to that place. Then one day she asked Delano Wright about the reason for his curiosity. His eyes had flashed with anger. He had ordered her to mind her own business, and his books on the subject disappeared. She never saw another sign of interest in the old missions.

Many times since then she had pondered this in silence.

Later, Delano had produced file folders labeled "abortion," "public prayer," "homosexuality," "Darwinism," and "atheists." Lupe had watched helplessly as the man spent hours at the table in his morning room, newspapers and scissors in hand, muttering to himself, clipping relevant articles, and putting them in the folders after underlining certain paragraphs and phrases. In the two years since Harmony's death, he had stuffed a filing cabinet with proof that evil prospers, as if such a thing needed proving.

How it saddened Lupe to have failed him. Often in her deep distress, her only comfort was Fray Alejandro's *retablo.* She would remove it from the velvet sack to stare at the miraculous images, seeking reassurance, taking solace in the proof it offered that she had been led by divine providence to that very time and place, even if the Holy Father did not deign to tell her why.

Once, at about three in the morning, Lupe dreamed again that she was burning. She awoke screaming. As usual she did not realize where she was at first. Normally in those first few moments her screams and cries would have continued after waking, but this night she was quickly called back from the horror by a pounding from the floor below. She arose and wrapped a robe around herself. She descended the stairs to the small interior landing, and opened the door. Outside in a pool of yellow light stood Delano Wright, also in a robe.

"Are you okay?" he asked.

"Yes, mister."

"I heard a scream."

Embarrassed, she said, "A bad dream."

"Oh." The older man nodded. "I just wanted to make sure you were okay."

"I am okay."

They stood in silence for a moment, awkward in their night clothes. Then Lupe said, "How could you hear me? Did I make so much noise?"

"I was right out here, sitting by the pool."

"You could not sleep?"

"I'm not sleeping very well these days. Sometimes I walk around outside."

Lupe looked up at the moon. "It is beautiful tonight to be outside."

He glanced upward too, and then returned his attention to her. "Since we're both awake, would you please come and sit with me awhile?"

"Yes, mister."

She followed him across the slate pavement to a group of teak furniture beside the pool. Settling onto a cushioned chaise lounge, she stared at the water. Stars were reflected in the surface, the cement underneath stained black, the liquid darkly infinite. It was as if Delano Wright had captured the night sky and laid it at their feet. From force of habit, Lupe rubbed her leg.

"Does it still hurt?" he asked from a chair beside her, pointing at her knee.

The wound, a deep cut from broken glass or jagged metal, had failed to heal as quickly as the others, but that was long ago. She pulled her robe over her flesh and moved her hand into her lap. "It is well, thank you."

After her release from the hospital he had driven her to every physical therapy session and every doctor's appointment. He had paid for everything. He had cared for her as if he were her father.

He said, "I've been thinking a lot about my life, Lupe. You know, in the Bible there's a place where Jesus talks about lukewarm Christians?"

"Lukewarm?"

"*Tibio*. To be not hot and not cold."

"Oh, yes. *Tibio*. Lukewarm. I know this scripture. It is in San Juan's Revelation, yes?"

"Exactly. And the thing is, I've been lukewarm, Lupe. It's what I've learned from . . . from losing Harmony. I've been lukewarm, and I have to be more passionate about the Lord."

"That is good, mister."

"Yes." He fell silent, and Lupe, as was her custom, waited. A slight onshore breeze had arisen, lifting up the distant roar of pounding surf from far below the hill. She listened to that peaceful sound and watched the stars' reflections dance on tiny ripples in the swimming pool. Finally, Delano said, "Lupe, I want you to know something."

She turned her dark eyes toward him. "Yes, mister?"

"I am much older than you are, which means I will probably die first. When I do, you will be taken care of."

"I do not understand."

"You're mentioned in my will, Lupe."

"Your will?"

When Delano explained the meaning of the word, Lupe remained silent. Delano said, "Don't you want to know how much I'm leaving you?"

"No. I would like to speak of something else."

He stared at her. He smiled. He shook his head. "You make me glad of my decision."

"Please, mister. This talk is very sad."

"All right. Just so you know I care about you very much, Lupe. These last few years you've become almost like a daughter to me. I have something to tell you now, but I wanted you to know that, so you won't take what I'm about to say the wrong way. I want you to understand this next part isn't about you, or anything you've said or done. I think you're just wonderful."

"Okay. . . ."

"You see how we are here, all alone in the middle of the night. We're both wearing our nightclothes. . . ." Something in his words made her uncomfortable. She pulled her robe a little closer around her neck. "Not that there's really anything wrong, of course. You and I know that. But the appearance of it, you and me living here, alone together, it doesn't look right. You can see that, can't you?"

"I understand."

"Appearances matter, you know. We Christians have to care about what other people think, because they judge Jesus by the way they think we live."

"I understand."

"Good. Then you will also understand why I have to ask you to leave."

"Leave?"

"Just the apartment. I want you to keep working here. I couldn't get by without you, but it isn't right for a single woman and a single man to live together as we do. I mean, you and I know we don't really live together, of course. But think how it looks to other people. That's what matters."

"What is in our hearts," she said. "Does it not also matter?"

"Of course. Of course. But no one knows what's in our hearts."

She thought about the Holy Father, who surely knew the content of the human heart, but it was clear the man's decision had been made. Who was she to speak against his will? Besides, might this be the beginning of an answer to her prayer, her constant plea to be more useful? For all this time she had preached each Sunday on the beach, and never once had any pagan Anglo been converted, not even after she learned proper English. How often she had begged to be more helpful to the Holy Father, to continue with her quest. Maybe now at last she could.

At dawn Lupe set out down the hill. In Blanco Beach she caught a bus to Wilson City, where she searched most of the day until she found a single room in the attic of a boardinghouse. It had low sloping ceilings and a separate bath and a tiny kitchenette against one wall, and a window in a gable that looked out upon a yard with patches of burnt grass and hard-packed earth scattered about with children's plastic toys and shaded only by the neighbors' drying laundry. Beyond the yard lay an alley, and between the alley and the yard stood a fence of woven wire adorned by many bits of trash, trapped like fish in a net by the current of the Santa Ana winds.

Lupe paid a deposit to the landlady in cash—like most people in Wilson City, she always dealt in cash—and she returned to Delano's house that night and worked as usual the following day, cleaning, cooking, and doing Delano Wright's laundry. She did not dine with him as she once would have done. Since his daughter's death, the man had made a practice of reading his Bible silently during meals, and afterward searching the newspapers for more clippings for his folders.

In the evening she prepared to go. After more than eight years in the apartment over Delano Wright's pool house she had only a few clothes, her toiletries, some small gifts she had received from Harmony and Delano at Christmastime each year, and a Bible. All of this she packed within a single bag. Then, with the apartment door closed and locked, she removed Fray Alejandro's burden from its crimson velvet cover. She unfolded the side panels of the triptych and stood it on a table. She knelt before the miracle. She clasped her hands together, fingers interlaced. She bowed her head and prayed. She had followed the *retablo* away from the longing of her heart, followed it to Blanco Beach and Delano Wright. She had remained. She had been faithful to Fray Alejandro's miracle. Now, finally, she had been forced to go. How she hoped her quest would resume in Wilson City. She dared not pray for this. She dared not admit her longing still remained. Yet she was filled with great excitement.

Lupe rose. She replaced Alejandro's folded *retablo* in the velvet bag and left.

Although Blanco Beach was only thirty minutes from Wilson City by car, to reach Delano Wright's huge house in time to cook his breakfast she had to rise at four-thirty, leave her room at five, and catch the bus three blocks away at five-twenty. There were four bus stops between her neighborhood and the canyon road, and three more stops along the canyon road itself, so the bus did not arrive in Blanco Beach until six-fifteen. Then she had to walk across downtown and climb the hill to arrive at the Wright mansion at seven. Every evening the process was reversed. She left work at six after serving Delano his dinner. If all went well, she arrived at her room at eight.

This left little time to meet the neighbors, but on Sundays, her one day off, she did her best. Once, as she was returning home from preaching at the beach, she saw a woman about her own age pinning laundry to the backyard clothesline. A small child hung upon the woman's back, a baby boy, bundled tightly in a multicolored *rebozo,* or traditional Mexican shawl. An older child, a girl, lay sleeping in the sunshine on a blanket near her feet.

"*Buenas tardes, señora,*" said Lupe.

"*Buenas tardes,*" replied the woman as she clipped another piece of clothing to the line.

"We are neighbors," said Lupe. "I am Guadalupe Soledad Consuelo de la Garza, from Rincón de Dolores, in Jalisco. How are you called?"

"I am Marisol Louisa Soto Guzmán, from San Blas."

"Much pleasure," said Lupe, extending her hand.

The women discussed many things. The town, the boardinghouse, the weather. Marisol Guzmán spoke of Mexico, of the ancient town of San Blas, and of her longing to return to the place of her birth, if only for a visit. She had not been home in nearly eleven years, and dearly wished to see her sisters and her mother. Lupe confessed she had no family in Mexico. "I am satisfied to be here," she said. "But I sometimes miss my village."

The child at Marisol's feet awoke and began to cough. The mother stooped to lay a palm first upon the girl's forehead, and then upon a cheek.

"Does she have a fever?" asked Lupe.

"Yes. She had been sick for seven days."

"Seven days is a long time. What is her name?"

"Louisa. My husband named her after me."

"You must take her to the clinic."

"I did. They prescribed some medicine, but my husband says we cannot afford it."

Lupe knelt beside the mother and her child. She too pressed her palm against the coughing girl's forehead. The little girl was extremely hot.

"How much does the medicine cost?"

"Two hundreds, ninety and six dollars."

Lupe stood and withdrew money from her pocket. She counted it, put enough for bus fare back into her pocket, and handed all the rest to the mother. "Here. Now you need only two hundreds, twenty and three."

"I cannot take your money."

"You must. For your daughter."

"But I do not know you."

"We are neighbors, are we not? Do you know what our Savior said about neighbors? To love them as you love yourself?"

"I have heard it. But I cannot pay you back."

"It is a gift. You must allow me to obey our Savior."

"In that case," said the woman as she took the money, "many thanks."

"That is all I can give you until I am paid next Friday," said Lupe. "Can you borrow the rest?"

"No, señorita. Everyone we know is very poor."

"My *patrón* is a wealthy man. He will give the rest."

"He is a gringo?"

"Of course."

"Then I dare take nothing from him. My husband would be very angry. He is a proud man, and does not like rich gringos."

"Have you asked your priest for help?"

Marisol turned her eyes toward the ground. "I have no priest, señorita. I have not been to Mass in many years."

"I am sorry to hear it."

The woman merely shrugged.

Lupe stared off toward the mountains which rose above the houses on the far side of the alley to the east. She thought of Tucker Rue, a gringo certainly, but certainly not rich. Perhaps this woman's husband would make an exception for one who had lived so long among them. She dreaded the thought of seeing Tucker. She feared the collapse of her resolve at such a pleasant prospect. The Lord, she thought, would not lead her into temptation. Yet she also felt a thrill at the possibility, and besides, there was no other way. "Do you know the place called Sanctuario?"

"Of course. It is just there."

Marisol pointed toward Tucker Rue's building, barely visible on the next block over through a gap between two houses. Lupe had not realized Sanctuario was so close when first she rented her room at the boardinghouse. Or had she known, even though her conscious mind denied it?

She said, "I am acquainted with the man who runs that place. If you tell him I sent you, he will help."

"Truly?"

"Simply ask for a man called Tucker and speak my name. Tell him you were sent by Guadalupe Soledad Consuelo de la Garza."

"May God bless you, señorita," said Marisol Guzmán as she knelt to lift her coughing child.

Lupe watched the woman pass through the alley gate. On her back the youngest child, the baby boy, stared directly into Lupe's eyes from his tightly bundled place within the *rebozo*. Lupe told herself the woman was too greatly burdened, with one child in her arms and another on her back. Then she told herself to turn away. Then she thought she ought to help the woman go to Sanctuario. In that way, back and forth, two people fought a battle in her mind. It was wrong to stand and watch when she could be of help. It was wise to ignore the baby's stare and stay far away from Tucker Rue. She only wished to help. She only wished to taste forbidden pleasures.

Lupe remained uncertain of her motive even as she called, "A moment, señora!" She went to the woman, who had stopped to face her in the trash-strewn alley. Lupe took the sick girl from the woman's arms and held her tightly to her chest. The girl laid her feverish head against the scar on Lupe's cheek, and it was as if the Mexicana's flesh were burning once again. Lupe said, "It will be better if I speak to him for you."

"Oh, thank you!" said Marisol Guzmán. "You are a very good woman!"

Ashamed to receive such praise, knowing that it was not true, Lupe said nothing. She only walked between the houses through the heat toward Sanctuario.

There, in the outer lobby they were greeted by a young man, a boy really, who called himself Vincente. Lupe explained the reason for their visit and the boy asked them to wait. Very soon Tucker came. He stared at Lupe as if she were the only person in the room.

"Hello," he said to her in English. "It's good to see you."

Without thinking she turned her face a little, to show him only her good side. Then she realized what she was doing and turned again to reveal her scar. "Allow me to present my neighbor, Señora Guzmán."

"Your neighbor?" At last he looked away from Lupe. "Do you live in Blanco Beach, señora?"

The woman smiled and shook her head. "No, señor. Such a thing would be impossible."

He looked at Lupe again and raised his eyebrows. She said, "I have moved here, Tucker. I live on the next block."

"That's wonderful!" He smiled and took a step closer. Lupe's heart was stirred, for it seemed he wished to touch her. She resented the coughing child in her arms who came between them, who interfered. Then, remembering herself again, she felt ashamed. She turned her face away, showing him the damage done by fire. His smile disappeared. He said, "Why did you quit? Has Señor Wright mistreated you?"

"Of course not. It is nothing like that. I still work for him. It is only because the mister does not wish to set a bad example, an unmarried man and woman living there together. Only for appearances."

"Ah, yes." Tucker nodded. "He cares a great deal about appearances."

She did not like his words, but with Señora Guzmán listening it would have been improper to admonish him. She said, "We have come for money. This child is very ill, and needs expensive medicine."

Tucker bent his head above the girl in Lupe's arms. "What is the matter?"

"An infection, señor," said Marisol Guzmán. "In her lungs."

As both women had done previously, Tucker laid his palm upon the small child's forehead. He was very gentle. The little girl stared at him with eyes that held no interest. He frowned. He removed his hand and sighed. He turned to the mother. "Señora, I regret very much to say I cannot help."

"But you do not yet know the amount of money necessary," said Lupe.

Tucker switched to English. "I have no money, Lupe."

"She needs only two hundred and twenty-three dollars."

"I don't have it."

"How is that possible? You have built these rooms, the kitchen, so many improvements here."

"All of this was done before the accident. Since then, it has been very difficult to keep Sanctuario open."

"But . . . why?"

"You should ask your boss that question."

Still speaking English for the sake of Señora Guzmán, Lupe said, "You felt how hot this child is. If she does not get the medicine, I think she may die."

Again, Tucker laid a palm against the small girl's cheek. "I'd give my last cent, Lupe. I hope you know that. But there are so many desperate people. . . . I've already given away everything I have."

Lupe felt an illness in her stomach. "How can I tell this to the señora?"

"I'll explain."

He spoke to Marisol Guzmán in Spanish.

With a nod and calm words of thanks, the mother received the news as if it were exactly as expected. She took her child from Lupe's arms and left the room. Lupe also walked away from Tucker.

Following them, he stood in the open door when they stepped onto the sidewalk. "This week I have a meeting with the benevolence committee at Grace Tabernacle. Maybe then I'll have some money."

Lupe turned back toward him. "That may be too late."

"It may be too late for many things."

Lupe stared at him, longing to deny it, to confess her feelings, but she was too slow to speak. As she struggled to find words, Tucker closed the door between them.

CAPÍTULO 20

AFTER FRAY GUILLERMO'S ABUSIVE REJECTION of the Indians' request for grain, Fray Benicio spent less and less time at the mission. The abbot pretended to take no notice, but Fray Alejandro brooded much about the schisms that divided them. Not only did it cause great damage to their witness to the unconverted, but he needed Fray Benicio's assistance in the refectory, where by that time neophytes were dying every day.

Still, Alejandro understood the young friar's hesitance to remain under Guillermo's influence. The abbot's actions defied logic. The whippings, the insults, the deliberate affronts to native customs . . . all of it seemed most unwise to Alejandro. Although awareness of his sacred vow of obedience filled him with misgivings, he had begun to think of writing to the Padre Presidente of all California missions to suggest perhaps Fray Guillermo might better serve the Holy Father in some other capacity.

Then, on the middle Sunday of the Lenten season, Fray Alejandro saw the Indian's strange sparkling hair as the man exited through the gate. Perhaps it was Fray Alejandro's exhaustion, having slept no more than three hours out of twenty-four in many days, or perhaps it was something less easily explained, but suddenly all thought of other obligations vanished as his mind became consumed with one thought only: he had to speak to the mysterious man.

The friar set out in pursuit. Once beyond the mission's gate, he glimpsed the neophyte just as he disappeared behind a stand of low mesquite. He followed. Beyond the mesquite lay still more of the low-lying trees. Alejandro paused and heard the sound of movement straight ahead. On he went.

In this manner the gentle friar trailed the Indian for almost an hour. Sometimes he went a league or more without seeing or hearing the man, who seemed to travel with deliberate purpose although to Alejandro's knowledge nothing but wilderness lay ahead. They reached a canyon where the land inclined more steeply. Breathing became difficult. Soon Alejandro was climbing, gripping bushes, searching out small level places for his sandals.

He reached a kind of gully carved into the hillside by centuries of downward-rushing water. There the going was a little easier. He moved from rock to rock, glancing upward often. Occasionally he caught glimpses of the man above. Usually, he did not.

Alejandro climbed as quickly as he could, and once atop the hill he looked down the far side. Below was a stand of sycamores. He saw the Indian moving toward them with the same determined, steady gait. Alejandro began to scramble down the hill. He reached the valley floor. He heard the sycamore leaves rattling listlessly in the breeze. A narrow trail of stones along the ground beside him, white and round like skulls, marked the course of a dry creek.

In the shade of the grove where he had expected to find the Indian, Fray Alejandro saw nothing. He hurried between the sycamores and on along the valley floor beside the winding creek. On his left and right the hills rose very steeply. The way between the hills was serpentine, with one slope pressing forward to conceal the valley floor beyond, and then the opposite side asserting itself back again the other way, the creek turning now left, now right, the view ahead never clear for more than a few hundred yards. All along the valley floor, on the hillsides, and in places farthest from the creek the plants stood parched in tans and grays, with a rare hint of olive green.

Closer to the creek the ugly friar saw more verdant life. Small red flowers balanced on delicate stems about hip-high. The petals like tiny splatter patterns, as if heaven had rained drops of scarlet paint. Another type of flower clung to even longer stalks, the coral-colored blossoms shaped like trumpets, the blooms so unexpected in that arid place, so distracting, that Alejandro became lost in contemplation of their rarity. Thus the friar was quite surprised to step around a boulder and find a crowd of people gathered down below him in a clearing.

Immediately the Franciscan knelt behind a dead *nopal,* or prickly pear cactus, its gray and lifeless pads a perfect match for the color of his robe. From the concealment of that vantage point he saw perhaps seventy Indians. A few wore the familiar sackcloth garments of the mission but most were quite naked, both neophytes and pagans gathered there together in pursuit of some mutual interest.

Alejandro's arrival had gone unnoticed because all were on their knees facing away from him, all except one man and one woman who stood gazing deeply at each other, and between those two another man, who was Fray Benicio. The young friar spoke loudly in Latin, the familiar liturgy of the Eucharist borne up to Alejandro by a gentle breeze.

Before Benicio and the standing couple was a large rock on which a cloth was draped as if it were a credence table. On the cloth were several objects, which Alejandro recognized as the silver chalice, paten, and ciborium from the mission chapel. The abbot would be furious to learn Benicio had brought such treasures to that place, yet in combination with Fray Benicio's words the sacred objects could only mean one thing: the young friar had somehow managed to convert a crowd of pagans from the village, who, although indecently exposed, nonetheless knelt reverently before the blood and body of the Christ. Alejandro rejoiced to see so many former pagans there in celebration of the Holy Mass, yet for reasons he did not completely understand the homely friar remained in hiding.

He watched as Fray Benicio led the recent converts through the embolism, fraction, and commingling. Then, guided by the few garbed neophytes among them, the naked crowd attempted the Agnus Dei, their mispronunciation rendering the ancient words completely unintelligible. Compelled by a lifetime of habit, Alejandro found himself whispering along with the others, "Lamb of God, who takes away the sins of the world, have mercy upon us."

As was right and proper, Alejandro pondered his transgressions while reciting the words. His thoughts turned to where he was supposed to be: not out in the wilderness, but in the refectory giving solace to the sick and dying. The faces of the suffering rose within his mind.

He was overwhelmed with guilt. Who was caring for them while he hid there like a coward? To whom would they turn for cooling cloths that day, or for a few drops of water on chapped lips? He had left them in their misery, abandoned them for hours without a thought, merely to follow a strange Indian, merely because of curiosity.

The moment for Communion came, and Alejandro almost rose to go among the people and receive it, for who there needed that reminder of forgiveness more than him? But before Alejandro thus betrayed himself, he saw Fray Benicio do a strange thing. The young friar spoke to the standing man and woman. At his instruction they moved close together, clasped hands, and turned to face the kneeling congregation. Alejandro frowned. This was not part of the liturgy. Was it some kind of wedding Mass?

At first the ugly friar blushed to see the woman's nakedness alongside the man's, but his embarrassment was forgotten when Fray Benicio removed the cover from the ciborium and poured its contents onto the silver paten with complete abandon, instead of gently placing each wafer of the Host upon the plate with reverent respect. Then, as Alejandro watched with horror, the young Franciscan raised the paten high above the standing couple's heads and spilled the precious body of the Savior down upon them. It was a sacrilege beyond imagination, yet what fell was not the Host at all, but only a small cascade of grain, caught up in the couple's tangled hair and tracing every aspect of their naked flesh as it tumbled to the earth.

Without a thought for stealth, Alejandro rose up from his hiding place behind the dead *nopal* and fled. Nobody followed. He spent hours wandering alone, pondering what he had seen: the Eucharist corrupted, the stolen grain in Benicio's possession. Eventually he found the dry arroyo and traced it to the mission, arriving just in time for vespers prayers.

To Fray Alejandro's amazement, Benicio awaited him within the chapel alongside Fray Guillermo. On the credence table was the Communion service, the same silver chalice, paten, and ciborium he had seen corrupted in the wilderness. The young man nodded to him as if nothing blasphemous had happened. Fray Guillermo began prayers the instant Alejandro entered, so he had no time to tell the abbot of Benicio's offense. Throughout their prayers Alejandro cast covert glances at the offending friar, ashamed that he had ever thought of taking Fray Benicio's side against their abbot. After the transgressions he had seen, Alejandro was eager to condemn the young friar as a heretic.

When the prayers were over, Fray Guillermo said, "If either of you would make your confession you will find me waiting." Alejandro paused, giving Fray Benicio one last chance to repent of his blasphemous behavior. When neither of them moved, the abbot continued, "Make haste, brothers, for I am told the sick have suffered long today without our care."

Only then did Alejandro's own transgressions return to memory. So concerned had he been about Benicio's offense, so convinced of his own superiority, the ugly friar had yet again forgotten his sacred duty to the sick and dying. Thus disgraced, he quickly made his confession, did his penance, and left the chapel for the refectory. He said nothing about Benicio's transgressions in the clearing.

As Alejandro crossed the moonlit plaza, he considered what a fickle virtue is humility. In the moment we achieve it, we are overcome by pride in our achievement. Countless others since that night have been caught within that very trap. Consider, for example, Tucker Rue, as he walked from a bus stop to the campus of Grace Tabernacle. Before the founder of Sanctuario stood a vast complex of princely structures: office buildings, classroom buildings, a gymnasium and indoor pool, freestanding chapels, and, of course, the massive auditorium humbly called a "sanctuary" by the wealthy Christians who had built it with a mere one-tenth of their income. Behind him was a bus ride necessary because he could not afford gas for his truck, and a mission built to feed and clothe and sanctify the poor, a mission which in the last two years had become more impoverished than the poor it served.

As Tucker trod a winding path between two buildings (ivy-covered monuments to misused blessings, in his estimation), a smug superiority overcame his mood. He thought of Jesus Christ, who had no place to lay his head. He thought of himself in much the same condition. Then he realized what his thoughts implied: the vanity required to compare oneself favorably with Jesus. He begged forgiveness. Secure in God's infinite charity, he enjoyed a fleeting moment of authentic piety, but upon turning round a corner and beholding a new gymnasium built from tithes that might have fed the poor, his indignation rose again and once more his humble circumstances seemed superior to those whom he had traveled there to see.

At last he found the proper building. The entry, trimmed in hand-carved limestone and guarded by a pair of richly paneled mahogany doors, did little to assist him in his struggle against condescending pride. Carrying a small black portfolio in his right hand, Tucker shook his head and entered.

A pleasant woman seated at a lovely antique desk offered him warm greetings. On the wall behind her was a famous image of Jesus washing Peter's feet. Tucker looked more closely, and realized it was probably the original. A large crystal chandelier hung from a shallow dome in the ceiling of the room. On the floor across from the antique desk lay a huge Persian rug, and around the rug stood a group of brown leather chairs and sofas. Pale yellow stone clad the floor itself and the lower portion of the walls. Tucker had once been told the stone was from a quarry near Jerusalem.

The woman offered coffee, which he declined.

"Are you sure?" she asked. "It's freshly ground French roast."

Of course it is, he thought. Something from a can would never do. But he only smiled and said again, "No, thank you."

There was a delay. He did not own a wristwatch, but he was sure it was at least fifteen minutes past the time of his appointment when an interior door opened and a man walked out. He was a minister of Tucker's acquaintance, a man who led a Tustin storefront mission similar to Sanctuario.

"Hello, Robby," said Tucker, rising.

"What? Oh, hello," said the fellow without slowing.

"Were they hard on you in there?"

"Just you wait."

The man walked out through the ornately paneled doors. Sitting down again on the leather sofa, Tucker Rue crossed his legs and watched the pleasant woman remove a small metal box from a desk drawer. She opened it to sort through a stack of money—petty cash, apparently—until she found a roll of stamps. She then began to affix the stamps one by one to a tall stack of envelopes, being very careful to align them properly. Tucker kept count as she did this, and had nearly reached three hundred letters before the inner door opened again and a man he knew slightly came out to shake his hand.

"Good to see you, Reverend," said Bill Miller .

"It's good to be back, Mr. Miller." Tucker thought it best to be polite. He had just remembered the man was a partner in a major L.A. law firm.

"Like I tell you every year at this time, you can call me Bill." He wore his hair long on one side and combed it over his bald head. His broad smile revealed a full set of very large white teeth. Clearly they were false. Leading Tucker toward the inner door, the man said, "Sorry we kept you waiting. Our last meeting went a little long."

They passed down a hallway and entered a conference room, richly appointed in dark wood paneling and leather. Eleven other men rose from their seats around a long table with a marble top. Most of them he remembered from years past. These were the usual gatekeepers of Grace Tabernacle's huge benevolence fund. Bankers, lawyers, and real estate developers. The senior pastor was also there, and Tucker felt his usual irrational surprise that the man looked just like his image in the media, yet up close he also seemed very normal.

When Tucker saw Delano Wright sitting at the table he felt his hopes for Sanctuario begin to fade, but of course he smiled and shook hands with everybody anyway. He unzipped the small black portfolio and began passing out his documents, walking around the table, giving a copy to each man.

"I thought you'd all be interested in this brief outline of Sanctuario's progress this past year. As you know, we've had to cut back on a few programs because money has been tight, but under the circumstances I think you'll agree we managed to accomplish a lot since the last time we met. If you look at the second paragraph, you'll see we added three more classes of English as a second language and we were able to continue our after-school tutoring, which has always been a great benefit to the community since there are so many working mothers. Unfortunately, we did have to stop offering the light snacks we were giving to our kids every day, but I'm hoping you'll be able—"

"Um, Reverend Rue," interrupted Arnold O'Connor, a slender, gray-haired man who wore gold cuff links. As Tucker recalled, he owned a chain of Mercedes-Benz dealerships. "We appreciate your preparation, but since we ran a little long on our last meeting, I wonder if I might make a suggestion?"

"Sure," said Tucker Rue, settling into his seat.

"Thank you. Um, some things have happened at Grace, which you might not know about. Del here has brought a new opportunity to us that, frankly, um, he's just about left everybody speechless. Could we just fill you in before you go over your presentation?"

Tucker felt his mouth go dry. He ran his tongue around to separate his teeth and gums. "All right."

"Great. That will save some time." O'Connor shifted in his seat. "You know about the development over on Blanco Canyon Road, of course. What you don't know is the details of Del's latest proposal. We'd like to share them with you, but first I need to ask for your word that you'll keep this conversation confidential."

"Okay. . . ."

"Thanks. We appreciate that. Um, the thing is, Del's idea means we need to make some changes here. All in all, I think you'll agree the changes are for the best, but it's going to be a little painful in the short term."

"Painful?" said Tucker.

"Well, difficult. Let's put it that way."

"What are we talking about, exactly?"

"An investment in the future. You know about the land Del donated, and about the church developing the land, paying for the actual development, the construction of the streets and utilities. That costs a lot of money, of course, which is why we've had to cut back on our support for Sanctuario a little the last couple of years."

"Seventy-five percent," said Tucker.

"Yes, that's right. Of course, with sales on the first phase coming in, we were planning to bump that up a little this year, as we discussed the last time you were here. But Del has this new proposition. Up to now we've only been participating in the sale of the land out there at New Harmony, but he just offered to let us get involved in the houses on the phase two. So what this means, Grace Tabernacle would actually be getting all the profits on everything from here on out. Land and houses both. Isn't that amazing?"

"Amazing," said Tucker flatly.

"Well, yes, we sure think so. It means down the road, there'll be no limits on our ability to fund mission work like yours."

"Down the road?"

"Um, it's going to take a while to get to the sales phase on the next stage. And of course with the added expense of building houses—the contractors would actually be working for us, you understand—um, that means even after reinvesting what's been earned so far we'll have to join forces with other churches in the area to raise what we need. We should be able to borrow most of it, but even the down payment will be substantial. Um, very substantial."

"So you're going to cut back on donations again?"

Arnold O'Connor adjusted his cuffs. "I'm afraid so. But only for the next twelve months, Reverend. Eighteen months at the outside. After that, Del's pro forma shows us getting to the, um, the advance sales on phase two, and the money should start coming in. Lots and lots of money."

Most of the men around the table smiled, although Tucker thought two or three of them looked uncomfortable.

"Grace Tabernacle used to be our biggest donor." Tucker's hands clenched into fists. He moved them underneath the table. "Two years ago you cut that back by half, and last year you cut it by half again. What's it going to be this year? Another cut in half?"

"Um, I'm afraid we won't be able to help Sanctuario this year."

"Nothing? You're giving *nothing*? You're going to spend it all on real estate?"

Bill Miller, the lawyer from L.A., leaned forward to say, "It's not about real estate, Tucker. It's about securing a future for the community. Once this deal is done, we should be able to double our original level of support for Sanctuario. Maybe even triple it. And the money will still be coming in to help Sanctiario long after all of us are dead and gone."

"I don't see how you're getting away with it."

Bill Miller frowned. "Getting away with it?"

"Yeah. What about the Fair Housing Act, or whatever they call it? How come the government is letting you build a Christians-only development?"

"Oh, I see what you mean. Yes, I wondered about that too. But speaking as an attorney, I can tell you Del and his people have thought that through pretty well."

Arnold O'Connor said, "You know, a couple of the new guys here haven't heard this part of it yet. Um, why don't you give us the top end on your strategy, Del?"

Delano Wright cleared his throat. "Okay. We couldn't legally exclude anyone on the basis of religion. Tucker's correct on that. So we solved the problem in other ways. We're giving the streets names like 'Ephesians Avenue,' and we have neighborhoods called 'The Way,' 'The Truth,' 'The Life,' and so forth, with those names carved in stone or etched in brass on the gated entry signage. We're building pocket parks with benches and fountains inscribed with New Testament verses. We're also putting Bible verses on access cards and chiseling them into fireplace mantels in the houses built on spec. We even carve them into the front doors. Of course, by now everybody knows about the three crosses we're building on Camel Mountain. The middle one will be so tall you can see it from the beach. We're surrounding all the neighborhoods with greenbelts that have walking trails and secluded places specifically identified for prayer. We require cable and satellite TV providers to scramble pornographic stations in return for doing business in the community and we have bylaws forbidding the sale of alcohol in stores. Schoolchildren are required to wear modest uniforms. We also have enforceable bylaws against public profanity, lewd behavior, and so forth."

"There still has to be a separation of church and state," said Tucker.

"True. But the state isn't involved in this. We modeled the plan on other private communities around the country, which are owned by corporations. The entire community is a corporate asset. So there's no government involved, and we don't have to worry about the Establishment Clause of the First Amendment. The Woodlands north of Houston started out kind of like this. So did Gleneagle in Colorado."

Looking away from Delano Wright, sickened by the sight of him, Tucker addressed his question to Arnold O'Connor. "What was that you said about joining forces with other churches?"

"Well, because the next phase is so much bigger with the houses added in, Del thought, and we agree, it's necessary to bring in some sister churches as partners in this thing."

Delano Wright leaned forward. "We're donating shares in the corporation to area churches in return for pledges to raise the necessary seed money for initial planning, fees, and infrastructure development."

"Basically, you're going to build a town and let the churches run it."

Del nodded. "Exactly." He sat back and stared at Tucker. "With everything I just described, we won't have many undesirables interested in living there, and with the level of security we have in mind, they won't be getting in to prey on the good people of the community."

Tucker swallowed. "Which other churches are involved?"

"I can answer that," said Bill Miller. He reached for a paper on the table before him and read several church names aloud.

"Every major donor I have is on that list," said Tucker.

For the first time, the famous pastor spoke. "The whole body of Christ is going to demonstrate its unity on this thing, Tucker. We're really excited about that."

"What about Sanctuario? Aren't we part of the body?"

"Of course you are. And don't think for a second we aren't proud to work with you, side by side."

"But you won't support us."

The pastor leaned forward, placing both arms on the table, looking Tucker directly in the eye. "Certainly we will. Our prayer ministry has always considered Sanctuario a priority. That's not going to change. And anytime you need hands and hearts over there, all you have to do is call. We'll send all the volunteers you can handle."

"I appreciate that. But you promised us more money this year."

"We didn't know Del was going to up the ante on this thing, Tucker. You have to understand, our financial resources are limited. Big as Grace has become, we still have to operate according to a budget. And Del's ministry here, well, it's going to consume pretty much all of our benevolence fund until it's off the ground."

"Off the ground? That means until you start those advance sales on phase two Mr. O'Connor was talking about?"

"Exactly."

"But he said that won't be for twelve or eighteen months! We'll have to close our doors a long time before then!"

The pastor sat back. "Come on, Tucker. You have more faith than that. The Lord will provide."

"What if he was planning to provide through you guys? I have sick children, hungry children, who need help right now."

"There's one thing I've learned as the Lord has built up Grace, and that is we always need to be ready to follow the Lord wherever he might lead. We make plans, and God laughs, as they say. This might be the Lord's way of telling you he has other plans for you and all those folks over there."

"Yes," said Delano Wright, still staring at Tucker. "He might want those folks to go back home."

Several men at the table shifted in their seats and looked down at their hands.

The pastor frowned. "Well, now, Del, I wouldn't go that far."

"Why not? They're breaking the law by being here. Since when do Christians help criminals break the law?"

Tucker's hands clenched into fists. He thought of Lupe, obviously illegal, and yet part of Delano's household for years. He wanted to ask the old hypocrite, Since when do Christians do one thing and say another? But he managed to restrain himself. He only said, "So that's what this is really all about? The immigration thing?"

The pastor said, "Absolutely not. You know we've always had a few who questioned some of your programs over there, but I stood up for Sanctuario. In fact, Del and I have a little disagreement about that. Right, Del?"

Delano Wright smiled. "We do until I change your mind."

Several people chuckled uncomfortably as the pastor continued. "This is not about the nature of your ministry, Tucker. It's just plain economics. Del tells us we have a limited window to raise the necessary funds. He needs every penny of our discretionary budget to go into this thing if it's going to work."

Tucker returned Delano Wright's stare. "Every penny?"

Without blinking, Delano bared his teeth. "That's the plan."

Tucker rose. He gathered up his papers and put them in his small black portfolio.

"The Lord will provide, Tucker," said the pastor. "You'll see."

"Yes," said Tucker. "I'm sure he will."

Bill Miller showed him out. In the hallway near the entry, Tucker felt a sudden wave of nausea. With a mumbled good-bye, he turned into the restroom, where he dropped his portfolio onto the marble lavatory counter and hurried to a toilet stall. There he knelt and waited, but although sweat rolled off his forehead and drool came from his lips, the nausea subsided. Eventually he rose and pulled some toilet paper from the roll and wiped his mouth.

Back outside the stall, he bent over the lavatory and splashed cold water on his face. He looked up into the mirror and tried to think of how he would tell his people. He thought of the woman who had come with Lupe, the one with the sick daughter who might die without her medicine. The nausea came again, in a violent rush this time, and he barely made it back into the toilet stall before his stomach emptied.

Kneeling before the toilet, Tucker thought, Lord, how can this be your will?

Of course he knew the answer. The Lord willed nothing of the kind. This was the will of powerful, greedy men who saw a chance to grab more power. It was the will of a bitter and vindictive father who could not let his daughter go, who felt he had to strike back at someone. The Lord had nothing to do with this. The Lord opposed it. The Lord hated everything about it, just as Tucker did.

He returned to the sink and ran some cold water, cupping his hand to take it into his mouth. He swished it around and spat it out, but the sour taste remained. He washed his hands. He removed a paper towel from the dispenser and thought about the little girl with the high fever. He removed another paper towel and thought about her vacant, hopeless eyes, then he removed another paper towel and thought about those fat white money changers in that conference room. Suddenly Lupe's lovely face was there before him. He thought of the entreaty in her eyes, of her purity of heart as she implored him to help the girl, and his shame as he confessed he had no money. He removed another paper towel, and another, and another, until he was pulling out the paper towels faster and faster, throwing them to the floor, on and on until the last one came and there was nothing left for his frantic hands to do except to beat upon the empty steel dispenser until his knuckles bled.

Tucker walked out of the restroom. He turned left and followed the hall to the door that opened to the entry area. Passing through, he saw the leather furniture where he had waited, and the lovely antique desk where the pleasant woman had greeted him. No one sat upon the furniture, and the woman was not at her place behind the desk. Alone in the light of the crystal chandelier, he crossed toward the paneled mahogany entry doors. He paused. He looked up at the image of Jesus on his knees before Peter, the original oil painting on the wall behind the desk, and he considered the humility it represented, the sacrifice, the willingness to do anything for the sake of love. He looked down and saw the stack of envelopes still on the desk, and the bright red, white, and blue of the American flag on the stamps. He turned and walked behind the desk.

Tucker bent to open a drawer. He removed the small metal box. He set it on the desktop. He thought about the carpet in the hallway on the far side of the interior door, how soft it was, the way it muffled footsteps, how he would not hear her coming, how that door could open any instant and she would find him there. He stood and listened for several minutes, staring at the metal box, listening for a reason to just walk away.

Finally, hearing nothing, he opened the box and removed the petty cash and counted out two hundred and twenty-three dollars, the exact amount needed for the little girl's medicine. He counted it again, getting blood from his knuckles on the paper money. He did not hurry. He wanted to be sure he did not take a single dollar more, or less. Then, when he had replaced the rest of the petty cash, Tucker Rue left the church.

CAPÍTULO 21

SHORTLY BEFORE EASTER, FRAY GUILLERMO ordered the leather-jackets to dig a mass grave near the bottom of the hill below the mission. Benicio protested, demanding that the dead continue to be placed in consecrated soil. When Guillermo refused this as impractical, their argument became terrible to witness. Fray Alejandro understood the abbot's reasoning. The raging disease had left too many dead. There was no more space within the chapel cemetery. But in spite of Alejandro's disgust at Benicio's corruption of the wedding Mass, he also understood the young friar's outrage. The dead neophytes were Christians. They deserved a sacred resting place.

The abbot's views prevailed, of course, and Don Felipe set his soldiers to work with picks and shovels in a clearing far below the mission walls. They dug until they could no longer see over the edges of the pit. Its length and breadth were large enough to hold at least a hundred bodies.

"There are but sixteen we must bury," observed Fray Benicio. "Do we truly need a grave of such proportions?"

"Not now," replied Fray Alejandro, remembering the empty houses of his childhood island home, the wagons stacked with corpses, the warships circling offshore to enforce quarantine. "But we may soon wish it even bigger."

That night after compline Alejandro lay awake within his little cell. He turned this way and that, perpetually discomforted by grief for the dead and dying. He thought of the pit beyond the mission walls, and wondered if the bodies it contained would decompose in that dry climate. He thought of spreading lye among the dead to speed the process, but it would be impossible to leach the lye in time, so quickly were the people falling prey to the disease. The friar rolled over in his bed, his grief replaced by worry. He tried to take some comfort from the fact that Don Felipe's men had dug deep.

A beam of moonlight angled through the single window high above his cot. It settled on his failure, the unfinished altarpiece. Staring at the empty wooden panels which he should have finished long ago, Alejandro heard his abbot's voice arise in anger elsewhere on the mission grounds, and then Benicio's reply. The good friar sighed. His brothers were again in conflict, probably about their activities that day: a single requiem Mass for all sixteen of the dead who had then been laid within the pit and covered by a mere handsbreadth of unconsecrated soil in order to leave room above for other bodies sure to come. Or perhaps the friars had found some new reason to contend against each other.

As the gentle Alejandro listened to their shouts, he wondered if the Misión de Santa Dolores might survive the pestilence which stalked it, only to succumb to his Franciscan brothers' mindless antipathy. Each accused the other of the very things they feared within themselves. Alejandro thought of Fray Guillermo's bleeding back and of Fray Benicio's corruption of the Mass. Both concealed dark secrets, and every secret between Christians was a shackle, every hidden thing an obstacle to unity. For his part, Alejandro carried his own secret: the secrets of his brothers. What they could not say divided them; what they dared not show they covered until fear and loneliness prevailed. Alejandro sensed his isolation in that most remote of Spanish outposts as he never had before.

In much the same way secrets had become an enemy to Ramón Rodríguez. For more than two years he had struggled to conceal his memories of a stranger burning in a car, a woman scarred forever, and a friend flung to his death. Then, just as he began to move beyond those horrors, Lobo's watery slide had come, and the earth itself, alive with bones, had reawakened his worst nightmares. Those secrets were his prison, and everyone he hid them from, a jailer.

It was like the early days again, like when he had first arrived. Now, as then, he feared his neighbors in the streets, the men who paid his wages, and the strangers on the bus and in the store. One slip of the tongue, one person who could read the secrets in his eyes, and he would be undone. He spoke no more than necessary. He looked directly at no one. He spent his days in careful maintenance of the very barriers he hated. He merely had to save three thousand dollars more and there would be enough to buy the restaurant in Hércules. How he longed to cast away his bondage! How foolish he had been to travel to this horrific land! He dreamed of going back through time, of living with Raquel and the boys in Hércules, in that gentle place before these awful walls arose, when he had been happy in his poverty and ignorant of secrets. But a secret once discovered cannot be abandoned; it can only be maintained or revealed. Desperate to avoid a revelation, Ramón Rodríguez maintained his secrets carefully, as did Trini, Paco, and Fernando.

It seemed Lobo did not share their discipline. He was instead inconsolable. Convinced he had been shown a vision of his future in that boneyard where he landed, an image of the punishment awaiting him in hell, Lobo made confession constantly, as if his friends were priests. Had he not killed their dear friend Felix and that gringa woman in his drunkenness? Yes, yes, yes, he acknowledged now that he had sinned an awful sin and surely deserved punishment. At his friends' insistence he had arisen from the pit that dreadful night, but he allowed no hand to touch him. He had stumbled to the bus stop on the canyon road and ridden home in morbid silence, muddy, dripping, nostrils filled with death. He was not among them anymore. He would take no absolution. He was a corpse upon the earth.

Deep into that dreadful night, his friends had tried to offer comfort. "It was only a cemetery," said Trini, sitting on a plastic chair. "An old one, which was lost. It has nothing to do with you, Lobo."

"Correct!" said Paco. "A few lost graves. It happens all the time."

Lobo sat with red-rimmed downcast eyes, alone inside his thoughts. Ramón too was silent.

It seemed Fernando would be Lobo's inquisitor. He said, "The bodies were not orderly, as they would be in a cemetery. They were mixed, all in a tangle."

"An earthquake shook them up," offered Trini.

Paco nodded. "That makes sense."

Fernando shook his head. "If they were bouncing on the surface, yes, an earthquake might explain it. But they were buried in the ground. How could any earthquake twist them while they remained packed within the earth?"

"And there were no coffins," said Ramón.

"That is true," replied Fernando.

"Are you trying to make our friend suffer?" asked Paco.

"I am sorry, Lobo," said Fernando. "I do not think it was a cemetery, but I also do not think you have been cursed."

"In that case, what do you think?" asked Rámon.

Fernando shook his head. "I do not know."

"It is God's condemnation," said Lobo. Then he rose and went to bed.

The morning after their dread discovery had dawned bright and dry. In the kitchen of their dwelling place, Trini, Paco, and Fernando encouraged Lobo to return with them to work.

"You need not worry about seeing it again," said Fernando. "That area has been abandoned. The *patrón* told us so himself."

"The *patrón* talked to you?" asked Lobo.

"It is true," said Paco. "Long ago he said we were digging in the wrong place, and sent us to the top of the hill."

An idea came to Ramón. "Do you think he knew about the dead, and moved you for that reason?"

Everyone fell silent. It was a question they had not considered until then. The answer was impossible to know.

"In any case," said Ramón at last, "Lobo will see it. We must pass by there when we come and go."

"No," replied Fernando. "We will take the long way around."

"Truly?"

"Of course. I do not wish to see it either."

Paco and Trini nodded solemnly.

"Will we tell someone?" asked Ramón, fearful of another weighty secret.

Again, all considered his question in silence. Then Fernando said, "I do not think it would be wise."

"There would be police," agreed Paco.

"Let them find it themselves, as we did," added Trini. "Why give them a reason to notice us?"

"They will never find it," said Ramón. "It is only bad luck that we did."

"It was God's will," mumbled Lobo. "A curse."

Ramón rested a palm upon Lobo's shoulder. "I do not think it is a curse, my friend. But I feel bad, letting those people lie there."

"Why?" asked Fernando. "They are dead and do not care."

"No one should be forgotten as they are."

"God has not forgotten," replied Fernando.

"Of course not," said Lobo. "God put them there, as he will me."

Ramón spoke to him. "If you do not want to go, I will stay with you."

"No," said Lobo. "I must make a little money in my final days. My family depends on it."

So it had been decided. They all went to work as usual that morning, and the next, and the morning after that, and so on for almost two weeks.

Ramón's obsession with their secret grew with every day that passed, until he thought of little but his fear of its release, the Anglos learning of the death that followed him, the curse he had encountered in their country. He knew it was not good to dwell on such possibilities. He tried to discipline his mind to think of other things.

Then Lobo became ill.

Fernando told them Lobo had caused the malady himself. His constant thoughts of judgment and disaster had called it forth. It was only psychological, said the wise Fernando, and would soon pass when Lobo realized he had simply caught the flu.

Ignoring this, certain he was dying, Lobo would not stay behind, but went with them out to the project in the hills. He wished to send a little money to his family in Puebla before he perished, so they would remember him with fondness.

"Lobo, my good friend," said Fernando as they left the duplex where they lived. "Please take no offense when I say you are a fool. You have a fever and a headache. You are very tired. You say your back is hurting. Stay in bed and sleep. Take some aspirin. We will bring you soup and crackers for your dinner. Let this flu pass by, and then you can return to work."

But Lobo would not listen.

At the job site in the hills that day, Ramón and Fernando were directed to the north while the boss sent Paco, Trini, and Lobo to the south. Soon after they separated, Ramón looked back. In the distance he saw Paco and some others following the road, with Lobo far behind, leaning heavily upon his shovel like an old man with a walking stick. Then a sudden wind stirred up the dust, and he could not see them anymore.

It was another hot and dry day in the hills. There had been no more rain; in fact, all signs of moisture in the soil had quickly vanished in the heat.

Fernando and Ramón were told to stack stones for a low retaining wall. Ramón enjoyed the work. It was like a puzzle. Among a pile of stones that had been dumped nearby, he sought the perfect shapes to fill the gaps within the rising wall. He took pride in the flatness of the wall's sides and top. He forgot his secrets for a while.

Then it was time for lunch. In the slender shade of a yellow earthmover he and Fernando sat apart from the other laborers, with their backs to a huge tire and their legs extended out into the sun. Ramón recalled a day in Mexico, many years before, when he had sat beneath a mesquite tree with his legs out in the sunshine, a day when he had helped a beetle pass and met the woman he would later burn. He and Fernando ate the sandwiches they had brought in paper bags, and drank ice water from a large orange thermos which had been provided by the company. In another time they would have discussed football, or the strange habits of Americanos, or the latest news from their families back home, but that day neither man desired to speak.

At the proper moment they arose to resume their work upon the wall, building it higher stone by stone. Time passed quickly. Evening approached. Ramón and Fernando and the others in their work crew began the long walk down the hill. When they reached the job trailer, the men turned in their hard hats and their safety vests. All the others set out for their cars and trucks, or the bus stop by the canyon road, but Ramón and Fernando sat down to wait for Paco, Trini, and Lobo. Eventually their friends appeared on the southern road where it came over a hill. Ramón saw them first, silhouetted against the dimming sky, the three of them abreast.

"There they are," he said.

Fernando only grunted. Even he, the wisest of them, had become taciturn with secrets.

As their friends approached, Ramón sat up straighter. "That does not look good."

Fernando turned, saw what Ramón meant, and uttered a quiet curse. "I told the fool to stay at home. You heard me."

"Yes. You did."

Lobo hung between Paco and Trini, his arms around their shoulders, his legs and feet trying to keep up, but often dragging back behind, his face turned downward toward the soil. The two smaller men clung to him, one on either side, with arms around his waist. When they reached the job trailer, they lowered Lobo to the ground beside Ramón and Fernando and went to return their hats and vests.

"I told you to stay home," said Fernando.

Lobo lay quietly, saying nothing.

"How long has he been like this?" asked Ramón.

"He sat down before lunch and did not stand again," replied Trini.

"Was he in the shade?" asked Fernando.

"Yes. There was a big rock."

"Well. At least he was in the shade."

Ramón stood up. "Come on," he said to Fernando. "It's our turn."

Grumbling, Fernando rose and stooped to help Ramón lift up their friend. "I told him," said Fernando.

"Yes," replied Ramón. "You did."

To avoid the dreadful secret and the climb over the hill, they did not take the shortcut, but walked the long way around to the canyon road. From there it was about a mile up to the bus stop. They moved slowly on the shoulder of the road.

"If a policeman comes, he will think Lobo is drunk," said Paco.

"Yes, that is very possible," said Fernando.

"What should we do if a policeman stops?"

"Run, of course."

"What about Lobo?" asked Ramón.

"I told him not to come."

"You are very wise," said Ramón. "But will we leave him here?"

"What else? The police would give us to La Migra, and they would deport us."

They walked a little farther, with Lobo's weight fully upon them. Ramón said, "Sometimes I think it would be best to be deported."

"What about your family? Your restaurant? Do you have enough money now?"

"No," replied Ramón. "It is just a thing I think sometimes."

"Listen, Paco," said Fernando. "You and Trini take this fellow for a while."

Ramón and Fernando paused to transfer the burden of the sick man to their younger friends, and then they all set out again. Their shadows were long upon the gravel shoulder of the road. Finally they reached the bench beside the little bus-stop sign. The upper fringes of the hills glowed orange in the horizontal sunlight. They lowered Lobo to the bench. He sagged to one side, but Fernando sat down to hold him up. Fernando said, "The driver will not take us if he looks too drunk."

Ramón was very tired. His fingers curled upon themselves with an independent memory of the stones that he had lifted. He tried to straighten them, but it was painful. At last the bus arrived with squealing brakes, its windows casting bright fluorescent light into the fading canyon.

The four friends boarded, furtively gripping Lobo's belt and shirt to hold him up, and doing their best to disguise his illness by moving close around him. If the driver noticed, he did not care. They passed many people, mostly other Latinos, as they walked back to the middle by the other door, where they could all disembark in Wilson City without walking down the central aisle again. Lobo fell into a seat beside a window and slouched against the wall. Ramón dropped into the seat beside him. No one said anything as the bus pulled away, rumbling eastward up the canyon.

Ramón tried to look outside, but it was not possible to see the passing hills beyond the windows, so strong was the reflection from the interior lights. Instead, he saw himself as if looking in a mirror. At first he thought it was a stranger in the glass. He absorbed the sight on a level beyond words, as people do when they first meet. The man he saw looked thinner than his self-conception, and more exhausted than he felt, with sunken, nervous eyes that did not seem to open up into him. It startled Ramón when he realized who that person was.

He wondered, if Raquel came on board the bus, would she know him? The boys would not, for they had been too young when he left Mexico, and he had only managed to send one set of photographs to his family in all the years since then. Ramón looked away from his reflection. He felt embarrassed, as if he had been caught staring at a person with a handicap, a deformity of some kind. His eyes fell to Lobo, riding on the seat beside him, undulating slightly with the motion of the bus, eyes closed, head lolling, both hands in his lap, palms up. Ramón saw something on his palms. He leaned closer. On the flesh were many tiny dots of red, a rash of some kind.

Ramón sat back and closed his eyes. Did people with the flu develop rashes? He did not recall. Perhaps he would ask Fernando later, when they were off the bus and the strangers all around them could not overhear.

CAPÍTULO 22

THE DAY AFTER EASTER, FRAY Guillermo discovered yet another theft of grain. He believed the culprit was a neophyte. When none of the recent converts would confess, he had Don Felipe select an Indian at random to be punished. The captain chose a young man, perhaps sixteen years of age. The neophyte was forced to stand with wrists and neck restrained by a pillory which had been hastily erected in the plaza. The other neophytes were warned not to give him food or water. Any comfort offered to the prisoner would result in a dozen lashes.

On the second day of punishment, just before the hour of none prayers, Alejandro emerged from among the dying in the dark refectory to refill the water bucket. Passing by the prisoner on his way to the well, the homely friar could not fail to note the terrible effects of almost two days in the unrelenting sun. The neophyte trembled in the stocks, his unsteady legs barely able to support his weight, the wood which pressed into his throat choking him each time he tried to grant release to his calves and thighs.

While drawing water at the well, Alejandro observed Fray Benicio near a chapel buttress on the far side of the plaza. The young friar paced in the shade next to the tall adobe wall, sometimes pausing to observe the suffering prisoner, then stalking back and forth again, shaking his head and talking to himself with wild gesticulations. Alejandro believed he understood this strange behavior. While the abbot had assumed the ongoing thefts from their storehouse were the work of neophytes, Alejandro had not forgotten the shower of grain Benicio had poured from the Communion paten at the corrupted wedding Mass. He resolved to wait awhile beside the well, to see what Fray Benicio would do. Surely the young friar would not allow the neophyte to continue suffering for a crime he did not commit.

Five minutes passed, with Benicio clearly in the midst of torment. Ten minutes passed. Fifteen. Still the young friar made no move to aid the suffering Indian. After twenty minutes had gone by, Benicio ceased his pacing back and forth and strode into his cell. Alejandro resolved to wait a little longer. Shielding his eyes, he gazed at the narrow rectangle of shadow above Benicio's threshold. Then the young friar closed his door.

Alejandro dropped his hand from above his eyes. He sighed and shook his head. He drew water with a ladle made from a dried gourd and approached the suffering Indian.

"Drink," he said in the young man's native language. Then in Latin he continued, "And may God be with you."

"Captain!" shouted Fray Guillermo from somewhere nearby. "Restrain that man immediately!"

The ugly friar did not raise his eyes from the neophyte's cracked lips. He wanted to be sure the Indian received every drop of water, but before he could complete his task a leather-jacket's hands were on him. The gourd was knocked to the ground. Fully half of its precious contents flowed into the dirt.

Over the shouted protests of Benicio, and even Don Felipe's mild objections, Fray Guillermo instructed Alejandro to strip to the waist. His wrists were then tied to the corral's fence with leather straps. There Guillermo had Alejandro whipped a dozen times.

As the lash bit into his flesh, Fray Alejandro sought escape in memories, but even those betrayed him. Inexplicably he thought of golden seeds flowing down along a naked woman's body. Oh, how he wished Benicio had not planted such an image in his mind . . . not profaned the Eucharist in such a way! The pain of that memory was even greater than the lash.

It was as if his entire world had been corrupted. For Fray Alejandro the Holy Mass was the center of the universe. All creation was part of its liturgy. The earth and moon revolved; the seasons overtook each other; the oceans rose and fell and the newly born grew up to conceive newborns. Such eternal patterns lent their rhythms to his worship. They inspired and informed it. He hoped to model their perfection with the holy rite. Although the faith of some might falter, nature with its endless cycles never shrank from mirroring God's constant fidelity, and if the universe did not forget its duty, neither did Fray Alejandro, even in the midst of suffering. As the lash came down, the gentle friar whispered softly, "Precious Savior, may my unworthy blood be commingled with yours."

It is true the liturgy of Holy Mass had been celebrated without ceasing for centuries, celebrated with confidence that the praises offered by entire congregations would transcend the flaws of any one believer in their midst. The sacred Mass connects each Catholic in space and time, in every place around the world and in the past and present, therefore as Guadalupe Soledad Consuelo de la Garza took Communion in the sanctuary of St. Catherine of Siena, Wilson City's smallest church, she was joined unknowingly with Alejandro and the brothers who tormented him. Indeed, as the Sunday Mass in Wilson City neared completion, Lupe too was tormented. Her mind should have been upon the Lord, but she was occupied instead with thoughts of Delano Wright. Although he was a Protestant, she longed to help him find the harmony of Holy Mass, for it seemed to her that he had lost his balance and was in grave danger of a fall.

Just as Delano had sent Lupe away for the sake of appearances, so he had sought to banish every other hint of impropriety from his life. He had moved beyond files filled with newspaper clippings that documented people's sins. He had caused all television sets to be removed from his house. Recently he had emptied the wine cellar, pouring several hundred bottles down the drain, remnants of his ex-wife's presence. Before that he had sold three oil paintings and two sculptures, all of which displayed nude human figures, and given all the proceeds to his church.

These pious measures did not seem to well up from a place of inner peace. On the contrary, every righteous gesture only seemed to increase his misery. Lupe feared it would all lead to madness. She had feared it from the moment on the beach when she first laid eyes on Delano, from that instant with the sun at his back, when he had been framed by solar flares which shot out all around like fire erupting from the Presence of the Lord. Or more precisely, she had feared it from a moment later when his features had emerged from the glare and she saw him as he truly was, as a man among the mocking crowd.

She agreed with Delano in principle that sin was rising in America. It was the very reason she had come, to save as many as she could, but rather than curse evil she preferred to reverence good, which was of course one purpose of the Mass.

How Lupe wished she had the words to remind Delano that their Savior could always be trusted, just as the planets, waves, and seasons never faltered, just as the Mass remained the same. But what she felt, what she knew, she simply could not seem to speak aloud in ways that made a difference. For many years she had preached the gospel every Sunday afternoon at Blanco Beach, yet not one pagan had repented. Who was she to speak of God to a great man like Delano Wright, she, who had known only failure?

In the little sanctuary, Lupe heard Father Herrera say, "The Lord be with you." The Mass was coming to an end. With all the people, she replied, "And also with you," using someone else's ancient words.

"May Almighty God bless you, the Father, and the Son, and the Holy Spirit," said the priest.

"Amen," said Lupe.

"Go in the peace of Christ."

"Thanks be to God!"

Father Herrera smiled and slowly made the sign of the cross over the congregation as the Virgen de Guadalupe stood on the altar high behind him gazing from among the golden flames with her beatific smile, and the boys in the choir began to sing a Latin hymn, their voices clear and high and bouncing from the concrete sanctuary walls.

Lupe followed her neighbor to the end of the pew, where she turned toward the altar and knelt before her namesake. She crossed herself and rose again to leave. As always, she felt a sadness that the Mass was over, a sense of anticlimax.

Outside on the little concrete plaza the air was hot and dusty, like sandpaper in her nostrils. Children chased each other in the stark sunshine while their parents lingered in small groups before the church, talking and laughing. It was their best chance all week to catch up on the latest news, busy as they were on every other day with work in Blanco Beach or in the fields from dawn to dusk. A man and woman who had recently returned from Mexico stood among a small gathering of friends who peppered them with questions about the recent Mexican elections, the weather down there, the economy, and road conditions . . . anything to keep them talking about home. Lupe wished she could linger, but the noon bus left in fifteen minutes, and she had to get to Blanco Beach to preach as usual along the boardwalk.

She set out across the plaza. As she neared the street someone called, "Doña Lupe! Can you spare a moment?" Startled to find herself thusly addressed, she turned to find Carlota Vargas waving from a bench beneath a eucalyptus tree. Señora Vargas was a fat woman who wore only high-heeled shoes and never missed an opportunity to tell people that her daughter had married an Americano and held a union job with the telephone company. Beside her on the bench sat another woman whom Lupe had seen before at church, but never met. Lupe remembered the other woman because she wore her hair short like a man.

"What did you call me, Carlota?" asked Lupe, stepping into the welcome shade of the eucalyptus.

"'Doña Lupe.' Do you mind? Other people call you so."

"It is too much."

"You are too modest." Carlota's chubby arm lay across the younger woman's shoulders as if to offer comfort. "This is my friend Isobel. She needs your help."

"I will do everything I can," said Lupe. "What is the matter?"

The woman with short hair looked at Lupe with red-rimmed eyes. "I have lost my job."

Carlota said, "She was accused of stealing."

"Not just me," said Isobel.

Carlota patted her shoulder. "Of course not, dear."

"Where did you work?" asked Lupe.

"That is why I thought you could help," replied Carlota. "She works for that Ramirez Janitorial? Over on Walnut Street?"

Lupe shook her head. "I have never heard of it."

"They do commercial cleaning. They clean that big Protestant church in Blanco Beach, Grace Tabernacle."

"I see. . . ."

"Does your boss truly run that church, as Carlota said?" asked Isobel.

Lupe shook her head again. "He is a member there. I do not think he runs it."

"But he is very rich, no?" said Carlota.

"Yes," replied Lupe. "He is very rich."

Carlota nodded wisely. "In that case, he could make them hire her back."

"What happened?" asked Lupe.

"They think Isobel stole some money," said Carlota.

"No!" said Isobel. "They did not accuse me personally. There were twenty others also. They said it could have been anyone, but since the thief would not admit his crime, all of us must go."

"They fired twenty people?" asked Lupe.

"Twenty and one," said Isobel. Her voice was very small.

"How much money was stolen? Could it be returned?"

"Two hundreds, twenty and three dollars," replied Isobel.

"That is all?" The number seemed familiar to Lupe. "Surely that could have been repaid by twenty and one people."

"We offered to do that, but they said the church would not agree."

Carlota said, "That is why I thought of you, Lupe. Could you ask your boss to make the church take the money?"

"I will ask," replied Lupe. "But the mister, he is a little strange these days." Lupe wore a small purse with a long strap. She opened it and removed her wallet. "In the meantime, here is all that I can give." She gave the woman forty dollars. "I am sorry it is not more, but I must keep bus fare for a week."

"God bless you, señorita," said Isobel.

"And you, my sister," replied Lupe.

As she walked away she heard Carlota say, "I told you she would help. Doña Lupe always helps."

Doña. A title once reserved for nobility, now also given by the people to a very few of excellent reputation or great age. At first Lupe was proud of Carlota's words, but later as she stood waiting for the bus she felt ashamed, for she could have given Isobel the bus fare too. She could have trusted God for a ride to Blanco Beach.

In such moments of weak faith she sometimes worried that the pagans in America were tempting her too much, with their big houses and new cars and fancy clothing. She had never cared for money before. In Rincón de Dolores there had been very little, yet everyone was fed and clothed and sheltered. In Rincón de Dolores, if a neighbor needed money she would give them all she had. She would not have kept some back because of faithless fears about the future.

On the bus to Blanco Beach a small boy stared at Lupe's scarred cheek. She did not mind; she knew it was an interesting oddity. She smiled at the little boy. He began to cry.

Lupe decided she would preach about money that afternoon. She would tell the pagan Anglos they were slaves to it, and as always she would offer them their freedom through the Savior. She knew no one would listen. Although she spoke the truth to them each week they never listened, for she was not good with words.

In Blanco Beach the bus stopped at the main station, with its public restrooms and trellised outdoor waiting area, usually occupied by a few homeless drunkards. Lupe stepped down onto the sidewalk and turned right toward the beach. Years before, when she had first arrived in Blanco Beach in the back of a gardener's truck, she had been shocked at the way the people there ignored her. Now she understood it was not her in particular, but the whole world they ignored. Sometimes she felt tempted to ignore them too. Sometimes she fell prey to that temptation, and failed to greet each person as she passed. But the memory of her shameful pride at Carlota's words remained, and as she walked along the sidewalk she was careful to look into the eyes of others, to smile, to say, "Good afternoon," in her now-almost-perfect English.

Among the nearly naked people on the boardwalk by the beach, Lupe was conspicuous in her American-style pale blue cotton dress with a wide white belt, and her pure black hair pulled back in a tight ponytail. During the early days she had always changed from her church clothes into something casual before going to the beach to tell them of the Savior. Then she had decided it might be better to stand out from the crowd, better to look respectful of the Lord by going there well dressed. She had become a Sunday afternoon fixture at Main Beach. Many local residents now knew her. Some even exchanged a smile and greetings, although none of them would stand and listen to her words.

On the southern end of Main Beach was a hill, which pressed right out into the ocean. Lupe followed the boardwalk to the base of the hill, passing beach volleyball players in little bikinis, and rows of multicolored umbrellas, and young men playing basketball on green concrete half-courts between the boardwalk and the Pacific Coast Highway.

Reaching her destination, she removed her little Bible from her purse and took her usual position by stepping up onto a bench near a set of stairs that climbed the hill toward a hotel. Across from her were public restrooms and an outdoor shower where sun worshippers could rinse off sandy bodies. She turned to her scripture for the day, took a deep breath, and began to tell the passing throng about the Savior.

She did not shout too loudly. She was aware most people thought her mad, and she did not want to ruin anyone's vacation. On the contrary, she wanted to make it the best vacation of their lives, so she spoke as if calling to a loved one across a crowded room, believing those who cared to hear would hear.

No one cared to hear.

With only short breaks to drink water, Lupe preached there for five hours. She spoke about money, about how it could become a god, about how hard it was for a rich man to enter the kingdom of heaven, harder even than a camel passing through the eye of a needle, and camels were quite large. She spoke of how the love of money was the root of all kinds of evil, and she told them of the wisdom of storing up one's treasures in heaven, not on earth where all treasure is eventually destroyed.

She spoke of the great freedom Christians enjoyed: freedom from the heartache of envy, freedom from the fear of poverty, freedom from the pain of loneliness, freedom from all the other sorrows people tried to salve with money. She spoke of the futility of gifts to charity and every other form of good deed, if one hoped to purchase entry into heaven. She spoke of the vast gulf between the tarnished benevolence of even the holiest philanthropists and the absolute perfection God had every right to demand of those who wished to live with him in heaven.

She spoke of the Savior, a man so poor he had been born inside a stable, who would nonetheless bridge the vast gulf between heaven and imperfect people with his broken body, a poor man who would wash away all their sins with holy blood if they would just believe him and accept him.

Nobody believed.

As the sun began to set and the people started packing up their towels and umbrellas and ice chests, Lupe shut her Bible with a sigh and stepped down from the bench. Her feet and legs were very tired from standing in one place for so long. She put the Bible in her purse and set out for the bus stop.

One and one-half hours later, she approached her boardinghouse in Wilson City, moving slowly upon tender feet. Weary though she was, on her way up to her attic room she rapped lightly at the first door on the second floor. The door was opened by Marisol Louisa Soto Guzmán, from San Blas. As usual the younger woman wore her brightly colored *rebozo* around her shoulders, but her baby boy was not bundled on her back at that time of night. Lupe assumed he was inside her room, probably asleep, for she heard no cries, just the blaring of a Telemundo melodrama on the television.

"Good evening, Marisol," said Lupe. "Can I do anything for you, or for Louisa?"

Little Louisa's horrific coughing had grown worse, and Lupe expected she would shortly die.

"Oh, Lupe! It is a miracle!" said Marisol.

"Indeed?" Lupe smiled. "Please tell me."

"A moment!"

The woman disappeared into her room. Lupe did not mind waiting in the hall. Probably Marisol's husband was at home. He was an angry man who did not allow visitors.

"Look!" said Marisol, returning to the door. She passed a small white envelope to Lupe. On it were the words, "For your daughter's medicine."

Lupe looked at Marisol. "Yes?"

"We have the medicine!" said Marisol. "When I woke up this morning, I found that envelope. Someone filled it up with money and slid it underneath the door."

"Enough money for the medicine?"

"Exactly enough!"

Lupe stared at the envelope again. "How much, exactly?"

"Two hundreds, twenty and three dollars."

Hearing that number, Lupe remembered Tucker Rue's words the last time she saw him at Sanctuatio: *I have a meeting with the benevolence committee at Grace Tabernacle. Maybe then I'll have some money.* She remembered sitting beside that handsome man in the early days, the two of them at a folding table in the empty warehouse, making fliers. Lupe remembered how his handwritten words on the fliers had flowed gracefully, like a work of Arabic calligraphy, exactly like the handwritten words on the envelope she held. She remembered all of this, and twenty-one people out of work because of two hundred twenty-three dollars taken from Grace Tabernacle, and she felt very tired.

"We only got the medicine this morning," said Marisol. "They told me at the clinic she should have started taking it a long time ago, but at least she has a better chance now."

"A better chance? Only a chance?"

"Yes, but God is good! Isn't that what you keep saying?"

"He is." She touched the desperate mother's arm. "God is very good."

Lupe climbed to her little attic room. She wished to rest as best she could, in order to be fresh for work at Delano's house in the morning. She changed into her sleeping clothes and ate a cold dinner: a little fruit and some cereal and milk. She lay upon her narrow bed and thought of Tucker, just one block away at Sanctuario, also lying on a narrow bed in that small cell of a room where he lived like a monk. It had surprised her when he asked Harmony to marry. She had believed he would make an excellent Franciscan, like Fray Alejandro in the olden days, eager to serve God in pagan places and remain celibate throughout his life, just as she had been.

Did she still believe that?

She remembered the way he had lifted her hand to his lips and kissed the place where barbed wire scarred her palm. How many times had she thought of that moment? She had often wished she had the gift of words, so she could have explained her feelings before it was too late, so he would have known how deeply she longed to return his kiss. She thought of all her sermons on the beach without one soul reborn. She thought of Tucker, and the trouble he was in. Had she made a terrible mistake?

Once she had believed her feelings for him were impious distractions. Obedience was sacrifice, and sacrifice meant suffering. But she had been naïve back then. It had never crossed her mind that God might grant her pleasure in the midst of duty.

Lupe's mind spun and spun and would not let her sleep although she lay a long time in the darkness. Or perhaps sleep fled before the soft sound of Louisa's coughing, which rose through the attic floor. She pressed her palms together at her chest and silently began to pray. She loved to fall asleep while speaking with her Father. But it was not to be.

After an hour she arose. She knelt in the darkness and reached below her bed and drew out a cardboard box. This she carried to the little table by the window. She turned on the light. She removed the contents of the box, a bundle wrapped in bright red velvet. She unfolded Alejandro's burden and set it upright on the table, the painted panels on the left and right of the central panel, which was blank. In the incandescent light she knelt before the triptych, the *retablo,* the ancient altarpiece.

As she had so many times before, she stared at the two thieves upon their crosses, one with the face of a stranger, and one with features she so dearly loved. Always before she had wondered which thief was unrepentant and which was on his way to paradise. Now, for the first time, she was afraid she knew.

CAPÍTULO 23

ALEJANDRO DID NOT KNOW EXACTLY how the pestilence was spread, but he believed physical proximity to the victims was a factor. None of the leather-jackets fell ill until the last part of the month. Probably their disdainful distance from the neophytes explained why they had not been laid low sooner. When contemplating this, Alejandro tried not to think about the fact that he was seldom far from the dying. In his efforts to ignore that fact the wounds from his flogging became a blessing, for his pain offered a welcome distraction.

When the first soldiers fell ill Don Felipe insisted on separate quarters for them, but there was no unoccupied space within the mission, so ropes were strung across the refectory and blankets draped down to establish a semblance of division. Fully one-half of the room was given to the three soldiers, while over twenty stricken neophytes were forced into the other half. When Alejandro's objection to these unjust accommodations went unheeded by his abbot and the captain, the friar moved among the dying on both sides of the blankets, tending to them equally.

One morning Fray Guillermo came to observe the situation. Holding a cloth to his mouth and nose, he took only one step into the refectory. "Have you made the soldiers comfortable, Brother Alejandro?"

"I have done all that I can, Abbot, but I am just one man and there are many here."

"You must devote your attention to Don Felipe's soldiers."

"Of course."

"I mean, if you cannot tend to everyone, first devote yourself to them. One must often choose the lesser of two evils. Do you understand?"

"I do."

"Good." The abbot stood silently for a moment, and it seemed to Alejandro he might be uncomfortable. Then he said, "When you disobeyed my orders I was faced with such a choice. I hope you also understand that."

"What choice, Abbot?"

"It was very painful for me to order your flogging, Alejandro, but it was the lesser evil. Discipline must be maintained. I could not let your challenge go unanswered."

"I only meant to give the man some water. I did not mean to challenge you."

"Your apology is accepted."

Alejandro did not know what to say, so he remained silent. The abbot glanced around the room. "This is difficult work."

"Yes, Abbot."

"How is your back?"

"I can bear it. How is your back, Abbot?"

Guillermo looked at him sharply. "Mine?"

Alejandro merely waited for an answer.

Finally, the pale man said, "You know, then."

"Yes, Abbot."

"In that case you also know I ask nothing of anyone that I do not first suffer."

At that the man turned toward the sunlit plaza and departed.

Ignoring Fray Guillermo's order, Alejandro gave the leather-jacket soldiers exactly the same care as all the neophytes over the next few days. If the three soldiers' disease followed the usual course, at least two of them would die. He wondered if Fray Guillermo would require them to be buried in the mass grave. The other soldiers might well desert the mission if they were offended in that way.

Fray Alejandro, familiar as he was with death, did not understand why people placed such great importance on their body's resting place. It is a question worth consideration. Prince or pauper, saint or sinner, are we not the same within the ground? All that rises from the earth returns to it again. Even our most cherished memories are pressed into the soil, as strata upon strata a record of all human folly is laid beneath our feet. We walk upon our past; with every step we drive it deeper.

Although we seldom pause to think that what is done today will lie beneath the paths of those who come tomorrow, other creatures live with it as constant knowledge. Consider, for example, the coyote. It has a sense of smell one hundred times more powerful than ours. It can detect a mole or groundhog through a foot of soil by scent alone. So it was that a particular coyote, trotting warily along a southern California hillside, stopped when a molecule of something interesting reached its nostrils. It lowered its long nose to the ground. It moved in a small circle, sniffing. It began to dig. It clawed and scratched at the dry soil. Unearthing one end of a bone, the canine gnawed and worried, but could not wrest it from the earth. After half an hour's wasted effort the coyote continued on its way, leaving the telltale sign of human history exposed.

For several days the bone remained exactly where it had been left more than two centuries before. Then a black Labrador retriever came, following the faded scent of the coyote. The dog's nose, while not as keen as the coyote's, could not have failed to sense a bone upon the surface. It sniffed the exposed prize. It began to dig. Using paws much larger than the coyote's, its progress was more rapid.

A boy on the hill above the Labrador retriever began to call her name. "Sunny! Sunny! Here, girl! Come on, Sunny!" The dog paused and raised her head to look up. She saw the boy, and beyond the boy a new neighborhood of houses hidden by a wall. Then, looking down again, she increased her efforts, digging frantically, torn between the urge to draw this prize up from the earth and a powerful desire to do her master's bidding.

"Come on, Sunny! Here, girl!"

The bone was free at last. Here was both a tasty treat and a toy that she could use to play her favorite game. Joyously, the dog ran up the hill with the bone between her teeth. She bounded straight toward her master over sun-baked stones and brush. She knew he'd want to play.

"Good girl!" said the boy. "What a good girl!"

Tail in rapid motion, Sunny dropped the bone at the boy's feet.

"What's that?" asked the boy. When he stooped to lift the bone, his fingers wrapped around a small fragment of flesh still clinging to its surface.

"A bone! Good girl!" said the boy.

The young lady beside him disagreed. "Yuck, Kenny. Drop that thing."

"It's only a bone."

"Where did it come from?"

"Some old deer or cow or something."

"It's gross."

Laughing at the girl's daintiness, Kenny Karlsson threw the bone ahead of them. This was just what Sunny had been waiting for. Playing her part of the game, the dog set out running. She reached the bone in seconds. She brought it back again. The boy removed it from her mouth, and again his fingers touched the tiny patch of flesh as dry as leather. Again he threw the bone. Again the dog retrieved it. On and on they played the game, to Sunny's great delight. But as always seemed to happen, the boy stopped far too soon.

"Here you go," he said, extending the bone to his female companion. "Why don't you take over for a while?"

"No, thanks," said the girl.

"Come on, look at her. How can you resist?"

Sunny watched the bone intently, with both ears cocked and furrowed brow.

"We should probably head back," said the girl. "I need to do my homework for tomorrow."

The two young people turned toward the far side of the hill, where their families' new homes stood. The boy threw the bone again, and Sunny dashed off after it.

"You don't like her, do you?" said Kenny Karlsson of his dog.

"She's okay."

"I've had her since I was a kid."

The girl said nothing.

"What's wrong?" asked Kenny.

"Nothing."

"Sure? 'Cause you seem kinda bummed or something."

"It feels spooky over here."

"What are you talking about?"

"I don't know . . . it just feels like someone's watching us or something."

The boy looked around. They could not be observed from their new neighborhood, having slipped outside its walls and traversed a small ravine and climbed over the hill beyond. They had followed a narrow cattle trail through the brush, established in the days before statehood, when vaqueros worked that land. Unseen insects all around them hummed steadily, low and powerful like a million volts of electricity. Above them soared a red-tailed hawk on inert wings.

Kenny said, "There's nobody out here."

"I know that. It just *feels* like someone's watching."

The dog returned with her tail high, her mouth around the slobber-coated bone, pure joy in her eyes.

"Maybe you should get a dog," said Kenny. "Sunny always cheers me up."

"I don't need to be cheered up."

"Okay, but if you'll just throw the bone for Sunny, I guarantee you'll feel better."

"I am *not* going to touch that nasty thing, so just back off."

Kenny Karlsson laughed, and the two of them continued on across the hilltop, returning to the safety of New Harmony.

CAPÍTULO 24

ANOTHER YOUNG GIRL DIED. GRIEVING, Fray Benicio forsook his habit, capuche, and cincture and went about dressed as a neophyte in sackcloth. He abandoned the comforts of his cell to sleep beneath the open sky. Fray Guillermo condemned this behavior strenuously. Alejandro agreed with the abbot, for it was a gross violation of the Rule, but he also understood Benicio's desire to join the people's suffering.

By that time the pestilence had taken thirteen children. Each of their deaths pained Alejandro as if it were a thousand lashes. He had always longed to be a father. It was the one regret he felt about his life within the Order. Thus when he thought of all the children in the pit he prayed with San Juan el Apóstol, *Sí, ven, Señor Jesús.* And for pity's sake, come quickly!

This special sorrow for the passing of a child is a common sentiment, yet if there is no doubt of heaven and no doubt about the Fall, should we not reserve our deepest grief for ancient ones who tarry overlong upon the earth? When an elder dies, we say, "At least he lived a full life," but only tribulations made it full. Should we not more kindly say, "At least his suffering is over"?

Perhaps we mourn ourselves when children perish. An old and wrinkled body only proves the Curse, but perfect newborns offer hope that finally the New Earth has arrived. With each child's death our happy future fades before the proof that children do not really bring perfection, and youth cannot prevail against this harsh and profane world.

So it was with Marisol Louisa Soto Guzmán and her husband from San Blas. They had brought their precious little girl to the meeting room at Sanctuario. In a simple wooden coffin quickly made by a kind neighbor, the child Louisa lay upon white satin taken from her mother's wedding dress. Around her were wildflower bouquets, yellow, lavender, and pink, gently picked by the callused fingers of rough and weathered men who worked with Louisa's father at a farm outside of town. There was no priest. Louisa's father hated priests. Indeed, it had taken threats of divorce by Marisol, Louisa's mother, to convince the angry man to let Tucker Rue speak at this, Sanctuario's first funeral for a child.

Standing by the little coffin, Tucker spoke long and earnestly of heaven. He spoke of God's delight in poor Louisa, and of her delight in God. He spoke of freedom from the damage done in her short life, of living every moment now with joy that far surpasses all the finest moments of Louisa's time on the earth. As Tucker spoke of paradise, he did not look at Louisa's father, who sat in the front row and stared at him with hatred in his eyes. Tucker looked instead above the heads of his small audience, at the blank wall.

How he longed to speak the truth, to tell them why this child had died. It was not God's will, nor was it inevitable, nor had she really perished from disease. Little Louisa Soto Guzmán had died of callousness, hypocrisy, and greed. She had died because of Delano Wright's revenge, because of wealthy Pharisees in Blanco Beach who measured ministries in terms of numbers. And had she died because—God help him—he himself had been too slow to act upon his outrage.

Because Tucker did not trust himself to speak the truth, he kept his eyes upon the blank wall in the back instead of on the people, and because his gaze was focused toward the rear he noticed Lupe instantly when she arrived. He thought her beautiful beyond compare. He barely saw her scar. He stared at her most shamelessly, for he could not do otherwise. He stumbled in his sermon. He had to check his notes. He carried on, glancing back and forth between the paper in his hand and the lovely woman in the back.

How he wished to make Lupe understand that he had done his

best. She had brought this child to him, and he had done his best to get the necessary money. He had compromised himself, his ministry, and his morals, for the sake of love, all love, not just love of Lupe. He had tried to save the child, but it had been too late.

Tucker Rue reached the end of all his useless words. He turned away from Lupe to gaze at the small girl in the coffin, pale and still upon her mother's wedding satin. He wished to add something to his words of heaven, something beyond words. He wished to show his faith by what he did. Where there was sickness, he wished to provide medicine. Where there was hunger, he wished to provide food. Where there was nakedness and poverty, he wished to give clothing and money. Gazing at the young life wasted by the falseness of religion, Tucker Rue vowed that he would never be too late again.

As Louisa's parents rose and went to look upon their daughter for the final time, a woman sang the old Mexican hymn "Pues Si Vivimos":

> In all our living, we belong to God;
> and in our dying, we are still with God;
> so, whether living, or whether dying,
> we belong to God; we belong to God.

Louisa's father looked around himself with glaring, streaming eyes, and then he closed the casket. Six short men in clean blue jeans and starched cotton shirts walked to the front. Three on each side, they bore the little girl out to a pickup truck, which had been decorated with black crepe and white flowers. There was no hearse, for this would be an indigent burial, paid for by the county. The county used a coroner's wagon for the transport of the indigent, and Louisa's parents preferred even a friend's open pickup truck to that.

Following the men out of the room, Tucker paused beside Lupe. He said, "Will you ride with me?"

Saying nothing, she stood and walked beside him.

As he drove out to the county cemetery behind the funereal pickup truck, Tucker wondered what Lupe would think if she knew he had stolen the money for Louisa's medicine. He was careful not to stare at her, sitting there beside him. Instead he watched the truck ahead, the black crepe peeling off and drifting to the gutters as they passed. He hoped that she might understand, but suspected she would not.

It did not matter. Louisa was dead anyway, and he would do what must be done.

The service at the graveside was soon over. Lupe rode back into Wilson City beside him in his old Toyota truck, just as she had ridden beside him into California. She touched his shoulder before parting. After so many years apart, what did that touch mean?

He could not sleep that night.

On Wednesday Tucker always hosted a potluck dinner at Sanctuario, which was followed by a Bible study and a time of prayer. Over the years it had become a great success, with over fifty people coming every week, and sometimes many more. This was possible even without money, since the people brought the food themselves. But Sanctuario traditionally provided paper cups and plates, and plastic knives and forks, and he was running very low on those. If the love of money was the root of evil, it seemed to him the lack of money was the trunk and branches.

To Tucker's amazement, Lupe arrived with a plastic bowl of fruit salad. She said, "Hello Tucker" in English, and offered him her hand. He shook it formally, then she was off to another corner of the room to speak with a pair of ladies there. He heard one of them call her Doña Lupe, and he marveled. Throughout the meal he watched her surreptitiously. She smiled and even laughed. He had seldom seen her smile. The unexpected radiance of it nearly overwhelmed him.

Why had she come? How did she know so many others? Some of the people at Sanctuario also attended the small Catholic church a few blocks away. Probably she had met them there. The priests might disapprove of those who worshipped as Catholics on Sundays and as Protestants during the week, but Tucker did not care. Anything that brought the people lasting comfort was a blessing to be welcomed. Besides, the differences in doctrine were nothing to him, not when compared to the vast gulf between what most churches said and what they did . . . a much more pressing problem.

Once he caught Lupe's eye across the room. She smiled at him. In his excitement Tucker almost stood to go to her, but at that instant her attention was distracted by a latecomer. Tucker turned to see Ramón

Rodríguez enter the large room. The man carried a grocery bag, probably filled with pastries. Ramón always brought *pan dulce* for dessert.

Tucker looked again at Lupe. She never looked away from Ramón as he walked to the food table. She watched him as he filled his plate, and as he took a seat, facing away from her. The intensity of her gaze disturbed Tucker. Had she returned into his life after all the passing years, only to tempt him now with jealousy?

Dinner was a great success, even though he ran out of paper towels and had to offer toilet paper for napkins. How embarrassing. There was some laughter, but no one really seemed to mind. On the contrary, they were all familiar with such compromises.

At the proper time Tucker rose to speak as usual, offering a short homily on the relationship between faith and blessings. Then came time for sharing and for prayer requests. He removed a small notebook from his pocket, and a pencil. He always made a note of prayer requests, so they would remember to praise God later when the answers came.

Flora Bolívar told them of her mother in Mexicali, who needed a knee operation. Raul Garcia wished his brother were a Christian. Diego Sanchez asked for help with the sin of worry. Tucker started writing. Then he stopped. He stared at the words for a moment. He drew a line through all that he had written. Come on, he thought. Give me something I can use.

Antigua Herrera complained about the insects that came through her front door, which she had to leave open to get cross-ventilation.

Tucker wrote: *Antigua—bugs.*

José Valles mentioned that his chronically ill wife wanted a beautiful painting to look at from her bed.

Tucker wrote, *Ramona, José V.'s wife—painting.*

Jesse Duran, José's widowed sister-in-law, worried that she could not afford clothing for the baby she would have in the early fall.

Baby clothes, wrote Tucker. *Jesse D.*

Someone mentioned the recent uproar in Sacramento over illegal immigration. Some worried they might lose their jobs or be deported. Others worried that their children would be forced to leave the Wilson City schools. One woman claimed she was the victim of a demon, which would not let her sleep.

Tucker sighed. He could help with none of it.

Then Katrina Juárez mentioned the high cost of birthday presents for her son, Eduardo, and Tucker wrote, *Katrina's son Eduardo—toys*.

Near the end of the prayer meeting, Lupe spoke. She mentioned a woman, an Isobel someone, who had lost her job. Apparently this woman and about twenty others had been fired together for some reason. It seemed to Tucker that Lupe watched him as she spoke. The look in her eyes was strange, as if she wished to communicate something right across the room, especially to him. Suddenly, just as she was about to tell them why these people were all fired, Ramón Rodríguez rose and hurried to the door. Lupe's eyes moved away from Tucker, following the man. Although it seemed she had more to say, Lupe picked up her purse and left the meeting hall, hurrying after Ramón.

Tucker felt his stomach roil.

He spoke a few final words about faith, then closed the meeting with a prayer and sent them on their way. Lupe did not return. He told himself it did not matter, indeed, it was for the best, for he had a long list of solid prayer requests, a lot of work to do, and she would not approve.

Three days passed and then on Sunday morning many miracles occurred in Wilson City.

Antigua Herrera awoke before the sun and made a pot of coffee for herself and for her husband, using yesterday's grounds. It was the one time all day when she was alone: those few minutes before the children woke. Even half asleep she did her best to savor the moment. Only when she had begun to drink the first cup was she alert enough to notice that her apartment was cool, yet there were no insects buzzing at the lamp. Curious, she went to the front room, and there to the everlasting glory of God Antigua saw a very fine screen door propped up in the front door opening, a nearly perfect fit, waiting to be permanently hung.

That same Sunday morning just two blocks away, José Valles entered the bedroom of his dearly loved wife, who was an invalid, and found her gazing at a beautiful oil painting in a golden frame which leaned against the wall below an open window.

Just down the street, Jesse Duran found a cardboard box containing baby clothes on her front porch, and four blocks in the opposite direction Eduardo Juárez, son of Katrina, discovered he was rich with birthday gifts. Little trucks and horses, fighter jets and locomotives, and army men and superheroes stood at attention on the hard-packed dirt behind his house, sent like manna from the heavens according to his mother, who was overwhelmed with charismatic fervor and stood with face and hands uplifted, shouting, *"Muchas gracias, Señor Jesús!"*

A week passed.

After a month of relaxation at their Caribbean home, Arnold O'Connor and his much younger wife, Elise, returned to Blanco Beach. With them were their newborn daughter, Katherine, and their son, Fletcher, who was eight years old. Mr. O'Connor, a slender, gray-haired man who often wore gold cuff links, a pillar of his community who owned a chain of Mercedes-Benz dealerships, a member of the benevolence committee at Grace Tabernacle, immediately noticed the screen door was missing from their side entry. He assumed their full-time chauffeur and handyman, John, had removed it for repairs while they were away.

On the granite countertop of the center island in the kitchen, he saw the family Bible lying open. Approaching it, Mr. O'Connor became angry, for someone had defaced the precious heirloom by circling a verse in bright red ink:

> *But the stranger that dwelleth with you shall be unto you as one born among you, and thou shalt love him as thyself; for ye were strangers in the land of Egypt: I am the LORD your God.*

Although Mr. O'Connor was outraged by this, he did not call the police until Elise realized the small Monet was no longer hanging on the dining room wall, and in all of the excitement about the missing painting—insured, of course, for more than one million dollars—it was many hours before they noticed baby Katherine's clothes were missing, as were most of the toys of her brother Fletcher.

CAPÍTULO 25

FOR EACH CORPSE ADDED TO the pit it seemed three neophytes abandoned the true faith, returning to their heathen villages and their strange god, Cooksuy. Fray Alejandro tried to reason with them, but he was met with unassailable logic. Their god offered something the Franciscans could not: an explanation for the awful pestilence. Cooksuy's sacred grove had been profaned, his high altar desecrated. Those responsible, the strangers from the south, refused to offer grain as recompense. Those who aided them were soon thrown in the pit. Who would remain among the Christians under such circumstances?

For his part, Alejandro's world had been reduced to the refectory and the paths across the plaza to the water well and to his narrow cell in the barracks, where he sometimes managed to sleep for an hour or two. Day and night he toiled alone among the dying, for Fray Benicio had abandoned his work within the mission in order to devote himself completely to ministry among the pagan Indians outside.

One evening the abbot joined Alejandro at the well. "How fare the infirm today, good brother?"

Alejandro dropped the dipping bucket to the bottom and began to draw it up. "Sadly, two more are now dead. Seventeen are with us still, including three new cases."

The abbot shook his head. "Such a blow to all our hopes."

"A blow to theirs as well, I should imagine."

"Of course. Of course." Guillermo watched Alejandro pour the water into his carrying bucket. "You are always careful to be sure those buckets never touch?"

"Indeed, I am."

"That is good. . . ." The abbot clearly wished to say something more. With his bucket full, Alejandro waited silently. Finally, Fray Guillermo spoke. "All of us—Fray Benico, Don Felipe, and his officers—we all appreciate your faithfulness in taking on this burden, Alejandro."

"Thank you, Abbot."

"It occurs to me you must need more time. It is one thing to miss a few nights' sleep, but on and on like this for weeks . . . it cannot continue. I have decided to release you from attendance at our prayers."

"Release me?"

"Indeed. You may use the extra time to rest."

"I can best tend the sick if I also pray for them."

"You may do that in your cell, beside your bed."

"Abbot, I appreciate your concern. Truly. But I believe it would be best if I continued to observe the vigils."

"It is not a request, brother."

"You are commanding me not to pray?"

The abbot's back stiffened. "Do not be impertinent. I am doing no such thing."

"But I must pray alone?"

"It is for the good of all."

The abbot turned and walked away without another word.

Later, when the hour of vespers came, Alejandro stepped outside the refectory to stand in the plaza. The sound of Guillermo and Benicio's prayers came faintly from the chapel to his ears. In the gloaming Alejandro whispered the same words, kneeling when he knew they were kneeling and rising when he knew they arose. In this way he prayed with his brothers just as he always had, but this one thing he added: the gentle Alejandro prayed for them as well.

Ever after that encounter Fray Guillermo kept a distance from the homely friar. Benicio did likewise, as did Don Felipe and his leather-jacket soldiers. Even the few neophytes who remained in good health seemed to fear his presence. Alejandro had been tainted by his contact with the dying. From cell to refectory to water well, he spent his days and nights alone.

Meanwhile, the abbot sent the leather-jackets out to capture every neophyte who fled. Some he flogged as an example to the others, publicly condemning them as heretics. Fray Alejandro was not so quick to judge. What had they done, except to seek more fortunate circumstances?

Many people known for wisdom have searched for much the same assurance. The three Fates, Clotho, Lachesis, and Atropos, once dominated Grecian lives. The Romans thrived or suffered at the whim of Fortuna and her wheel. Saint Augustine of Hippo once chanced upon predestination, and Muhammad sheltered in a cave to dream of *quadar,* the destiny Allah has written. The neophytes knew little of the Christian saints and nothing whatsoever of the Muslims, ancient Greeks, or Romans, but life had schooled them well in the caprice of providence. Karma, kismet, fortune, fate, or destiny—call it what one will—as they fled the fearsome harvest at the mission for their little stone god Cooksuy, what they wanted more than anything was luck.

Good fortune is a universal hope, a hope that spans the generations to include the time of Ramón Ernesto Rodríguez Obregón, who wanted the same thing. Yet it seemed to him the God of all creation was intent upon the opposite, for surely the woman's appearance in the meeting hall at Sanctuario could not be a blessing.

Had she not appeared in the moment long ago when he decided to risk everything on one last desperate border crossing? Had she not suddenly been there again when Lobo's madness drove him to kill Felix and the Anglo woman? Two terrible mistakes distanced by many years and miles, yet both times she was there. Now, more than two years after the accident, she was there again, just as Ramón Rodríguez came seeking help for his sick friend. It must be a bad omen.

He had not noticed her when entering the meeting hall, filled as it was with so many, and late as he had been. Even when she began to speak of people losing jobs, at first her identity was hidden by her scar and his deceitful memory. But her voice . . . she spoke, and Ramón slowly recognized the voice. He had stared at her with the sudden dismal revelation that he had caused the scar, and his guilty realization made him rise and hurry from the room.

Now, outside the front door of Sanctuario, Ramón paused to glance around. He looked up, and saw only blackness. He was immersed in destiny. Sweat flowed from his pores. Suddenly he could not recall his own address, or where he was, or who he was, exactly. He had come to the United States a husband and a father, a simple man with desperate hopes. He had lost that person. He was lost to fate.

"Señor Rodríguez," came a soft voice from behind him.

He turned, and it was she, standing near him in the starless night. He touched his own cheek. "If I may ask, how did you get this?"

"I burned."

"I let you burn? I was cowardly?"

"Do you not remember?"

"It seems sometimes I do. At other times . . . I wonder."

"You could not help me, señor. You were hurt yourself. Your head."

He thought of their first meeting, when he had seen something of Raquel in her. He wished to remember his wife by looking at this woman with a scar, but she did not resemble his Raquel anymore. Or did she? Viewed in a certain way, the woman was still beautiful. Might Raquel be scarred as well? Might Raquel be changed as he himself had changed? Might this woman have been sent to show him how his dear Raquel had suffered?

He asked, "Why are you here?"

"I have a friend at Sanctuario. I believe he is in trouble. I think he needs my help."

"But why are you here, in Wilson City? We are very far from where we met."

"You told me of this place."

Shocked at such a simple explanation for the mystery of so much time and space compressed, he replied, "Did I?"

"In Naco, yes, señor, you did."

"In Naco. When I lost you in the desert?"

"You risked much to help me, señor. I am very grateful."

He wished to remember, but ever since the accident his memory was not good. Those first days in the United States only came to mind as heat and desperate thirst. "I don't know how I lost you."

She shrugged as if it were unimportant. "Why are you at Sanctuario?"

"I too have a friend in need of help."

"You came to ask for prayer?"

"Yes. And medicine." He nodded toward the door behind them. "Inside they spoke of anger toward us. They said the government is angry."

"That is true."

"If my friend went to the hospital, they would deport him?"

"I do not know. I was in their hospital for many weeks, and no one asked to see my papers. But I speak English well, and I was visited by Americano friends. Does your friend speak English? Does he have friends from the United States?"

"No."

"In that case, it is possible they would send him back."

Ramón rubbed his sweating forehead. "Do you think I would have saved you from the car? If I could?"

"You do not know?"

"I do not."

"I think you are a good man, Señor Rodríguez."

"Am I?"

"Your sick friend, is he the one who tried to take the wheel, or perhaps the one who carried you away?"

"Sadly, he is the one who caused the wreck, señorita."

"He is very sick?"

"I think so."

She turned her eyes to him. In the darkness they were darker still, like his Raquel's eyes. She said, "Please escort me to him."

"I do not remember where we live."

"There is no need to fear. I only wish to help him."

"Señorita, you must understand he meant no harm."

"Of course."

It was strange, but he truly did not know the way to where he lived. His head was very hot. His boots were very heavy. He said, "You will not report him to the police?"

"I only wish to help him if I can."

He wiped the sweat from his eyes. He stared at her. To help the one who caused such damage, scarred her cheek, killed her friend . . . it was something he would like to see. Pointing to the left, he said, "I believe it is this way."

She began to walk. A remote siren wailed. Nearby dogs replied with fearsome howls. A man shouted. A woman screamed. In the distance, shots were fired, a door was slammed, and footsteps slapped the pavement. Ramón hung half a step behind, allowing her to part the darkness as they walked through Wilson City. From high upon a metal warehouse wall a strong light shone onto the sidewalk. The woman walked into the whiteness. The warehouse floodlight sparkled in her midnight hair like all the missing stars. A moth writhed in the glow above her, drawn to it as we are drawn to heaven's light in death. The woman paused. They were at the corner. He tried to remember, and pointed onward hopefully. She set out again. She must have been Fortuna after all, for they were somehow safe.

It was not so far from Sanctuario to the little duplex house where Ramón and his friends lived. They walked another block and turned a corner and arrived. How could he have forgotten? What was this strange lethargy that filled his mind? They turned the corner and arrived to find the front door open and light spilling out onto the broken concrete porch, and Paco standing by Lobo's truck, which was no longer hidden in the garage, but instead stood in the front yard near the door.

The woman walked beside the truck, passing by the front, trailing her fingers along its crumpled metal. In the light from the open door she touched the yellow places where the car's paint still remained upon the whiteness of the fender. Ramón wondered what was in her mind. Did she know this was the truck? Did she know that was the paint from her friend's car?

"He is in the house?" she asked.

"Of course," replied Ramón.

She entered through the open door.

Ramón turned to Paco. "Are you mad? Get this truck back inside the garage."

"Who is she?" asked Paco.

Ramón could not explain, so he simply said, "A woman from that place. Sanctuario. She will pray for him. Perhaps she will heal him."

"She may pray for him, but he will not be healed," said Paco as he laid a hand lightly on Ramón's arm. "Our friend Lobo is dead."

Ramón stared at him. "But . . . but . . . I left him sleeping just an hour ago."

"Perhaps he was already gone and you did not know."

"But . . . dead? *Dead?* How can he be dead?"

Fernando appeared at the door. Whispering into the night, he said, "Who is this woman?"

Ramón replied, "I met her back in Naco. She came across the border when we did."

"She was not with us!"

"She did not have the money. She followed."

"Followed? No one could have followed. That dung heap of a coyote was always watching."

"Fernando, my friend, why does it matter?"

"Lobo is dead! That is why it matters! He is dead and we must bury him. We must do it tonight. We must do it secretly, before anybody knows. Imagine if the police learn of this."

Remembering he had no papers, remembering he had no Americano friends, Ramón said, "It is well. Let us bury him."

"No, it is not well! Now this woman knows!"

"She is a good woman. She will cause no problems."

Trini emerged from the house. "I just met a woman in there. Ramón, is she not the woman from the car, the one who lived?"

"Yes," replied Ramón.

Paco drew his breath in suddenly.

"Fool!" hissed Fernando. "With this very truck her friend was killed! And you say she will cause no problems?"

"One moment," said Ramón. "Let me think." He rubbed his palm across his face, wiping away sweat. "We will bring her with us. She will be a witness, an accessory. Then she cannot tell."

The three men stood in silence as the town of Wilson City popped and howled and screamed around them in the night. At last Fernando said, "Paco?"

"I trust Ramón," said Paco.

"Very well," said Fernando. "But if she cannot keep a secret, we are ruined."

Paco shrugged. "What else can we do?"

"Come," said Fernando, speaking softly. "We must hurry."

Ramón followed Fernando into the house with Paco at his heels. Inside, he found the woman standing by a bundle on the floor.

Ramón stared at the bundle, his friend Lobo, wrapped in sheets. Filled with grief and wonder, he said, "It was only *la varicela*," meaning chickenpox. "No one dies from that."

"He was very sick," said Fernando.

"Yes, but *la varicela*?"

Fernando said, "It is God's will."

"What are you going to do?" asked the woman.

"We must give our friend a proper burial," said Ramón. "Will you come and pray for him?"

"Now? Tonight?"

"We are afraid to wait," replied Ramón. "If we could not safely take him to the hospital, as you said, all the more so we must not let the Americanos know of this."

The woman stared down at the body in the sheets. Ramón, Paco, Trini, and Fernando watched her closely. Finally she nodded. "I will come. I will pray for your friend."

"You know who he is?" said Trini. "This one caused the wreck that scarred you so."

"I will pray for him," she said again.

The others stared at her in wonder. Ramón wanted to tell them what she was: an omen sent by God. Fate in human form. But how does one pronounce such things aloud? Instead he simply joined the others as they gripped four corners of the sheet and lifted their friend Lobo.

Ramón was surprised at the weight, but perhaps the real heaviness was not his friend. Everything that night seemed heavy, even his own arms. They walked clumsily outside through the door, shuffling sideways to fit through, nearly dropping Lobo. It was a good thing they had brought the truck so close. Ramón did not believe he had the strength to go much farther.

Fernando got behind the wheel, with the woman up beside him. Paco, Trini, and Ramón all sat in the back, to hold the sheets down in the wind.

"Where are we going?" asked Ramón.

"Fernando says he knows a place," replied Paco. "But first we must get shovels."

With only one headlight working and the smell of burning rubber coming from beneath the crumpled hood, Ramón hoped Lobo's final resting place was near. The truck rolled through the vicious night. The white sheet flapped and beat against Lobo's head and chest, offering brief glimpses of his pustulated face. Ramón shivered in the rushing air and moved behind the cab to get out of the wind. He wrapped his arms across his chest and hugged himself for warmth. He leaned back. He closed his eyes. When he opened them again, the truck had stopped.

"Where are we?" he asked, looking around sleepily.

"At our workplace," said Paco. "Fernando and Trini have gone for shovels."

Ramón turned to see the woman in the cab, staring forward through the windshield. The clouds had parted. Her silhouette was sharp against the moonlit hillside opposite, but he could not see the details of her face. With her scar invisible in the shadows it was Raquel he saw, the high cheekbones, the curving nose, the gently sloping forehead. A Mayan queen was his Raquel, and so she always would be in his memory. He sighed, leaned back, and closed his eyes again. He was so very hot.

CAPÍTULO 26

FRAY ALEJANDRO FELT AN AWFUL heat. It was much like that which once consumed him at the chapel of San Francisco de Assisi, but unlike the first of Alejandro's burnings, this fire had not lashed out from the Holy Presence. He felt no consoling sense of fellowship, no holy passion. Forsaken by all others at the mission, this time he was utterly alone. It even seemed he had been shunned by his Creator, for the conflagration came from down below, and this, his second burning, would surely put him in the pit.

Having seen the telltale spots of red upon his palms and felt them on his face, knowing the pestilence had marked him at last, the good Franciscan lay abed and stared at the unfinished altarpiece. How was it possible so many months had passed yet he had failed in such a simple task? Such a privilege, yet he had dismissed it. How was it possible? How had he come to this?

Sobered by his imminent demise, his mind wandered widely. He contemplated all the little blessings he had failed to celebrate. Such a fine life he had led; a quiet, normal life. Decades passed by in his beloved friary in Spain, years of glorious normalcy when he should have blessed the Lord at every opportunity, blessed the Lord with all that was within him, yet as trickling water carves a canyon, so it seemed he had allowed his joyfulness to suffer slow erosion by routine.

Only the most obvious of blessings had been noticed in the moment. A birth, a good saint's timely passing into glory, a confirmation, or a marriage . . . these floods had overwhelmed him, buoyed him, driven him tumbling into gladness. But subtle daily undercurrents had spanned a vaster distance, moved him further, shaped the greater portion of his journey. How much grander would his life have been if he had remembered to rejoice in quiet streams as well as rapids?

Alejandro sighed. Perhaps it was a moan. He moved in his narrow cot. He saw a vision. Perhaps it was a dream. For reasons that he did not understand, he pondered how a child perceives a garden.

The air is heavy there with pollen, and she smells it. The sun there serves a purpose greater than illumination, and she knows it. The plants unfurl new glories every instant, and she sees it. She leaves the garden rich with tales to tell, but we who have no time for wonder merely tolerate her passion. We are waiting for heroic moments. Thus it is that almost everyone except a child or dying man will miss the signs of God, and thus it was a kind of miracle that Guadalupe Soledad Consuelo de la Garza truly saw the gardener.

He came with several others, all of whom, like him, wore khaki shirts and dungarees. These men, Latinos all, fanned out across the property with clippers, lawn mowers, and rakes. She paused to watch them through a narrow window in the entry hall, her hands in yellow plastic gloves around the handle of a mop. Every week on Thursday morning these men labored in the flower beds that her employer never truly saw and mowed lawns where he no longer walked. The roar and whine of their machines destroyed the sullen silence of his empty mansion. For the assistance—the distraction—of their presence, she was grateful. Yet even in the midst of gratitude she did not fail to note the meaning of the man. Wearing the same uniform, brown of skin like all the others, dark of hair like all the others, busy with his work like all the others, still she saw him clearly, as a child might see.

Throughout that day she often paused to look outside. No matter where she was inside the house, he was there beyond the window. Once she saw him run a palm along a peeling eucalyptus trunk in passing, and she saw the huge tree's branches gesture down in gratitude. Another time he raised a finger and a hummingbird alighted. She saw him pause and stoop to smell a cluster of deep purple heliotropes and, with them, turn to face the sun. In the late afternoon she went out to him.

He stood with his back to her, shaping a tall hedge with hand clippers. The wind was from the inland hills. The sun and stars were in his hair. She could not hear the breakers or the traffic of the town below. Silently she watched him work, the clippers constantly in motion. Finally, the gardener paused. She took it as permission.

She said, "I have been here many years."

The man resumed his clipping.

"I have tried to tell the good news to these people, but they will not listen."

He only cut the hedge.

"Have I done enough? May I return home?"

The tool he used made smoothly snipping sounds as shrubbery leaves went flying. Lupe wondered if she was truly present, or if this was a dream. It did not matter. So many questions must be asked of someone.

"I know the Savior told us not to worry, señor, but how can I leave things as they are? My concern is for the mister, not myself. I fear he is sinking into something, and I cannot lift him up. I fear his soul is dying."

The clippers clipped. The little leaves descended.

"I fear also for Tucker. Am I right in my suspicions? Has he really turned to unrepentant theft?"

The clouds above his silence started to flow faster, rushing from the east across a yellow sky.

"Tucker breaks my heart, señor. I fear I have betrayed him. I fear I should have stayed with him. I fear I have misjudged my quest. I fear I should have acted on my love for him."

The leaves began to rise up like a pillar from his furious chopping. Spiraling slowly as if in a placid cyclone, the leaves climbed into the sky, up and up they drifted toward the rushing clouds; on they flowed for miles against the wind. Unsurprised, she watched this. She had seen such things before.

"Has it been forbidden you to answer?" asked Lupe. "Because of my failure?"

When he remained silent, she stepped forward and touched him. He turned and was a gardener, only a young gardener, a boy surprised to find her there. He smiled. "*Sí, señorita?*"

"It is nothing," she replied. "I was mistaken."

"Lupe! Come here!"

Delano Wright stood waiting by the door. She approached him. Staring past her shoulder, he said, "Is that man here illegally?"

Following his gaze, she saw nothing but the gardener. "I do not know, mister."

"I don't want people working here illegally."

She almost said, "I work here illegally," but he had known this all along, of course. It was not worth the words.

He looked away from the young man by the hedge, but he did not look at her. "Soon I have go to Sacramento for a few days to tend to business. Would you like to spend the nights here while I'm gone? I would be more comfortable knowing the house is occupied."

"Of course," she said.

"Then it is decided. And you remember that my guests from church are coming in two hours? You will stay to cook for us, and serve us?"

"Of course," she said again, for she had done so many times in recent months.

After she had begun to work for Delano, he had hired a chef to teach her how to cook. This she had learned well. That evening, as the gardeners packed their tools and drove away, Lupe prepared dinner for eleven. It was not difficult in Delano Wright's kitchen, with its multiple refrigerators and bank of ovens and eight-burner range. A cold peach compote would be followed by a richly seasoned leg of lamb, garnished with cloves and pineapple and grilled over hot charcoal. Also she tossed fresh asparagus, new red potatoes, onions, and tomatoes with olive oil and salt and pepper. These she roasted. She added a pair of sourdough loaves. For dessert she made eleven little flans, her country's famous recipe. To simulate crème brûlée, she covered them in sugar, which she would caramelize. Delano Wright entered the kitchen just as she prepared to light the torch.

He said, "Would you like me to do that?"

"I can do it, mister."

"I know how much it frightens you."

"I am fine." She lit a wooden match and fired the torch. She began to pass it slowly over the sugar-covered flan.

"You know," said Delano, "I've always meant to ask. Why are you afraid of fire?"

His question surprised her, after all their years together. She did not answer quickly, and when she did, she kept it simple. "My house burned down. I lost my parents. My little sisters too." The sugar browned and bubbled. She moved to the next little custard.

"I'm sorry," said Delano.

Lupe remained silent.

"Why didn't you ever tell me about it?"

"As you said, you never asked." She did not mean it as an indictment, yet it was a sad fact.

"Did it happen long ago?"

"Yes. Very long."

"How did it happen?"

She moved to the next dish. "I was in my bed, and then it came, the fire. I saw the smoke uncurl across the ceiling. It was the devil coming for me. I saw the devil's face in it."

Delano remained silent. She glanced up and saw his eyes were on the torch as it scorched the flan. She turned her eyes back down to her work. The hissing flame was blue. It looked cool, but the browning sugar made it out to be a liar. "I lay under my blanket and watched the smoke expand. I did not move. I was a child. I believed it was an act of faith, you see. An *auto de fe*."

"Children sometimes have strange ideas."

She heard a note of sorrow in his voice. She thought of Harmony, defying him with wedding plans even as she burned. She pitied him. "Yes, mister. That is so."

"How did you escape?"

"Did I escape? I am never sure."

"I don't know what you mean."

"You see how my hand shakes, mister."

"Yet you brown the flan."

He watched a little longer, and then left the kitchen. The guests arrived at seven. She met each of them at the door and showed them to the front living room. One of them, a man with long hair strangely combed across his baldness, greeted her with a smile. His teeth were very big. He said, "Hello, Lupe. Here we are again. Making a habit out of this, aren't we? Everybody coming over here to eat your good cooking? Say, how are you anyway? Getting along okay, are you?"

"I am well, Mr. Miller. And you?"

"Just fine, Lupe. Just fine. And like I always say, you can call me Bill."

"As you wish, Mr. Bill."

He laughed. "Say, I'm parched. Do you suppose I could get a scotch and water? Just a short one would be fine."

"I am sorry. We have no liquor in the house."

"Oh, that's right. I keep forgetting Del's a teetotaler. Then how about a little chardonnay?"

"No wine either."

"No wine? But Del keeps a fine cellar."

"He poured it out."

"Poured it *out*?" The man laughed again. "Oh, Lupe, you're funny. I've seen Del's cellar. That would take a while."

"Yes," said Lupe. "It did take a while."

The man's smile disappeared. He glanced at his host, who stood in earnest conversation with a pair of other guests on the far side of the large and richly furnished room. "Say, Lupe, is our friend okay, do you think?"

"You should ask him that, Mr. Bill."

"Sure. You're right. Of course I should."

"We have tea or lemonade. Many kinds of soft drinks. Mineral water too."

"Anything at all," said the man with the big teeth.

She served drinks to everyone. She waited while they lingered in the front living room. They spoke as if she were not there. Like a ghost among them she heard everything: their complaints about a government man who was slowing down construction on their big development, their new Christian community. She heard their strategy to work around him. They would call in certain favors owed. It was the American way. They knew many people. They were powerful men. They assured themselves the government man would no longer be a problem. Even Christians have a right to politics in this great nation.

Finally, when they moved into the dining room, she began to serve. Two at a time, she brought them sustenance. They talked and laughed as she worked all around the table. They told each other stories. She recognized the famous preacher among them. She recognized several others. She had seen them on the television and in newspapers. She re-filled their glasses, took away their plates, brought the flan and coffee.

It was then she overheard one man tell another, "They took the strangest things. The Monet is understandable, but I mean, why steal our screen door?"

"What's that, Arnie?" asked a man across the table.

"Didn't you hear?" said another. "Arnie and Elise got burgled."

"We did too!" said the first man. "Just five nights ago."

Yet another man said, "That's strange. Our house was robbed the night before last."

All eleven men fell silent as Lupe moved among them, filling coffee cups.

"Can't be a coincidence," said someone at last.

"We should tell the police," said another.

The great men began putting theories forth, suggesting potential suspects. They asked themselves who had reason to hate them all, and assured themselves the robber would be caught, now that they had found this clear connection. Yes, indeed, they said. Now he will be quickly caught.

The three men who had been robbed began to list their stolen property. Lupe listened carefully. She had heard the list before. She was certain of it. She had heard it in a holy place, as requests from humble saints. She thought of Tucker taking notes. She thought of the devil's face in curling smoke. Her hand shook as she poured the coffee. Oh, she thought. What a painful thing is love.

CAPÍTULO 27

THE MISSION FELL INTO A disheartening routine: each morning a kind of roll was called, missing neophytes were identified, and Don Felipe sent three leather-jacket soldiers to their villages to capture and return them. Two days after Alejandro fell ill, the soldiers failed to return. The captain sent five more. They found the missing soldiers' bodies in the arroyo, stripped of armor and of pikes.

"It seems we are at war," said Don Felipe.

"Then we will fight for God," replied Fray Guillermo.

Alejandro could only lie within his little cell. Prayer was burdensome, for his mind wandered in its fever. Driven by reports of violence, wracked with a disease from the devil, he found it easier to contemplate the evil that consumed him.

A student of history, he knew the pestilence had nearly overwhelmed humanity four hundred years before his time. Some said eighty million died in Europe as it reaped its morbid harvest; others said two hundred million. The dead were half the Western world, at any rate, and still in Alejandro's day the doctors did not know the cause.

He had read ancient parchments in Spain filled with many foolish theories. The malignancy was attributed to cats. Others warned of evil airs. Some said birds. Some said Jews, some said women, and others blamed it on the foreigners, any foreigners. This ignorance was the devil's bread and meat, for it led to many crimes. Jews were massacred.

The sick were buried prematurely. Those deemed responsible were sometimes scourged or flayed or burned alive.

Men called "doctors" went about in full-length coats of black, with pointed hats and leather gloves and breeches, and masks with hideous curved beaks to frighten death away. They stuffed the beaks with aromatic herbs as proof against miasma and the stench. To avert evil, they gazed out at their hellish world through eyepieces made of crimson glass. With wooden canes they prodded patients from a distance as a test of life, and beat back those who tried to come too close.

Today's doctors maintain their distance differently, of course, with hazmat suits and isolation wards, and lab results received from a distance via telephone calls or facsimile machines. That is how it was for Earnest Winchell—"Ernie" to his friends—a doctor of internal medicine at Northport Medical Center, the small hospital in Blanco Beach.

Dr. Winchell stood in a nurses' station. In his hand was a telephone. In his ear was an explanation for the horrific suffering of young Kenny Karlsson, a boy of high school age, lately of New Harmony. The doctor heard the words, spoken calmly by a lab technician on another floor of the building, but he did not believe them. He said, "That's impossible."

The technician replied, "We thought so too, but there's no chance of a mistake. We took secondary specimens and triple-checked everything."

Dr. Winchell's knees began to shake. He dropped into a chair and hung up the telephone. He thought about the technician's words. They were not twenty-first century words, not something to be heard in modern times at all. The woman might as well have warned him that barbarians were at the gates, or Pompeii had just been buried by the eruption of Vesuvius.

He thought about the patient's presentation. It had been many years since he had studied the disease in medical school, but to the best of his recollection the symptoms agreed perfectly with the laboratory's findings.

He thought about the fact that he had touched Kenny Karlsson's skin. He felt his courage wane. He thought about his wife, Gilda, and his twin five-year-old daughters, Sam and Kelly. He had gone home and touched each of them as well. He searched his memory, trying to remember the contagious period and how it was transmitted. Might Gilda and the girls already be infected?

Oh, how gladly Ernie Winchell would have donned medieval bird-like armor to avoid that foolish touch if only he had known! How gladly he would have viewed the world in shades of red and prodded Kenny Karlsson with a cane!

Control yourself, he thought. You're a doctor. Act like one.

He took a few deep breaths and rose and walked a short distance down the hall to stand outside the patient's door. He tried to think of what to do. Place a guard, certainly. Do that first of all. No one in or out of the room. And verify that the ventilation system to the room is isolated. Then make a call to Atlanta, to the Centers for Disease Control. Send them a copy of the lab report. And try to get the names of everyone who had been in contact with the boy: the people in admissions, janitors, visitors, nurses, lab techs . . . everyone.

Within the next half hour all these things were done or under way. When he could think of no other measures to be taken, Ernie Winchell called his wife. "We have a little problem here," he said. "I'm going to have to work an all-nighter."

"Really? Why?"

"It's just this one patient. I need to stay to keep an eye on him."

"But tonight's the parent-teacher thing."

"I know. I'm sorry."

"Ernie, I don't understand. What's so special about this patient? Why can't the night shift handle it?"

"Listen, I'll explain tomorrow, okay? Right now I'm late for a meeting."

"Ernie—"

"I'm really sorry, sweetie. They're paging me. I have to go. Just pretend we're back in the bad old days and you're an intern's wife again, okay?"

"Okay. . . ."

"I love you."

"I love you more."

"That's impossible."

Less than two hours after Dr. Winchell hung up the telephone, seven men and women arrived in full-length suits of white, with gloves and hats and plastic masks to ward off death. Many special measures were imposed, the entire floor detained, doctors, nurses, visitors, and patients forced to stay. Doors were sealed with tape, specimens taken, vaccinations given, and additional hospital security guards were posted with instructions to allow no unauthorized entry or exit.

One of the people from the Centers for Disease Control asked a question Dr. Winchell should have thought of long before. "Where does this kid go to school?"

Calls were made, and it was quickly learned that more children had called in sick that day than usual. The school officials were unconcerned, believing it to be an outbreak of chickenpox, rare at high school age, but not unheard-of.

Yet of course it was not chickenpox. It was instead the early symptoms of a spreading evil, with many friends from Kenny Karlsson's school displaying all the same first signs that had afflicted him, children with parents who went to work in office buildings all around the county, who rode in elevators, and had business lunches; children with younger siblings who attended a different school; children whose families employed maids and nannies who traveled home to Wilson City every evening in packed commuter buses. The possibilities for widespread infection were already almost uncontainable.

As contagious disease specialists considered all the ways the malevolence might spread, a team with a different specialty arrived in Blanco Beach, special agents of the FBI, wearing suits and holstered semiautomatic pistols. They were there because the Department of Homeland Security suspected terrorism. How else could such a pestilence have reappeared after so many years?

Information was power. To control it, they collected the cell phones of everybody on the floor. All the landlines to the isolated floor were shut down. The hospital security guards were replaced with Marines on special detachment. The hospital staff, patients, and visitors unlucky enough to have been caught up in the quarantine were warned not to test the new guards, who would use lethal force if necessary.

Only eight hours had passed since Dr. Winchell had called Atlanta, and his wife.

The Karlsson home was searched and left uninhabitable. Upholstery was stripped, carpet pulled, drywall punctured. No possible hiding place remained uncovered. Even the doghouse in the backyard was examined, and that was where a CDC technician found the well-chewed human tibia, or shinbone, which still retained small fragments of dried flesh. Six hours later a laboratory in Los Angeles reported two remarkable facts: First, the bone had indeed belonged to a victim of the disease, and second, the victim had perished more than two centuries earlier. It would be another forty-eight hours before test results could determine if the diseased tissue was still infectious, but all search teams were ordered to assume the worst.

When this possibility was met with widespread skepticism among the FBI special agents involved in the investigation, a pair of specialists were called in for a briefing. One was an infectious disease and biohazard research fellow at Scripps Research Institute in La Jolla. The other was an authority in the field of sociocultural anthropology, archaeology, and bioarchaeology at UC Santa Barbara. The infectious disease specialist spoke first. Her information was remarkable both in terms of what was unknown as well as what was known.

It seemed scientists had disagreed for many years about how long some of the world's most virulent diseases might survive after the death of their human hosts. The University of Michigan Health System had recently proven that *Bacillus anthracis*, the bacterium that causes anthrax, could not only subsist outside its host, but actually reproduce and grow in contaminated soil. This finding merely confirmed the empirical beliefs of ranchers and excavation contractors. Natural gas pipelines had long been routinely diverted around ranches where cattle had died in anthrax outbreaks.

But anthrax was only the beginning. The city of London's subway system had been deliberately designed to skirt known plague pits from the 1600s, and new research at the University of Liverpool suggested that the bubonic plague did indeed lie dormant throughout Europe. Also, a paper published in the prestigious medical journal *Lancet* detailed research completed in 1985 suggesting smallpox could survive for at least a century in a victim's casket.

A special agent raised his hand. "How could this bone still have skin on it after more than two hundred years?"

The professor from UC Santa Barbara spoke up. "There are several possibilities. The body might have been intentionally mummified. It might have been frozen, although that seems unlikely in this case. It might have been preserved with tannic acid somehow. Many bodies were unintentionally preserved that way in the peat bogs of northern Europe. Or it might have been preserved in a very dry place. A cave somewhere in the hills, perhaps. Or buried several feet below the ground in a well-drained area. As you may know, this part of California only gets about a foot of rain per year. Most of that is consumed almost immediately by the desert and savanna vegetation, and most of the re-mainder escapes as runoff. A body buried six feet deep or more in an area with sloping topography might well remain almost completely dry. Add the lack of oxygen and insect life at that depth, and it's entirely possible the body would fail to decompose, at least not completely."

"How come I've never heard about any of this?" asked another spe-cial agent.

"Think about it," replied the biohazard specialist. "If you were a terrorist and this information came to your attention, what would you do?"

After a brief pause, the grim-faced special agent said, "Head straight to the cemetery for some raw material, I guess."

The biohazard specialist only nodded.

When thorough background checks were made on Kenny's parents, it was discovered that one of his mother's parents was a second-generation immigrant from Lebanon. In spite of this red flag, no evidence was found of terrorist connections. Under lengthy question-ing both of the parents consistently maintained they had no knowledge of how the human bone had come to be in their backyard.

"Sunny found it somewhere," said the exhausted mother. "It's just Sunny's bone."

Sunny was released outside the Karlssons' home and shooed away. As the dog wandered through New Harmony, special agents followed at a distance, watching with binoculars, hoping the animal might lead them to the source of the tibia. This scheme yielded nothing useful.

Despite the pleas of Kenny's parents and the objections of Dr.

Winchell, the FBI tried to question the boy from outside the plastic tent which contained what was left of him. He was far past answering.

"Doctor," said a female special agent, "Isn't there something that would perk him up a little?"

"Perk him up? Are you crazy? I've had him on sedatives for days to kill the pain."

"We must have answers, Doctor. Lives depend on learning how he was infected. You know that as well as we do. How about some kind of amphetamine?"

When Ernie Winchell refused, she made a call on her cell phone. Soon one of the doctors with the Centers for Disease Control came down the hall with a syringe. To Dr. Winchell's dismay, the drug was injected into Kenny Karlsson's intravenous drip.

The boy awoke almost immediately, but in response to their insistent questions he could only scream.

Kenny's devastated parents fell ill that evening, as did his younger sisters. The family maid was brought in with symptoms. It was too late in their case for vaccinations. Dr. Winchell assumed they all would succumb over the next few days, an entire family, gone.

A situation room was established in a space normally reserved for waiting friends and relatives. A meeting was held. Officials from Atlanta and Washington, D.C. were included via speakerphone. At issue was the proper balance between containment and publicity. How much should be communicated to the general public? At what point would they panic?

A man from Homeland Security said if this was the work of terrorists, surely it was best to do whatever possible to minimize the news. Why give terrorists the publicity they wanted?

A woman from the Centers for Disease Control said it was essential to disseminate the news, to allow citizens to protect themselves, to get them early treatment, to administer vaccine. Besides, too many people were involved. The press would surely get wind of the story soon. Better to control the way the news got out instead of risking that the media would decide for themselves how to spin it.

The officials on the speakerphone said they needed time to gather information and consider options carefully. The situation must be contained a little longer. One did not announce such information willy-nilly. A plan would be formulated, a decision would be forthcoming, perhaps in as little as one day.

During that one day Kenny Karlsson died, twenty-seven more became infected in the recently constructed Christian community of New Harmony, and Dr. Earnest "Ernie" Winchell became feverish and noticed several red spots on his palms.

CAPÍTULO 28

ON THE FIRST SUNDAY AFTER Pentecost, eighteen days after the pestilence attacked him, Fray Alejandro awoke. To his very great surprise it seemed he had survived. His body was a mass of sores; his face was deeply scarred forever, yet he felt fortunate indeed. From his cot the good friar praised the Holy Father ceaselessly. He even did his best to celebrate the Holy Trinity as the day required, although there was little he could do in his weakened state. Then, just after vespers Fray Guillermo appeared at his door.

"I was told you are well, brother."

"Indeed not, Abbot. I do not think I could rise from this bed if it was burning, but it does seem I will survive."

"God be praised."

"Most earnestly, yes."

"You have heard the news of Fray Benicio?"

"I have heard no news at all these last two weeks or more, nor would I have understood it if I had."

"Of course. I meant today. You have heard today?"

"What do you wish to tell me, Abbot?"

The abbot's face worked strangely in the candle light. To Alejandro it seemed as if his head were an egg in the process of hatching. His cheeks flushed in stark contrast to his pale complexion. His mouth contorted. His eyes bulged. When at last he spoke, the words rushed from the crack between his lips like steam under great pressure. "That boy has abandoned us completely! He has thrown off his clothes and gone to live entirely nude among the heathens in their village! He paints himself with mud, just as they do! He brandished a spear against Don Felipe's soldiers when they attempted to return him! A spear! *Against us!* He has gone completely mad!"

Alejandro closed his eyes against a wave of weakness. He could only whisper, "I am sorry."

"Sorry? Sorry? I tell you a Franciscan has given himself over to apostasy and you tell me you are *sorry*?"

"Indeed I am very sorry, Abbot. And I would go to try to save him from his error if I could, but as you see, that is quite impossible."

Fray Guillermo raised both hands toward the ceiling. "What am I to do? I find myself abandoned! One brother has become a pagan and the other cannot leave his bed. The heathens lie in wait beyond the mission walls. The neophytes betray us. What am I to do?"

Alejandro opened his eyes to see Fray Guillermo's face quite changed. In the place of rage he now saw fear. "Perhaps you could do one thing."

"Yes? Anything!"

"Upon the floor beside my bed you see my chamber pot. It is completely full and I feel the need to relieve myself. Would you kindly empty it for me?"

The superior's face began to writhe again. His teeth ground. His lips trembled. "I will send someone!" he snapped before turning on his heel to leave.

Alejandro sighed. Lying on his cot, he thought about Benicio's decision. He understood it. He too sometimes longed to become what the people were, to erase the differences between them in order that he might save a few. But which differences stood in the way of the pagans' salvation, and which were evidence of that same salvation? For Fray Alejandro this was not an easy thing to know, not nearly as easy as Benicio and Guillermo seemed to think.

Murder is forbidden in the commandments given to the prophet Moses, indeed God condemned the Canaanites to destruction because of their child sacrifices, yet Abraham, having also been commanded, raised the knife above his son. In all its forms idolatry is anathema, yet divine decree demanded Israel must gaze upon a graven serpent for salvation from the poison coursing through their veins. It is a simple-minded man indeed who views obedience in terms of absolutes, for in this fallen world even the Creator sometimes makes good use of evil.

Thus, although the eighth commandment bids us not to steal, Tucker Rue, a minister of Almighty God, moved among the rooms of absent Christian homeowners with his conscience clear. His soul was bound about with certain ethical resolutions. He would not steal from those who could afford no loss. He would not steal from those who freely gave. He would not steal when owners might be present, nor would he bear arms, nor resist capture with anything but flight. He would not steal from unbelievers, for those still lost in sinful natures can but only sin, and who was he to punish that?

He would steal from Christians only, and only from a certain kind of Christian, from those who claimed the cross, yet lived for themselves. Above all else he would involve no other in his enterprise, for Tucker Rue knew there was a slight chance he was wrong and he dared not lead another to temptation.

He had heard of Delano Wright's trip to Sacramento. He knew the man had traveled there to lobby for the second phase of his development, the abomination on the canyon road. He also knew, of course, that Lupe now lived in Wilson City, so the old Pharisee's huge house would be empty. Thus it was with confidence that Tucker Rue arrived on foot at the gate below the hill, wearing a ski mask and leaving his old pickup truck a few yards down the driveway until he could disable any security cameras Delano might have installed outside.

He applied a screwdriver to the keypad at the gate and removed the faceplate. He made adjustments to the wiring. Soundlessly the ornate sculpted barricade slid open. He felt a hint of pride. He had studied burglary as diligently as any seminarian or philosopher ever studied epistemology. He had learned each doctrine well: how to defeat photoelectric alarms, passive infrared alarms, ultrasonic alarms, where to look for the proper wiring, how to create bypass loops on keypads and magnetic contacts. He was an intelligent man. A doctor of theology. These concepts were not difficult for one so steeped in scholarship.

With the gate safely open, he returned to his truck and drove onto the property. He parked beside the garage, in a place not easily seen from the driveway. He backed into the spot, the better to escape quickly.

Still wearing his ski mask, he approached the rear door by the kitchen. From his pocket he removed a small Allen wrench, which he had previously bent to a thirty-degree angle and ground smooth on the end. Also, he held a tiny screwdriver. He slipped the screwdriver into the lock and twisted, then inserted the modified Allen wrench. Working from the back of the lock forward, one by one he pressed the pins up, using the tension of the twisted screwdriver to hold them in the raised position. This took several minutes, then he was inside.

He had no time to listen, to verify his solitude, to assure his safety. He moved quickly to a keypad in the kitchen near the hallway to the garage. He might have removed the keypad from the wall, removed the insulation from the wires behind, and jumped them with a set of alligator clips, but to his surprise those measures were unnecessary. On the face of the keypad, a pair of green lights glowed. Strangely, the system was not armed.

He hurried to the bedroom wing, where he ripped a cover and two sheets from the first bed he found. Returning to the kitchen, he spread the bedcover on the floor outside the pantry. He made quick work of piling much of the pantry's contents in the center of the fabric, cans and jars of vegetables and beans and sauces, bags of noodles and boxes of cereals and rice, as well as savory little nothings, artichoke hearts, caviar, Grecian and French delicacies, escargot, rich man's food. Gathering the four corners together, he staggered underneath the burden all the way outside to his truck. It was the seventh rich man's home that he had robbed, and their food was always his first priority. He sometimes thought of Saint Peter, of the sheet filled with unclean animals that rose before him those three times. Kill and eat. Kill and eat. Kill and eat. God has made this clean.

Back within the house again, he spread both of the sheets on the floor in one of the living rooms. He removed a notebook from his hip pocket and began strolling through the house, glancing back and forth between the list in his hand and the boundless luxury around him. With his assistance, Delano Wright would tithe well, even if unwillingly.

This for Pablo and Lenora, thought Tucker, removing a set of towels from a bathroom.

This for their little boy, Juanito, he thought, taking an exquisite handmade model sailboat from its cradle in the living room.

Still he wore the ski mask. He might not have sufficient time to delete the video recordings before he left, and it was impossible to avoid every camera, some of which could be smaller than a pencil tip. Checking off the prayer requests as if his notebook were a shopping list, he took a foot massager for old Carmen, who suffered so from bunions. From the garage he took a fine set of wrenches for Henrique, whose ancient Ford was broken down. He took an alarm clock for Nana Dominguez, who could not afford to be late to work again.

Tucker Rue piled all these things and more onto the sheets upon the floor, then he went down the long hall to the master bedroom, and straight into the massive walk-in closet there. He removed a pair of shoes and pressed against the wooden back of the rack where they had been displayed. The back swung open. He pushed a set of numbers on a keypad mounted behind this little hidden door. The numbers were Harmony Wright's birthday, a date he would not forget, no matter how much time might pass since she had playfully revealed this family secret to him. After he pressed the final number, an entire set of shelves on the far side of the closet moved an inch. Tucker gripped and pulled the disguised entrance to Delano Wright's safe room, and the shelves swung wide on silent hinges.

Stepping inside the windowless space, he saw a little kitchen along one wall, and a well-stocked bookshelf, several comfortable chairs, a dining table with more chairs, and two sets of bunk beds. He also saw an oaken rolltop desk, and on the wall above it, a group of video screens. There were seven of these screens and all but one were active, showing different rooms. The blank screen would be the disabled gate camera, he thought with a smile. It was indeed a wise choice to remain masked when robbing rich men's houses. Moving to the desk, he removed a disc from the small computer there, the record of his presence. This he slipped into his pocket. He typed commands into the keyboard, shutting down the cameras and deleting every trace of his image from the computer's memory. He then went through the desk drawers. He found quite a bit of cash and a few bearer bonds. He left the bonds, but took the cash. With the first handful of money he thought, This for Sanctuario, because the rent is due. With the second handful he thought, This for Wilson City, because the taxes must be paid. Render unto Caesar what is Caesar's.

Slipping the bills into his pocket, Tucker felt a sudden urge to leave. Too much time had passed.

In his haste to go he almost missed the little painting propped against the wall beside the desk. But with a glance in passing he saw its primitive style, not at all the kind of art that fit in Delano Wright's house, and he wondered why the man had bothered to conceal it in the safe room. In spite of his desire to leave, he bent to look closer, saw its subject matter, saw the Spanish words, and suddenly a memory came flooding back, an image of a different man than he now was, a naïve man, the kind of man who went into the wilderness to look for God.

He remembered a remarkable vision coming to him there, a suddenly appearing saint there in the desert's midst, and the strange burden she had carried, those wooden panels bearing images which he had only briefly seen, and had not been allowed to study. Suddenly he knew why the painting had been hidden in that secret place. It did not belong to Delano Wright. The similarity to what Tucker had once seen in the wilderness could not be a coincidence.

I can tell you this: it is a guide for me. To help me find my way.

This, he thought, for Lupe, lifting up the painting, which had so obviously been taken from her.

Out of the safe room, out of that closet large as houses, out of the master bedroom, and down the hall he went. He held the prize for Lupe like a baby. He did not know if she had prayed for it, but God often bequeathed unrequested blessings. He had to go; he felt the Spirit warning him that time was short. Yet when he passed a closed door in the hallway, Tucker paused. This too he remembered from that afternoon so long ago, when Harmony had given him a tour of her family home. This too must be entered.

He opened the door.

Inside, all was as it had been. The whole room was a shrine, an altar to a father's love. Everything was perfectly arranged and perfectly clean. Every piece of French Provençal furniture, every frilly pillow on the bed, every velveteen stuffed animal along the wall, every doll, every snapshot of a high school friend, every rock band poster, every ribbon won on horseback spoke to him of a Harmony whom he had never known, the Harmony who once became the woman he had met and tried to love.

Overwhelmed, Tucker sat heavily upon the narrow bed. His eyes moved around the room, taking in each clue about the person who grew up there. From precious little girl to brave young woman leaving home, she had filled that place with signs. Such innocence. Such beauty. Such a glorious creation. Suddenly Tucker gasped, sucking in the air. He had not been breathing. He pulled the ski mask off his face and drew in oxygen, knowing surely there must be a molecule or two remaining that had passed through his fiancée's lungs. Undisguised, he thought about the terrible thing that he had almost done to her, the damage he had verged upon, and finally, more than two years past the proper time, he began to cry. Dear Lord, he thought, gasping at the air, with eyes awash. Did you have to go so far to save her from my selfishness?

A sound. The sharp rap of something falling or bumping into something hard. Someone else was in the house.

Tucker sprang to his feet. The painting was still in his hands. His face was still exposed. He drew down the ski mask. He moved silently across the carpet to the door. He paused there to listen. It had sounded like an object hitting the tile kitchen floor. Tucker Rue had always known it might end like this, but if he could get to the front door before they reached the middle of the house, he still had a chance. He took a step out to the hall. He stopped. He wiped his streaming eyes. He could not run. Not yet. It had not been finished.

Turning back into Harmony's room, he scanned a bookshelf by her little desk. He found what he sought. With the primitive painting tucked beneath his arm, he pulled a red pen from a copper cup upon the desk. He quickly turned the pages in the book and then he underlined a passage. He replaced the pen. He left the book open on the desk.

Down the hall he went, as quickly as he dared. He must not make a sound. He had worn shoes with rubber soles for just that reason. In the living room he turned away from the cased opening that led to the more private rooms, the morning room, the kitchen. He hurried toward the front of the huge house, toward the formal living room. To him it seemed that Harmony was waiting there to meet him, the woman he had nearly ruined with his ill-conceived proposal. She encouraged him to hurry, endorsing his enterprise in spite of the damage he had almost done. Such a saint could do no less. But who was he to be forgiven?

Tucker reached the front door, and behind him came a voice. It was not Harmony's, of course. Under the circumstances, it was remarkably calm. It said simply, "Hello."

In terror Tucker Rue fled from Guadalupe Soledad Consuelo de la Garza's unwise greeting and Harmony Wright's posthumous forgiveness. He thanked God for reminding him to put the mask back on. Lupe could not have seen his face or known that it was him. But had she seen his truck? Would she recognize it if she saw it? These thoughts overwhelmed all others as he drove along the canyon road, the truck bed heavy-laden with so many answered prayers.

Imagine seeing a burglar and saying hello. How he worried about Lupe's innocence! He should not have run away; he should have turned around and scolded her. For her own sake he should help her become hardened, more aware of danger. He should have warned her not to greet strange men wearing masks, advised her not to call to them in such a way, but to flee from them instead.

Tucker laughed. Imagine it: a burglar turning back to warn a woman against burglars. What would he say, exactly? *Don't be so polite; I'm robbing you.* He laughed again. His laughter grew, and grew, and then he was crying again.

Overwhelmed, he pulled to the side of the road. He prayed as traffic passed, and as the sun slipped down behind the hills.

Oh, God, what am I thinking? Is this right? Is this just? Am I doing any good, or am I only adding one more wrong to all the others? Must Lupe be warned of *me*? I don't know. I don't know. Maybe I should stop. But how can I stand by doing nothing while they live the way they do?

Oh, God, do you demand that much? Must I watch my people bear this crushing poverty while those who claim to love their neighbors drive vehicles so needlessly immense it takes a picker's daily pay just to buy the gasoline to drive an hour? Must I ignore the way they numb their minds with gigantic television sets and hoard food enough to feed a village and walk into the closets of their homes to choose between a dozen pairs of shoes for church and time their pastor's sermons on thousand-dollar watches and spend their stingy tithes on softer pews or bigger stained-glass windows?

The familiar righteous anger rose again to do its cleansing work. His hysteria faded, replaced by something cold. On he drove.

He passed the mighty gates of New Harmony. Up beyond the gates Camel Mountain was now partially obscured by lawns and lovely homes and winding landscaped roads, the people up there safe against the gathering darkness, safe behind the walls that bound their Christian world. He saw Delano Wright's huge monument on top of the mountain, the giant concrete crosses, multimillion-dollar crosses glowing in the floodlights like three upright whitewashed tombs. He saw a pair of ambulances at the lordly gates and wondered who was ill or injured, and then he thought he did not care, and immediately he hated the thing in him that mocked sympathy. How these people tempted him! Tucker Rue ground his teeth. It was either that or curse.

He drove on, and in a few more miles he came upon a billboard by the road. It stood all alone, far from any other man-made thing; a blight on God's creation, especially because of what it bore:

NEW HARMONY, PHASE II
SAFETY, SERENITY, SANCTUARY.
JOIN THE CONGREGATION.

Congregation! Think of that. To sell real estate as if it were Christ's body. To hide from obedience behind walls and gates and guards and call the hiding "sanctuary."

Suddenly his foot was on the brake. The old truck skidded to a halt. Ahead and behind he saw no other vehicles. He rolled over to the shoulder. He emerged. Above him insects swirled within the glaring whiteness of the billboard lights. He reached into the truck bed and removed a little plastic tank of gasoline, his emergency supply, a precaution he had learned while in the desert leaving water for dehydrated immigrants.

With the gasoline in his right hand, he waded through the thick brush between the road and the sign. He reached the first of its three poles. He uncapped the gas and shook it out, covering the pole. He moved on to the next pole, and there he did the same. He did it again on the third pole, and then he lit a match. He was Abraham knifing Isaac. He was Israel raising up the serpent.

The sign was a bright pyre in his rearview mirror as he drove away from the shoulder. Had he but looked down he would have seen its flickering light absorbed into the darkness of the painted panel on the seat beside him while, in the truck bed at his back, the corners of the white sheets flapped and beat against his answered prayers.

So much for your congregation, he thought with his eyes upon the fire. So much for your sanctuary.

He neared Wilson City. He had many other homes to visit in the night, many blessings to distribute. For this, however, he would have to wait. He always started placing things at people's doors around three in the morning. They must be asleep. They must not know the Lord's mysterious ways. He drove aimlessly, avoiding Sanctuario and his neighborhood. He dared not risk a chance encounter with a member of this flock.

Tucker found an empty lot and parked. In the darkness, he sat still and stared out through the windshield, thinking about Lupe, and Harmony, and Jesus Christ. Once he raised his hands to his nose and inhaled the scent of gasoline. Again he thought of warning Lupe away. He was not a man to follow, not a man to call back with a greeting. He was beyond her now, beyond everyone. He thought of Moses, who also wore a mask when he descended Sinai, whose great love had been poisonous to everyone but God.

The painting lay beside him on the seat, the details of it very dark and hard to see in that empty parking lot. Suddenly he had a thought: if Lupe was calling out to burglars at Delano Wright's house, it meant she was not at home. He need not wait to bless her. He could return her property immediately.

He drove to her boardinghouse, and parked out at the curb.

Tucker Rue, accomplished man of God and burglar, used the tiny screwdriver and crooked Allen wrench again, although this time his intention was to leave more than he took. The simple lock on Lupe's door soon clicked. He pushed into her attic room. Moonlight streamed across a little table by the window. He put the painting there and began his search. It did not take him long, for she had made no serious effort to hide the thing he sought. He found a cardboard box. From inside the box he removed a bundle, the crimson velvet black in the dim moonlight. This he also carried to the little table by the window.

From the velvet bag he removed the strange paintings, the secret Lupe had once carried through the desert of Sonora. He unfolded the two images on either side of the central panel. Glancing very quickly at the object, he could see she had replaced the stolen panel in the middle with a blank piece of raw wood. It made him angry to think of her treasured possession broken up that way. Had Delano Wright taken the central panel as a payment of some kind? Had he simply stolen it? Why had he not taken all three panels together? Tucker shook his head. All that mattered was the fact that part of Lupe's treasure had been separated from her, hidden from her in the man's safe room, and now the pieces would be reunited. Tucker smiled to think how this would please her.

Details of the paintings were unclear in the moonlight. It was just as well. He was not there to view art. In fact, he did his best to avoid looking at the images on the other panels. Lupe had concealed them from him in the desert. She would not wish them seen there in her room. He merely hoped to give a gift to her. To do so this intrusion had been necessary, but he would respect her privacy in every other way.

He compared the size of the painting he had stolen from Delano against the panels of Lupe's triptych. As he had expected, they seemed to be a perfect match. He turned Lupe's three-part painting over. Examining the rear, he saw several hinges made of leather, which held the pieces of wood together. Each bit of leather was attached with small iron nails. He rose and went to search Lupe's small kitchenette. Returning with a knife, he set to work upon the nails. It was slow work in the moonlight, but thirty minutes later he had replaced the blank piece of wood in the center of Lupe's painting with the painting he had recovered from Delano Wright.

Satisfied, he left it there: Fray Alejandro's wonder, the three small painted panels standing upright on the little table. Because of the darkness and his respect for Lupe's wishes, he might never have seen his part in the miracle if not for losing his truck keys. When he reached the street below and realized they were missing from his pocket, he knew he must have left them in the attic room, so up he went again, and again he used his homemade picks to make short work of Lupe's simple lock. Once inside the room, he stood still by the door and scanned the floor, the table, and the little kitchen counter.

He saw no keys, and yet he had to find them. Imagine if his truck remained there through the night, and in the morning all the answered prayers were seen. With no other choice, Tucker switched on the overhead light.

The keys were where he'd left them on the little table by the triptych. He saw them very plainly now. He quickly crossed the room, and lifted them, and then it happened.

In spite of his resolution not to violate Lupe's privacy, he beheld the paintings clearly. He saw, and felt the power in his legs give way. As had Lupe many years before him, Tucker Rue sank onto his knees before the power of Fray Alejandro's burden. He knelt there as if praying, but he had descended in mere weakness, not in faith. Both of his shaking hands gripped the table for support. He was lost to everything except the paintings. He saw the background of the central panel, Golgotha with Christ upon his cross, and the little chapel with its own anachronistic cross upon a steeple, and the horrible open pit below, Gehenna possibly, the burning garbage dump of hell, or possibly a tomb engorged with bodies piled on bodies, flesh corrupt with bursting boils, and beneath it all the enigmatic Spanish words. *El Cristo resucitado ha enterrado el infierno*. The risen Christ has buried hell.

Yet for all its unearthly power, this was not what dropped him to his knees.

On the panel to the Savior's left he saw a very different image. Mary graced the dark field of Golgotha, that cursed terrain which was somehow also that of southern California, with Camel Mountian's profile unmistakable. But this was not just any Mary; it was Mexico's own Virgen de Guadalupe, replete with turquoise robe and folded hands and rays of light or flames arrayed around her. There also stood the Magdalene, and John, whom Jesus loved, and several other mourners, while on the cross above them hung the faithful thief, who stared at Jesus with the hope of heaven plain upon his face.

Still, for all its mystery and beauty, this too was not what laid him low.

It was not even the rampant evil on the opposite panel: the demonic faces of the mocking crowd, the common Jews, the Pharisees, the Roman soldiers with their shouting mouths and deep-creased scowls and upraised fists. No, Tucker had been beaten to his knees by the man upon the other cross. That unrepentant thief had overwhelmed him, that mocking face so very clearly painted in detail, that face which was, incredibly, somehow, Tucker's own.

CAPÍTULO 29

THE GALLOWS HAD BEEN BUILT in perfect alignment with Alejandro's cot and the narrow doorway of his cell. How earnestly he wished it might stand elsewhere, out of sight. Then he could have gazed into the world outside the confines of his tiny room and seen a sky the color of a robin's egg and clouds like cotton bolls and a distant hillside clothed in tan and olive green. Then he would not see the swaying neophytes whom Don Felipe had hung for the murder of his leather-jacket soldiers. But Alejandro was trapped by the aftermath of his own affliction and had only two choices: gaze out through his door across the narrow strip of plaza to see three corpses dangling brown and bloated, or stare at the unfinished altarpiece upon the table by his bed. It was a devil's alternative. One vista brought him heartbreak; the other, accusations.

He could not bear to watch the bodies sway, so instead he gazed at the symbol of his failure, the *retablo* on the table, and he thought about that day at San Francisco's little chapel many years before when he received his calling to the mission. *Go and save my children.* He had come two thousand leagues since then, a million steps from the far side of the world to the most remote outpost of Christendom, only to completely fail.

Whom had he come so far to bless? Whom had he come to save?

The images he should have painted mocked him; the empty wooden panels whispered, *No one.*

The lost still perished in their sins, the sick still died, Christians were the same as pagans, and the gospel was mere empty words to everyone but him, it seemed.

Eyes unwavering upon the failed *retablo,* Alejandro marveled that he had not recognized his uselessness much sooner. He had led a sheltered life at the friary in Spain, naïve in the assumption that he understood his Maker's wishes. He had blithely followed fantasies to California, so blindly certain of the Church and crown, so convinced of his own understanding, that he overreached.

The homely friar turned from the convicting sight of three mostly bare wood panels where three sacred images should be. He looked to the doorway, willing himself to gaze beyond the corpses on the gallows, to block the bodies from his mind, to concentrate on the lovely hillside far beyond. There he saw several *chinampos* grazing, a hearty breed of cattle they had brought to Alta California to be consumed by soldiers, friars, and neophytes alike, their hides transported south to answer the endless call for leather in New Spain. Although the brutes were raised for slaughter, they enjoyed the peaceful circumstances and protection of the mission. They were amply fed and fattened to the very end.

Alejandro wondered, in that final instant when their lives were taken, did the cattle recognize those comforts were but gentle lies enticing them along a path that ends with gutting? Did they realize everything had come to naught? How easy to believe one could control the future, how tempting to place hope in plans and projects.

It is a mistake still made today by millions.

Consider the economy of California, for example. Many worldwide empires are directed from the offices and homes of San Francisco, Los Angeles, Orange County, and San Diego. Collectively they surpass the economies of most nations. Indeed, depending on one's source of information it is variously said the economy of the aptly named Golden State is the tenth or seventh largest in the world.

For generations Delano Wright's family had played a major role in this, yet for all his comfort, peace, and fat portfolio, when that wealthy man deplaned at the airport he strolled from private jet to waiting limousine with no conception whatsoever of the plague his obsession with New Harmony had unleashed.

After a fruitful series of meetings at the state capital in Sacramento concerning certain local objections to Delano's plans for phase two at New Harmony, he looked forward to a quiet meal at home and a good night's sleep. He rode alone, isolated from his driver behind glass, passing rows of palm trees as the limousine crossed the city toward the Pacific Coast Highway. He was glad he had arranged for the car and driver instead of leaving his Bentley at the airport. He was too tired to drive.

Soon they reached the ocean and turned along the shore. All around him were Maseratis, Bentleys, and Ferraris. He was an island in a sea of money. He was content. He remembered to thank God for his blessings.

He thought of Sacramento, so far inland. He did not like to leave the coast. He did not like the inland towns or cities, places bound about with nothing but more land, places with no clear-cut borders, nothing to contain a person. Where was the edge of civilization in a place like that? How could you know? Along the shore there could be no mistake. You had the land. You had the sea. You had the beach in between; your world defined. You knew where things ended, how far you could go.

His cell phone murmured softly. He answered.

"Del, this is Arnie O'Connor. We have a problem."

"Could it wait until tomorrow? I spent all day with those bureaucrats at the capital, Arnie. I'm just beat."

"I wish it could wait, Del. I really do. But this thing is just . . . it's just the worst thing. . . ."

Del felt a flutter in his stomach. He sat up straighter, suddenly alert. Arnold O'Connor was a seasoned businessman, yet his tone of voice bordered on the desperate. "What's wrong, Arnie?"

"They won't say exactly. That's part of the problem. I mean, how are we supposed to defend against this thing when they're being so vague?"

"Who's being vague about what, exactly?"

"The deaths, of course."

"Deaths? What deaths?"

"Out here at New Harmony, Del. I *told* you that."

"You haven't told me anything."

"I've heard it's up to five so far, and there's thirty more to come. At least. I don't know how many, really. But I've seen . . . I've seen some of them. Jill Hadlock across the street. I watched them put her in an ambulance. They wore those plastic suits, you know? To keep out chemicals? They put her in the ambulance, and she was . . . she was . . ."

Del heard a choking sound. He said, "You need to be specific. I don't know what—"

"Welts and blisters, Del! Puss and blood! Horrible. Horrible."

"What are you talking about?"

"I *told* you! Why don't you just listen?"

"Hey, Arnie? You need to calm down, okay? Calm yourself and start at the beginning."

"Don't tell me to calm down! You talked us into this! You promised it would go smoothly! You said everything had been considered!"

"I'm just trying to catch up with you here. You've got to tell me wh—"

"I guess you didn't think of *everything*, did you? WE'RE ALL GOING TO DIE!"

"Arnie, you're not making sense. I'm going to hang up now. I'm sorry."

Delano pushed a button on his phone. Immediately he dialed another number. After a moment he said, "Hi. It's Del. I just got a call from O'Connor. He sounds like he's lost his mind."

On the other end of the connection, Bill Miller, the man with the hair combed over his bald head, sighed heavily. "Well, it's bad. We're all badly shaken."

"I've been out of town. Assume I know nothing, will you? Tell me everything."

Miller began to talk. As Del listened, he had a sense that his driver must have made a turn into some alternate reality. Beside him a gated neighborhood gave way to a state park, and past a level field of brush he could see the moonlight on the ocean. He was isolated from the passing world by glass and steel and chromium. There was very little road noise in the limousine, just a whisper of sea air passing over the compartment and the low hum of tires on pavement. He might have been up in his jet, crossing a continent, or leaving the earth's atmosphere, shooting into empty space. Nothing he was hearing could be real.

Bill Miller spoke of the entire Karlsson family, dead of some disease. Del remembered the Karlssons. They were among the first to buy in to his dream at New Harmony, a fine Christian family. One son and two beautiful little girls. One of those girls had looked a lot like Harmony when she was a teenager. He had felt such pride when they signed on at New Harmony, such joy at what he had accomplished for them and thousands more just like them.

Miller spoke of many other families gravely ill, of three more on the verge of death so far, a father and his son in one family, the wife and mother of another. He spoke of a quarantine, of thirty or more people taken from their homes in New Harmony—taken by force in some cases—and placed under the control of some government operation, incommunicado. He had been out to the hospital, but they had not let him near the floor where some of the victims were being treated. They had not answered any questions. They had forced him to leave.

"They had soldiers at the hospital, Del."

"What do you mean, soldiers? What kind of soldiers?"

"I mean that's who kept me from going in. A bunch of guys in uniform with weapons. I don't know what kind they were."

Del asked many questions, but it all came down to how, and why. Beyond the grim statistics and what little he had been able to learn from Arnold, Miller knew quite little. "A man at the hospital took me aside. Not a soldier or a doctor. A guy in a suit. He asked who I was, and made me show my driver's license. He wrote down my address. He warned me not to talk about it. Said it's a national security matter. National security, Del. He threatened me with prison if I talk."

"Prison?" asked Delano Wright, astonished. "*Prison?*"

"I'm not even sure I should be telling you about this."

"But it's our development! These are our people!"

"If they found out . . . oh, no. I just thought . . . what if they have this phone tapped or something?"

"Come on, Bill. That's ridiculous."

The connection was dropped.

Delano slipped his cell phone in his pocket. The coast highway descended a hillside into a long depression which curved along a beach. Ahead he saw a tall bluff and a house upon the promontory, angled roofs and chimneys silhouetted by the moon. He was shooting out along the very edge of everything. On one side lay civilization, on the other, empty space. He tried to think of what to do. Should he go to the hospital? To New Harmony? Should he just go home as planned?

He wondered if there had been a mistake. Maybe Arnold had suffered a nervous breakdown and imagined all of this. The man had certainly sounded unstable. But no, what about Bill Miller and the hospital? Surely both of them had not gone crazy simultaneously. No, there must be something to it, but how could things be as bad as that? Five dead people and another thirty sick to the point of quarantine? What could make that many people that sick all of a sudden?

He thought about that man at the hospital, the conversation Miller mentioned, the man who had said something about national security. Suddenly he wondered if that meant terrorism.

Dear Lord, protect us.

Could someone involved with New Harmony have a terrorist connection? Surely not, but why else have the soldiers at the hospital? Why mention national security? Delano needed more information. Removing his cell phone from his pocket, he dialed a number in Sacramento. "This is Delano Wright," he said into the mouthpiece. "For the governor."

"Yes, sir, Mr. Wright," said the woman on the line. "May I tell him why you're calling?"

"I'm afraid it's confidential."

"Yes, sir. Of course. He's in a dinner meeting at the moment, but I'll just check to see if he can interrupt it for you."

"Thank you."

"Not at all, sir."

Delano waited as the limousine climbed the hill beyond the beach and the ocean on his right slipped out of sight. He was bound about by land again. Anything could happen. He thought about those crazy things O'Connor had said.

Welts and blisters. Puss and blood. Horrible. Horrible.

Suddenly, for no logical reason, a painted image came to mind. He saw himself lifting a painting from the ground, a painting of Camel Mountain with a pile of bodies, pale skin covered with welts and blisters, puss and blood. He remembered the strange figure he had chased the day he found that artifact, the trespasser with the oddly shining hair, the one who disappeared as if by magic in a grove of sycamores.

He had assumed that man was a Latino, but what if he was from the Middle East? What if his intentions were much worse than mere illegal immigration?

No. That was preposterous, of course.

Yet his instincts warned of *some* connection, somehow, between the image he had lifted from the ground and the tragedy unfolding in that same place. It showed the exact location of New Harmony and corpses in that place afflicted just as Arnie had described. Could it really be a complete coincidence?

"Mr. Wright?"

"Yes, I'm here."

"The governor asked me to tell you he's very sorry, sir, but he just can't break away at the moment. He wanted to know if there's a number where he can reach you later on tonight, or if you'd rather talk tomorrow."

Remembering his discovery the day he chased the trespasser, the secret he had found, remembering his fears of bureaucrats and politicians, archaeologists and the news media, endless red tape and delays, remembering his choice to break the law for the sake of New Harmony, to not report the painting, and thinking now about the painting's hellish image, Delano said, "No. No, tell the governor I appreciate it, but there's no need to call back. I think we're supposed to see each other at a thing in Pasadena next week anyway. It can wait until then."

"Very well, sir."

Delano put away his cell phone just as the driver turned up the hill toward his estate. Strangely, the gate was open.

The limousine climbed the long curving driveway until the house came into view. Several cars stood in the parking area. Two of them were police cruisers. All the windows of the house glowed brightly. He closed his eyes and forced himself to take deep breaths.

The limo stopped. "Bring my bags, please," said Delano when the driver opened his door.

As Delano approached the entry, he saw a man searching behind shrubbery along the front wall of his house, shining a flashlight along the planting bed. A woman in uniform stood just inside his front door.

He said, "I'm Delano Wright."

"Yes, sir. They're just in there." The policewoman pointed toward the front living room.

Lupe sat on a brown leather sofa. Across from her was a man in a wrinkled suit. The man stood up. "Mr. Wright?"

"Yes. What's going on here?"

"My name is Sauter, sir. I'm a detective with the Blanco Beach Police Department. I'm afraid your home has been burglarized."

"Burglarized?"

"Yes, sir."

"This isn't about the disease?"

"Disease? What disease?"

Careful, thought Delano. Careful what you say. He looked at Lupe. "Are you all right?"

"Yes, mister."

The detective said, "She surprised the robber in the act, sir. She's a very lucky lady."

Again, Delano asked, "You're all right? You're sure?"

"I am fine, thank you."

"Thank God."

"Yes, mister. I have thanked God very much."

"What did they take?"

Detective Sauter said, "So far Ms. Garza has been able to identify a few things. . . ." He checked the notebook in his hand. "Quite a bit of canned food from your pantry, a model boat, some books—"

"Excuse me," said Delano, interrupting. "Did you look in my closet?"

Lupe shook her head. "No, mister."

Delano said, "I'll be right back."

He crossed the living room, walked along the gallery, and turned into the hall that led through the bedroom wing. Along the way he saw men and women looking at his things, taking photographs, dusting for fingerprints. He crossed his bedroom and entered the closet. He saw the shelving unit ajar. His stomach roiled. Inside his safe room were two men: one tall, one overweight. The fat one had a camera.

Thinking of the painting he had left in the safe room, Delano said, "Please don't take photographs in here."

"Who are you?" asked the tall man.

"Delano Wright. This is my house, and there are things in here I don't want photographed."

"We need to do it for the investigation," said the fat man.

"Not in here, okay? This place is very private."

"Sorry," said the fat one. "It's procedure." He raised the camera, pointed it at the video monitors about the desk, and pressed the shutter button.

"Hang on a minute, Lenny," said someone from behind Delano. He turned to find Detective Sauter standing there. "We can waive the photos of your safe room if you want, Mr. Wright."

"Thank you."

"Just understand it might mean we can't prove a case against the perpetrators."

"I do understand."

"Okay. Lenny, Mike, why don't you guys go cover the garage?"

"We did that already," said the tall one.

"Then do something else for a while, okay? Mr. Wright needs some space to check the damage here."

When the two men had passed Delano, he entered the safe room, walking directly to the desk.

Behind him, the detective spoke. "The perpetrators took the disc from your surveillance system, Mr. Wright. It looks like they also deleted the video files on your hard drive. We've got a consultant who does wonders with these things. She might still be able to pull an image off the drive, but these guys are professionals. They found this safe room. They knew about the cameras, and what to do with the computer there. I'd bet a lot of money they wore masks and gloves and clothing that won't offer much."

Delano stared at the empty place upon the floor beside the desk, the place where he had left the painting propped against the wall.

"Do you see anything missing?" asked the detective.

Delano made himself look away from the empty space. He scanned the safe room quickly. "No. It all looks untouched."

"Take your time, Mr. Wright. Look around."

Delano's hand shook as he opened a desk drawer. Of course, the cash was missing. They had been smart enough to leave the bonds alone. "There was some money here . . ." he said.

"Cash?"

"Uh-huh."

"How much?"

"A hundred thousand dollars. I keep it for emergencies."

The figure did not seem to surprise the detective. Probably he had worked among the rich in Blanco Beach for many years. "Was it uncirculated? Straight from the bank?"

"I think so. Yes. It was new hundreds, taped in bundles."

"Which bank, sir? When did you withdraw it?"

"I think . . . First Capital, down in the village. I guess it was about five years ago. I can get you an exact date."

"Okay. Good. That's a while back but the Feds make them keep good records on cash transactions of that size. Maybe we can get some serial numbers. Anything else missing?"

Delano continued to ignore the empty space beside the desk. "No," he said. "That's all."

"All right," said the detective, writing in his notebook. "Uh, I was looking at your access to this room. It's pretty ingenious. Who did the work on it, do you know?"

Delano said, "What?"

"The security system, this room, that hidden door. Were they all installed by the same outfit?"

"When we had the house built, yes."

"Do you remember who did the work?"

"Oh, I see. You mean that might explain how they knew about the room."

"It's possible."

"Okay. I think it was . . . let me think . . . oh, wait a minute." He bent and tapped a few keys on the computer. A file came up on the monitor. "There it is. Left Coast Security, up in L.A."

The detective said, "Well, that's a dead end."

"Why?"

"Left Coast is Harry Simmons. I know him. Used to be on the job with the LAPD. No way he's involved in this kind of thing."

"Maybe someone got access to his records," said Delano.

"I doubt it. Harry's a professional. Runs a real tight ship up there. No, sir, they most likely got in here some other way. Who else knows about your safe room?"

"Nobody."

"Just you?" asked the detective. His tone of voice was skeptical.

"Well, my wife. My ex-wife."

"What's her name?"

"Ana."

"Has she remarried or gone back to her maiden name?"

"I don't think so. It's been a couple of years since we talked."

The detective wrote again in his notebook. "Where does she live?"

"Someplace in Florida is all I know. We really don't stay in touch."

"Do you know how I can contact her?"

"I can give you the last number she gave me, but I don't think she's involved in this."

"Why not?"

"I changed the access codes a long time ago, right after she left. Plus I added a few more security measures she didn't know about."

"I see. And there's no one else who knew about this safe room?"

He thought about Harmony, who used to love to hide in their "secret compartment" when she was young. "No," he said. "I'm the only one."

"How about your maid? I heard you ask if she'd been back here."

"Well, sure. Lupe knows about it. I forgot about that. But she's not involved in this."

"How can you be sure?"

"I told her never to go into the safe room."

"She always does what you tell her?"

"You make her sound like a . . . a slave or something. It's not like that. We're very close."

The detective raised an eyebrow. "Close?"

Delano felt blood rush to his face. "It's not like that either. She's just . . . she's worked for me a long time. She's like part of the family. I mean, if I had a family." He began to move around the safe room, touching things, a way to avoid facing the detective. "Lupe, she could just ask me for money anytime. She knows that. She knows she's in my will and everything. So, I mean, why would she do this?"

"You're absolutely sure about her?"

"Absolutely."

"You'd be surprised how often it's someone you least expect, Mr. Wright. Think about it. Someone you already suspected could never pull it off."

Delano thought about Ana, driving out of his life in the Porsche, and Harmony, making marriage plans behind his back. "Yes," he said. "I see what you mean."

"Good. How about if I just ask you a few question about Miss de la Garza? Would that be okay?"

"All right."

"Okay. Let's start with her background. Where's she from, exactly?"

CAPÍTULO 30

WEEDS SPROUTED IN THE MISSION garden. Horse manure lay uncollected where it fell. The Indians who had been hung by Don Felipe for the murder of his soldiers still dangled from the gallows, turning slowly as they decomposed, but the warning was wasted, for the plaza beyond Fray Alejandro's cell, once vibrant and alive with workers from sunrise to sunset, now lay desolate and empty.

Almost all the healthy neophytes had fled, and the few converts who remained among the Spaniards in the Misión de Santa Dolores were harassed both day and night by shouted threats from the nearby brush. A leather-jacket soldier who failed to take the threats seriously exposed himself to view above the eastern palisade and was shot through the shoulder with an arrow. Don Felipe's men ventured beyond the mission walls only when it was necessary to add more bodies to the pit, and only with a major show of arms.

As for the Franciscans, Alejandro remained bedridden, severely weakened by the aftermath of his disease. Without the good friar in attendance, the sick and dying suffered unassisted as the pestilence continued its grim work in the refectory.

Fray Benicio had last been seen moving in and out of the brush outside the mission in the company of Indians, completely naked as they were, his body smeared with pagan markings drawn in ochre-colored mud.

Fray Guillermo rarely ventured out-of-doors, preferring to make endless counts of the supplies, compiling lists which cross-referenced each other, and writing many letters, which he read to Don Felipe and Fray Alejandro while pacing to and fro with wild gesticulations. The letters expressed his outrage at Benicio's behavior, demanding the young friar be excommunicated, demanding more soldiers, demanding additional Franciscans, demanding more supplies. It was a useless occupation, for none of the abbot's letters could be sent south to his superiors in New Spain. Who would carry them?

Alejandro received news of the outside situation mainly from a faithful neophyte who brought him food, refreshed his water, and emptied his chamber pot each morning. As the news became more hopeless, Alejandro began to sense a connection between the bleak events beyond his cell and his own uselessness. The Misión de Santa Dolores was a failure, just as he had failed. One was an external expression of the other. The homely friar begged God's forgiveness. With many prayers for grace he sought his Savior's peace which passes understanding, but it seemed he spoke to empty air.

One afternoon Fray Alejandro awoke to find an Indian seated on the three-legged stool beside his table. The little window high upon the wall bathed the man in a narrow beam of sunshine. His dark hair shimmered slightly in the light, like feathers on a crow.

"Good day to you, my son." Alejandro yawned and wiped sleep from his eyes. "Have you come with bread?"

Stooped over the tabletop, the Indian did not indicate in any way that he had heard this greeting. Curious, the Franciscan examined him more closely. To his great astonishment he saw the man apply a paintbrush to the unfinished altarpiece.

"Stop!" cried Alejandro. "Oh, no, my son! You must stop at once!"

Drawing the brush along a wooden panel, the Indian ignored him. Outrage overcame Fray Alejandro's weakness. Feebly he strove to leave his bed. The Indian paused. He turned and raised a hand. To Alejandro's great astonishment he made the sign of the cross as if to bless the friar. Then he raised the wooden panel from the tabletop and held it upright in the narrow beam of sunlight.

Alejandro gasped. The lifelike figures added by the Indian seemed to move upon the wood. He had seen such vivid images only once before, at San Francisco's Porziuncola, in frescoes painted with such absolute perfection many said they could not have come from human hands.

For many hours the ugly friar lay abed and watched the stranger's brush. Weakness overcame him sometimes, and he slept. Always when he woke again the Indian was there, working on the altarpiece. The friar began to wonder what was truly happening and what was just a dream.

Images of mystery were born before his eyes. Strange things. Horrible things. Wonderful things. He saw Benicio appear within a mocking crowd as if the Indian had brought him living from the fiber of the wooden panel. He saw a furious Guillermo there as well, produced as if from dust. He saw himself among the mourners on another panel. On the center panel he saw the living God made flesh upon a cross.

"Who are you, señor?" asked the friar, but the Indian ignored him.

"What are you?" he asked, but the Indian continued painting.

Fray Alejandro prayed aloud with open eyes, watching the miracle unfold like flower petals in the springtime, asking God for explanations, sensing no reply. In spite of the Indian at work beside his cot the good friar felt alone within his tiny cell, exactly as he had before. He felt alone, yet he still prayed, exactly as he had before.

Although centuries had passed between Fray Alejandro's time and hers, Guadalupe Soledad Consuelo de la Garza shared this sense of solitude. Indeed, the years might have been seconds, for she too lived in a foreign place at the end of a long journey. She too begged God for an explanation and heard only silence. She too believed herself a failure, yet she still prayed.

In her childhood and her early adult years in Rincón de Dolores, Lupe had seldom lived a minute without some small exchange with her Creator. In the morning it was, "Señor, thank you for this pretty sunrise." At her little shop it was, "Señor, please allow these eggs to sell before they are too old." At christenings and weddings she praised God every second. At funerals she asked unceasingly for comfort. She was never without conversation. When she spoke with one friend, there were really three. Her Father, God; her Savior, Jesus; her conscience and her help, the Holy Spirit . . . these were all combined in one, and always, always there. She never felt alone.

Then had come the quest.

The journey had been an easy trial. Barbed-wire fences, border guards, deserts, thirst, and awful sun, all easy. But those Sunday afternoons upon the beach, the hours and hours of speaking about the Savior, the flood of passing pagans, apathetic or amused, the walls they lived behind, the endless, endless failure . . . they had worn her down.

She had watched the children on the beach, and her thoughts had been of Tucker. What a father he would make, with his gentleness and passion! How often she had wished it could be so. How often she had dreamed of him, even as she spoke the holy Word of God to passing pagans. Her dreams had robbed her words, for her love had been divided.

Once, the flow of smoke against a northern wind had been the hand of God to her, a sign external, a moving of el Señor outward from her heart. Now she barely noticed fresh-cut leaves that spiraled slowly up into a yellow sky. She did not trust such signs, for who could say if they were real?

She thought of Tucker, and she wept. She thought of Delano, and wept. If such men made such choices, who was she to dare to dream that love might matter most? Where now was the Presence? Where the Holy Indwelling? Worn away by others' apathy. Eroded by amusement. Ended by her failure. Lupe had come to save Americanos by the millions, and accomplished nothing. How she longed to leave!

Yet if she was alone within her soul, in her mind she persevered. She would not depart that heathen place without permission. She would await divine approval for her going, even if it took a lifetime.

Disturbed by all these things, Lupe slept fitfully before the *retablo*, her head cradled in crossed arms upon the table. The night before she had returned home very late, driven in the mister's limousine, barely able to remain awake along the way. Unsuspecting, she had plodded up the steps to her small attic room. She had entered, and turned on the light, and there was Fray Alejandro's burden upright on the table, miraculously complete.

How this could be possible, she had neither known nor cared. She simply knew the *retablo* had been made whole, a miracle in answer to the prayers of many generations. If only they could see this in her pueblo! Padre Hinojosa would be so proud, so joyous! But what did it mean? Had el Señor heard her pleas even when she thought him absent? Throughout the night she had gazed upon her sacred charge. Did it offer guidance? Oh, she longed to know! Late into the night she had begged the Lord for understanding, but received no answer. All was silence. At last her flesh had betrayed her, and she had slept.

Outside her single window the sun arose to send a shining beam across her eyes. She stirred. She moaned. She raised her head and saw the altarpiece. The image briefly came to life within that abstract waking landscape where consciousness is incomplete. She saw the evil in the mocking crowd, the corruption buried in the ground, the anguish in the little group of people on the right. The risen Christ has buried hell.

The *retablo* strained to share a secret. Was it in the crosses? In Golgotha? She could almost see the meaning . . . then her mind was fully here and now; she was awake, with the fleeting hint of revelation lost.

Lupe bathed and dressed and ate a sparing breakfast. She knelt before Fray Alejandro's burden, the holy altar there upon her little table. She prayed to silence once again, and crossed herself. She rose. She left.

Midway down the canyon road her bus passed a blackened hillside. Near its ridge she saw a crew of men in yellow struggling against a line of burning brush. The wildfire was a long and crooked serpent crawling right across the land. Smoke streamed from it toward the sea and swirled around the speeding bus. Soon the sight was lost beyond another hill, but the scent of burning lingered. Lupe sank lower in her seat. She touched the scar upon her neck and cheek. She shivered at the thought of such a fearsome thing unleashed.

Arriving at her employer's house, she sensed something was amiss. Even after she had straightened up the pantry and gone through all the other rooms, correcting small disturbances left by the intruder, something wrong remained. She felt a malevolence. She did not know its source. She murmured prayers throughout the day, asking for protection. She sensed no answers. Nonetheless, her prayers continued.

At lunchtime she prepared a sandwich and some soup for Delano, who was working in his study. There, she left the food upon a table for him, entering and exiting as quietly as possible. Since the death of Harmony it had become their normal ritual. She would return in an hour to take away the empty plate and bowl. Usually he thanked her as she did these things, but that day he was every bit as silent as her God. Her apprehension grew.

All through the afternoon she cleaned. It seemed essential that she scrub and wipe and disinfect all surfaces. She was almost certain of the thief's identity, but what if she was wrong? What if it had been a stranger, someone wholly given over to the dread disease of sin, leaving profane or demonic traces? As she mopped, Lupe blessed each tile upon the kitchen floor. As she vacuumed, every yard of carpet got a prayer. She called on God to purify the sinks, the tubs, the toilets. Never had she put such heart into this work.

In the evening, she went to say good night to Delano. Throughout the day he had never left his study. She opened the door. She said, "I am going now, mister."

His head was bent above a Bible on his desk. He did not seem to hear.

Again, she said, "Mister? I am going."

Still he showed no sign of hearing.

She stepped into the room, moving closer. "Mister?"

At last his head snapped up. "What is it? What do you *want*?"

She stared at him.

"Well?" he said.

"I only want to say good-bye."

"All right. Good-bye. Please leave and close the door."

She did exactly as he asked. Outside in the hallway she stood still a moment. Never had he spoken to her in that way. Even in the weeks and months after the accident, when his grief for Harmony had seemed all-consuming, even then he had always spoken with respect. She closed her eyes. Silently, her lips moved. Expecting nothing, she entreated the Almighty to have mercy on him.

The scent of smoke was strong when she set out for the village. As she descended the hill toward Blanco Beach, it was as if her fears had filled the hazy air. Every acrid breath reminded her of suffering. At the bus station she sat upon a bench to wait among the many other Latinos bound for home. She was greeted with smiles. She knew many of them had begun to call her "Doña Lupe" but she took no pride in it. They were not the people she had come so far to save. They had been believers all along.

At last the people boarded the canyon bus. It was an hour past the scheduled time. The driver warned them they might not get through to Wilson City. "Big fire," she said, speaking loudly in case they did not understand English. "Lots and lots of smoke up there, *comprende?*" No one answered.

As the hills of Blanco Canyon gathered in around them, it seemed the smoke became more concentrated. Many in the bus began to cough. The headlights of the bus reflected on the haze. The driver slowed the bus and leaned forward in her seat. At an upward incline the diesel engine roared. Near the top the smoke cleared slightly. Lupe looked back to the west, directly at the setting sun. It did not hurt her eyes. The sun was feeble, weaker than the moon, perfectly round and solid red, like a child's rubber ball.

Lupe tried not to think of fire as the sickly sun settled down behind the hills. In her seat beside the window she tried to pretend the whiteness was just fog. She watched it for a sign of clearing. She kept her eyes up high, hoping for a sight of stars, and although she sensed no possibility of an answer, she closed her eyes and begged her Maker for a parting in the muteness that so wounded her. She begged him to explain the sign, the message in Fray Alejandro's reunited burden.

At first her prayers were formed of urges and desires, tacit gestures of sincerity and hope, then she formed the words. I have come so far to serve you, Señor. Please reveal yourself to me. Why this distance? Why this silence? How have I offended you? I am weak, but you are strong. Deliver me, O Holy Father. Please deliver me. Please allow me to complete this quest. Allow me to go home.

The bus slowed as it came to a stop. She opened her eyes. The doors opened. Four people climbed the steps, coughing, bringing smoke inside with them. Although it terrified her, Lupe rose. She alone descended.

On the shoulder of the road she stood within the gloaming as the bus doors closed behind her. The diesel engine roared. In a moment, all was silent. Cinders settled down like snow. Alone in the wilderness, she held out her hand, and bits of ashen leaf and branch fell weightlessly upon her palm. She thought of stories of Pompeii. She pulled the neckline of her T-shirt up over her mouth and nose. Breathing through the fabric, she stared at a vision.

High above, floating on miasmal vapors, three gigantic crosses glowed in the gathering darkness, and through the haze behind them, illuminated by their radiance, she saw the place of the skull. Yet it was not Golgotha at all. It was the tall hill they called Camel, its shape a perfect match for the undulating painted line between the land and sky on Alejandro's burden.

Lupe closed her eyes against the stinging smoke and visualized the *retablo*, the center panel, blank for generations. She considered the miracle: her Savior's image somehow on that panel, and a chapel, and a pit of horrors down below, and the Spanish words. The risen Christ has buried hell. Yet although Golgotha was clearly Camel Mountain, what lay below the crosses was not hell at all. It was just New Harmony.

Hot upon her unscarred cheek a new wind blew. The smoke now drifted inland, east, away from the sea, back the way it had come. She sensed a different evil in it. Despite her itching eyes she forced herself to watch.

The wind accelerated. Before, it had been silent. Now it built within her ears. From a whisper it grew louder, louder, until she had to brace herself against the roar. It clutched at hair and clothing. It bent the grass and branches. It drove the smoke along the ground like rushing waves across the ocean. She saw the devil dance within the curls and tendrils.

As the air above her cleared, Lupe watched dim flickers in the darkness, bars of light moving through the haze below the crosses. Intrigued, she walked a dozen steps before she realized she was climbing up the hill. Drawn toward the dancing luminance, she walked up, and up. Father, please reveal your will at last. Free me from this limbo. On she walked. Let my quest end here, or let it properly begin at last. Up she went. Do not hide your face from me. Show yourself. Show yourself.

A beam of light detached itself from all the others. It wavered to and fro. It came. Lupe stood still upon the earth and saw the figure come. Garbed in a sand-colored uniform and boots, it came. With the shining light attached to a rifle, with a hood beneath a helmet and a gas mask for a face, it came. She heard shouted words, stolen by the roaring wind. Uncomprehending, she continued up the hill.

Beyond the figure Lupe saw a great pair of ornamental gates, and stucco walls that ran into the smoke on either side, and before those gates and walls were many soldiers, and sandbag emplacements with machine guns, and floodlights on tall poles, and armored vehicles with headlights slicing through the haze as they slowly crawled alongside the walls. She saw an army there to guard New Harmony, or, if New Harmony was really hell, to guard the outside world.

Then the figure stood against her, shouting one more time. Still not understanding, she went on. Its posture changed. It crouched lower. In that howling, windswept moment it aimed the rifle at her chest.

EACH DAY THE TAUNTS OF Indians lurking in the nearby brush grew louder and the number of voices increased. Stones and arrows rained down on the mission without warning. No more residents were harmed, but the neophytes and soldiers could not move about inside the walls without fear.

When a stray arrow struck Don Felipe's favorite horse in the flank, the captain shouted for a sergeant to assemble thirty soldiers in the plaza. Fully armed with swords, muskets, and iron pikes, these men rode out against the Indians. With nine of Don Felipe's men dead or dying from the pestilence and three already murdered by the Indians, this left only six leather-jacket soldiers within the mission walls. They, along with the remaining neophytes and Fray Guillermo, watched the sortie from behind the palisade.

Out through the gate charged the thirty at a gallop. They entered the brush, which stood shoulder-high around their horses. Once they had ridden deep into the cover, they began to thrash about themselves with swords and pikes, fighting an enemy who remained unseen by those who watched the battle from the mission. Smoke from musket fire drifted in small plumes around the action. Shouts and screams were heard. More than one Spaniard went missing from his saddle. At last the soldiers turned and fled. When they arrived back in the mission, there were only twenty. One of the missing was Don Felipe.

From the cot within his cell, Fray Alejandro heard it all, and through his narrow door he saw Guillermo berate the surviving soldiers. The abbot danced around them as they dismounted. "Cowards!" he shouted, his pale face glowing red with rage. "Little girls and women! Why have you retreated? Return to your duty! Return and deal most harshly with those vermin! Are you frightened boys? Are you timid mice?"

The sergeant struck Guillermo in the face, knocking him to the dirt.

Alejandro marveled that the abbot had chosen that moment for insults. It seemed a foolish strategy, if strategy it was. More likely Fray Guillermo had given no thought to his words, even though the Franciscan Rule said friars "must not be quarrelsome, dispute with words, or criticize others, but rather should be gentle, peaceful, and unassuming, courteous and humble, speaking respectfully to all." Should not a man of God use words in godly ways, even in the face of violence? Words were sacred things. After all, it had been written in the Scriptures, "The Word was God." Alejandro did not claim to know how this was possible, yet he did believe God and God's own word were somehow one, and he suspected this was connected to the fact, also recorded in the scriptures, that the Creator merely spoke, and all things came to be.

The good friar was aware that poets and philosophers sometimes claimed they too created with mere words. In this it might appear philosophy and poetry had aligned with his theology, yet he believed there was a difference.

Let us not become concerned with such distinctions here, except to note the role of language. Whether we are gods whose speech can form creation, or creatures formed by godly speech, all agree creative power emanates from language as heat does from the sun. Words are not inert tools to be wielded haphazardly like a hoe or spade. Words can heal a broken heart, or cut as deeply as a sharpened sword. Thus we should not be surprised that Delano Wright could be so deeply injured by the words he had found in his daughter's childhood Bible, words crudely underscored in red as if a man might impose the power they contain:

> *For the poor shall never cease out of the land: therefore I command thee, saying, Thou shalt open thine hand wide unto thy brother, to thy poor, and to thy needy, in thy land.*

The book lay open on his desk. He hung above it, head cradled in his hands, elbows pressing down on both sides, staring at the words which had been roughly underlined. He and Ana had given Harmony the book when she was baptized. Bound in pink leather, full of pictures, liberally pasted with gold stars on the flyleaf, a star for every verse his daughter had memorized, Delano remembered this book well, this, his little girl's first Bible.

The pressure of the ugly lines below the words had driven deep into the sheets of tissue-thin paper underneath. The thickness of the red ink almost made the words themselves illegible.

If this defacing was an act of sacrilege, an abomination meant to break his heart, it was a foolish enterprise, for his heart had been broken long ago. If it had been done to prick his conscience, in that too it had failed, for all he felt was anger.

The policeman, Detective Sauter, had asked many questions about his primary suspect: Where did she live, exactly? (An apartment in Wilson City somewhere.) Where did she come from, exactly? (Mexico, somewhere.) Did she have a boyfriend? (Delano did not think so.) Did she have other friends in Wilson City, or family? (He had never asked.)

For each question, such vague answers. For over eight years Lupe had cooked and cleaned and organized his house. Delano had thought he knew the woman. In fact, if anyone had asked, he would have said he knew her very well, but by the time Detective Sauter finished with his questions it was clear that he and Lupe were strangers.

Staring at the crude lines in his daughter's Bible, Delano recalled the convicting power of the detective's words. It seemed the details of the burglary were the same as several other recent thefts in Blanco Beach. Did he know Arthur O'Connor? (Yes, he did.) Did he know Bill Miller, and Kenneth Joplin, and Frank Lender? (Yes, and yes, and yes.) Did Lupe have some connection with them all, some way to know when they were out of town? (She had served them several dinners at his house. She might have overheard them speaking of upcoming travel. Yes, it was very possible.)

To take the woman into his home, into his family, to provide for her as he had in the event of his own death and yet to know so little of her, to let her overhear his plans and meet his friends, to tell her—to *tell* her—of his safe room and *to give her the combination* . . . Delano had felt the detective's eyes upon him, judging him a fool, and he had known the judgment was unerring.

Then had come the last humiliation.

"Mr. Wright, is she in the country legally?"

And his debasing answer, "I don't know," which was as good as a confession of complicity in her crime. Yet he was not a criminal. It was not that way at all.

How could he make the policeman realize what life was like with Lupe? How could he explain? Yes, she'd had no English when she came, but he was fluent in her language so they had communicated perfectly from the beginning. Yes, she had needed training in a few things around the house, proper cooking and so forth, but she had always been completely *there* somehow, as if her presence were as natural as air. With the detective listening, his eyes never leaving Delano's face, it had been impossible to find the words. Everything he thought to say seemed wrong, so he simply said it never occurred to him to question her legality.

But he did remember wondering. In the early days, when he only wanted some stability at home, it would have been inconvenient to ask about her legal status. Then he began to see Lupe's effect on Harmony, the way his daughter's depression seemed to lift in Lupe's presence, and he could not bring himself to ask. In time, it no longer crossed his mind. He had not thought of it in years. Did she have a right to be there? It would be like asking if she was a human being, if she was a woman, if she was alive.

What had Lupe become to him? A friend? A confidante? Role model? Saint?

The answer could not be explained. But he knew he had been foolish. He saw it in the detective's eyes alongside disbelief, justified of course, for he must confess that he had known the truth about her all along; he had known she was illegal, known it in a subliminal kind of way. Perhaps even consciously once upon a time. Still, Delano refused to think himself a criminal. If he had anything to confess, it was only living in denial for eight years.

"Will she be deported?" he had asked.

"That's probably the least of it," replied the detective.

Eventually the police all left, and what a trial he had endured then, awake and wondering about her through the night, and today, knowing she was in the house, wanting more than anything to confront her, to get the truth out of her somehow, to force her to confess or somehow prove her innocence. But the detective had been very clear. He was not to let her know of their suspicions. He was to act naturally. They would be watching her quite closely. They hoped to catch her in the act. If she had stolen from so many homes, there was no reason to believe that she would stop. Also, given the scale of the crimes, it was likely she had accomplices who should also be brought to justice.

Could he really believe that of her?

It was not the theft itself that made this all so difficult, of course, but the fact that Lupe—Lupe in particular—might do such a thing. He now realized he had sincerely, if unconsciously, believed that she was perfect. It was why he had put her in his will: never at any time had he seen her act in selfishness. Such a person ought to be rewarded.

But what if she was a thief? How did one make small talk with a woman capable of such monumental deception? It was impossible, so Delano spent the entire day hiding in his own house, avoiding her, although he could not keep the anger from his voice when she came to say good night.

Anger. Yes. He refused to call it grief. And his anger only grew after she left. If the tension was unbearable while she was there, it was all the more so in her absence. Although his dignity was in a shambles, at least when she was in the house he could confront her if he wished. Now she was beyond his reach, and even that last shred of control was gone.

Furious, impotent, he rose and paced the study. Somehow in his thinking all doubt of her guilt had been removed. He only wished to know why she had betrayed him. The hundred thousand dollars had been in the safe room for five years at least. Why not take it earlier? Did she have a boyfriend, as the detective had implied, someone who had pushed her to commit the crime? He made a fist and pounded on his hip in time with every step around the room.

He wondered if she would return tomorrow as she had this morning, putting on an act of innocence. How much longer would she keep up her charade before escaping back to Mexico? Was she even *from* Mexico? He only had her word on that. He knew so little of her. She had kept her secrets close. Never in a million years would he have dreamed her capable of this.

He paused in the middle of his study. He raised his voice up to the heavens. "How many times, Lord? How many times?" Thinking of betrayal, thinking of Ana running away with Harry Martin, a Sunday school teacher of all things, a man who taught their daughter about Jesus, and thinking of Harmony, planning to get married over his objections, going behind his back to marry that pompous little minister who so clearly thought himself superior, and Lupe with her on that day, with her in the car, helping with the marriage plans, joining Harmony's deception.

Lupe had stolen something more than just his trust and dignity and money. She had threatened his ministry, his service to the Lord. She had taken the strange artifact, the painted piece of wood he had lifted from the ground exactly where the next phase of New Harmony soon would rise.

Clearly, it was ancient. Clearly, it depicted Camel Mountain. What if Lupe tried to sell it and someone recognized the landscape, as he had? What if someone saw the chapel on the hillside and began asking questions about a lost Franciscan mission, as he had? Questions about that painting now, added to the tragedy of the strange disease which had ravaged New Harmony, might mean the end of everything he had worked for since his daughter's death.

He had to get the painting back. He should have destroyed it. It had been a silly superstition, really, to keep it just because of what it showed. After all, it was not Christ himself, but only an image of him on the cross; not a miracle, just the image of a miracle.

Pacing, pacing, Delano Wright thought about his options. Obviously he could not tell the authorities about the missing painting and therefore risk exposure of the secret it revealed, if indeed a Spanish mission truly had been there. How could he explain his own concealment of the thing? There were laws—legal technicalities, in Delano's opinion—requiring archaeological finds at construction sites to be reported. Of course, the morality of his choice to keep it secret was quite clear, but it would be difficult to explain to the police. They might not appreciate the full importance of New Harmony. No, he could not let them know about the painting.

He considered making a few calls. He knew people who knew people. They had ways to deal with problems such as this by working at the fringes of the law, but the risks in that approach outweighed the risks inherent in the problem. He could not control such people. Things might go too far. He was an example to the world, a well-known Christian role model. He could not get involved with criminals, not even to resist the acts of criminals.

But he had to get that painting back before someone guessed what might lie beneath New Harmony and ruined everything. If he could not let Lupe keep it, and if he could not send the police or criminals to recover it, what then could he do?

He had no choice. He had to go and get it personally.

Out in the pool house apartment Delano found what he needed: a notepad with an address in Wilson City. It might be Lupe's address. It might not. At least it was a place to start.

Minutes later he was in the Bentley on the canyon road. Minutes after that he passed New Harmony and saw military vehicles blocking the main gates. Gripping the steering wheel more tightly, he whispered, "Deliver us from evil."

He drove around a long bend and into a pale wall of smoke. Concentrated by the canyon walls, it was very thick. Wildfires were quite common in southern California, but still he was surprised. Added to the rest—disease, theft, betrayal—it seemed as if the world were ending, as if humanity's follies had finally descended into Armageddon.

His Bentley crawled through the canyon. Driving nearly blind, he strained to focus on the white line at the shoulder, which came and went within the smoke. Then he saw the dull red glow of taillights, a bus, moving even slower than he was. Glad of the company, he pulled close to follow. He worked his shoulders to ease the tension in the muscles. He and the bus driver climbed a little rise together, and he saw the setting sun in his rearview mirror. The weakness of it startled him. It was bizarre to stare straight at the sun without blinking, as if the ground had softened underneath him or gravity had faded. A weak sun was the end of life for everything.

The road ahead dropped down, the smoke gathered back into itself, and the view in his rearview mirror became solid white. On he drove.

Darkness draped its mantle on the canyon in mere minutes. He thanked God for the taillights on the bus. He began to wonder if this might have been a terrible mistake. Were the authorities so busy fighting the inferno that they failed to think to close down the road? Was he driving toward the fire? He wished to turn around, but how would he find his way back without the taillights up ahead?

Then the bus rounded a bend with Delano close behind, and the awful shroud of smoke lifted as quickly as it had fallen. Suddenly he could see stars above, and moonlight, and the hulking shapes of giant boulders on the hills.

It did not cross his mind to thank his Maker for an answered prayer. He only thought of finding Lupe and the painting. The bus accelerated. So did Delano. Five minutes later he came to Wilson City.

He entered an unfamiliar part of town, where zoning ordinances did not seem to apply, where dilapidated houses and apartment buildings stood alongside aging commercial structures. He passed a group of young men standing underneath a streetlight, wearing undershirts and bandannas on their foreheads and khaki trousers and dungarees hung low around their thighs. They stared hard at him as he rolled by. He watched his rearview mirror nervously. Every car in the mirror seemed a threat. A pair of Latinos in a pickup truck pulled beside him at a stoplight. Both of them stared at his car. He wished the Bentley were an old Ford or Dodge or Chevrolet. He pressed a button and his doors locked. Immediately he worried that they might have heard the soft clicking of the locks. It was important not to show fear.

He made a right turn, just to get away.

The building at the address on the scrap of paper was an old house, a small mansion really, two stories of stucco and brick with a steep roof. In better times it must have been a beauty, but even in the darkness he could see discolored places where the façade had been stripped of shutters, and peeled and missing paint where the wooden trim had been abused by desert heat and dust. One of the windows on the second floor was patched with cardboard. In the yellow light of the front porch, about a dozen people sat on mismatched plastic and metal chairs.

He parked at the curb and emerged from the Bentley and immediately smelled wood smoke. Standing still, he sniffed and looked around. The wind had shifted. A sickly halo ringed a streetlight half a block away. Other lights farther down the road were nearly swallowed up in growing haze. It seemed the smoke had followed him. He pressed a button on his key fob and the Bentley sounded a low tone to let him know the security system had been armed. As with the clicking locks, the sound added to his anxiety. He felt an irrational desire not to be insulting, not to let the people on the porch know he felt the need to set his car alarm in their neighborhood.

He stared at the Bentley, thinking he could simply get back in and drive away. As he thought of this, something white appeared on the pristine black paint of the hood. It was soon followed by more white spots, which seemed to appear from out of nowhere. He touched one, and it disintegrated on his fingertip. Ash was falling from the sky.

He approached the small group on the porch. "Good evening," he said in his Castilian Spanish.

"Good evening," replied several of the men and women.

"Is this the house of Lupe de la Garza?"

He received no answer.

"I am Delano Wright. I am her employer."

"Doña Lupe is not here," said a young woman with a baby in her lap.

"Doña? You call her that?"

"Everybody calls her that."

"But why?"

"She is like a mother to us all," said a very old man sitting at a folding table. He was older than Delano. He might have been three times the age of Lupe. He held playing cards in the crooked fingers of a hand much damaged by arthritis or hard labor. Across from him two other men also held cards. All three of them looked only at their hands.

"Please, I am curious. How is she like a mother?"

"How is any mother like a mother, señor? She does her best to care for us." The old man laid a card upon the table.

"She got medicine for my daughter," said the young woman who had spoken first. "She has given money to everyone here."

"She walks with me to the clinic," said the old man. "To be sure I do not fall."

"She brought groceries when I lost my job," said another man, a little younger, who seemed to have no teeth.

"Groceries?" asked Delano. "What kind of groceries?"

"Rice and beans. Milk and eggs. Soft food I can eat."

"Did she bring more fancy food? Salted fish eggs, maybe? Snails?"

"Snails!" The toothless man laughed. "Are you crazy? Who would eat a snail?"

Delano forced himself to smile. "I was only joking."

"Of course, señor."

"What about other things? Books with leather bindings? Paintings? Perhaps a nice model sailboat?"

Everyone fell silent.

"Have I said something wrong?" asked Delano.

The young woman with the baby said, "Señor, you say you are Doña Lupe's boss?"

"Yes. That is correct."

"What does she do for you?"

"She is my housekeeper."

"What is your name?"

"Delano Wright. I already told you that."

"Where do you live?"

"In Blanco Beach."

The old card player leaned forward to wipe ashes from the table with the side of his twisted hand. "Of course he would say that. They all live in Blanco Beach. It does not mean he knows her."

"My house is on a hill above the downtown. Lupe used to live over the pool house in my backyard."

"Yes." The young woman nodded. "That is what Doña Lupe told me. She once lived in a fine apartment by a swimming pool, new and clean, with a separate room for her bed. I believe her too. Such a one as she would never lie."

"Do you know when she will come home?"

"She should be here already. She is a little late."

"A little late? It has been an hour since she left my house."

"It takes her at least an hour and a half to get from there to here, señor."

"That long? Surely not. The drive is only half an hour."

The young woman shrugged. "One must wait for the bus, and it has many stops, and there is the walk from the closest stop to here, but you may believe what you want."

"An hour and a half? Truly?"

Nobody replied.

He said, "I wish to leave a note, to let her know that I was here. Please, which apartment is hers?"

"She has only a small room, señor. It is in the attic."

The wind rose suddenly as Delano passed among them toward the house. It pressed against his back. Cards flew off the old man's table. Women's skirts fluttered like flags about their legs. The front door, which was propped open by a rock, blew loose and slammed shut with a mighty crash. He opened it and entered.

Inside was a foyer. Along one wall were eight aluminum mailboxes. Spray-painted graffiti covered the plaster walls. Spanish obscenities, mostly. A wooden staircase rose along the left. Delano ascended, and as he climbed he thought of gangs on street corners, and hard-packed dirt yards, and neighbors who were too poor even to buy food, much less get their teeth fixed. He assured himself he had been right to make her leave his home. It simply was not proper for an unmarried man and a woman to live in the same place. But if her neighbor had been truthful, his decision had added three hours of travel to and from his house. Three hours, round trip. He thought of losing that much time from every single day. Perhaps he should have been more helpful, found her an apartment in Blanco Beach, someplace closer, someplace safer. Less exposed to undesirables.

Delano considered what it would be like to go from living high upon a hill above Blanco Beach to a bare existence such as this. Such a change in circumstances must have been depressing. Perhaps it was understandable that this life might drive her to desperate measures. But he had paid her well enough to live better than this; he was almost certain of it, although of course he really did not know the cost of rent. All those people out in front had said she gave them money. Might she only live this way because she gave too much away? If so, that was her choice. It did not justify the way she had turned against him. She was not his daughter. He had no obligation to her, other than that of an employer. What right had she to betray him for insufficient benevolence? She had no idea how many millions of dollars he had given to the poor throughout the years, how many thousands of hours he had devoted to the Lord.

He reached the third-floor attic landing and a single wooden door defaced by graffiti. He thought of his daughter's defaced Bible. *Thou shalt open thine hand wide unto thy brother, to thy poor, and to thy needy, in thy land.* Who did she think she was?

He knocked and waited. There was no answer. He tried the doorknob, and to his surprise, the door swung open. Light from above him on the landing spilled into the room. Stepping in, he found a switch. Another light came on. Beneath low sloping ceilings he saw a bed to his left, a row of clothing hanging on an open wooden rod, and a set of cabinets along the far wall with a sink and an electric hot plate and a small refrigerator underneath the counter. Straight ahead, alongside the wall he saw a little wooden table with two chairs. Beside the table was the small room's single window. On the table was a painting.

In two steps he was at the table. He took the strange painting in his hands. Unlike the artifact he had found in the hills, it was made of three separate panels. At first he thought it was not what he sought, but then he looked more closely at the center panel and saw the crucified Christ above a chapel and the mouth of hell below, the Spanish words along the bottom, and the unmistakable profile of Camel Mountain above.

His hands began to shake. She knew the secret of the painting's hiding place, and here it was within her room. It was damning evidence, incontrovertible, that Lupe was indeed the thief. All thought of his own guilt for her circumstances perished in a wave of righteous indignation.

Strangely, the other two panels seemed to match the stolen one. To his unpracticed eye, the colors and the style appeared identical. The figures in the angry crowd upon the left all stared precisely at the Christ upon the stolen middle panel. The mourners on the right also gazed directly at him. The hilltops on both of the side panels aligned perfectly with the distinctive Camel silhouette in the middle. A thief hung on a cross on each of the two flanking paintings, much as one would expect, and these figures also focused directly on the Savior. Both of the side panels were the same size as the one he had uncovered on the hillside, and both seemed every bit as ancient.

Delano took the painting to the middle of the room and stood beneath the single naked bulb. In that brighter light he saw a small network of cracks in the surface of the paint, identical on all three panels. He saw the same yellowed patina, as if they had been coated with some kind of oil or varnish which had aged the same on all. She had possessed the central panel for perhaps thirty-six hours. Was that long enough to create two matching paintings? He was not an artist and did not know for sure, but it seemed impossible to him. Besides, even if Lupe did paint two other panels to match the one she stole, could the paint have dried so quickly? Surely not. No, the other two panels must have been already painted. She must have gone into his safe room and taken measurements and photographs. She must have planned this for along time, long before she stole the center panel and one hundred thousand dollars from him.

Determined to uncover her motive, he began a slow search of the images inch by inch: the three figures on the crosses, the Virgin and her entourage, the chapel, the horrific view of hell, the Spanish words, the ancient date, and then the mocking crowd, each one of whom had been given a unique personality, each with ugly anger painted clear upon their face, each with . . .

No.

It could not be.

He cocked the panels to get better light.

There, right there in the center of the mockers, was his face. His face on a man who hated Christ. His face on a raging Pharisee. His face among those who mocked his Savior with the heartless words *Save yourself!*

From some distant place within him rose a growl. It grew into a roar, and Delano Wright swung the cursed thing against the tabletop. Like Moses casting down the tablets, with both hands he swung it down, and again, and yet again, intent upon the absolute destruction of that hateful lie. One of the panels cracked. Still he beat it down. The panel broke into four pieces. It fell away from the other two. It lay upon the floor. He stomped the pieces even as he beat the other panels down against the table, howling like an animal, screaming without words, his entire body reaping this destruction. Down came the remaining panels, down and down and down again, until they too split asunder. Shouting unintelligibly, weeping, Delano Wright took one broken piece into his hands and tried his best to bend it, to twist and snap it, tried to destroy every hint of the foul accusation it represented.

Then somehow Lupe was there beside him, begging him to stop. She gripped his arm and called to him as if from a great distance.

In his heaving, overwhelming, all-consuming rage, with every bit of strength that he possessed Delano Wright swung the broken painting hard against the unscarred cheek of this, his judge and cruel betrayer. She staggered back against the wall. She sank to the floor. She sat there propped up like a rag doll, legs extended, arms limp, eyes unfocused, head cocked toward her shoulder. With a final wordless curse he flung away the broken proof of her vile treachery.

He might have left her then, or perhaps he remained a while to rail against her. He might have stormed down her stairs, or maybe he had walked away in benumbed silence. He did not recall. He was not himself. He only knew he came back to this world as if awaking from a dream. Suddenly he stood in the smoky air outside the boardinghouse, staring at an empty street where his Bentley had been parked. It had been stolen, of course, stolen in the time it took for him to be destroyed by the last person on the earth for whom he cared, the one person he had dared to think might care for him.

He stared blankly at the spot where his car should be. The image of the street began to fade and dance before him. He pressed both palms against his eyes and felt a wetness there. He took his hands away and saw them smeared with tears and ashes. He stepped onto the street and sat down on the curb. Bits of incinerated bushes fell like snowflakes through the darkness all around him. His eyes burned. He began to cough.

He gazed unseeing deep into the night as the ashes fell. He considered Lupe's painted accusation. A Pharisee. A hypocrite. A judger of all people but himself. A viper. A whitewashed tomb. Strange, but he no longer raged against it. He felt empty now. Perhaps it was exhaustion, some kind of emotional bottom. He felt calm, but not peaceful, like a condemned prisoner who had lost all hope.

Ashes gathered on his legs, his shoulders, his head. He reached up with both hands and gripped his hair and pulled. Rocking forward, rocking back, he groaned and pulled his hair, for he could not escape the sight of Lupe sprawled below him, felled by his own hand. Everything had fallen with her, the wife he had abandoned in every way that mattered, the daughter he had tried to make in his own image, the town he had built on fear and vengeance, all of it had fallen with her and continued falling even now, in the swirling, drifting ashes, the truth now unavoidable, for he could not deny that Guadalupe Soledad Consuelo de la Garza had painted him exactly as he was.

CAPÍTULO 32

A SOLDIER AT THE PALISADE beside the gates called out, "Fire! Fire! They have fired the brush!" Thus began the second assault by Indians that Fray Alejandro would suffer in his lifetime. Unlike the first, when he had arisen from behind a boulder and startled two escaping Indians, this time he would not suffer alone.

Through the narrow doorway of his cell the friar saw Guillermo run across the plaza with the leather-jacket soldiers. They stared out over the wall, their backs to the bedridden friar. In the sudden slumping of their shoulders Alejandro saw the bitter truth. Here was more bad news, more evidence of failure. He sighed and fell back against his cot. Beside him in the tiny room, the Indian still painted.

Leaving three men to stand guard along the palisade, the sergeant called the soldiers and remaining neophytes to the center of the plaza. He spoke loudly. Alejandro heard him from his bed.

"Compadres, this is very bad," said the sergeant. "You have seen yourselves that they have fired the entire countryside upwind of our position."

"The Holy Father will defend us!" shouted Fray Guillermo. "He will withhold the flames!"

"I do not think so, Abbot. Very soon the wind will drive the wildfire to the mission gates. There is no other possibility. Even now you can see the smoke."

It was true. Beyond the palisade on the far side of the plaza a massive wall of smoke unfurled toward the heavens. Already Alejandro smelled it.

The sergeant said, "If you or any of your converts wish to remain and perish here of course you may; however, as for us, we will ride out and try to fight our way around the outside walls toward the downwind side. There must be four hundred of them out there waiting, but we have horses and much better arms. If we can get clear, we will go south to New Spain. I most strongly suggest that you come with us."

"What about the sick?" cried Fray Guillermo. "Would you abandon them?"

"They are all dead now, Abbot. Did you not know? We put the last one in the pit two days ago."

Although Alejandro felt his heart break at these words, Fray Guillermo did not even pause. "And the mission?" asked the abbot. "Would you forsake your duty to the king?"

The sergeant turned his back on the abbot to give orders to his men.

The pale abbot's face contorted. "You are a convert to Satan! A heretic!" He stomped his feet in time with his words, left and right as if pounding sour grapes. "You will *not* leave this mission! You *will* remain and defend it! God *will* stand with us!"

Ignoring him, the leather-jacket soldiers dispersed throughout the grounds, gathering supplies and arms as Fray Guillermo raged against the devil's alternative, calling curses down upon the pagans out beyond the walls, making threats against the Spaniards there within.

Alejandro did not fear the choice. The sickness which had scarred the good friar's flesh had made an even greater change within. Before, he had been caught in a dilemma, torn between Benicio and the abbot, between his conscience and the Rule. He had not dared oppose his wayward brothers, but after the disease he cared not what any man might think, nor did he fear death. Fray Alejandro resolved to go out to the heathens without Benicio's bribes or Guillermo's violence. Instead, if he could but summon up the strength required he would rise to face them with the simple love of Christ. He lay at peace as foul smoke raced across the plaza to enter the narrow doorway of his little cell. He watched the Indian paint calmly, and his sole regret was for his brothers, who were both so clearly lost.

A broken man is capable of anything. No debauchery is beneath him, no selfless martyrdom too lofty. Such a man will risk all, accept all, oppose all. He is a hollow vessel, ready to assimilate the weaknesses or strengths of any pestilence or benefit that comes. In this state are murderers made from decent men, sinners transformed into saints, grand and foolish gestures offered to the world. Nothing is more dangerous on earth. Nothing is more ripe with possibility. Nothing better described the state of Fray Alejandro Tapia Valdez. Nothing better described the Reverend Tucker Rue.

Throughout the night after leaving Lupe's room Tucker had wrestled with the curse in her painting. At first he tried to convince himself the *retablo* on Lupe's table was the vengeful work of Delano Wright. The man had hidden part of Lupe's painting in his secret room. He must be to blame somehow. Perhaps he had hired an artist to add Tucker's face, as a kind of bitter joke. But the unrepentant thief resembled Tucker far too perfectly. It was the work of one who knew him very well, and even half dead from the heat and thirst Lupe knew him fully from the start.

At one time he had believed he saved her, but in truth it was she who led him straight to his own purpose, straight to his life's meaning, to Wilson City, to Sanctuario. With that artwork in her hands she had helped him found his ministry. He had loved her then. He would always love her. But she had seen the truth in him. Wisely she had refused him, and wisely she had expressed the wicked truth of him in paint.

That truth had bound him helplessly before the painting in her room. Lupe's unrepentant thief had clambered down and come for Tucker, had driven nail-pierced hands between his ribs and clutched the throbbing muscles of his heart. Denial could not defend against this attacker, nor could apathy, nor ignorance, for if such a saint as Lupe saw him in this way, he was well and truly guilty.

At dawn he had arisen from the narrow cot in his monkish room. He would return the stolen goods. He would accept his punishment, exchange one cell for another. In the alley stood his old truck, filled with everything he had taken from Delano Wright, everything except the painting. He only had to drive it to the police station.

But what of Sanctuario? He had no funds for a bail bond. He might not be free for months, or even years. Before he went, he had to make arrangements. He had wandered back and forth across the building. He had entered the empty meeting hall. He had sat upon a folding chair and waited.

At eight o'clock as usual the first volunteers had appeared. He had asked them to join him in the meeting hall. He told them he would make an important announcement when everyone was there. They passed the time with small talk. By eight thirty all the others had arrived. They sat on the folding chairs, nine of them in all. He stood before them. He had their full attention. He saw their expectant faces, their openness and love. He spoke of his first days in Wilson City, a pale Anglo among dark people, a stranger, not to be trusted.

They had all smiled, amused to think of their beloved Pastor Tucker as a stranger.

He did his best to return their smiles, even as he spoke of Doña Lupe going door to door with him, serving as an intermediary, an ambassador between cultures, saying this is a good man; you can trust him; he is for you; God is with him. He spoke of their first days in that building, an empty shell, and the token privacy of blankets hung on ropes, the shining future, the certainty of youth. He remembered the day she left, his misery, the unquestioning assumption that his ministry had gone with her. Then had come a visit from a mother and her children needing food, and his sad news:

Lupe is gone. Everything is over. I am very sorry.

And the mother's naïve question: But señor, are you not still here?

Most of a decade had gone by since then, and he was still here. Yet somehow he had lost himself. He did not know how. He only knew he had forgotten who he was, or whose he was, and in forgetting he had sinned great sins.

He had explained this, providing exact details, and their smiling faces changed. Tears began to flow. They had cried, No, Pastor! No! They wrung their hands. They bowed their heads.

When he had completed his confession, he asked for their forgiveness. Confused, they had stared at him. Who are we to forgive? You did this for us. We led you to this. We thought only of ourselves. Always asking, asking, asking. We are the ones to blame. We must return everything, somehow, everything. We must beg forgiveness for ourselves.

Faced with such humility, Tucker Rue's shame increased tenfold, and he had cried before them.

Throughout that day they had worked hard to close the mission. Saying nothing of the reason, for they would not add to Tucker's disgrace, they had sent their children out to spread the news of the closing, and the people came. They had given everything away that was not stolen: the contents of the refrigerators and the pantry, the used clothing, the furniture, the cooking utensils, the office supplies, the books in the library, the computers . . . everything. The stolen things they had collected in one room, to be returned. There were many questions among those who came, those who did not know. But why are you giving everything away? Why, why, oh, why? Yet Tucker and the volunteers would give no answer. They had only given, and cried, and trusted in God's mercy.

At sunset on that day the mission of Sanctuario was almost empty. After tearful farewells the volunteers departed.

As Lupe climbed the hillside at New Harmony, as Delano Wright drove through blinding smoke on Blanco Canyon Road, in that very moment Tucker Rue walked the empty space alone, preparing his mind for the trial that lay ahead. In his old room he found a little pile of personal effects upon the floor. His Bible, a suitcase with his clothes, a framed photo of his parents, and a little radio he sometimes listened to at night when he could not sleep. He wished these things had been given away too. He could not take them with him to the police station and jail, and he did not want to leave them here.

He heard someone knocking on the front door. He sighed. Parting with his friends had been so painful. He did not think that he could say good-bye again. He remained where he was, standing in the little room. The knocking continued. It quickened. It seemed urgent. Sighing again, he set out for the entry.

Outside the door stood a young father with three small children. The father had not heard the news until after he returned home from work. Was it true? Had everything truly been given away? Everything? Truly?

"Not quite everything," said Tucker Rue. And he offered them his own possessions. The clothing was too large, of course, and the Bible was in English. The people in the photograph meant nothing to them. But the radio was received with gladness.

As the young father led his children off into the night, Tucker heard him tuning in a Spanish-language station. He heard a newscaster speak about a wildfire in the canyon, the result of thoughtless vandals who had burned a billboard. So far it had done no further property damage, but the weather forecast called for a change in the wind. A front was coming in across the ocean. It could drive the fire directly down on Wilson City.

Tucker ran into the kitchen where a ladder had been mounted to the wall. He climbed up and emerged from a metal hatch and stood on the flat roof and looked across the town. From that high place he saw a glow among the western hills. He felt a slight breeze at his back. Please don't let the wind change, he prayed. Please don't let it change.

Even as he prayed it, the wind against his back began to fade. Helplessly, he felt a first brush of air against his face. Soon it was obvious that the wind had indeed begun to shift. It now blew from the hills into his town. He smelled smoke. Alone upon the roof, he looked into the blackness of the sky and saw white flecks come streaking down, seemingly from nowhere. He began to cough. His eyes stung, so he closed them. He knelt. He clasped his hands together on the parapet. He pressed his forehead to his hands. The wind roared in his ears, and scripture came into his mind.

I have eaten ashes like bread, and mingled my drink with weeping.

For nearly an hour, Tucker Rue remain in that position, begging God for mercy as the hot wind rose and the smoke gathered and the ashes drifted into piles. Finally, at the sound of screaming sirens he looked up. Beyond the distant rooftops flames poured down from the canyon like a glowing lava flow. Wilson City had begun to burn, and he had lit the fire.

He rose and moved toward the ladder. He stepped through the roof hatch. Buffeted by the wind, he lost his footing. He fell, and his left arm cracked against the metal ladder as he tumbled fifteen feet below. He hit the kitchen floor and lay unmoving, lost to all his errors, liberated from the cares of consciousness.

Eventually he awoke, and back came recent memories. He moaned, not only from the pain of broken bones, but from the deeper agony he bore. He rose, cradling his shattered left arm with his right. He felt along the length of it. The pain was nearly overwhelming when his fingers touched the strange bulge where the bone pressed out against the skin. He backed against the wall and stood with his eyes closed, willing himself to remain conscious. The pain subsided slightly. He found it possible to think again. He unbuttoned the front of his shirt and tucked his useless arm inside. He left Sanctuario and walked into the night.

More than half an hour later, having walked many blocks from Sanctuario, he came upon an apartment building overwhelmed by an inferno. At the far end of the block two houses burned. The flames cast a flickering orange glow on everything. A fireman dragged a hose across the road. Tucker walked beside him. Above the roaring fire he shouted, "I'm Pastor Rue, of the Sanctuario storefront mission. How can I help?"

The fireman shook his head. "You need to get out of here!"

"I'm a minister and these are my people. You must need me for something."

With a sudden mighty crack, the apartment roof gave way, sending a million angry sparks into the sky. The fireman flinched and spun toward the apartments with a curse. Once he realized what was happening, he turned back toward Tucker. "I don't have time to argue!" He waved toward the street downwind. "Run toward the far side of town. This thing is spreading fast."

Tucker set out for the closest house. With every step a spike of pain shot up from his broken arm. He beat on the door with his good fist, crying out in Spanish. When a frightened couple answered he explained that they must leave, take their children, and flee to the east side of town. "Get some blankets and go to Sanctuario," he said. "You can stay there tonight."

He had forgotten Sanctuario was now an empty shell. He ran from house to house, apartment to apartment, trying to ignore his aching arm, beating on the doors, screaming through the doors, begging everyone to hurry. "Tell your neighbors," he said. "Don't leave anyone behind!"

The street filled with people fleeing eastward through the haze, coughing, carrying the littlest children, and suitcases and pillows and blankets. "Hurry!" shouted Tucker. "Run to Sanctuario!"

At one door a young man answered fearfully, "I thought you were La Migra."

"La Migra?" said Tucker. "Are you crazy? The fire is coming and you worry about them? Come on, man! We have to go!"

"I cannot. My friend is here."

"Get your friend and come!"

"He is ill, Pastor. He cannot move."

"Where is he?" Without asking for permission, Tucker stepped inside. Favoring his damaged arm, he charged through the house. "Where is he? I will help you carry him."

"We cannot carry him, Pastor," said the young man, following.

"You look strong enough." Tucker flung open a door and looked into an empty room. "Surely the two of us can do it."

"No, I will not touch him."

Astonished, Tucker looked at him. "Why not?"

"It is death to touch him."

"What do you mean?" asked Tucker, opening another door.

Through the door a putrid stench enveloped him. He gasped and covered his nose and mouth. Inside on the floor lay two dreadfully disfigured men. Their faces were masks of oozing pustules, their features swollen almost beyond human recognition. Tucker turned and ran. Outside in the yard, he knelt and vomited into the bitter smoke. Waves of pain from his shattered arm almost overwhelmed him. When his stomach had been emptied, he wiped his mouth and rose up from his knees and went back in the house. There, the young man waited.

"What happened to them?" asked Tucker.

"I do not know," replied the young man.

"Why are they here? They should be in a hospital."

"They would not go, because of La Migra."

"Hospitals don't turn people in to immigration," said Tucker. "They must go to the emergency room right now."

"They are dead, Pastor."

"Dead?" Tucker thought about this strange fellow living with two dead men in a house, two men looking as if they had been boiled alive. He wondered if the young man had lost his mind. He tried to speak calmly. "You spoke of a friend."

"Ramón," said the young man. "In the last room down the hall."

"He has the same affliction?"

"Yes, Pastor."

"Yet he lives?"

"Yes, Pastor."

"Show me, please."

The young man led him to a room. Inside, the sick man lay upon a mattress. Like the others, he was covered with a thousand little blisters. His eyes were swollen shut. Horrible. Horrible, thought Tucker Rue. He wondered how the man could breathe through those obstructed nostrils, yet his chest did rise and fall.

Tucker stepped into the room. "His name is Ramón?"

"Yes, Pastor," replied the young man, hanging back.

"I know a Ramón. Ramón Rodríguez. He works construction at New Harmony."

"It is he."

Tucker tried to see Ramón's face beneath the stricken man's nightmarish mask. He found nothing familiar there. He turned back toward the young man. "I am sorry. I do not remember your name."

"We have only met one time, last Christmas at Sanctuario. I am called Trini."

"Oh, yes. Of course." Tucker nodded. "Well, Trini, we must get your friend out of here. The fire is coming quickly."

The young man shook his head. "We cannot."

"Trini, you have been very brave. You remained here with your friend when many others would have fled. Now be brave a little longer. Help me carry him outside."

"Pastor, if we touch him, we will die. Lobo died. So did Fernando and Paco."

"We cannot let him burn."

"We cannot touch him."

"Trini, you can see my arm is broken. I cannot save your friend alone."

The young man shook his head. "Surely he would rather burn than die like that."

Tucker turned to look at Ramón on the mattress. Who did he know who might join him in a risk such as this? Only one name came to mind. "All right," he said. "In that case, will you do something else for me?"

"Yes, Pastor."

"Do you know the house of Doña Lupe?"

"Of course. Everybody knows her."

"Would you please go there and tell her Tucker needs her help?"

Suddenly the young man would not meet Tucker's eyes. "You want her to come here?"

"Certainly not, but what else can I do? Leave this man to burn? Now, will you go very quickly? Will you bring her here to me?"

"I will do my best, Pastor. But she might not come."

"She will come. Now, please, go quickly!"

When the young man had departed, Tucker went into the kitchen, where he filled a drinking glass with water. The smell of smoke was strong. Even the air within the house had become hazy. He carried the glass of water to the bathroom, where he found a washrag. He returned to the sickroom.

A set of dresser drawers stood beside the door. On the top Tucker saw two tall votive candles, one adorned with an image of the Virgin of Guadalupe surrounded by golden flames or rays of light, and the other showing Jesus Christ, pulling back his robes to reveal his sacred heart.

Tacked onto the drywall above the dresser, just behind the candles, were several clippings from a newspaper. Tucker leaned a little closer. The clippings all concerned a traffic accident more than two years before. A car had collided with a hit-and-run driver and flipped over. The passenger escaped with severe injuries. The driver had been killed. Scattered across the top of the dresser were many *milagros,* little pieces of punched tin, tiny images of praying men and women mostly, symbols of a penitent's desire for mercy or forgiveness. Above the clippings on the wall, above the little altar, a word had carefully been written in red ink on the drywall: *perdóneme.*

Forgive me.

Tucker stared down upon the afflicted man. How different things would be if there had never been an accident. Harmony alive, and married to him. The two of them, working side by side at Sanctuario. He might even have learned to love her in his way. Delano Wright would certainly have come around eventually. And Lupe's perfect bronze complexion would not be marked by fire.

He stared at the afflicted man and thought of all the lonely years, of Sanctuario abandoned, and incarceration looming. He stared at the afflicted man and wondered: What must it be like to live beneath those boils? To become a monster on the surface, and yet remain yourself inside? Tucker thought he knew. He thought he understood it perfectly. The man moaned and moved his head a little. Tucker wondered what to do. What would Lupe do?

"Ramón," said Tucker Rue. "I am with you."

He knelt beside the man, wincing when the movement jarred his broken arm. He poured a little water on the washrag and began to wipe the suffering man's forehead. Again the fellow moaned. "Have courage, Ramón," said Tucker Rue. "You are not alone." Gently, gently, he did his best to cool the burning fever as smoke from the wildfire slowly filled the room. He began to hum a familiar tune, a hymn all Mexicans would recognize. Softly, then, he sang the lovely words.

> In all our living, we belong to God;
> and in our dying, we are still with God;
> so, whether living, or whether dying,
> we belong to God; we belong to God.

As he sang, Tucker Rue laid aside the washrag, and he took Ramón Rodríguez's ravaged hand in his one good hand, touching his boils very gently for fear of causing pain, but touching the man nonetheless, for it is not good to be alone.

CAPÍTULO 33

THE PAINT WAS WET. FOR that simple reason Fray Alejandro could not take the center panel with the others. He summoned strength enough to rise from his bed and place the two side panels in a bag, but he had to lay the center panel in the small stone vault below his cot, lest it be ruined during his escape attempt. He hoped to return one day and reunite it with its brothers, but that was not to be.

The mission burned around his cell. Above the roar and crackle of the fire he heard the heathens outside shouting, "*Muerte! Muerte! Muerte!* Death to Spaniards! Death to traitors!" Kneeling by the stone vault, weakened by disease, he feared he could not rise and walk. Then the Indian said, "Fear not," and Alejandro saw the man beside him, hair alive with a fierce light as if it had caused the fire, and he was somehow strengthened.

Following the Indian, the friar walked out through the narrow door. Carrying the altarpiece, he entered the flames of hell. There, Fray Alejandro encountered heaven.

In years to come he would try but fail to adequately describe what happened during this, the third of his three burnings. At the end of murders, wars, and carnivores, the lion and the lamb will be at peace, or so the prophets say. Such harmony may seem impossible today, but it was the first condition of our world, a flawless peace profaned when human teeth attacked the flesh of fruit. Violence begets violence. Evil ripples out but miracles remain, and even now, in the death throes of creation, a tender soul may sense a remnant of tranquillity. For the rest of his long life Fray Alejandro knew this, because he once walked a gauntlet of swirling sparks and murderous pagans, yet he was not burned and not one person saw him pass.

Many other mysteries remain with us today. Who can understand why Lupe's reaction to Delano's assault was neither fear nor anger? Who could recognize her thoughts as she slouched where she had fallen, alone upon the attic floor, her back against the wall? In her ears was the echo of his pounding feet upon the stairs as he descended. Before her was the ruination of Fray Alejandro's burden, her precious guide in pieces scattered all about the room. In her fingers was a single bloody tooth, the broken proof of Delano Wright's fury. Yet, awful as these losses were, she most mourned the death of fellowship with him.

She longed to ask him, *Why?* but his single blow had been too powerful. She could neither rise nor clearly think until long after he had gone. She could only try to understand. She put herself in his place, and slowly, slowly she remembered.

It was his image in the crowd, of course. For some reason he had come to see her, and he had entered, and seen the likeness that had drawn her to him on that first day long ago in Blanco Beach. Always she had hidden the *retablo* lest this very tragedy occur. What a foolish thing, to leave it in the open. Had not Padre Hinojosa warned her solemnly to guard it? She remembered well his words: *Others must not see it, daughter, lest they find themselves within it and despair.* What a shock it must have been for Delano to see his face among the mockers, to see his destiny so plainly.

Lupe had dared to hope her quest included saving Delano from his fate, yet in that hope, as in all others, she had clearly failed. The *retablo* showed him as a man in love with violence, and now the very thing it had predicted, it had also caused.

Oh, her failure was so absolute!

Through the drifting smoke above New Harmony she had seen the crosses and the mountaintop and she had felt such joy. It was the very image of Fray Alejandro's burden. Foolishly, she had dared believe it might be proof she had been faithful, proof that all the years away from her beloved Rincón de Dolores, and her unending grief at leaving Tucker, and her fruitless preaching to the empty wind in Blanco Beach, had not been wasted after all. Foolishly, she had dared believe it might mean her quest was ending.

Then ferocious men with masks and weapons had appeared within the smoke to drive her back. What sin had she committed, that she could see Fray Alejandro's promised land but not go in?

Lupe had returned to her little attic room to gaze on the *retablo*, desperate to understand. But just as warlike men had barred the path to Alejandro's vision, so Delano's destruction of the ancient treasure left her lost without its guidance. She had indeed reached the end, yet she had saved no one. All was failure, failure everywhere.

Through the open door beside her, Lupe heard footsteps ascending on the stairs. Might it be the mister coming back? Might this be a second chance? She stirred herself to gaze toward the stairway landing hopefully, but when the visitor arrived she saw he was only Trini, the young friend of Ramón Rodríguez.

"Doña Lupe," said the young man at her door. "Are you ill?" He stared at the bloody tooth she clutched in her lap.

She sighed. Pressing down upon the floor, she tried to rise. "No. I only fell."

Trini hurried forward to assist her, his hand upon her arm. "In that case, can you come to my house? Pastor Tucker is there. He said he needs your help."

She laid her tooth upon the table and began to gather up the pieces of the shattered *retablo*. The taste of blood was like a metal peso in her mouth. "Of course," she said, hiding bits of broken miracle within the crimson bag. "But why?"

"Ramón is very ill. The pastor needs your help to carry him."

"Surely I can do no more than you."

The young man looked away from her. "I cannot touch him, Doña Lupe."

"No?"

"You remember our friend Lobo? It is the same."

She closed her eyes for just a moment. "I understand."

"I would not go if I was you, but I promised to say the pastor needs you quickly."

"I must do this first," she said, stooping down again to pick up the pieces.

He took another step into her room. "May I help?"

"No, thank you. It is better done alone."

"I do not mind," he said, bending to touch a painted fragment.

"No." She gripped his arm. "Please wait for me downstairs. I will be there as soon as possible."

Minutes later, Lupe descended to the building lobby. There she found most of her neighbors crowded near the doors.

"What is it?" she asked.

Marisol, who had never been the same since her daughter died from lack of medicine, stepped back to let her see. Beyond the glass was only chaos. Driven sideways by the roaring wind, ashes streaked from out of darkness, through the porch light's glow, and back into darkness. Lupe could barely see the gleam of windows on the far side of the street. It was difficult to believe so much had changed in the short time since she had returned to the boardinghouse.

"We must hurry," said Trini, who stood waiting there among the crowd.

"Yes," she said, pushing the door open. Immediately her eyes began to burn from streaming smoke.

"Doña Lupe!" shouted Marisol above the wind. "Take us with you! Save us!"

Lupe knew she could do no such thing. In everything she was a failure after all, and nobody's savior. "You are safer here."

"No, we are not. Look!"

Lupe followed Marisol's gesture toward the west, and saw the unmistakable glow of raging flames. Surely the wind would drive the wildfire toward them. "Let us go," she said.

With Trini there beside her, Lupe led the people of her building out. Some of them used the fabric of their shirts to cover their mouths and noses. They carried the smallest children and held the older boys and girls by the hand. Two young men helped one old man move a little faster. Even so, they made slow progress through the darkness and the smoke. Indeed, they had gone only twenty meters when Lupe saw Delano Wright's vague form. He sat upon a concrete curb beside the road with arms wrapped around his legs and chin between his knees.

"A moment," said Lupe to Trini. The small crowd paused as she approached her employer. "Mister?" she said. "Mister, you must go."

"I can't." His voice were strange, distant, as if he were not conscious of his words. "They stole my car."

She bent to touch his shoulder. "Then you must come with us."

"That painting in your room, is that really what you think of me?"

"Come with us, mister."

He looked at her with wonder in his eyes. "Why would you want that, after what I did to you?"

"Quickly, mister. Come." She put upward pressure on his arm. He rose as if he had been lifted. "Come," she said again. "Come."

"Lupe, that painting in your room. You didn't steal it, did you?"

Her eyes went wide. "How could that be possible? One cannot steal a miracle."

He rose. He reached down and touched the scar upon her cheek, very tenderly. "I . . . I . . ."

She knew what he wished to say, this man who never spoke his heart. She smiled, reached up, and took his hand. She gave it a squeeze. "I love you too, mister. Now come with me, okay?"

He nodded and fell in with the others.

Leading them, Lupe blinked against the stinging smoke. She wiped her streaming eyes and coughed almost constantly as she walked across the town of Wilson City. The air was full of shouts and barks and sirens. Cars passed at a crawl. Towering flames cast an eerie crackling glow into the haze beyond the row of houses on her right. Behind her, children cried. To offer comfort to them, Lupe began to sing as loudly as she could.

> De colores, de colores
>   se visten los campos en la primavera.
> De colores, de colores
>   son los pajaritos que vienen de afuera.
> De colores, de colores
>   es el arco iris que vemos lucir.

On and on sang Lupe in spite of scorching in her lungs. She sang of the colors that dressed up the country in springtime, of the colors that dressed the little birds outdoors, of the colors of rainbows that stretched across the sky. Soon the parents joined her, encouraging their children, and in another minute even the old man began to sing the folk song of his youth, the words of divine colors that his people dearly loved. Thus it was that the neighbors strolled through the inferno, coughing, singing, voices drawing others to their side, until there were perhaps three dozen of them following the woman who believed herself a failure.

They reached the duplex where Trini had lived for eight years with Ramón Rodríguez. Behind it and beside it, the houses were on fire. The flames rose high into the smoky haze. They mingled, making it impossible to tell which angry burst of orange and red and yellow came from where. Lupe shivered at the sight. She asked her God for courage. She called out to everyone, "You must keep walking." She pointed to the east. She shouted over the roar of the flames, "Remain calm, and do not fear. The Lord is with you."

"You are coming also, yes?" asked Marisol.

"I cannot," she replied. "I must stay to help a friend."

"Then I will stay also," said the old man. "I cannot walk much farther anyway."

"Neither can my children," said a woman standing near him.

"You must all go," said Lupe. "Soon it will not be safe here."

"Sadly," said the old man, "I cannot."

Lupe looked at Trini. "We must have your truck."

"The truck is not mine, *madre.*"

"We must have it."

"As you wish," said Trini, and within three minutes he had backed the pickup out of the garage.

"Señor," said Lupe to the old man. "Will you ride in front?" Then she spoke to the parents, saying, "Put your children in the back. This is my friend Trini. He will drive slowly and you will walk behind."

The old man climbed into the front seat with the help of strong hands on his back and shoulders. The children climbed into the truck bed.

Before Trini could drive away, Delano Wright stepped into the truck's path and would not move.

Lupe went to stand beside him in the beam of the truck's one working headlight. "Look at this," he said. "Look at the paint here on this fender."

"Yes, mister."

"It's yellow paint, from a yellow car. And see that fringe inside the cab? And the letters in the back window? Someone's name?"

"Yes, I see."

"This is the truck that crashed into Harmony."

"Yes."

"Don't you care? You don't seem to care."

"We need it for the children."

He turned suddenly toward her. She flinched away. In the firelight she saw anger leave his face. "Don't be afraid," he said. "You don't have to be afraid of me."

She stared at him, saying nothing.

He pointed toward the duplex. "Is the driver who killed Harmony in there?"

"I think so."

"You said you were here to help a friend. Is he your friend?"

"Yes," she said. "Tucker is there too."

Lupe felt a weakness rise. The sparks from the fire seemed to drift into her mind. She touched her temple. There was pain. She knelt to the dirt, and then slipped slowly sideways.

Instantly, Delano was down beside her. "What is it? What's wrong?"

"I do not know," she said. "My head aches very much."

"God forgive me," said Delano. "You must have a concussion."

"What is a concussion?"

"*Una concusión,*" he said. Then, switching back to English, "I never meant to hurt you. I was just so angry, and you came up behind me, and I wasn't thinking."

"Yes, mister."

"Please forgive me, Lupe."

"Mister." She reached through her pain to touch his hand. "Before it was even done, I forgive you."

Trini came to kneel beside her too. He spoke to her in Spanish. "Doña Lupe, you are on the ground again."

"Yes." She smiled up at him. "I seem to spend a lot of time down here."

Delano joined their Spanish. "We should get you into the truck."

"No. I must go help Tucker."

"I think it is too late," replied Trini. "Look."

Turning toward the duplex, Lupe saw its roof alight with flames. An overwhelming terror then engulfed her. She was a little girl again, lying in her bed, lying motionless and trusting that her father would appear to save her from the pungency of burning pine and the silent smoke that fanned across the ceiling. The heat caressed her skin, the cost of faith approaching. Still she lay unmoving, for to rise would mean she did not trust, she had no faith, she was not worthy of this test. Her father would come. She lay unmoving though her blanket smoldered, though the air no longer satisfied her lungs. Yet her father never came.

Before the burning duplex Lupe clawed at the dirt. She rubbed it in her hair and on her face while rocking to and fro. She wailed like a widow. She heard the crackling of fire and thought of Tucker in the burning house. She thought of losing him forever. She thought of Señor Rodríguez, who had helped her in her quest, and had spoken of a loving wife and children waiting back in Hércules. Wild with fear, ashamed of faithless terror, she arose somehow in spite of the damage in her head. She staggered toward the burning building.

Delano Wright followed. He laid a restraining hand upon her arm. Oh, bless him for such welcome temptation!

"What are you doing?" he said.

She allowed him to restrain her even as she said, "I cannot let them die." She should have fought against his hand, but the urge to live was overwhelming.

Trini offered more temptation, saying, "Ramón will not survive anyway. He is covered everywhere with boils."

"Boils?" said Delano. "What do you mean?"

"He is very sick, señor. He has something like *la varicela*. Already three of my friends are dead from the same thing."

Lupe felt Delano's hand fall from her arm, her last excuse, removed. She prayed, Father, give me courage. She started for the burning duplex. Delano walked beside her, saying, "If the fire doesn't kill you, that disease will. They're as good as dead already. There's no *reason* to go in there."

"I must." Her head throbbed as the heat of the flames caressed her scar.

"But it's *fire*, Lupe. Aren't you afraid?"

Such was her overwhelming terror that she did not trust herself to speak. She could only look at him, and in his eyes she saw an understanding come, and something else, which she did not deserve.

He said, "My God. You're going to do it anyway."

On she moved toward the conflagration. Her scar ached terribly, as if the flames already scorched it. She must not think of that. She must not think of fire, or smoke, or tests of faith, or death. She must think only of the ones in need, of Tucker and Ramón, especially Tucker, her dear Tucker, whose love she had traded for a life of failure. She felt her body shaking, hands and jaw and knees, yet she walked toward the flames.

"Lupe."

She looked up toward the one who called. In the doorway of the house she saw the man's fine dark suit, his Mayan features, his black hair which shimmered in the firelight like the feathers of a crow. Might his hair be burning? Even as she looked, the light within his hair rose to hover in a circle around his head, much brighter than the fire. Did he beckon? Silhouetted as he was by leaping flames which shot out all around, she could not be sure. Was this a blessing that he offered? A benediction? She could only gaze upon him. He was untouched by the golden flames, as untouched as her namesake, the Virgen de Guadalupe. He was at peace. He was magnificent.

Lupe's teeth rattled with the sound of bones. Oh, how her head ached! She stepped closer. She felt the contents of her stomach rising. She longed to flee, yet she took another step. The heat upon her face was horrible, yet she could not let them die.

She saw the devil in the smoke. How could she move into that? Yet what of Tucker's kiss upon her hand? What of Ramón's joy in Naco, thinking she was his wife, and his disappointment when he found that she was just a stranger? What of a woman she had never met, a woman in a small town much like hers, and that woman's children, waiting, waiting for a father who would not return? In the name of mercy, how she feared to go! In the name of love, how she longed to enter in for all of them!

She thought of timber stacked beneath a martyr's stake. She thought of sticks within her father's fireplace. She thought of Moses in the wilderness, a man of uncircumcised lips following a column of fire.

She stepped closer to the burning, yet she was no saintly martyr. She would enter, but she could not do it fearlessly, therefore in this as in all other things it seemed that she had failed.

From among the flames she heard again, "Lupe."

"Here I am," she whispered.

"Stop, for it is finished."

Strangely, there was no relief. She could only think of Tucker and Ramón. Above all other earthly things, in that moment she desired to save them. But she bowed her head before the command. "Let it be with me as you have said."

She collapsed onto the yard. In that instant someone touched the scar on her cheek. She looked up, and saw Delano gazing down at her with awe. His hand lingered on her cheek a moment, then he walked away, toward the doorway where she ought to be, his arm cast across his face against the heat, his body bent beneath the roiling smoke, and he disappeared into the flames.

She saw this act of faith, this *auto de fe,* a thing beyond all words, and when the fire ascended to the middle of the walls some within the crowd began to yell, *"Salid! Salid! Salid!"* Come out! they called, a few of them at first, mostly girls and women, until the minutes slowly passed and this call became predominant and everybody shouted it as one—Come out! Come out! Come out!—and she knew those inside could flee the fire with honor.

Yet they did not come, even when someone shouted, *"Agua!"* and nearby men with garden hoses hurried toward the crackling walls. *"Agua, rapido!"* they shouted, and the men aimed slender streams to douse the flames, but the fire would not be vanquished as the smoke rose up and traveled west, against the wind.

CAPÍTULO 34

WITH A QUILL IN INK-STAINED and arthritic fingers, an old man labored painfully, scratching words on precious paper. It was the good Fray Alejandro, that ugly Spaniard now made even less attractive by his scars and advanced years. He worked at a crude table in a room beside the transept of the chapel of Santa Dolores, a building small but pleasing in proportion, which had been recently completed by the people of his village.

It was a good village, Rincón de Dolores, a place of almost five hundred souls, which he had helped to build from only three small houses and a barn where two trails came together. He had served these people as their priest for more than thirty years. Against his will, they now treated him as if he were a living saint. But as he neared the age of eighty, it occurred to Alejandro he should try to document the truth about himself for the sake of humility and honesty, confessing his role in the tragedy that took place long before in Alta California, when he and his Franciscan brothers lost the Misión de Santa Dolores through their sins.

The friar had been at work upon his story for five days. He had reached the final words of his memoir, although such a humble man would never think of what he wrote in such a way. For him it was a record of the facts and only that.

He had just finished writing of the escape from the inferno. Long ago he had realized his survival could never be explained, and so he did not try. He merely described facts. He wrote of neophytes and leather-jacket soldiers killed in most horrific ways. He never knew what had become of Fray Benicio. He saw poor Guillermo pierced through by many spears, but although burdened by his weakness and forced to walk quite slowly through the burning gates, Alejandro himself remained unseen and untouched by the frenzied heathens who surrounded him.

Once beyond the mission walls, the gentle friar had suddenly realized the Indian was no longer near. He stopped. He turned and saw the man at a great distance, standing on a hillside, looking down. Silhouetted against the raging wildfire, the Indian's long hair reflected reds and oranges as if it were alight. He raised his palm toward Alejandro. Something in the gesture seemed to go beyond a mere acknowledgment of parting. Could it have been a blessing? A benediction? Alejandro smiled his ugly, crooked smile and raised his hand as well. In an instant, the Indian was gone.

The friar had not returned to Mexico City. What future could remain there for an utter failure, a man with his defacing scars? Instead, he had wandered southward in the wilderness for months, until he reached a remote place high in the Sierra Madre mountains, a crossroads which had been his home ever since.

Fray Alejandro had tried to teach the good people of Rincón de Dolores what he learned in Alta California. Once each year he led them in a reenactment of his failures so they would remember. He prayed someone would return one day to show the lost souls of Misión de Santa Dolores a more saintly model of obedience, but as his years advanced it seemed unlikely to occur within his lifetime.

He paused in his writing. Was there more to tell? Recently a visitor had come from the valley down below to say the people in the lowlands were at war with Spain. In another village called Dolores a priest had begun this war. A *priest,* may the Holy Father forgive him! The homely friar sighed. Must mankind always make the same mistakes? Oh, he was glad to be so old. He wished to avoid the coming days. He bent back to his work, and wrote the final words.

So Alejandro's story ends, as all stories must, but in each ending a beginning may be found. Consider for example what a lovely day it is in the gardens that were once the central plaza of the Misión de Santa Dolores. On this day many tourists stroll within the adobe walls, pausing at the reconstructed granary and palisade to read placards which explain each aspect of early Spanish mission life, taking snapshots with their cameras and gazing across the plaza at the re-created barracks, which are said to be much like those that housed the leather-jacket soldiers and Franciscan brothers, before the Indians arose against the Spanish in that place.

Adjacent to the barracks stands the chapel. It is not the largest of the California mission chapels, nor is it the most ornate. Only the foundation of the structure is original. All the rest has been re-created as faithfully as possible from clues found in the soil and from a journal written by Fray Alejandro Tapia Valdez, a Franciscan friar, the only Spaniard to escape the Indian revolt. But of all the old Spanish mission chapels in the state of California, Santa Dolores is most fascinating, for it alone was lost for more than two hundred years, only to be found and raised again.

On this day a small woman with a scarred cheek passes among the garden flowers. She wears no jewelry and no makeup. Her graying hair is restrained only by a plain black plastic clip. Beside her is a man even more severely scarred by countless blemishes across his face and hands and forearms. Both the woman and the man are dressed humbly, she in a cotton skirt and blouse covered by a traditional peasant's apron, and he in a western-cut cotton shirt and blue jeans. They walk slowly, as old people will. They do not touch, but something in the way they move together speaks of many years of friendship.

Around them in the lushness of the garden, hummingbirds dart from blossom to blossom. Butterflies flit everywhere. The scent of roses drifts upon a gentle breeze. A ten-foot limestone fountain trickles water down from basin into basin, the calming laughter of it constant in the background.

They pause beside a low place in the plaza wall, where it is possible to look down the hillside toward the canyon. Below and to the left and to the right they see hundreds of small houses on the hills and canyon floor. These humble homes are the famous second phase of New Harmony, known throughout the country as a shining example of low-cost housing for the poor.

Closer to the mission, but still below it on the hillside, is a park, perhaps thirty acres in size, where the land is undeveloped. It is a level place, built up from soil which was excavated from the mission site. On this land we see a grove of sycamores, planted almost thirty years ago, and sacred to the memory of a vanished people who once highly treasured places such as this. In the desert soil below the sycamores lie more than two hundred bodies, their bones still wearing patches here and there of pockmarked flesh. No one knows of them, or of the dreadful secret that they keep.

Although the mission is a public monument, it is also a functioning church. In that capacity, the chapel bell begins to ring, the first call to Sunday morning Mass.

"We should go in," says the old woman.

"With much pleasure," replies the old man.

As they cross the plaza, she says, "How is business at the restaurant?"

"We do well. Raquel sends her love and her regrets. She would have come with me this time except she has the flu."

"I feel bad for taking you away. You should have stayed to care for her."

"It was not necessary. Our children and grandchildren grant her every desire."

The woman smiles. "It must be good to have children and grandchildren."

"Oh, yes. And how are things in your hometown?"

"Much the same as always."

"Well, not exactly the same. There is the hospital, the school, the library, and the public swimming pool."

"All old news," replies the woman with a smile. "No one thinks them special anymore."

"You have made no other improvements in Rincón de Dolores recently?"

"No. I must give to other places where the need is greater."

"But you still work in your little shop each day?"

"Of course. How else would the children get their Chiclets?"

"And the fortune that he left to you . . . you still spend none of it on yourself?"

"For what purpose?" The old woman waves a crooked hand as if shooing a fly. "I have all I need."

"As do I," replies the man.

They pause outside the chapel. By the entry is a bronze plaque with words in English and in Spanish. Already standing there are an obese woman and a small man with a mustache. The American tourists ignore them. The man with the mustache peers at the plaque and reads aloud in English, "'Reconstruction of the Misión de Santa Dolores chapel, outbuildings, plaza, gardens, and park were made possible through the generous philanthropy of Doña Guadalupe Soledad Consuelo de la Garza, of Rincón de Dolores, Jalisco, Mexico.'"

"Doña Lupe," whispers the man with the pockmarks, making a little bow.

"Stop it." The woman with the scarred cheek smiles. "You embarrass me."

"But you are a great woman. Look what you have done."

"A great woman? Me?" Lupe's eyes go very wide. "I am a great failure. I did nothing here. This is all because of the mister's money."

Ignoring the two Spanish speakers behind him, the small American with the mustache reads from the memorial again, "'In loving memory of Reverend Tucker Rue, and with eternal gratitude to Mr. Delano Wright. "Greater love hath no man than this. . . ."'"

The obese woman says, "I heard she was just a wetback until she inherited her money from that Wright person. I heard they lived together, but they weren't married."

"You don't say," replies the old man.

"Imagine sleeping with the man to get all of his money, then using it to build a church." The obese woman sniffs. "Some people think they can buy anything."

When the tourists have moved on, Ramón asks, "Those people, they used Señor Wright's name, yes? What did they say?"

"Nothing important," replies Lupe as her finger, bent now from arthritis, touches the bronze, tracing the letters of a name. Tucker.

The two of them stand silently awhile, then the chapel bells begin to ring again. Unrecognized by all inside, they enter. The chapel is dark and cool. Votive candles flicker on a tiered display beside the entrance. Rustic wooden pews stand in rows along each side of a single central aisle, which is paved with Saltillo clay tiles. Great logs, called *vigas*, hand-shaped by axes for authenticity, cross the ceiling high above. At the far end of the chapel in a niche in the adobe wall stands a little altarpiece. On a wooden table covered by a white cloth are the elements of the Eucharist.

During his homily, the priest announces this is a Requiem Mass, held annually in honor of all who perished in the famous Blanco Canyon epidemic and wildfire.

When the time comes to receive the host, Lupe and Ramón approach together. In the aisle with them are many short and brown Latino maids and gardeners from Wilson City and New Harmony, and an equal number of tall and pale millionaires from Blanco Beach. Before the little altarpiece, they all kneel. They all receive the same body. They all receive the same blood. They all rise and return to their pews, sitting there together. Since the twin disasters many years ago, the Misión de Santa Dolores has become a place of peace and comfort for them all.

After Mass the doors are opened. The worshippers go out. The tourists come in. Lupe and Ramón are the last to rise from their pew. They move forward to stand before the altarpiece.

"I cannot tell that it was ever broken," says Ramón, staring at the small *retablo*.

"You say so every year," replies Lupe.

"Is that truly what the señores looked like?"

"Yes," replies Lupe. "You do not remember?"

"I only know I rose and walked out of the house somehow. Other than that, it is all confused. The fever, you know, it took many memories."

"Well," says the woman with the scar upon her cheek, "That is how Tucker and the mister looked."

They gaze at the three panels of the *retablo*, which have been almost perfectly restored. Only Lupe sees the subtle differences. For example, among the heavenly host above the crosses is a face that calls to mind stone carvings of the ancient Mayans, a smooth sloped forehead, pendulous earlobes, cheekbones high and proud, and full black hair surrounded by a gilded halo that shimmers slightly in the chapel candlelight. It is rumored that this is a self-portrait of the artist. These rumors cannot be proven, for his identity is a mystery. He came from Wilson City and repaired the artifact and then he disappeared, never to be seen again.

The mysterious artist has included Delano within the picture as before, except now he stands among the devout mourners. Also, Tucker is still there, but now he is the repentant thief upon his cross, his image lifelike and compelling. The Virgin is not much changed. She remains in beatific prayer, burning yet unburned just as she once appeared in Guadalupe, Mexico, with leaping golden flames which shoot out all around as if erupting from the Presence of the Lord. To Lupe's great embarrassment, there is just the one small difference in her namesake, the sole remaining sign of the *retablo*'s destruction, the blemish in the paint upon the Virgin's cheek.

"Ramón?" says the woman. "Do you sense God's spirit in this place?"

"Indeed I do. And you?"

The woman waits long before she answers. "I have not felt his presence anywhere in many years. But I believe that he is here."

Together they walk toward the front doors of the chapel. There beside the votive candles, they pause to gaze at a glass display case which contains a little book. It is bound in leather, clearly very old, and open to the first page, where Spanish words are handwritten. Beside it is a plaque which says it is a gift from the people of Rincón de Dolores. As she has each year for many years, Lupe bends down close to read the words:

> *In spite of the fading of memory that accompanies my age, I, Fray Alejandro Tapia Valdez, servant of Almighty God and brother of the Franciscan Order, shall do my best to record the strange and terrible history of La Misión de Santa Dolores in Alta California, just as it occurred. . . .*

When Lupe is done reading, she whispers a prayer for Alejandro, and then she and Ramón step outside into the glorious California sunlight.

Ramón asks, "Will we travel here again next year as usual?"

"If God allows it."

"God, and La Migra," replies the old man, smiling.

The rich old woman laughs, and together they walk on into the garden.

THE
Author, Book & Conversation

ATHOL
DICKSON

In the same year Albert Einstein died, Rosa Parks made history, and Disneyland was founded, Athol Dickson was born in Oklahoma to a traveling salesman and his wife. His first bed was a drawer lined with towels in a travel trailer. When he was three months old his family settled in Texas, where he lived until a recent move to Southern California. Athol and his wife, Sue, once sold their house and cars to buy a boat. They moved aboard it and cruised over 4,500 miles along the North American coastline between Galveston and the Chesapeake Bay.

Athol's novels have been favorably compared to the work of Octavia Butler (by *Publishers Weekly*), Daphne du Maurier (by Cindy Crosby, fiction critic for *Christianity Today* and FaithfulReader.com), and Flannery O'Connor (by the *New York Times*). His last four novels were all finalists for the prestigious Christy Award. Two of them, *River Rising* and *The Cure*, went on to receive the award, and *Winter Haven* remains a Christy finalist as of the *Lost Mission* printing date. Athol Dickson's novels have been honored by a *Romantic Times* Top Pick, by a *Library Journal* starred review, by *Booklist* as one of their Top Ten Christian Novels of 2006, by *Christianity Today* as a Best Novel of 2006 finalist, by *Christian Fiction Review* as one of their Ten Best Novels of 2007, and by the Audio Publishers Association in 2008 with their coveted Audie Award.

Q: What inspired this story?

A: I started hearing about bishops from Africa and Latin America coming to the United States to offer guidance and assistance to Episcopalian churches, and I learned that churches in South Korea now send more missionaries around the world than America does. That got me thinking about what it means to go from being a country that offers spiritual help to other nations, to being a country that needs spiritual help from those same nations. On one level that's frightening. On another it's wonderful. When fear and wonder come together you can be sure you're in fertile territory for a novel, so I decided to write about the reasons for this shift, and what it means to live in these drastically changing modern times.

Q: Yet much of the *Lost Mission* story takes place more than two hundred years ago. Why is that?

A: A couple of reasons. What we're living through today is nothing new. It's all been lived out before, and it all has roots in what went before, so I thought to understand the present, it would be best to start by looking at the past. Also, I wanted to explore the inevitability of our mistakes, the fact that they almost seem to be in our DNA. What does that mean for us as individuals? What does it mean for us as a community, as the human race? Are these awful choices we keep making really unavoidable, or is there a way to break the cycle?

Q: So, what's the verdict? Will the circle be unbroken?

A: Ha! That's a great old song. But I'm not a big believer in black-and-white, easy answers, so I'll leave the verdict up to the reader. *Lost Mission* spends a lot of time weaving in and out of some very difficult dilemmas. Nothing is easy in it, just as nothing is easy in this deeply flawed world of ours. In the end, I think it does point to a way out, but I don't know if many of us are prepared to go that way. Some things you can't know about yourself until the moment of decision is upon you. That's the way things work out with the characters of this story, too. Each of them has a hard choice to make, and none of them knows what they will do until the end has come.

- What mistakes were made by the main characters in this novel, and what (if anything) did each of them learn from their mistakes?

- How many connections did you notice between the 18th century and the modern storylines? What does the existence of so many connections imply about the mistakes made by the central characters?

- If you met a real life person who left their home, risked death in the Arizona desert, and entered the United States illegally just to try to save our souls, how would you respond?

- Consider New Harmony and Sanctuario. What are Delano and Tucker's true reasons for building them? Are the things they symbolize fundamentally different, or the same? Are there any "New Harmonys" in your life? Any "Sanctuarios"?

- What is more important: the way Lupe came to America, or the reason why she came? Think of all the other ways characters in this story face the ethical dilemma of choosing the lesser of two evils. What does the story have to say about that topic?

- Consider each of the following things in terms of what they symbolize within the story: fire, the Spanish mission, borders, unconverted Indians, the retablo, the man with shining hair, smoke, disease, scars, and the quest. How does the symbolism in each of these cases communicate an important truth?